DESERTS OF NAROOSH

DESERTS OF NAROOSH

RISE OF THE GRANDMASTER™ BOOK THREE

BRADFORD BATES

MICHAEL ANDERLE

LMBPN Publishing
PMB 196, 2540 South Maryland Pkwy
Las Vegas, NV 89109

First US edition, February 2021
Version 1.01, March 2021
eBook ISBN: 978-1-64971-450-3
Print ISBN: 978-1-64971-451-0

THE DESERTS OF NAROOSH TEAM

Thanks to our beta readers
Kelly O'Donnell, Mary Morris, Larry Omans, Rachel bBeckford

Thanks to the JIT Readers

Dave Hicks
Dorothy Lloyd
Veronica Stephan-Miller
Diane L. Smith
Jeff Goode
Angel LaVey
Allen Collins
Rachel Beckford

If I've missed anyone, please let me know!

Editor
The Skyhunter Editing Team

LIST OF TIM'S CURRENT STATS AND SKILLS

"Tim" Level Fifteen Battlesworn

    Primary Stats

    Strength: 13

    Endurance: 14

    Dexterity: 20

    Intelligence: 32

    Wisdom: 44

    Perception: 5

    Vitality: 3

    Revitalization: 3

    Luck: 6

Notable Gear

    Simple Dagger of Dexterity, +1 (X2)

    Staff of Divine Retribution, +4 Intelligence +5 Wisdom

    Circlet of Wisdom, +1

    Boots of Swift Regeneration, Increase base movement speed and Mana regeneration by 1%

    Battlesworn Robes of Justice, +4 Intelligence +6 Wisdom

Belt of Wisdom, +2

Wristband of the Goddess, 10% damage reduction to dark-based attacks

Leather Wraps of Divergent Health, 10% chance for single target healing spell to jump targets and heal the secondary recipient for 50% of the value.

Ring of Marginal Transcendence, +2 Wisdom

Necklace of Unshakable Will, +3 Wisdom +1 Intelligence

Pants of Recovery, Increases mana regeneration

Jerkin of Unmeasurable Delight, +1 to all base stats

Paul's Gloves of Mending, +4 Wisdom +7 Intelligence

Skills

Healing Orb: Journeyman rank one

Dodge: Apprentice rank one

Flame Burst: Apprentice rank three

Cleanse: Apprentice rank seven

Appeal to the Goddess: Novice rank one

Infiltrator: Novice rank three

Small Blades: Apprentice rank six

Throwing Knives: Apprentice rank two

Sneak: Apprentice rank three

Night Vision: Novice rank five

Backstab: Novice rank seven

Flame Burst: Apprentice rank three

Weaken Undead: Apprentice rank five

Divine Light: Apprentice rank five

Healing Storm: Novice rank one

Curse of Giving: Novice rank five

Behold My Power: Novice rank six

Who Needs a Shield: Novice rank five

Quick Feet: Novice level one

Stances

Way of the Boulder: Novice rank nine
Way of the River: Novice rank nine

Buffs
Armor of Eternia: Novice rank six
Attacks of the Faithful: Apprentice rank one

Open Quests
The Deserts of Naroosh

CHAPTER ONE

"Wake up!" ShadowLily yelled.

Hey, it wasn't his fault he fell back asleep after the last time she told him to do something. Mornings weren't his thing, and it sure didn't smell like coffee. Tim pried his eyes open, wondering why his mouth tasted so bad.

Never bet a fire mage how many different foods you can eat at once without getting sick.

He wanted to laugh but wasn't sure if it would make him throw up again or intensify the ringing in his head. Why was there this horrible pounding noise?

Something jabbed him in the ribs.

"Grahh." Swatting her hands away, Tim mumbled, "It can't be morning yet. Go away."

"If you answered the door as I asked you to, then we'd know who's been out there for the last ten minutes." ShadowLily climbed out of bed, looking for her clothes.

Damn, they must have had a good night if her clothes were on the floor and not in her inventory.

The pounding in his head didn't stop when whoever was

beating on the door finally relinquished their furious barrage of hate against such an innocent barrier, and it took him a moment to realize he was hungover. He must have been out of it if he didn't remember to cleanse himself. A quick cast of the spell made him feel a million times better. As the pounding faded from his ears, he tossed the sheets aside and stood.

They needed to invent something back in the real world to take the edge off a bad night out. He'd heard of IV services that would come to your house, but he'd always hated needles, and an IV hydration service seemed a little extreme. Maybe when it got to the point you started hiring someone to pump you full of liquids, it was a better idea to tone down the drinking a wee bit.

Sure would be helpful after a good party though.

He tried to equip his clothes and realized that they must have been in the tangled mess on the floor. It looked like a laundromat exploded in their room. Clothes mixed with sheets, combined with towels, and what was that?

Fuck it. He didn't have to get dressed to answer the door.

Now that his senses were coming back to him, he realized there was no way it was morning yet. It was still dark outside the windows. It was damned inconsiderate to bang on someone's door in the middle of the night unless it was an emergency.

Holy shit, could it be an emergency?

Was it already time to save the world again? It hadn't been more than a few hours since they wrapped up their last adventure. Eternia already dropped their next quest on them. Not that he was complaining. It wasn't like he entered the game to sit around and drink beer. It was just that a full night's sleep would be nice, and if he couldn't have it then whoever showed up better have coffee.

Tim reached the door and pulled it open. "What?"

JaKobi gave naked Tim a solid once-over. "It seems as though Vitaria sent us one last surprise. Seraphina asked us to meet her at the city gates."

"That was fifteen minutes ago, so you better hurry," Cassie snapped as she took a hearty eyeful.

Lorelei yawned. "And maybe get some pants. While I'm sure Seraphina has seen one before it's probably considered quite rude to go around with that thing flopping about."

He'd almost forgotten that he'd decided not to put on clothes before answering the door. His cheeks burned as he felt the fury of his awakening fading. There wasn't anything to do now but put a brave face on. "Pants are overrated," Tim casually replied as he sauntered back into the room, trying to find the damn things before anyone figured out he wasn't nearly as comfortable with this as he was letting on.

If Seraphina was calling on them in the middle of the night, it must be important. The city's leader had her bit of mischief to attend to. *I doubt she'd give that up just to screw with my sleep.* Tim wondered what kind of horrible monster Vitaria dumped on their doorstep this time. With the passage under the mountain clear, the city of Tristholm should have been safe. It just went to show that it never paid to take your safety for granted.

Tim looked up, wondering if ShadowLily had found his pants, and saw that she had climbed back into bed while he was gone. He wasn't the only one who didn't feel like doing anything right now. Not sure if she was hungover, Tim cast Cleanse on her.

"Apparently we have a monster to fight." He pulled the covers off ShadowLily's head. "This is why you never open the door."

"I didn't open the door. You did." ShadowLily hit him with a pillow. "It wasn't like we were going to get any sleep with them pounding at the door anyway."

ShadowLily was right, but that didn't mean he couldn't grumble about it. What was life without a few well-placed gripes? As long as you kept them in moderation. No one wanted to hang out with someone who bitched about everything.

He smiled and decided it was his turn to return the poke she'd given him earlier. He gave her a gentle nudge in the ribs and squawked as she grabbed his wrist and flipped him onto his back. A second later, she straddled him with a giggle. The move was so unexpected that he completely forgot he left the door open.

Shit, with her on top of him, he forgot what his name was.

ShadowLily looked down at him with a stern face and waved her finger back and forth. "I do the poking around here. You do the things the poker tells you to do."

Her expression turned hungry, and Tim knew today would be a good day.

Cassie cleared her throat from the doorway. "I don't think you have time for that."

ShadowLily rolled off him, taking the blanket with her. Tim was left lying there at full salute and nothing he could do about it. Why did his brain move so damn slow without coffee? Not to mention how his critical thinking skills were cut by ninety percent as soon as he saw boobies.

"Five minutes or I'm sending the guards in to haul you away," Cassie yelled, and their door slammed closed.

Tim leaned over the edge of the bed into his girlfriend's furious face. "So I have four minutes to kill."

"That line would have worked before I almost had sex with you in front of our friends." The assassin's clothes appeared as she stood up.

It wasn't as if she didn't have a point, and maybe it wasn't as funny as he thought it was. "It's just…" Tim waved at her gorgeous body as she strapped her weapons into place. "When I see you, sometimes I forget about everything else."

A dagger appeared in her hand, and the blade slowly spun in her flat palm. "If you weren't so damn cute, I'd toss you out the window." The knife stopped spinning, and she slashed the tiniest papercut of a scratch across his chest before putting it away. "Next time, the door is closed, or the clothes stay on."

Tim healed himself. "Sounds like a good rule of thumb."

It wasn't like he wanted to put on a show for the world. He just needed more sleep to make better decisions.

Two minutes later Tim tracked down his last item of clothing from the floor, and they were out the door. Cassie smirked at them before turning and leading the way to their destination. It didn't take long for the sound of shouting to reach his ears. It was the kind of noise you heard and instantly knew trouble was brewing. Cassie glanced back, and he motioned for her to get going. He knew it meant running, but sometimes an adventurer had to do what an adventurer had to do.

The world didn't save itself.

Cassie slid to a stop inside the courtyard holding her arms out to make sure no one went past her. There was a giant cobra in the center of the open space and a guard lying six feet away moaning in agony. Five or six of Seraphina's men had their spears out and were trying to back the giant snake away from their fallen comrade without much success.

The soldiers didn't seem able to get close enough to the wounded man without putting themselves at risk. The best they could do was keep the cobra from finishing off the wounded warrior. A rescue attempt would take a full-out assault, and Tim was pretty sure he didn't get called down here to deal with one snake that a handful of Seraphina's archers could kill from the rooftops.

Violence should be a last resort, the failsafe for when all other options turn to shit.

Tim quickly cast Cleanse on the wounded guard. The man stopped moaning, and his eyes almost bugged out of his head when he saw the cobra. He back-peddled, looking like a crab going after a tasty treat it spied down the beach. When he was back in the arms of his fellow soldiers the guard's wits returned, and he gave Tim a firm nod of thanks before letting two of the soldiers escort him away.

The rest of Seraphina's men still held the giant cobra at bay, but its movements were growing agitated. There was no chance the cobra would live in an attack on her men, so what were they waiting for? Something else was going on here, something he hadn't figured out yet with all the commotion.

Tim drew a deep breath and let his eyes move past the snake to take in the rest of the room. Looking completely relaxed as it used a dagger to cut slices of orange fruit before tossing them into its mouth was a creature Tim had never seen before. It was a Were of some kind, that much was certain, but he couldn't quite put his finger on which. The thing in front of him was shorter and more compact than the werewolves but was easily over six feet tall.

A six-foot-tall were of any kind wasn't something to fuck with.

At least not alone. Thankfully, he brought backup.

Tim took a minute to look the creature over and thought about where he had seen the dog-like features before. The name of the Discovery show he'd been watching escaped him, but Tim knew what type he was looking at now. He'd always thought hyenas were kind of cute.

Like big furry love balls with razor-sharp teeth.

The kind of thing that was super cute on TV and terrifying in real life. Not that he ever planned on meeting a hyena in real life, let alone its Were counterpart in a game.

A quick scan of his interface showed that the creature was titled Jabari's Chosen. Tim wasn't sure if that was the creature's name or its classification. It sounded a lot more like a generic title so probably not a name. After letting his pet attack one of the guards, Tim was pretty sure the thing's name didn't matter. A messenger didn't stroll in armed to the teeth if they weren't looking for a fight.

The spear in the werehyena's hands looked like it had seen some heavy use. It never paid to take a skilled fighter lightly. The difference between a trained fighter and your average street-tough was like the difference between the guys at the "Y" and the ones in the NBA.

Thankfully, Tim and Seraphina had a few skilled fighters of their own.

Before taking charge of the situation or addressing the monster, Tim wanted to observe Jabari's Chosen for a few moments longer. He was more than willing to let the guards continue doing their jobs while he took in the situation. The more you knew about an opponent, the easier it was to defeat them.

He wore loose-fitting clothes that looked made from a soft, handwoven fabric. His cloak had a hood, but it was down for the moment. Leather straps that continued up his calves tied his sandals to his feet. The outfit would have been at home in ancient Greece or maybe even Rome, but neither of those options felt exactly right.

Looking over the werehyena again, Tim realized the creature was almost Egyptian. The shirt and leggings were a dull, practically colorless material, but the beast had a sash that went over one shoulder and hung below his waist that was dyed vibrant colors marking his wealth or position in society.

It made a certain kind of sense. Their next stop was in a desert after all.

Holy shit, were there going to be pyramids?

Tim started to get excited as he turned away from Jabari's Chosen and looked for who was in charge. It didn't take him too long to spot Jon. He made his way over to the man and extended his hand in greeting. "What's going on?"

Jon looked relieved as he clapped Tim on the back. "Thank Eternia you're finally here. This thing demanded the right to deliver a message to the one who opened the passage. He hasn't been taking our efforts to keep him here while we summoned you very kindly."

"Let's find out what he has to say." Tim motioned for the group to come with him.

Jabari's Chosen took one last bite of his fruit and tossed the rest away. A quick flick of his wrist shook the worst of the juice off his blade. The werehyena looked satisfied as he tucked the dagger away before picking up his spear and moving to stand by the cobra.

His eyes moved over the new arrivals with a cold and calculating gaze. As their group turned and made their way toward the creature, Jabari's Chosen watched their progress like a cop outside the bar at two in the morning.

Holding his back straight and full of pride, Jabari's Chosen addressed Jon. "Is this him? The one I've been waiting for?"

Tim smirked. This guy better watch that shit, or Cassie would rip him a new one. He might have been their de facto leader, but it was wrong to assume it couldn't have been any of the women. There was no way in hell he'd be anywhere in this game without the superior play of the women around him.

Not to mention the fact that because Cassie's death didn't count due to her resurrection, he was the only member of their party to die in combat. Pretty nice badge of honor that none of the people he was tasked with keeping alive had met a grisly death.

Not that there weren't a few close calls.

Still, he was in charge for now, and it was time to accomplish leaderly things.

"I speak for the Blue Dagger Society," Tim called. It was easy enough to put on a brave face when he had Cassie standing between himself and the danger. Normally there would have been an assassin right by the tank's side, but she was conspicuously absent.

Wait, where was ShadowLily?

When the going got tough, the stealth got going. That was something his buddy Captain Waffles used to say when the stealthers would drop out of combat and leave the rest of the group to die just to save a few gold on repairs. In this case, Tim knew ShadowLily wasn't abandoning them to save a few repair fees. The assassin was simply putting herself in a position to attack from behind if he failed to handle things diplomatically.

Smart lady.

Still, the fact his girlfriend thought so little of his conversational repertoire was slightly disheartening.

The werehyena stepped forward and slammed the butt of his spear onto the tile three times to make sure he had their group's full attention. "I have a message for you from Jabari the Great, second only to the Pharaoh himself."

The werehyena gave a barking laugh. "The people of the desert are happy with the way things are. If you enter our territory, it will be considered an act of aggression and will be dealt with accordingly."

Tim smiled as he thought about what the messenger said. He wanted to be pissed off that the ruler of a kingdom wanted to bar their access before even meeting them, but all his mind kept shouting over and over was the word Pharaoh. Pharaohs meant pyramids, mummies, traps, and all the things that made games like *Tomb Raider* and *The Prince of Persia* great.

Get the fuck out of the way Indiana Jones. I've got this.

Tim was pretty sure the rest of the group felt the same way he did. All he wanted to do now was get to the deserts of Naroosh sooner and find out how it would have felt to be alive way back in a time where everything seemed magical.

Plus, it wasn't like Promethia couldn't survive for a while without them. Ernie would send them a message if things went sideways back home or if Gaston got into too much trouble cavorting for Lady Briarthorn. The healing shack was in Judy's capable hands, and Paul had promised to send someone of sufficient worth to make sure people were healed in his absence.

With access to the portal system, they could return to the city in a flash and deal with any drama before heading back to the desert equally as quickly.

Tim pulled himself out of his thoughts of the future and addressed Jabari's Chosen directly. "Please inform Jabari the Great we cannot abide by his proposition. We have business to complete in the deserts and cannot be dissuaded from our course of action." Tim offered a small bow. "I'm sorry you've had to travel all this way. Maybe we can find you some fresh water and food for your return journey."

He felt a little poke in his ribs and knew Lorelei told him to tone it down a little.

The werehyena looked over them dispassionately. "Jabari the Great." The messenger paused to look up as he made a symbol over his chest with the fingers of his left hand. "He who is wise in all things anticipated your response and has already devised a response of his own."

The creature sprang into action and stabbed a soldier that let his guard down. As the were pulled the spear free from the body, he stared boldly at the soldiers. "Death is all that waits for you in the deserts of Naroosh."

The cobra darted forward and sank its fangs into a man's arm. A second later, ShadowLily cut the snake's head off. Being dead didn't stop the cobra's venom from tearing a strangled cry from the monster's last victim. Before the poison could cause any further harm, Tim cast Cleanse on the guard, quickly followed by Healing Orb.

Cassie was engaged with the werehyena when he turned. Her staff made the perfect match against his spear. Their tank moved with precision, slowly backing the creature away from the wounded soldier so the others could get him out. A few men took wounds as Jabari's Chosen threw some kind of tacks at them as they retreated. It was the perfect time for Tim to cast Healing Storm. The relief on Jon's face as his men made it to safety, healed and alive, was palpable.

Now all they had to do was take care of one last problem.

Cassie circled the messenger until his back was to ShadowLily. Somehow the hyena must have sensed the assassin's presence. The beast threw its spear at Cassie, grabbed its sword, and spun a slashing strike behind it. An arrow *plinked* off the blade, sending the sharpened iron into ShadowLily's arm instead of her throat.

His girlfriend went down faster than someone facing Iron Mike in the ring.

A strangled cry erupted from Tim's chest as he ran toward her. A Healing Orb was already flying from the tips of his fingers as Jabari's Chosen pulled his blade free.

Cassie stopped the next attack from ending ShadowLily's life with her staff. During the ruckus, Lorelei moved into a flanking position and was presently filling Jabari's Chosen with enough arrows to make his back look like a pincushion.

With enough arrows sticking out of you, one would imagine that fending off a fireball was probably impossible. Tim smiled as he thought about how right those people would have been as the flaming ball slammed into Jabari's Chosen, instantly vaporizing most of the were. Whatever magical protection the messenger had employed must have ended.

Tim cast a quick Cleanse on ShadowLily, in case the messenger's blade was poisoned, then he put every ounce of his strength into making her whole again.

Her eyes fluttered open as the muscles of her arm knit back together. "JaKobi's right. This shit hurts."

Tim kissed her and pulled her to her feet. "Tell me about it."

"You two can canoodle later. Right now I only want one thing from you." Cassie looked at them expectantly. "Just say we're going to the desert to kick this guy's ass."

The tank waved away Tim's concerned look. "Of course I mean in the morning, you giant turd muffin."

JaKobi grinned. "People need to find out what happens when you fuck with the Blue Dagger Society."

ShadowLily put an arm around Tim and led him away. "Sleep now, decisions on who and what to kill later."

"I guess we'll talk about it at breakfast, but I don't see any reason to delay our trip," Tim called as she dragged him from the courtyard.

Sleep was important, but there had to be another reason she was pulling him away from the victory. "What's up?"

"Oh, I know you heard the word Pharaoh and lost your shit. If I didn't get you out of there, the others would have convinced you to leave right now. I'm not ready to give up our last night with a bed and a roof so easily." ShadowLily smirked.

"You just named three of my favorite things." Tim started to pick up the pace.

"Oh yeah, what are those?" ShadowLily giggled.

Tim couldn't stop grinning like an idiot. "You, me, and the word bed."

She slapped his shoulder. "You're lucky I'm into you."

Didn't he know it.

CHAPTER TWO

"What's that wonderful smell?" Tim rolled out of bed.

After stumbling into the next room, he saw the pot that must contain the sweetest of life's blessings.

Coffee.

He poured a cup and looked back at the bed. ShadowLily was gone, but she'd left behind his favorite drink in the hope of rousing him. Tim appreciated the gentle touch after the violent poking attack she'd subjected him to earlier. The scent of fresh-brewed coffee did the trick that a thousand pokes would never accomplish.

It got him out of bed with a smile on his face.

Tim never missed the chance for another cup of coffee. It was kinda funny to think he could still catch a buzz from his morning cup of java inside a game, but he could, and he didn't have plans to stop that particular ritual anytime soon. Coffee was his autopilot drink for the morning. Some people wanted juice, but not him.

It was coffee or nothing at all.

One sniff of his armpits confirmed that addressing his caffeine addiction wasn't the only thing Tim needed to take care of that morning. A bath before breakfast was probably a good idea unless he didn't mind a few stares and pinched noses. A small sigh escaped his lips as he dug his toes into the thick rug and stretched his back. It was a shame the inventory trick only worked on his weapons and equipment.

He had to scrub the rest of himself clean the old-fashioned way.

And baths. Tim hated baths when he came into the game, and while they had grown on him slightly, what he really wanted was a shower. It wasn't until right now he realized how much he missed the one back in his room at the Blue Dagger Inn.

Maybe the people of Tristholm didn't know how great showers were.

Who knew, with Joe and Seraphina spending more time together, maybe he could get the restaurateur to put in a good word for him. Or it was time to buy a place in Tristholm. With a place of his own, he could put in as many showers as he wanted.

A shower in every fucking room.

Tim chuckled to himself as he sipped his coffee. *Every room might be a little excessive.* Still, it always paid to have your space.

What he didn't have time for was taking on another project. Between the healing shack, the slums, learning to smith, and his adventuring, he didn't have the time to take on something else. He already kind of felt like he was half-assing four things instead of focusing on one. That didn't mean he wasn't having a lot of fun.

It just meant he was busy.

Maybe being busy wasn't such a bad thing. Idle hands were the devil's plaything, or perhaps it was a drill sergeant's worst nightmare. Either way, life seemed to be better when he was busy. Between school and work it didn't give him a lot of time to get into trouble, and somehow he'd found a way to stay so busy in the game that trouble would have to seek him out. Maybe it was time to start being a little bolder and a little less planny.

There was a point when he assumed that his entire time in the game would revolve around his adventures in the capital city of

Promethia. Revitalizing the slums and the healing shack were long-term projects that he now realized he might not always be able to attend to himself.

Thankfully, the game made managing those projects easier. Instead of having an interface he had to watch constantly, he had contacts in the form of Mr. Applebottom and Paul the High Priest. While he was out of town or detained on other business, they made sure that things went smoothly in his absence.

At least that was how it worked in theory.

The last replacement at the healing shack hadn't exactly been up to the task, but this was new for all of them so he'd expected a few bumps in the road. What was life without a few hiccups?

Smooth sailing didn't build character.

Tim slipped into the warm bathwater and let the sudsy liquid wash away any lingering worries. What was there to be worried about? He had some of the best people in the world in his party, all of them wanted the same things out of their time in the game, and somehow his favorite place to eat was now only a portal hop away.

A deep sigh escaped his lips as his muscles relaxed. Tim reached out with a wet hand and found his coffee cup on the stool next to the bath.

Who said you couldn't have your cake and eat it too?

A few delightful mouthfuls later, Tim's brain started to move at a more desirable rate. This was the perfect time for him to go over his skill increases and select his item from the city guards' stockpile.

The list of items offered from the guards' armory had a rather pitiful selection of things that might be useful to his class. Most of the stuff was geared toward fighters, which made sense considering the source. It was kind of nice not to have to look over every item and scrutinize which might be best. In this case, there was a clear winner, and it wasn't even close.

Tarnished Circlet of Divine Wisdom

Luther The Great once wore this circlet. After hundreds of

years of less-than-worthy successors, the circlet now finds itself in your hands. Will you be the one to return this item to the splendor of its heyday?

+3 Wisdom +1 Intelligence

The Tarnished Circlet of Divine Wisdom can be upgraded twice. Once to Circlet of Divine Wisdom, and again to Polished Circlet of Divine Wisdom. Each time the item upgrades, its stats will increase.

To reach Circlet of Divine Wisdom, you must heal five hundred people.

Whoa!

Tim knew that the game had a few upgradable items because one of his group members had received something similar. While he knew this particular item wouldn't be with him at the endgame, it was nice to have something to work on while he worked toward whatever the endgame ended up being.

If *The Etheric Coast* had upgradable items at endgame, that would be super cool. Sometimes it was nice to have something to work on during a raid encounter besides beating the boss. Upgradable gear was another way to deepen the endgame experience, but to have the items while leveling was some next-level stuff.

It was so cool when you were a huge fan of a game, and the developers dropped some good news on you. Sometimes it felt like all the devs did was rain on your parade, but now and then they could make you smile too.

This was a time to grin like an idiot.

Tim pushed away his thoughts of what might be coming down the pipeline for them as they continued to level. The last thing he wanted to do was go down the rabbit hole of possibilities only to get yelled at for taking so long. Plus, his coffee was starting to run low, and he didn't see anyone magically appearing to refill it no matter how hard he wished for it to happen.

Before climbing out of the tub, Tim decided it was a good time to look over his stats and skills.

Interesting.

The system now sorted his skills from lowest ranking to highest. Tim wondered if he could change it to the other way around but decided to worry about finding out if the system had options later.

Skill Increased: Quick Feet

Rank: Novice level four

You used this spell to get out of danger, and that's the right way to do things. Keep using this spell to see further increases.

Quick Feet saved his ass from George the Lizard rat. Sometimes a small burst of speed made the difference.

Skill Increased: Night Vision

Rank: Novice level six

It's now five percent easier for you to see in low light conditions.

That little bit of extra light made things easier under the mountain and in the tomb. He would have to start spending more time in dark places to drag the skill up to the apprentice ranks.

Skill Increased: Flame Burst

Rank: Apprentice level four

You don't use this skill often, but when you do, it's always in new and unexpected ways.

It wasn't that Tim deliberately forgot to use this spell. It was that Divine Light was a more effective offensive strategy. The skill was pretty damn handy when he used it, and getting it up into the journeyman ranks would be a major boost to his limited offensive capabilities.

Skill Increased: Behold My Power

Rank: Novice level nine

This skill is so close to the apprentice ranks you should almost be able to taste it. Keep doing what you're doing and reap the benefits.

Behold My Power was such a tricky skill to use. Having to decide the right time to use it was tough. When could they afford to lose ten percent of their health, and was the fight going to be long enough for him to use it twice? There was a lot to consider when casting the curse, but it was so close to the next rank that Tim would have to use it in his next fight.

Skill Increased: Healing Storm

Rank: Apprentice level one

Using a skill regularly is the fastest way to increase your proficiency with it. You've used this spell very efficiently. Congratulations on reaching the apprentice ranks. The base amount healed by Healing Storm has increased by ten percent, and the spell now also applies a heal over time component. Ten percent of the ordinal heal will be applied as HOT over the next six seconds.

It wasn't a huge amount of additional healing, but any amount of free AOE healing was a welcome addition to the toolkit. The small heal over time component would be enough to take the edge off any nicks or bruises and let Tim apply his larger heals more judiciously.

Skill Increased: Way of the River

Rank: Apprentice level two

Use this stance more often to see greater results.

This stance was great for him when they were all taking damage, but it was highly situational. His first job would always be making sure Cassie stayed up. If the tank controlled the battle, the rest of the things would fall into place.

Skill Increased: Who Needs a Shield

Rank: Apprentice level three

This curse now applies an eleven percent reduction to an enemy's damage for ten seconds and increases the entire party's dodge chance by one percent.

Words couldn't describe how fond Tim was of this spell. Reduced damage meant he could contribute a few offensive strikes to the fight. He was pretty sure this spell was also a big factor in how JaKobi survived their fight with the blacksmith.

Skill Increased: Way of the Boulder

Rank: Apprentice level four

Your tank must love you. Not every healer can provide a flat-out damage reduction buff to their main source of protection, but you can. Continue using this skill to reach the journeyman ranks.

Tim felt like this skill would get a decent boost at the journeyman ranks after getting a big fat pile of zip at the apprentice ranks. It was funny how Cassie's class lined up with his. Her job was to avoid taking hits, but when she did, he reduced the damage by ten percent, twenty if he managed to cast Who Needs a Shield first.

It looked as though his Armor of Eternia and Attacks of the Faithful were both boosted to apprentice level four without much fanfare. He was interested to see if these skills would evolve over time or if they would become situational as they moved into new areas. One thing he knew, it didn't cost him anything to cast or maintain the buffs so he'd keep them up, even if they weren't effective.

Skill Increased: Curse of Giving

Rank: Apprentice level four

You must like this spell a lot. A LOT. That said, you use this curse with great efficiency. When isn't the right time to damage your enemies all while healing your group? Never. You should be using this spell all the time. This curse now returns ten percent of the damage done to the recipient(s) of your stance.

Tim couldn't help but agree.

This curse provided healing to his entire party if he slipped into his Way of the River stance. If he stayed in his main stance, it reduced the amount of attention he had to pay to Cassie, freeing him up to make calls to the raid. Curse of Giving was quickly becoming one of his favorite casts.

Skill Increased: Cleanse

Rank: Apprentice level eight

Hangover Spangover. Thankfully you've also used this spell for other things. Such as removing toxins and poisons from people's wounds. You know, the stuff Cleanse should be used for.

Hey!

Some would argue that being able to cure a hangover was more important than reattaching an arm. Tim chuckled as he took another sip of his coffee. Not having to worry about waking up with the spins, and spending the day tied to the porcelain throne is what made life worth living. He could have always stopped drinking, but now he didn't have to.

Skill Increased: Weaken Undead

Rank: Apprentice level eight

Dead things don't like you, and you don't like them. This is a perfect spell for getting rid of evil. Weaken Undead now lowers the resistances of the undead by twenty percent and all other creatures by ten percent.

It was a good skill to have, especially for undead boss monsters. The average dungeon boss had resistances that would make a normal MOB as jealous as Tim was of Ryan Reynolds' abs.

Who in the fuck has abs like that anyway?

Ryan does, that's who.

Skill Increased: Divine Light

Rank: Apprentice level nine

Crushing your enemy and seeing them flee before you, nope, you'd rather burn holes of holy fire through them. Divine Light does ten percent increased damage. The spell now also applies a DOT (damage over time) on the target for ten percent of the initial damage inflicted over five seconds.

If the spell didn't cost so much he'd use it all the damn time. Who didn't like shooting Ironman-like bolts of holy energy at people? Sure, Tim used a staff and not a super cool suit with a talking AI, but his thing was still cool as fuck. This was his default attack after Curse of Giving, and he was excited to see how it would change at the journeyman ranks.

Skill Increased: Healing Orb

Rank: Journeyman level four

Oh, the old tried and true. There's a bet going on that you wouldn't stop using this skill even if the developers made it suck. Not to worry, that kind of thing is totally unethical, and a developer would never dream of nerfing your favorite skill into oblivion.

;-)

This spell is thirty percent more effective than at base level and applies thirty-five percent of the initial heal as a heal over time.

Those bastards better leave my Healing Orb alone!

Tim would be so pissed if they nerfed his bread-and-butter ability. It wasn't his fault that he used the heal so well in conjunction with his curses. Despite how effective his healing seemed to be, he was pretty sure he was in the middle of the road when it came to heals per second numbers. His class choice gave him a ton of utility while sacrificing pure healing numbers, so it was his ability to do more than heal that made his class shine.

With his curses applying damage to a lot of their targets, it shrank the workload on the DPS, or if his damage-dealing compatriots decided to push it, then he could ease off and focus on pure healing output. It was a near-perfect situation for Tim. Although they had come close to getting wiped out more times than he was willing to admit.

Living on the edge wasn't his style.

Play it safe and have a plan was the way Tim liked to handle his business. If there was time for it, he also preferred not only to have a plan but a backup and a contingency as well. You never knew when your first couple of options would turn to shit, and you had to pull a rabbit out of your ass to survive. There was no reason to go through life flailing around when all you had to do was take a few moments to set yourself up for success.

"Hey, what are you still doing in the tub?" ShadowLily walked into the bathroom. "Get out and get dressed. Everyone is waiting for you. *Again.*"

"Damned ungrateful morning people is what you are." Tim laughed. "I'm also not saying I'd hate you if you got me a little more of that coffee."

ShadowLily stopped and stared at him. "Lucky I don't pour the pot out on your big fat head." Her tone softened. "If it gets you out of the tub faster, one cup of coffee coming right up."

"Thank you!" Tim shouted as he pulled himself out of the cast-iron monstrosity of a tub.

It took him a second to figure out why she snapped at him, but then he realized his mistake. It was a good rule of thumb never to ask someone to do something for you that you could easily do yourself. It was also polite when you got up from the table to ask if anyone needed anything, but he sucked at doing that too. Realizing the mistake was the first step to success.

Not repeating it was the second.

Little moments like this also reminded him to be thankful for the special people in his life. Sometimes you needed someone to give you a little reality check. It was always easy to get caught up in your hype. Every single thing he'd accomplished in this game wouldn't have been possible without his friends. From Gaston the assassin up to the Goddess Eternia herself, there were many people responsible for his success. It wouldn't hurt for Tim to tell them how much he appreciated them more often.

Maybe after another cup of joe.

He took a few moments to make sure he was dry before equipping his clothes. He'd made the mistake a few times of not completely drying off first, and there was no worse feeling than underwear sticking to your wet skin. Who wanted to spend the day like that?

So far, the best thing about the inventory system for him was that it didn't matter how much gear you had. It could always be equipped in an instant as long as you were out of combat. Tim also found the ability to save items into sets incredibly helpful for when he wanted to change outfits in the market or simply go from using his assassination skills to his healing. All he had to do was think of which of his five active slots he wanted to activate, and the magic happened.

New clothes would appear on him instantly. It was the kind of thing that would make every runway model in the world jealous. Not to mention his clothes always smelled awesome when he put them on, as though he pulled them from the drier moments before.

ShadowLily was stomping her foot impatiently when Tim exited the bathroom. She pointed at the cup of steaming coffee on the table. "It's grab and go time."

Ignoring the cup of steamy hot perfection, Tim moved directly to the woman of his dreams and wrapped her in his arms. "I love you." He kissed her. "And I couldn't do any of this without you."

"Don't you forget it." She shoved him away as she smirked. "We don't have time for your sweet-talk right now. We have people waiting for us."

Tim sighed dramatically. "If sweet-talking is out, I guess we should go." He motioned for her to lead the way.

He followed ShadowLily for five steps before turning and running back for his coffee. Tim sipped the delightful liquid and hurried to catch up, cup in hand. The best part about the day was that whatever they faced, it would be new and exciting. The deserts of Naroosh awaited.

But not until there was more coffee.

A proper day of adventuring could never be accomplished without the requisite amount of caffeine.

CHAPTER THREE

Breakfast was a meal of indulgence.

At least it could be when someone felt the urge to be a little naughty. Tim liked living on the wild side of the menu for brunch, especially after a long night out or in celebration of a recent accomplishment. Sometimes he wanted to pretend he was celebrating so no one could judge him for eating slices of pumpkin bread French toast with cream cheese frosting. Sometimes it was okay to give in to temptation, and eating something bad wouldn't end up with him getting his balls cut off like a night with another girl would.

There was also something to be said about the power of a good Denver omelet when you paired it with hash browns and biscuits and gravy. If Tim felt like waddling home, he added a side of corned beef hash. It felt like there wasn't a problem in the world that couldn't be hashed out over a good breakfast. Whenever he had a big problem that didn't solve itself in the shower, he figured it out with a fork in his hand.

Better than the guy who figured it out while pooping.

Not that being in college was all sunshine and daydreams. If you wanted to do well, you had to work your ass off. They told you about the credit hours upfront. What they didn't tell you was that for each hour in the classroom, a student had triple those hours of work outside it. Toss in a part-time job and an active social life, and sleep became something of an indulgence, and full meals a weekly luxury.

On the weekends, Tim liked to knock out both of those activities at the same time. Eat enough food to feed a village followed by a nap that lasted late into the afternoon. Saturdays were a gift from the gods and should never be wasted with such idle things as working or catching up on chores.

Saturdays should be celebrated with an extra slice of carrot cake you brought home to give you that special kind of sugar rush upon rising from second napsies.

Sunday was when he caught up on all the things he'd put off during the week. A.K.A. panic and spend the entire day studying. Tim wasn't amassing massive amounts of student loans so he could get C's in class.

Imagine paying someone to be mediocre.

Michael Jordan didn't show up to work every day thinking, you know if I just slack off a little today no one will notice. No sir, the guy invented insults and slights to keep himself motivated. While Tim was no MJ, when it came down to failing, he was only prepared to do it if he'd given it his all.

Tim picked business as his college major because numbers made more sense to him than words. Despite his best efforts, his coding skills stayed somewhere around the average fifth grader's. Meaning he could create a half-assed blog or a forum, but that was about it.

So he took the safe route.

Right up until he met a girl named Sierra, and she planted the idea of going into *The Etheric Coast* in his head. Of course, he'd thought about it before, but it never seemed like a viable option until he sat down and did the math. It wasn't as if the woman of his dreams influenced his decision at all.

The plan had been to enter the game and work as an apprentice to a blacksmith. Tim would have left the game with a huge chunk of his student debt erased and a little spending money. Somewhere along the way, he'd decided to lay all his dreams on the line and become an adventurer.

With the guild they had, it was worth the risk.

Although at the time it felt like Tim was taking a major leap of faith, now he had a streaming contract that erased most of his immediate worries. Tim didn't even have to edit the videos. All he had to do was mentally hit record. It'd become so easy for him to do that he didn't even think about it anymore. No one wanted to be bogged down with video editing and worrying about buttons when they were inside a new world and fighting to bring down the baddest creatures the developers could throw at them.

In a world of magic and monsters, what most players wanted to do was kick ass. The little intrusion streaming put on his life was easily outweighed by the benefits of having his POD fees covered and money going home to his parents. They deserved to be able to take it easy for a while. The money he was sending them wasn't the kind of cold hard cheddar that would let them quit their jobs, but it was enough to take care of an unexpected expense or two, and who couldn't do with a few less bills?

It wasn't like Tim's parents wanted to be millionaires and live in a big mansion. His folks were simple people. All they wanted was to give their kids the best opportunity to succeed they could. If that meant sacrificing things like new cars, or eating out so their children could have the best, then that was what they did. Tim realized how much he owed them the more he thought about it.

His folks were hard on him, but they were also the reason he was successful.

Without his parents taking such an active role in his life, Tim probably wouldn't have gone to college. Most of the kids from his neighborhood didn't. He remembered how they mocked him for caring about class, for actually doing his homework. Teased him for being scared of what his parents would do if he skipped school with his friends.

In the end, he'd made it to college, and now he was a graduate.

How fucking cool was that?

Tim knew his parents wouldn't stop sacrificing things until they gave his brother and sister the same opportunities he had. The fact he could help out in some small way made him feel good. Family was what made life worth living. Sure, sometimes those two brats were frustrating as hell, but at the end of the day, no one had your back like family.

Tim's family bubble now extended to a few more people.

There was no other word that could better describe the members of the Blue Dagger Society than family. All of them would give everything they had for every member of the guild. Being in the guild was like moving into a neighborhood where your best friends owned all the other houses. Joe took the place of all of their fathers, making sure they were fed and looked after one another. JaKobi might as well have been his brother, and Cassie and Lorelei his sassy sisters.

Then there was ShadowLily.

The woman was quickly becoming the love of his life. If he had to describe how much she meant to him in one word it would be Buttercup. Although his princess was a whole lot more deadly, and he liked it that way. He tried to justify coming into the game rationally, but at the end of the day, all he really wanted was a chance to spend more time with her. It didn't matter how much Tim tried to rationalize it. Facts were facts.

Risky, sure.

Unwise, some might think so.

For Tim, it was the best decision of his life.

"Pass me the pecan syrup." JaKobi nudged Tim out of his daze.

Tim picked up the warm jug and handed it to him. "You know, with all the magic we have access to, you'd think one of us would have learned how to levitate things."

"I like fire." JaKobi poured steaming syrup over a mountain of pancakes. "Lifting things with your mind doesn't seem nearly as useful."

Tim snickered. "Only when you run out of toilet paper and that roll under the sink is just out of reach."

Cassie slapped the healer on the shoulder. "No bathroom talk when we're eating."

"Yes, Mother." Tim eyed her over the rim of his coffee cup, but Cassie ignored him and turned back to Lorelei, and started talking about Joe and Seraphina.

Not needing to know more about his girlfriend's father's dating life, Tim turned his attention to his plate of food. He didn't know if he got hungry in the game or that he simply wanted to eat. Either way, the result was the same.

He stuffed his face full of delicious.

Tim's first plateful went down faster than that guy Leonidas kicked into the well. Halfway through his second plate of sunny side up eggs over skillet potatoes with biscuits and gravy on the side, he slowed down and savored the taste.

Why was it that biscuits and gravy were so damn good?

It was one of those questions that didn't need an answer. Sometimes things were awesome, and they stayed that way forever. Unlike some of his favorite movies as a kid, biscuits and gravy would never go out of style. The real trick was getting Tim to try something new. He was a tried-and-true kind of guy. He knew what he liked, and he ordered it all the time.

Then he met someone who wasn't afraid to challenge him. ShadowLily could break him out of any rut, even a food rut. No matter what they did together there was an almost infectious energy around her, and he was starting to think of things as theirs instead of his and hers. As long as their nights didn't end up with her drunkenly throwing knives at things he was holding on his head everything would be fine.

He looked up when she walked into the room. It was like he just knew she was there. Like he wasn't complete without her by his side. He shook his head for a moment trying to get rid of the mushy crap that was filling it, but he couldn't do it. Love wasn't a battlefield for the weak.

Tim stopped with his fork halfway up to his mouth to watch her sit at the table, then realized that he probably looked a little ridiculous with his mouth wide open and a spoonful of yolky potatoes dripping back onto the plate. Hurriedly shoveling the bite into his mouth, he chewed it as quickly as he could and finished it off with a swig of rumpleberry juice.

Trying to pretend he was cool as a cucumber, Tim grinned from ear to ear. "Nice of you to join us, sleepyhead."

Laughing, ShadowLily speared a sausage from the tray in the middle of the table. "As if. Who do you think carried in all this food?"

It dawned on Tim that ShadowLily probably grew up working in the restaurant business because her dad owned a diner. That meant Joe raised her on early mornings and hard work. Tim's dad worked the late shift on Fridays, which meant he usually spent Saturdays watching cartoons and eating cereal from a mixing bowl on the couch.

Was half a box really too much?

It felt like a hasty retreat was the best approach in this case so Tim decided to play things smooth. "I guess it could have been me who slept in."

ShadowLily didn't seem impressed with his effort so he moved on to plan number two. Blame the other guy. "That late-night fight took it out of me."

"Don't blame the freaky hyena because you didn't get up with the rest of us," ShadowLily scolded. "It's like you forgot all about going to Naroosh today. It was all I could do to hold these guys back."

Tim slapped a hand against his heart. "You wound me. I promise that I will be of no further delay."

Cassie snorted. "I won't believe that until you get a few more cups of coffee in ya."

"Touché." Tim grabbed the carafe and refilled his mug.

Looking around the table, he decided it was time to get the spotlight off of himself before he ended up in a deeper hole than he was already in. "So what's the plan for today?"

"I think I can answer that," Seraphina boldly commented as she walked into the room. "Or at least the first part."

This was one of the moments Tim instinctively knew it was better to keep his mouth shut. ShadowLily might put up with his crap, but Seraphina probably wouldn't enjoy it nearly as much. Tim watched the city's leader and waited to find out what would happen next.

"Joe and I will join you on your journey to The Hallow, along with a small retainer of my men. With the passage open and less-than-friendly creatures making their way through it would be better to have a warning system in place. Last thing we need is a hundred of those things wreaking havoc in the countryside."

"Sounds good to me." Tim smiled. "But instead of riding there, why don't we use the quick travel?"

Seraphina gave him a sly look as if that had been the reason she came along. "I guess we could bring a smaller advance party and have the rest of the men meet us there on horseback." She glanced at the group. "We'll need to have a ride back."

Tim hadn't thought of how Joe and Seraphina would get back to Tristholm once the rest of them went into the desert. It seemed logical that they would have full access to the portal system. Or maybe she wanted to get the guy alone in a carriage for the afternoon. It wasn't the right time to harass her about the details—there were pancakes to finish before they left.

Plus, who wanted to ride a horse when they could get there instantly? Sure, it was all nice and relaxing until your horse saw a werewolf, then your balls ended up pulverized faster than someone shotgunning a beer.

CHAPTER FOUR

Khalid peered into the cavern, looking for any sign of the monster lurking inside.

He glanced over his shoulder and motioned for the small band of hunters to move into place. This was the last place he wanted to be, but after the woman and child had disappeared while fetching water at the river, it was the logical spot to go.

Jabari had ordered him not to pursue the matter, but leaving one of the people under his protection to be killed by a river dragon was madness. A leader protects his people and looks out for them, cares for them. He doesn't sacrifice them to the monsters of the wild.

A noble who refused to protect his people wasn't noble at all.

Not that he'd been fuming about it since he stormed out of the palace after his morning prayers. His time in the temple had only hardened his resolve that something had to be done. If he couldn't handle the task officially, he could hire two hunters and some porters and do it on his own.

It had taken the entire day to find the right men for the job and track the monster to this cavern. How the water dragon covered so much ground with the woman and child in its jaws was astounding. It was one thing to kill a person and quite another to carry two bodies for miles.

The sun dipped on the horizon, bathing the cavern's entrance in shadows. The perfect time for them to attack would be in the morning, but by then the woman and her daughter might be dead. He was probably kidding himself that they were alive now, but he knew if it were him out here injured and alone he would want someone to come and save his ass. The sun was setting behind the cavern, but inky black shadows had already covered the interior.

Slow-moving water eddied and swirled around the cave's entrance. The monster could have been waiting for them right there if the water was deep enough. There was no way to tell in the low light until it attacked or got lucky. Spotting the eyes of a crocodile at night was almost impossible.

Hunting a crocodile was dangerous at the best of times.

Despite being lone predators, the massive animals often congregated together on the riverbanks. It wasn't unheard of to see great packs of the reptiles sunning themselves on the shores, not unlike Jabari's many wives at the palace's sapphire pools.

The crocodiles of the river Euz were stronger and larger than those of its many tributaries. It must have been the river's fertile waters, or maybe it was the healthy fish population they had cultivated to help feed the crops that lined the muddy banks. It wasn't unheard of for the city's fishermen to report tales of seeing twelve and even fifteen-foot specimens. Of course, there were tales of larger crocodiles, but Khalid paid them no mind.

Fantasies were for the ears of children.

It wasn't as if they were some backwater people. They didn't only have canoes. Their flotilla sported many barges. Some were for sailing, others for making war. It would take a massive river dragon indeed to destroy one of Jabari's finer vessels.

Khalid made the sign of the goddess over his chest and thanked her that it wasn't one of the river cows instead. While the giant hippos looked docile and kind of cute, they were the most deadly creatures around. He'd seen a man snapped in half, a whole group of canoes overturned by a single one of the hulking brutes.

Then they would disappear underwater.

It was well known that the hippos could hold their breath for remarkable periods while they traveled along the river bottom. It made them frustrating creatures to hunt. It wasn't until he thought of attaching bamboo rods and rope to the ends of some of their arrows that the annual hunt became productive. With the simple invention of a buoy, they could follow the underwater beasts' progress and be in position to kill them when they surfaced for air. Tonight, they weren't hunting for their annual feast. They were doing something of much greater importance.

Trying to save lives.

Being out here against orders was one thing, but killing the monster was worse. Still, the lady of light called to him. It was as if his heart was filled with light. If the goddess wanted him here, there was no other place he would rather be. Not that his master was very understanding. He had spoken of praying to the gods himself and getting a very different answer.

Were they even praying to the same gods?

It fell on his shoulders to act. Khalid would follow his heart and do what he must, despite Jabari's decree. Displeasing a man of such importance was a risky business. As the head of the city's soldiers, Khalid held a certain amount of leeway in how he handled his orders. The short amount of leash he had didn't extend to openly defying his master's will.

In this life, sometimes we do what we must.

Once a water dragon tasted human flesh, it never stopped hungering for it. The woman and child would only be the first of many taken if they didn't end this now. It was the honorable thing to do. Something he would have expected any of his men to do for any of the villagers. What kind of man would he be if he turned around now?

"Light the torches!" Khalid roared.

He found that when he was nervous or a little scared, it helped to act with a confidence he didn't feel. Nothing was worse in battle than doubt. It was okay to be cautious, but doubt was never an option.

Not if you wanted to live.

Now that they had come so far, there was nothing to do but see their mission through. Sleeping in the marshlands was out of the question, and so was walking back in the dark. All of them would have been easy prey for the giant crocs at night. The river dragons were notoriously nocturnal hunters. While this one had been awake most of the day, the lure of a feast right outside its den might be too much for the crocodile to ignore.

If they wanted to live, they had to end this now.

The two hunters lined up behind him. Each of them was equipped with a bow and followed by a servant holding a torch. Khalid was blessed to have been able to lure two of Nar'ha's famous archers away from the pub with promises of glory. The two archers were the perfect backup to Khalid and his trusty spear.

It took him a moment to strap the small leather buckler to his wrist. Khalid still wasn't sure why he was bothering except out of tradition and his hope that the goddess' words etched into the wood by his wife would keep him safe. It wasn't like the wooden shield was strong enough to stop a bite from a river dragon, but entering the battle without the item wasn't an option.

Sometimes a little luck was all that kept you breathing and your opponent dead.

The spear in his hand filled him with confidence. Three times the weapon had been blessed by the gods during the hunt and once again in the arena. The spear had become so important he even gave it a name—Sekhet.

Tonight, Sekhet would become the great leveler.

"Stay behind me and keep your eyes open," Khalid commanded as he walked forward.

Keeping his body angled behind the shield, he slowly moved down toward the water's edge and followed the slow-moving liquid into the caverns. Hefting his spear above his head allowed him to throw the weapon or to stab with it. Keeping the crocodile at a distance would be the key to his survival.

Khalid cast one look behind himself to make sure the men still had the heart to see this through. Leaving now would bring great dishonor to their names, but fear couldn't always be controlled. He'd seen war-hardened veterans piss themselves in fear before a battle, but they always fought. He didn't know these men well enough to rely on their ability to summon courage when it was called for. The two had the look of men who would fight until death snatched them away.

Still, looks could be deceiving.

Jabari appeared to be a great man. He had many wives, he owned all the land, and people bowed at his feet. However, it was all for show. Unlike his father, Jabari was petty and cruel. One wrong word could end with a man ruined in reputation and wealth. Sycophantic followers surrounded him, and he wasn't someone to be trifled with on the best of days.

The cavern's interior was darker than Jabari's heart and a good deal more than Khalid would have liked. As the men followed him inside, their torches reflected off the water and spread the light farther than it would have gone without the liquid assistance. The cavern must have been immense for none of their light to reach the back. He'd expected the space to be big enough for a few of his men, but he could have fit an entire company inside.

How was it possible that he never knew this place existed?

It wasn't as if Khalid hadn't spent the entirety of his youth hunting in the marshes of the great river. His skills as a hunter were why Jabari's father plucked him from obscurity and sent him down the path he was on now. Such a great man deserved respect, and it was the main reason he stayed in his position after the man died.

Some decisions haunt you longer than others.

The choice to come here wouldn't keep him awake for even a night. The right thing to do wasn't always easy. It was kind of like a person admitting they were wrong. It took effort and resolve, but it was worth it.

Plus, it wasn't as though all the cards were stacked against them. At least they only had one pool of water to keep an eye on. A river dragon big enough to carry two people away wouldn't fit anywhere except the main space of the cavern. Although today it felt like every blessing was a curse as if when he flipped a coin, one side was light and the other only darkness.

The only downside here was that the space was too big for him to keep watch over the entire surface of the water all at once.

Keeping his head moving from side to side, Khalid looked for any sign of a body or the crocodile as he circled the edge.

"What manner of place is this?" one of the torch bearers mumbled in hushed awe.

Khalid heard a *thunk* from behind him and looked back to see one of the hunters smiling as the torchbearer grimaced and moved both his torches to one hand so he could rub the back of his head.

"Hold the torches high, and let the goddess protect you. A righteous man has nothing to fear." Pili the hunter motioned with his bow for the man to get moving.

Knowing that the situation was under control, Khalid continued deeper into the cavern. The sound of slowly moving water was loud enough to drown out their footsteps, but the fact they hadn't laid eyes on the monster yet was disturbing. The river dragons weren't exactly known for their subtlety.

The sound of breaking wood made Khalid's head snap to the left faster than a cobra could strike.

A crocodile bigger than he'd ever laid eyes on stomped into the room from some hidden recess at the back of the cavern. The snapping sound came from a human leg the beast was chewing on like one of Khalid's hunting dogs with a bone. Seeing the size of the monster, Khalid knew he should have turned and tried to run, but the thrill of the hunt was on him now, and there was no turning back.

A kill like this would etch his name in the histories right below the gods themselves.

Readying himself for the battle, Khalid called upon Eternia for strength and Mosi to guide his hand. The goddesses wouldn't let him down; they never had before. Three wars, two fights to the death, and one rebellion later he was still standing.

With the gods on your side, nothing was impossible.

The twenty-foot crocodile moved past the men as if they weren't there. It slid into the water as it finished off the leg. Khalid watched the ripples for a moment, then all signs of the monster disappeared.

This was where things would get interesting.

They stood zero chance with the predator in the water. The only way for them to hurt the giant monster was to get him out. Attacking the croc across the room would have been ideal, but the sheer size of the creature had momentarily stunned him from charging into battle. Now they had to lure the beast out of the water so he could keep it busy while the archers did most of the work.

A loose stone brushed against his boot. Khalid bent to pick up the rock, then threw it by the side of the pool so it bounced along the edge before plopping into the water. The river dragoon exploded from under the surface, its jaws snapping at the air as it slid forward on its belly into the cave.

"Arrows!" Khalid cried.

Rolling to the side so both archers could have a clear line of sight, he prepared himself for what was coming next. Before the river dragon could do more than turn its head, three arrows were sticking out of its side. Not that they seemed to have slowed the monster at all.

Khalid had the creature's full measure now and knew that one snap of those jaws and it wasn't only his shield that would break in half like a toothpick. Fear robbed a man of courage, and when there was none to be found, a warrior could only do one thing.

Charge!

Khalid ran toward the crocodile, closing the distance between them in an instant. A scream tore from his lips as he beat his spear's haft against the rim of his shield. *That's right. Your tasty snack is right here you big motherfucker.*

The gods chose this path for him. Live or die, Khalid knew this was exactly where he should be.

The river dragon was shifting its focus to the archers despite his taunts. It was time to remind the giant crocodile that the problem right in front of you was never a good idea to ignore.

Khalid's spear lashed out, catching the mighty beast behind the jaw. His arms never trembled in battle before, but now they were shaking like leaves caught in an autumn breeze. He fought to hold onto the weapon as the monster whipped its head around in a fury.

"Oh, shit!"

Why was the ground rushing toward his face?

Khalid managed to twist at the last second and take the fall on his side. His hand still gripped the shaft of his spear so at least he hadn't lost the weapon. There was no way to know if he got hit with the tail or if the massive beast had merely shaken him free. It didn't matter. He had to get back up.

"Goddess grant me the strength to banish this monster back to the depths." Khalid glanced to the heavens before flipping back to his feet. There was no way he'd make it back to the crocodile before it killed the hunters, so he squared his stance, cocked his arm, and lined up his shot.

Something hit him from behind, and Khalid hit the ground hard, again. The air flew out of his lungs as he struggled to figure out what happened. It must have been the monster's tail. This time he rolled back to his feet, controlling how his body moved, so when he was finally standing, he could throw the spear in one fluid motion.

With nothing left to lose, he let Sekhet fly.

The gods must have been smiling upon him today since the spear flew with a falcon's grace. At the last possible second, the tip dipped a fraction, and instead of skimming the top of the monster, it plunged deep into its side.

The river dragon roared in rage and snapped at the nearest thing to him. One of the torch bearers disappeared in a gout of blood. The crocodile shook his head so violently that one of the man's legs flew off and landed on the cavern floor twenty feet away. The creature spat out the rest of the man's body and turned to focus on the source of his torment.

"This isn't going to be fun!" Khalid clutched the sword on his hip.

Maybe the gods didn't favor him nearly as much as he thought.

That was the thing with the gods. Their love could be as fickle as a springtime rain. Khalid smiled as death approached him on four legs and a tail. The monster was faster than a chariot pulled by a team of Jabari's finest horses, and it seemed the fates would determine the outcome of this battle in moments.

If the gods ordained his death, then Khalid would meet it with honor.

The only way to ensure his place in the heavens was to make sure that the creature came with him. Arrows filling the river dragon's side reminded Khalid that he wasn't in this alone. A grin spread across his lips as he looked over the shafts. Then his eyes settled on the rent caused by his spear. The battle was almost over, but would the gods see him through it to the end?

Jaws the size of his first house opened, ready to crush him like a pesky mare would crush an apple. Khalid threw his body to the side not caring about anything except getting away. He hit the ground hard but was happy to be sore and not missing a limb. He couldn't sense the monster anywhere, but he knew it must be coming for him so he whipped the sword around in a wild slash as he leapt to his feet..

The blade bit deeply into the crocodile's tail with a meaty *thunk. The tail, not what I was expecting.* The attack seemed like a good idea when Khalid thought the jaws of death were closing in on him, but now that the thick hide of the crocodile's tail trapped his blade, his plan seemed to have some minor flaws.

The first of which became apparent as the river dragon started to move.

Holding onto his sword seemed like a feat of Herculean strength. Every step the crocodile took threatened to rip the blade from his hands. The muscles in his shoulders burned, and ever so slowly Khalid's fingers started to slip. Rather than risking his grip faltering before he could secure the blade, he simply let the sword go.

He stood there in the darkness feeling the weight of his destiny crushing down upon him. Fear tried to creep into his heart, but Khalid shoved it away. Being hard-headed as a mule also seemed to have blessed him with a short memory. He would not go whimpering off into the night like a scared child on his first hunt. He would show the monster what it meant to be a true warrior of the light.

"Eternia!" Khalid screamed as he rushed forward with his dagger in hand.

Although the weapon was only as big as one of the river dragon's teeth, Khalid would do what he must. The monster ignored his screams and reckless charge. His feet thumped against the cavern floor with growing intensity, and he lifted the dagger above his head. Seeming to sense him at the last second, the crocodile started to turn in his direction.

This was it, his chance to end it.

Khalid's dagger buried itself deep into the river dragon's eye, and for the first time since the fight started, he felt as if victory was assured. But the gods were a fickle bunch, always giving with one hand and burning with the other.

The strike to the crocodile's eye was a killing blow, but it wasn't instantly fatal as it would have been if he used his sword. Which probably meant he was in for a world of hurt. The beast whipped its head frantically back and forth as the blade turned the crocodile's eye into a pile of jelly, trying to dislodge whatever had plunged into it.

The massive snout slammed into Khalid's ribs and sent him flying through the air. He had enough time to appreciate the sensation of being a falcon on the hunt before his left side and back collided with the cavern wall.

His left arm cracked as he tried to slow his impact. It must have worked a little because he wasn't dead, only sore enough to wish he was. Every inch of him screamed in pain as he rose unsteadily to his feet. Cradling his broken arm against his chest, Khalid watched the river dragon's death throes as a grin spread across his lips.

A broken arm was usually nothing to smile about, but after this fight, it seemed like a blessing. The monster was dead, and now it was time to see if they could find the two women. The elation he felt over the battle quickly faded as he remembered the sound of snapping bones.

If even one of them is alive, this was worth it.

Turning away from the greatest kill of his life, Khalid pointed at the remaining torchbearer. "You, bring one of the torches to me."

Seeing that the servant was moving to carry out his order, Khalid turned his attention back to the two hunters. "Go and get the porters. The people of the valley will sing about this battle for ages."

The torchbearer handed Khalid one of the torches and started to back away. He stopped the man with a stare. "Can you collect my dagger?"

Looking at the blade sticking out of the giant crocodile's eye the man simply replied, "Sir?"

Not wanting to waste more time than he needed to, Khalid thrust his torch back at the man and strode toward the dead river dragon. It took him three tries to wrench the blade free with only one arm, but it slid out with a wet *pop*.

After wiping the worst of the gunk off the weapon, he slapped the dagger home in its sheath and looked around the cavern floor for his sword. Khalid motioned for the torchbearer to follow him but realized the man was still staring at the monster they had slain and not paying any attention to him at all.

Khalid cleared his throat. He was about to rip him a new one but knew that it wouldn't do any good. Even dead, the monster was a good deal scarier than it had any right to be. So instead of chewing the man out, he simply instructed, "Follow me and keep the torches held high."

A few moments later, Khalid found his sword. He picked up the blade and swooshed the weapon through the air a few times. After deciding on the best way to use the blade without exposing his left side and useless arm to a potential foe, he spoke to the torchbearer trailing behind him. "I'll handle security. You keep me bathed in light."

"Yes, sir."

He really should have learned the man's name, but the servants they used changed so frequently it was damn near impossible. Although this man had shown some stones by not running after the croc ripped the other torchbearer to pieces. It took real courage to continue doing your job when people were dying around you.

If they had found the women already, this would have been a massive celebration, but Khalid was starting to worry that they might not have made it to the cavern in time. A song worthy of a hero's epic battle wouldn't have a fitting end unless they saved the damsels. No one wanted to sing songs about the hero that almost saved the princess, even if they did kill a big-ass monster first.

Was that someone crying?

Khalid followed the sounds deeper into the cavern. It could have been a trap, but he doubted anyone was ballsy enough to do that behind the crocodile. Slowly he followed the winding cavern until he found a small recessed alcove. Inside the space were one very traumatized teen and five or six hard maple crates with heavy iron lids. The trunks were big enough they couldn't have been carried here by men alone. It would have taken a team of oxen and an army of porters to move the chests way out here.

The only reason someone would go through all that trouble was if the contents were worth a fortune. His eyes sparkled at the thought of potential riches, but the look quickly faded as they settled on the teen.

"It's okay to come out. The monster is dead." Khalid held out his hand for the girl.

As she climbed out of the space, he realized he knew her. It was Neema. She was about the same age his daughter would have been if she was still alive. If he remembered correctly, a long time ago the two girls might have been friends.

The girl clutched a wound on her leg as she limped out of the alcove. "My mother?"

All Khalid could do was shake his head. There was nothing he could have done to save the girl's mother so he shoved the guilt he felt to the side and focused on the tasks at hand. While Neema's mother couldn't be honored in the traditional way, surely her spirit would still find the afterlife and be waiting for Neema with open arms upon her death.

Khalid laid an arm over the girl's shoulders and spoke. His voice was rich with empathy and held the promise of better days to come. "I will go to the temple with you myself, and we will ask the gods to look after her."

"I will sacrifice one of our sheep to see her safely into the next life." The girl looked up into his eyes. "Thank you, Khalid."

This was a girl on the very edge of womanhood. In her, he saw the strength he would have been proud to see in his daughter. "Know that if you ever need anything at all, if it is in my power to give it to you, it will be yours."

"I want to get the hell out of here. I keep waiting for that thing to wake up and try and eat us." Neema looked past Khalid and the torchbearer into the darkness beyond.

The entire cavern filled with bright orange light as they made their way back toward the dead river dragon. The hunters had returned with the porters and were harnessing the crocodile to a large wooden travois. The men ignored Khalid and continued with their business as he limped past them.

At the cave's entrance, Khalid stopped and focused on Neema for a moment. "You can leave the cavern but do not go too far. I will join you when it's time to leave."

Before they left, he had to find out if what was in the crates was worth taking with them. It was dumb of him not to have checked while he was there, but getting Neema out of the caverns seemed more critical at the time. He motioned for someone to watch the girl and for a few other men to follow him back into the cave.

The lid on the crate was too heavy for him to move aside on his own so he had two of the men do it for him. He was surprised to see that treasure filled the crate to the top. The next one was equally full.

"Load these up, and not a word to anyone." Khalid looked over each of the men. "I don't have to tell you what Jabari is willing to do to keep a secret."

With his business taken care of, he started back toward his men, intending to find someone to take care of his arm and maybe something he could chew on to take the edge off. There was still something about this that didn't make any sense. What kind of man would hide his treasure out here?

The dangerous kind.

Still, there wasn't a scarier son of a bitch out there than Jabari, unless of course, a person had the displeasure of meeting the Pharaoh himself. Khalid almost laughed at the thought. The man rarely left the palace. He'd never store anything this important out in the middle of nowhere. They had probably taken some warlord's recent spoils. Sucked for whoever lost it, but everything was coming up for Khalid today.

May the gods be praised.

CHAPTER FIVE

J abari's palace courtyard was illuminated like it was a feasting day.

Instead of the happy faces of the villagers, the grim and determined faces of his soldiers greeted Khalid. Instantly, he knew there would be trouble. At this time of night, shadows should have bathed the courtyard with one or two men patrolling the perimeter. With this many men present it could only mean that Jabari was coming to address them.

Khalid had trained most of these men himself, if not all of them. How was it that he couldn't find a single friendly face among the bunch? Had he not earned enough respect among them to get a simple smile upon his glorious return?

It didn't seem like warm and fuzzies were on the menu tonight.

Maybe going after the women was the wrong choice after all?

No, doing the right thing was never the wrong choice. He had done as he must, as the goddess would have commanded. That didn't mean he wasn't standing hip-deep in a pile of shit right now. The only way out of this now was to beg for forgiveness and hope that his position as head of the guards bought him some leeway.

Khalid felt the walls closing in. He was always listening to his heart instead of his head, and not for the last time it was going to cost him. It was one thing to be lax in the enforcement of certain decrees and another to openly defy his master. The choice had seemed simple at the time. The river dragon had been a menace, and its attacks on the village would have only gotten worse as time went on.

Standing in the courtyard surrounded by soldiers, the decision didn't feel so simple anymore.

If killing the river dragon wouldn't make Jabari happy, then maybe the six chests full of golden coins would? Hadn't he seen several of the nobles bargain their way into favorable contracts by offering large sums of gold in return? The treasure might not be enough to let him keep his position, but it might be enough to spare his life.

Khalid motioned for the porters to drop their loads and leave.

Most of the men looked relieved to be allowed to flee. All the laughter they shared during their return trip vanished with the soldiers' appearance. No one wanted to end up being the next person Jabari threw from the top of the palace. The man had only taken a bite of bread before their leader. Yes, tradition was important and needed to be honored, but punishment for a crime should be delivered with prudence.

Every situation shouldn't be met with the final door.

Still, Jabari was their noble and had to be respected. The man sat on the throne of Naroosh, seated there by the Pharaoh himself, and therefore his actions were above reproach. Unless one of the gods or the Pharaoh himself ordered otherwise, Jabari's word was law. If his master wanted something done, all he should have to do is ask Khalid to do it. In that regard, Khalid had utterly failed in his duties.

The courtyard emptied faster than he would have liked, and his men still wouldn't look him in the eye. He knelt, knowing it wouldn't be long until Jabari made his appearance. When his master didn't appear, he looked around to see Neema standing next to him.

The girl squawked as he pulled her to the ground. "Stay down, and keep your mouth shut."

Jabari appeared flanked by four of his finest warriors. As a noble, he never went anywhere without protection. He moved toward the crocodile's corpse and laid one hand on the beast's massive head. "Impressive."

"He saved me from the river dragon," Neema shouted. "Eternia be praised. Without her intervention, I fear the creature would have eaten me."

Khalid glared at the girl and hissed, "Be quiet."

If Jabari heard either of them, he gave no indication. "Is this the very river dragon I asked you not to hunt and kill?"

Having been addressed directly, Khalid felt comfortable speaking. "It is."

His mind was screaming at him to justify his actions, but he already knew Jabari wouldn't be impressed. The noble had given an order, and in going after Neema and her mother, he had broken his word. Since the new Pharaoh had ascended there was only one suitable punishment to administer for defying a noble's will.

Death.

Khalid thought maybe his hand in raising Jabari would have made the choice to spare his life a simple one. It was the choice the boy's father would have made, but this younger generation was of a different sect. They wanted to return to the old ways, whereas the people who had lived through those times never wished to see them return.

There was a time when working for a noble was an honorable profession. Now he spent as much time investigating crimes committed by his men as the ones committed by the general populace. A few black eyes he could overlook, but a few scraps with the locals was nothing compared to what he found.

Thefts.

Beatings.

Rapes and murders.

All committed by the men and women who were supposed to protect the people. Khalid's general philosophy on policing the city was to find the truth of the matter and act on it. He expected the men under his command to treat each encounter with the commoners as respectfully as possible and for their actions to be above reproach.

Until now, that policy had served him well.

Jabari was of the mind that rules should be enforced to the letter of the law despite the circumstances. Of course, if you could afford to make a large enough donation, he'd overlook certain misunderstandings, and no one was dumb enough to accuse the soldiers of anything in their leader's presence. It was as though a petulant child ruled them. Khalid could almost feel the gods laughing as they watched the people of this land struggle in futility.

"Do you know why I asked you not to kill this particular river dragon?" Jabari's voice was calm like the whisper of the desert sands before a storm.

Khalid lowered his head so that he was looking at his master's toes. "I am ignorant as always, Jabari."

"Yes," the noble hissed. "Yes, you are."

While circling the captain of his guards, Jabari held out his hand for a sword. A second later a blade found his waiting palm, and he placed the naked edge against the back of Khalid's neck. "The Pharaoh himself asked me to protect something for him and provided me with a guardian. What do you think he will say when he finds out that one of his most prized possessions is dead?"

Khalid was starting to get a sense of just how badly he'd fucked up. Disobeying an order from the Pharaoh was tantamount to spitting on the gods themselves. No one would be so stupid, and yet here he was.

"I am sorry for failing you, Jabari." The sword pressed against his neck hard enough to draw a few beads of blood, and he stopped speaking immediately.

"I can forgive failure." Khalid heard the sounds of men being forced back into the courtyard as Jabari continued speaking. "Betrayal is something the Pharaoh won't let stand. My word is law for a reason. Not so you can pick and choose which of my commands to follow."

Khalid felt the weight of death sitting on his shoulders. "I never meant to betray you."

"And yet you did," Jabari hissed in his ear.

There was a commotion behind him, but Khalid couldn't turn. He heard the sound of shuffling feet coming from behind, then the first of the men passed him. It didn't take long for him to figure out these were the porters that helped carry the crocodile and chests back to Naroosh. The soldiers shoved men to their knees in a single-file line.

An execution line.

Jabari removed the sword from Khalid's neck and laid a warm hand on his shoulder. "Imagine what the Pharaoh would think if he knew it was my very own captain of the guard who slew his guardian and not some wayward hunters?" His face pulled into a mask of rage. "You put me at risk. Me!"

Spittle flew from Jabari's lips as he snarled, "If I thought killing you would solve this for me, you'd already be dead." He tapped his sword against Khalid's broken arm. "Instead, I'm going to scrub you from the histories so thoroughly it will be as if you never existed. The Pharaoh must never hear of this betrayal. I will not be perceived as weak."

"If you promise to spare the girl, I'll do whatever you want," Khalid pleaded.

All of this was for nothing if Neema died too.

"She is rather fetching." Jabari ran his fingers through Neema's long black hair. "I think I may keep her for myself. Can't let her go running around the kingdom telling everyone about what happened."

Jabari motioned with one hand, and one of Khalid's soldiers sprang into action. He stepped up to the first man while pulling a long thin blade from a case. With practiced ease, he slammed the blade down between the vertebrae on the man's neck, killing him instantly. One by one he moved down the line, and the soldiers dragged the fallen bodies away.

It was a death factory.

For every one of the men that died, Khalid felt part of his heart wither and die. He had led these men to this fate. None of them knew what they were signing up for. All of this was his fault. There had to be a way for him to make it right. Why would the gods hand him this amazing victory only to have him laid so low?

Maybe there was something greater going on here, a struggle between the gods. If he let himself be killed like the others, would he be letting Eternia down? There wasn't much time for him to make a choice. The line of men in front of him was rapidly shrinking.

Would he die like a dog, or would he take a chance that Eternia had greater plans for him? When death was on the line, the choice was easy. He wanted to live. Khalid would fight, and if the gods wanted him to live, then he would live. If the soldiers cut him down, he could only hope that the scales would tip in his favor as he stood before the gates of the afterlife.

Moving with speed born from decades of training, Khalid rolled forward and out from under Jabari's grip. His master expected nothing but total subservience and wasn't prepared for the move. Now that he was back up on his feet, it would be easy enough to dodge Jabari's blade. For all his ruthless talents, Jabari was a shitty fighter. For someone who killed as many people as he did you'd expect a little more talent with a blade, but it was clear he was more comfortable giving the order than executing it himself.

Khalid dodged inside a wild slash by Jabari and slammed the elbow of his broken arm against his opponent's elbow. He fought against the explosion of pain long enough to pluck the sword from Jabari's fingers. Everyone was frozen. Not a single person moved as they all watched in shock. What manner of man would be so foolish as to lay a hand on the noble?

Khalid grinned as Jabari backed up, but it wasn't the right time to press his luck.

It was time to get the fuck out of there.

"Time to go." He slid the sword into the empty sheath on his back and grabbed Neema's wrist with his free hand, dragging her to her feet. There was nothing left to say. They would need all their breath sprinting for their lives.

The soldiers moved to encircle Jabari. His immediate safety was more important than cutting Khalid down. He didn't know if the further delay was a gift from the goddess or if it was a final show of respect from some of his soldiers, but he wouldn't waste the opportunity to flee.

They ran. "Can I trust you to stay with me? Khalid shouted as they sprinted.

Neema pulled her wrist free. "Just get us the fuck out of here."

He shoved the girl away as he dodged a lazy strike from one of the newer soldiers. Without the girl to hold onto, he pulled Jabari's blade from his back. This man was no match for his skill even with one broken arm, but he didn't need to be. All the soldier had to do was slow him down, and when the others caught up, his and Neema's fates would be sealed.

He faked a slash to the left and spun in a quick circle to the right. The man was as pitiful a swordsman as he thought, and now Khalid stood right behind him. It would have been easy enough to cut the man down, but he didn't want to fan the flames of hatred any more than they had been already. Instead, he kicked the man in the back and sent him sprawling on the ground.

Then the real race to freedom began.

In a flash, the two fugitives were out into the cool desert night. The wind he'd felt stirring as they entered the outlying village was turning into a gale. Just the kind of thing that would make tracking the two of them through the desert impossible. At least one of the gods was smiling down upon them.

There was no time to think. All they could afford to do now was run. Jabari would send an army after them when the storm cleared so they had to be gone by then. This wind was their chance to make a clean escape. As they ran through the winding streets, the reality of their fate dawned on him.

Khalid was an exile.

"There is something wrong with this new Pharaoh, and I swear to the gods I will find out what it is," Khalid huffed to the moon as he ran. "Evil will not be allowed to swallow the land of my people. I will give my last breath to see the people of Naroosh free again."

"What about me?" Neema cried as she struggled to keep up with his relentless pace.

For the first time, he considered what to do with the girl. He couldn't leave her alone. If she went back to Naroosh, Jabari would kill her. If he left her anywhere else, she'd be sold into one of the pleasure houses or worse. He didn't see very many options in front of him.

"You will come with me, and I will train you. One day you will carry on my quest for justice when I am no longer able." Khalid meant every word.

There was something evil happening in the deserts. The new Pharaoh wasn't a man worthy of respect. If the gods had seen fit to let him escape, they must have agreed. It was time that someone stood against the spreading madness before their kingdom was lost to darkness forever.

CHAPTER SIX

Brother Colton liked being in charge.

He found that it was always easier to give the orders than do the grunt work. Although if he told himself the truth, he'd rather let someone else handle the hassle so he could go back to his alcove and continue his research. It seemed as though no one liked to read about the past to save the future anymore, but whenever shit hit the fan, who did they call on?

Researchers like him.

Sure, the field agents liked to take all the credit for the temple's success, but without the power of the research team, no one would know the correct anti-curse to use or even how to break the seals on something as simple as a reaper chest without getting their damn heads cut off. Brother Colton had always found the true heroes rested well behind the action.

It was much safer there, and they had cookies.

Getting chased around the countryside by murderous were-wolves wasn't exactly his thing. He needed a bookshelf, a desk, and somewhere to heat his tea. Brother Colton snorted in disgust as he thought about what some of Tristholm's new priests were drinking. Some invention brought in by the travelers, and it had a rather foul name. It was on the tip of his tongue, but he couldn't quite think of it.

Coffee.

Who would drink the vile stuff? He'd overheard two travelers in town talking about a special kind of seed that could only be harvested after a large feline ate it and shit it out. What kind of crazy person saw a cat shitting and thought, hey, I wonder if I can make a drink out of that?

None of that weird brown bitter crap for Brother Colton. He only drank the finest imported teas. It was his one little eccentricity, at least that was what he liked to tell himself. It wasn't as if he needed his pay for anything else, so he spent his coin on fine tea and rare books. One of these days he might even get back to his books if the High Priest got tired of torturing him with forced social interactions.

Thankfully it was only ten in the morning, and he was done interacting with humanity for the day. The afternoons were his time to read and pray. Sometimes, if he thought he could get away with it, he even snuck in a quick nap.

You couldn't work hard all the time.

A nap sounded like a damn good idea at the moment. He might lose his temper if he had to settle another petty dispute before lunch. The thought of some tea, a few of those delicious cookies his chambermaid baked daily, and a quick nap eased his mind quite a bit. Brother Colton didn't know how anyone else felt, but a good cup of tea, an old book, and a little nap was all it took to set the world right again.

When he woke up, he'd be more than happy to preside over another battle of "who was the most devout." It was amazing what young people could find to fight about. Eternia only cared that you believed, not how many times a person made her symbol in front of their chest as they prayed.

Brother Colton was just starting to indulge himself in the

daydream of a relaxing afternoon when he spotted a group of people walking toward the temple gates. If he wasn't mistaken that was Seraphina herself, and it couldn't be.

Not them again.

The thought of a nap quickly evaporated as Brother Colton straightened his robe to receive guests. He hoped Tim didn't want to drag him out on some kind of crazy adventure again. One carriage ride of death was enough for him.

As he walked to meet his guests, Brother Colton saw a blur from the corner of his eye.

"Just when today looked so promising!" He let out a weary sigh.

The last thing he needed was Jessi pestering the travelers with her insane babble about trouble at the farm.

"Oh, no."

Brother Colton hiked up his robes in a very unpriestly way and started to run.

CHAPTER SEVEN

Tim felt a grin spread across his lips as he saw Brother Colton.

It always expedited things when you knew the man in charge. Although at this point, Tim would be kind of surprised if any of the temple priests didn't know their little band of travelers. They had made quite a name for themselves so far. He still wasn't sold yet on notoriety being a good thing, but having friends in high places sure seemed to help them along.

Lifting his hand to wave, Tim noticed the expression of greeting on the priest's face turn to one of concern. It wasn't until the rotund priest started running toward them that he grew concerned. If there was one thing Brother Colton didn't do, it was run. If the man was sprinting toward them, the situation must be dire indeed.

There wasn't time to think of what to do. Tim spun in place, darted between JaKobi and Cassie, and fired off his Snare spell. He watched the spell fly hoping that it would be strong enough to contain whatever horror was charging at them now. His eyes followed the spell's progress as it collided with a young woman.

What in the fuck?

Why would Brother Colton be so worried about the girl coming toward them? Tim decided he wanted to find out before the man reached them. Ignoring his friends' questioning gaze, he ran toward the startled girl.

"I can't move," the young woman flatly stated as she looked up at Tim in confusion.

Tim waved away her concern. "It will be gone momentarily."

There was no need to tell the young woman that the level of his Snare spell was so low that she didn't have much to worry about. If the girl put a little more effort into her fight, she might have already been free. For now, she was stuck in place, and Brother Colton was far enough away he'd have time to ask her a few questions before he arrived.

"Honey," ShadowLily laid a hand on Tim's shoulder. "I know we've all been on edge lately, but I don't think Paul would be too pleased if you started attacking the temple's acolytes without provocation."

"He didn't attack her exactly." JaKobi knelt and poked the acolyte's legs.

"Hey! Stop that!" the girl shouted as she swatted JaKobi's hand.

Cassie stepped forward and pulled the fire mage back to his feet and away from the girl. "Sorry about him. He's all curiosity and no manners."

"Well, how often do you get to see a Snare spell at work up close?" JaKobi exclaimed in excitement. "Normally we use them and run away."

Tim's spell broke, and the young woman stumbled forward, landing in his arms. She obviously wasn't there to cause any of them harm, but he hadn't figured out exactly what she wanted yet.

Gently setting the young lady back on her feet, Tim asked, "Was there something you needed?"

"Yes, you big oaf." The acolyte swatted his arm. "I need to talk to her." She pointed past Tim at Lorelei.

Cassie grinned. "That's a first."

"Probably a real blow to the ego." JaKobi snickered.

"You know I liked it better when you two weren't on the same side," Tim grumbled.

Lorelei stepped forward, looking as shocked as the rest of them. "What can I help you with?"

"There's a problem…"

Brother Colton barged into their circle around the girl. "Jessi, I told you not to bother anyone with this nonsense."

"It's not nonsense." Jessi stamped her foot in frustration. "People are dying."

Seraphina stepped forward and laid a hand on the young woman's shoulder. "Calm your heart little one, and tell us what you've found."

Jessi looked around at all the expectant faces, her eyes finally settling on Brother Colton.

The priest had the same kind of worried expression a dog walker gets when they reach in their pocket and realize they're out of bags. "You have their attention now. You might as well tell them your story."

It wasn't exactly a ringing endorsement, but it gave the young woman the strength to continue. Jessi drew a deep breath and plunged into her tale. "A harpy is attacking farmers along the southern field. No one has died yet, but several men were injured."

"Jessi, the foreman told us that the injuries were due to accidents. It makes more sense than a monster attacking them." Brother Colton shook his head sadly as if he felt bad for wasting their time.

Face scrunched up with determination, Jessi continued, "People say things when I'm around that they wouldn't when they see one of the priests coming. Sometimes it's as though they forget I'm even in the room. Trust me. There's a problem."

Tim wondered if they had time to go off on a goose chase when the deserts of Naroosh were calling to them. If they got distracted by every little side quest, they'd never make any progress toward the endgame. On the other hand, it wouldn't do much for their reputation if they left without looking into it and people died. Being a hero wasn't easy work. Thankfully, this time the burden of making the decision wasn't on him.

Tim gave Lorelei a slight nod letting her know whatever choice she made they would all stand behind her.

The ranger looked around at all the faces, clearly pleased that everyone trusted her to make the right call. A grin spread across her lips as she looked down at Jessi. "I think we have the time to check it out."

"Weren't we about to…" JaKobi's words trailed off as Cassie's elbow slammed into his ribs.

"No." Cassie frowned at the fire mage. "We weren't."

Tim felt for the guy. He'd been on the receiving end of a few elbows in his day and knew that the hits didn't feel very good. It probably didn't help that in this game Cassie was extra strong, and JaKobi was what was commonly referred to as a squishy. Although if you asked the fire mage, he would probably call himself a glass cannon.

Lots of firepower but easy to break.

The same thing could be said about Tim's class, but his ability to pull health from his targets and to heal gave him a better chance of survival. Not that Tim spent much time deluding himself about his prowess in battle. If he found himself facing multiple opponents without a tank to hide behind, the results wouldn't be pretty.

When things got ugly, Tim got to spend time with Barbara.

Deciding it was time to save JaKobi from himself, Tim took the lead. Turning to face Seraphina, he knelt on one knee. "It seems our trip to the desert has been slightly delayed, but I would be more than happy to take you and your men through the portal as planned before we depart."

Seraphina lifted Tim. "I'd tell you to stop bowing, but truth be told I kind of like it." Tristholm's leader flashed him a quick smile that said, please make sure to go out of your way in the future. "My men are already on the way with our carriage for the return trip. It would be such a waste to have sent them all that way for nothing."

"Plus, it will be nice to get some time alone together." Joe took Seraphina's hand and gave it a gentle kiss. "Between her ruling a city and me trying to open another restaurant, we've been kind of swamped."

JaKobi held up a finger and exclaimed, "Busy bees get the honey." He looked around at all the confused faces. "Early bird gets the worm and all that."

"Stop talking." Cassie nudged him again.

Seraphina almost giggled. "It's not getting the worm I'm worried about."

Joe looked like he was about to faint. ShadowLily's cheeks turned bright red. Everyone else smirked. It wasn't as if Tim hadn't said worse himself. It was just he tended to make his overtures in private to cut down on the humiliation factor.

Trying to wipe the grin off his face, Tim turned away from the couple and focused his attention on Brother Colton. "We require access to the quick travel portal."

"Of course, of course." The priest looked flustered. "I'm so sorry about all this. I told Jessi not to bother you, and now we've delayed your plans over what might amount to nothing."

ShadowLily casually draped an arm over Brother Colton's shoulders. "If we get out there and find nothing, I'm holding you personally responsible."

"Me? But I don't want you to go," the priest stammered.

Tim couldn't help but laugh. If he were in the same spot as their rotund friend, he would have been equally worried. Thankfully, he knew she was only screwing with him a little. If they lost a few hours chasing down a lead that didn't pan out, it wouldn't be the worst use of time in history. He simply wanted to make sure they weren't always getting sidetracked.

"Leave the poor guy alone. He's worried enough," Tim called

from behind them. "If the foreman's lying, I'm sure Brother Colton's punishment will be swift and severe."

The priest stopped walking as if the idea of someone lying to him had just occurred to him as a possibility. "I don't think Jim would do such a thing. If there is a harpy, he certainly won't be in charge any longer."

"Wait, the temple owns a farm?" Cassie blurted from behind them.

Brother Colton smiled and nodded with satisfaction. "Several. We don't do anything fancy, only grains and potatoes, a few fresh herbs for our kitchens. You'd be surprised how many hungry people you can feed with bread and potatoes."

"So the farm we're heading to is one of the temple's?" Tim grinned. "Wouldn't surprise me if we found something then. Vitaria wasn't exactly thrilled with us the last time we saw her."

ShadowLily nudged Brother Colton back into motion. She turned her smirk on Tim. "You always think everything is a trap."

"That's why we're still alive." He held up one finger like a very important person making a proclamation. "Prudent planning and proper timing are the keys to every victory."

Cassie barked out a harsh bray of laughter. "Fuck off. Normally, I just run forward and hit things with my stick."

Brother Colton snickered while leading the way into the temple's portal chamber. "Oh, I'm sure there's more to it than that. Otherwise, anyone could be an adventurer."

Tim laughed while thinking back to some of the bad players he'd been unfortunate enough to play with in other games. Some people honestly didn't know what they were doing wrong and improved greatly with a few hints about positioning and rotation. Others seemed almost willingly bad, like a DPS that managed to do less damage than if they auto-attacked the entire fight.

One of his favorite MMOs didn't have an in-combat resurrection mechanic, so if someone died, that was it. They were out the rest of the fight. When his guild had content on farm, a death or two didn't mean that much, but when you were working on progression, staying alive mattered.

Sometimes raiding was amazing, and other times it felt like someone repeatedly punched you in the boys and asked you to thank them for it.

Hardcore gaming wasn't for everyone.

When it came to raiding, Tim used to be proud of his elite status and always looked down on those he perceived not to be putting in the effort. Going to college quickly dispelled any misconceptions that he had on how much time a person should dedicate to their time in the game. He also stopped caring about different difficulty settings for the raids. It didn't matter to him if you raided on the hardest level. Raiding was supposed to be fun, and it didn't lower his enjoyment if someone else could beat the game on an easier setting.

He used to bitch endlessly about how creating different levels of the same encounter took away precious development time from creating new content. Now he understood that part of the reason they always had shiny new content is that more people played the game when they could have fun at their pace.

Not everyone was raiding four hours a night, six days a week, pushing for world firsts. Most people raided a couple of nights a week and maybe popped in for some dailies or simply to chat. Real life had to take precedence over raid life unless you found a way to get paid for it.

The best part about being in *The Etheric Coast* was there wasn't really a work-life balance to flesh out. His work literally was his life. Tim loved that every day in this game he got to wake up and take on new challenges.

Although a little extra time to plan wouldn't hurt.

In some regards, deciding to live inside a virtual world made things easier for him. He didn't have to worry about much right now. His streaming contract took care of his POD fees, and everything else they did, while sometimes stressful, really was for fun.

No one ever wanted their fun to feel like work.

He laid his hand against the portal and thought about where he wanted to go. The wavering blue light formed into an image of a cavern. "Your destination awaits."

Joe scooped Seraphina up into his arms and stepped through. Tim could hear her scolding him before they vanished from sight. Seraphina's guards stomped through the opening after them.

Maybe this delay was a good thing. Knowing Seraphina, by the time they stepped through the portal into the city of Elmore's Hallow, there would be all kinds of conveyances set up. Merchants hawking wares and doing repairs. As well as food.

They might not have taco trucks in *The Etheric Coast*, but maybe Joe could have a little sandwich stand. If he could use the portal to send orders back to Tristholm, he wouldn't even need to set up another kitchen.

Magic was so amazing. It could accomplish just about anything.

The last of the royal guards tromped through the portal, and Tim took his hand off the cool metal surface. He turned away from the device and looked at his group. "Who's ready to hunt down a harpy?"

"Lorelei already went to get the horses." ShadowLily shrugged.

It seemed as though Tim wasn't the only one ready to get back out there and kill some things. Despite his grumpy attitude over the morning, there wasn't anything he'd rather be doing. There would be plenty of time for sleep after they dealt with this little issue, and another night staying in the castle didn't sound so bad.

Walking down to the temple's stables didn't take long. The area looked different now that zombies weren't covering it. It kind of took him by surprise. Tim hadn't been back on this side of the temple since the incident with the werewolves. Brother Colton had done a masterful job getting the place back in order. He'd have to remember to tell the High Priest how impressed he was next time he saw him.

Lorelei waved at the group to get their attention. "These are the best of the bunch. Make sure to treat your horse with respect, and if you have any treats, it never hurts to share."

Three of the horses whinnied and one stamped its foot.

The ranger pointed at a large bucket with the word treats painted on a makeshift sign above it before flipping onto her horse with a casual grace Tim knew he'd never be able to match. He might not be able to flip onto a horse like an elven rider from the myths, but he could certainly bribe his noble steed better than the rest of them.

Tim reached into the container and grabbed two juicy green apples. He tucked one into his robes for later and kept one out for what would surely become his newest friend. Moving down the line, Tim stopped in front of a beautiful black mare and remembered his father reading him the book as a child.

He reached out and scratched the horse's nose. "I think we're going to be good friends."

The horse nudged Tim's other hand, and the jig was up. It only took him a moment to make sure his hand was flat before he felt comfortable lifting the tasty treat for his glorious steed. Foam frothed from the horse's mouth as it finished up the snack, which ruined the image of him riding majestically to their destination.

She's lucky I like them a little rough around the edges.

The horse nudged his arm out of the way, searching his robe for the other apple. Tim pushed her nose away with a laugh. "That one's for later."

An attendant came forward and slipped a saddle onto the horse for him. Tim noticed there was a name stenciled into the saddle's leather.

Sadie.

"What a beautiful name for a beautiful horse." He kicked his leg up high to get it in the stirrup and vaulted into the saddle with a *thump*. Sadie seemed to grunt as she took his full weight. "Come on. It's not that bad. You could have had him." Tim pointed at Brother Colton as he climbed onto a stool and into the saddle.

Sadie whinnied in a way that said same-diff.

"Better watch it, or you're not getting that other apple." Tim laughed as they followed Lorelei out on the trail.

This was it. They were off on another adventure. Tim didn't know why, but these little quests that felt like side missions always ended up providing him with the best rewards. This wasn't even a quest really, only a hint that something might be happening. The smell of opportunity was in the air, and he loved it.

He pointed his finger in the direction they were already going. "I said to the cabbie, yo Holmes, smell ya later."

"Babe, I don't think we're going to Bel Air," ShadowLily purred as she moved her horse up next to him.

"Well, we're going somewhere, so my statement still stands." Tim laughed. "In other words, that's my story, and I'm sticking to it."

ShadowLily gave him a look as if she was seeing him for the first time. "It's a good thing you have a cute butt."

Tim thought about being offended, but he did have a great butt. So instead of mock indignation, he smiled into the sun and leaned back in the saddle for a long ride. A single notification appeared in his vision as Lorelei shared the quest she'd received from Jessi with all of them.

Quest Received: Farm To Table

Jessi thinks a harpy may be attacking a farm run by the temple. While Brother Colton says it might all be nonsense, the girl was extremely persistent. Go to the farm and find out the truth of the matter. If there is a harpy, deal with the problem.

Reward: Why does everything in life have to come with a reward? Can't you help someone out of the kindness of your heart?

Tim accepted the quest.

/ CHAPTER EIGHT

The farm was bigger than Tim expected.

Rolling fields of golden brown wheat stretched onward for what seemed like miles. Tim remembered the chill and the cold he'd felt on their way to Tristholm and wondered how this was possible. Then he realized they were in a world of magic, and literally anything was possible. In fact, if Tim really thought about it, fields of shimmering wheat growing in a winter climate were one of the least remarkable things he'd seen since coming into the game.

It was still cool as shit.

Without magic, fields of crops like these in such a cold climate wouldn't have been possible. Tristholm would have to rely on trade and the summer harvest to see them through the winter. One wrong move and a lot of people would die from starvation. Eternia and the temple creating fields like this changed the game for the people living out here. Year-round growing and keeping the price of flour down was probably doing wonders for Seraphina's reputation as a leader.

Many a ruler lost their head over the price of bread.

It was crazy to think that people in the real world could still starve to death. With all of the world's access to technology, a reasonable person might believe that starving kids would be a thing of the past. While Tim hated those late-night commercials where they tried to scam you out of money using the images of kids, he still knew there was a real need out there to make sure this didn't continue to happen. It kinda felt like being able to eat, and access to a decent education should be more of a right and less of a privilege.

Still, there were plenty of dedicated scientists working to solve the problem back in the real world. It was amazing how they could breed different traits into plant genetics. Drought-resistant if you needed it, or maybe it was cold, or the heat that would kill a crop in a certain location. Those problems were quickly becoming issues for past generations. It was amazing what people could do with science. Most of it went right over Tim's head, but he sure loved to read about it and imagine where the future would go.

I'm going to drive a hovercar before I die. I just fucking know it!

As nice of a horse as Sadie was, nothing beat kicking back in a comfortable seat for long trips. If you had a nice enough car, it was like you couldn't even feel the road. Riding a horse to your destination was a little rough on the legs, his ass, and it kept smashing his two coconuts together in the most uncomfortable way.

Maybe cowboys had padded balls.

Sometimes he felt maybe his generation was soft. It wasn't as though they woke up, had to walk a mile down to the stream to get water for breakfast, then spent the day doing hard manual labor. Tim's normal morning routine consisted of a small hit off his vape, a ginormous cup of coffee, and plopping down in front of his laptop to game or catch up on the homework he missed while gaming the night before.

At least I don't have to try and write a ten-page paper in four hours again.

Tim snickered to himself as they drew closer to a large cluster of buildings. *What was with college and all the papers anyway?* It wasn't as if a person didn't retain knowledge without writing a massive essay and listing the thirty million resources they found on the internet.

Life must have been so much simpler when all people had were encyclopedias.

Sometimes he wished he could tell someone he knew something without giving an hour's dissertation about where he garnered the information. Granted, people were starting to get used to fact-checking things they heard from others. In the age of social media, a person was only a scroll away from being bombarded with fake news or someone screaming that real news was fake.

Life must be infinitely easier for a horse.

Sadie tossed her head and craned it to the side. Tim swore she looked at him from one eye and sneered around her bit for a minute. The look said, you think you have it rough? I have a metal bar stuck in my mouth and a two-hundred-pound asshole on my back.

He leaned forward and patted Sadie's neck. "I get you. As soon as we stop, I'll get that thing out of your mouth and produce another tasty treat."

Brother Colton trotted into the lead. "Follow me. I'll take us directly to the foreman."

They followed the priest until they dismounted in front of a gorgeous white farmhouse. Tim had always loved the idea of one. The buildings were usually one story with lots of windows and vaulted ceilings. The older ones tended to be broken up a little on the interior, but some of the renovated ones had wide-open living spaces.

Just because he liked to fall asleep to HGTV didn't make him any less of a man. It simply ensured he knew what ShadowLily was talking about when she told him how she was decorating their place.

Tim shook off any future thoughts of farm living as the smell hit him in the nose like a knockout punch from Iron Mike. It was weird how an odor could hardly be there one instant, and the next, it enveloped a person like a bubble. It was worse than a summer road trip with the family, and you heard someone discreetly or not so discreetly roll a window down.

Nothing said family fun like long road trips and farts.

A man rushed out the front door, tucking in his shirt as he came. "Brother Colton, I wasn't expecting another visit so soon."

"Yes, and I wasn't expecting to come." The priest frowned, clearly not enjoying having his presence questioned. "Sadly, my acolyte Jessi roped these fine young people into traveling all this way. She still believes there's a harpy out there."

Giving their group a once-over before turning back to the foreman, Brother Colton leaned closer to the man as if sharing a secret. "These adventurers have a mission to complete for the Goddess Eternia, so please give them a tour of the grounds, and explain why their presence here isn't needed."

The foreman looked a little taken aback by their appearance and credentials but managed to compose himself quickly enough. He extended a hand to Tim. "I'm sorry if you wasted any time coming all this way. There really is nothing to see out here."

ShadowLily looked around the empty yard. "Things must virtually run themselves if you can take a break in the middle of the day."

Brother Colton wore a look of shock as if it had only now registered that it was odd for someone in charge of the farm to be inside while everyone else was out working. "Jim, the young lady has a point. Maybe we should step inside and see what's going on."

Jim's face turned white as a sheet. Tim had the feeling the man might have been sneaking away for a nooner with one of the ladies on the farm. Not that it was any of their business what two consenting adults got up to in their spare time. He was about to suggest they should go on the tour and save the man a little embarrassment when a wail of misery filled the air.

Brother Colton stepped back from the door in shock but moved out of the way quickly enough that he didn't get barreled over by ShadowLily and Cassie as they stormed through the farmhouse's front entrance.

Jim didn't move out of the way fast enough and wound up sitting on the patio after Cassie shouldered him out of the way. Tim still didn't know what was going on, but a scream like that didn't come from a pleasant nooner. Something was wrong. It was the kind of wail you'd expect to hear from someone who had been locked in a house for ten years or had just seen someone die.

Holy shit. Tim motioned for everyone to follow the ladies inside.

A woman huddled in a corner sobbing. Blood covered her hands, and only someone dealing with intense grief could make the screeches coming from her throat. The sheer emotion the woman gave off made his knees feel weak. Tim felt an intense desire to flee the room. He'd never been great at dealing with the emotional stuff, but maybe he could help in another way.

Solving problems was kind of his specialty.

A young man was laid out on white linens on the dining room table. At least, they used to be white. Now the color matched the blood-stained towels that littered the floor around the corpse. While some of the young man's wounds had been stitched closed, others were still exposed. Tim didn't know a lot about weapon wounds versus animal, but these certainly could have been claw marks.

Or maybe talons.

It was starting to look like Jessi was right. At the very least if the farmers weren't dealing with a harpy, there was something else out here that clearly needed to be dealt with. Tim wasn't sure why he was surprised. It was like Eternia to slip in a little extra work before they reached the next zone.

Goddess going to do what a goddess is going to do.

Looking at the boy on the table now, Tim felt kind of bad

that he had hoped for some action. It was one thing to kick evil's ass and bask in the loot shower and infinite praise of the people you helped. It was another thing entirely to see the reactions of the victims' families when their loved ones weren't coming back. It certainly made the situation feel more real. Tim wouldn't wish the kind of agony that woman was going through on his worst rivals, let alone a lady who worked to feed the kingdom's hungry.

Brother Colton took one look at the boy, and his face turned red. By the time he rounded on the foreman, the priest's face was almost purple with rage. "What is the meaning of this?" The fury rolled off his words like an old-time southern preacher working his parishioners into a frenzy.

Jim held his hands out in front of him as if to ward off a blow. "I thought they were telling stories, trying to get out of doing a full day's work." All the energy seemed to drain from the man in an instant. He slumped against the wall, slid to the floor, and cradled his head in his hands. "I was so wrong. I never thought anything like this would happen."

Brother Colton moved to Jim's side and placed an absolving hand on his shoulders. "There is still time for you to redeem yourself in the eyes of Eternia. Take them to the harpy, and I will see to this young man's body myself."

Turning away from Jim, Brother Colton knelt and helped the grieving mother to her feet. "Would you do me the honor of accompanying me for a cup of tea?"

The woman looked dazed. "Yes," she stammered.

"I would so love to hear about your son and what made him such a valuable member of the temple's faithful." He smiled warmly at the woman in a way most people wouldn't be able to do in the face of such a tragedy. "When we finish our tea and our stories, I will see his soul delivered into Eternia's waiting arms myself."

"You would do that for my son?" the woman stammered with

appreciation. She pulled Brother Colton into a warm embrace. "Thank you."

Brother Colton returned her hug, looking slightly embarrassed. "I only serve at Eternia's will. It's what she would want me to do." Brother Colton escorted her out of the room and toward the back of the house and the kitchen.

Cassie had Jim up on his feet and pinned against the wall. "Pull yourself together. We've got work to do."

"You saw what that thing did to Gary. I don't want to go out there and end up like that." Jim tried to break free of Cassie's grip, a look of pure panic in his eyes.

Their tank's grip might as well have been made of iron. Try as he might, Jim couldn't get away.

Tim stepped forward before things could devolve further. "So you know where the harpy is?"

"Of course not." Jim sounded flustered. "I thought the stories were all bullshit. No one's seen a harpy in a thousand years!"

Cassie slapped the man. It was more of a snap out of it slap than one with any real violence behind it, but it did the trick.

"I can show you where Gary was working today." The panic fled as his mind started working on the task at hand.

Lorelei patted the bow on her back. "Just get us there, and don't run off."

Tim was starting to think things might be going a little too far. There was always a possibility that Jim really thought it was all bullshit, and he didn't send those people out to die so they could meet their quota for the day. Although the foreman had clear and concise evidence of an attack right in front of him, and the yard wasn't full of workers.

Holy shit! Where were the workers?

Moving Cassie gently out of the way, Tim addressed Jim directly. "You *did* recall the rest of the workers, right?"

The look of panic returned to Jim's face, although this time it seemed to be fraught with concern. "We have to hurry."

Tim made sure the man focused on him. "Jim, how do we get them back here?"

Pointing to something behind Tim and out the front doors, the foreman stuttered, "There's a bell."

"Cassie," Tim said as he guided the man over to a seat. The foreman was clearly not cut out for dealing with anything more stressful than someone showing up late for work.

"On it." The tank moved toward the door, JaKobi trailing behind her.

Looking down at the man, Tim tried to remember something about how to snap someone out of a daze. He'd read enough military science fiction to know that the way they did it in the books was to give them work. Military men couldn't think about their impending doom at the hands of alien forces when they had to lug crates around the cargo bay, now could they?

"Jim, we're going to get everyone back here, but that's not the only thing. We'll need you to get them inside and organized. We need to know if everyone is here and if not where they were supposed to be today." Tim laid a hand on Jim's shoulder and hit him with a Healing Orb. "Can you handle that for me?"

The foreman came around. "I can do that, but we need to do something about Gary."

ShadowLily looked at the young man on the table and shook her head. The look on her face was one of regret. The lines created by her frown might as well have said, if we only got here sooner.

"This obviously isn't where everyone lives. Is there a dining hall or a bunkhouse that can hold everyone?" She looked at Jim. "If we can direct them there, we can give Brother Colton time to handle things properly."

"Whatever you need." Jim looked at the body and down at the floor. "How could I have been so stupid?"

Clapping her hands snapped the man out of it before he could wallow. "Let's get out there and get ready for the farmers."

"You're right, of course." Jim moved toward the door, a little confidence coming back with each step. "We'll get them in the dining hall and lock it down." Jim looked at their party for a moment, then at the men and women running toward the buildings. "Maybe we should send word back to the temple, in case you can't handle the monster yourself."

JaKobi moved away from the ringing bell. "We'll handle it."

Cassie dropped the ringer. "Plus, you might have noticed the guy inside is kind of important. While no one might come looking for us, if Brother Colton doesn't return soon, someone will come for him."

"In other words," Tim put a hand on Jim's back and guided him out to meet the first arrivals. "Stay inside and don't come out until you get the all-clear." Jim nodded in understanding, and Tim continued, "If you would be so kind as to point us in the right direction, that would be great."

Jim turned in a slow circle, clearly thinking about the workers and their assignments for the day before pointing off in the distance. "He was working in that field, but at the far end closer to the hills."

The entire party turned and followed Jim's extended finger.

Now they had a direction to go and knew for a fact there was a monster waiting for them. It was time to do what they did best and kick some ass. Turning until his eyes rested on the tank, Tim gave her a little bow. "Care to lead the way?"

Cassie stomped forward and pushed her way past him. "You're such a pussy."

JaKobi snickered as he followed in her wake.

"Me squishy, you buns of steel." Tim grunted like a caveman. He pointed at Cassie, then in the direction Jim told them to go. "You, go do steel things."

Lorelei rubbed his head affectionately as she walked by. "Don't worry. You can hide behind me, tough guy."

"I might take you up on that." Tim grinned. "But Cassie might take better care of me if I hid behind JaKobi."

ShadowLily slapped Tim's ass as she walked past. "I don't know about that. You should never underestimate the man's ability to upset her."

"Lorelei, I hope your offer still stands." Tim grinned as he followed the others.

"Try and keep up." The ranger dashed forward twenty feet in the blink of an eye.

Guess that's a no.

Tim felt good about their chances. The team seemed focused and ready to roll. The harpy didn't stand a chance.

CHAPTER NINE

Khalid's words rang in Neema's head like a gong in the temple.

Do not fail.

Had it really been ten years since he had saved her from the monster that killed her mother? She didn't feel any differently, but she'd changed from a teen into a woman. From a girl into a warrior. There were those amongst the nobility who needed to pay for their crimes against the people they swore to protect.

One day the resistance would see to it they did.

Neema kept her pace slow and deliberate to not draw any attention to herself in the mostly open streets. Worshippers on their way to squeeze in their morning prayers before a long day of work rarely moved faster than a snail's pace and almost never in the kind of large groups that would have made hiding easier.

By the gods, she hated moving slow.

She liked to run ever since Khalid had trained her in the ways of the hunt. There was a reason she could shoot a dove from the sky while sprinting across the sands, and it wasn't because she liked walking. Now when their land's entire future depended on her mission's outcome, she had to move as slow as a turtle.

Oh, how the gods loved their tricks.

At least this mission didn't have to be completed in the heat of the day. Sometimes a girl had to be thankful for the little things. It wasn't that she was a delicate flower that wilted under the sun's intense rays. It was more that she hated how the sand stuck to her skin when she was sweaty. As anyone who had lived in the desert or who had been to one of the great seas could attest, once you got sand in some places, it was damn near impossible to get it out. If things went well, she'd be back to Khalid before the heat of the day had time to make her skin a sticky trap for it.

When had things gone to plan?

Neema nodded to a woman she passed before continuing up the street. She reminded herself to slow her pace again, but her feet had problems obeying the order. It might have been her nerves getting the best of her. She needed to calm down. Sneaking past the sleeping soldiers at the gate had been easy enough, and all she had to do now was deal with the guards at the temple.

The temple guardians weren't exactly the finest warriors. They were more like brawlers who found a purpose. Still, the men were fiercely loyal to the priests and wouldn't be shy about defending them from Jabari's men if it came to it. There was no love lost between the two factions.

That was the thing with Jabari the loathsome. He wanted complete control, and the priests were the one thing that kept him from having it. It wasn't as if their city's ruler could stand before the people and claim he knew the gods better than their priests. No one would believe such madness.

Not yet, anyway.

That was the thing with tyrants. Their rule didn't require the populace's belief to be there. They ruled because they had the power and the soldiers to keep it. For a man like Jabari, the fear was always insurrection, so they answered every problem with ruthlessness. The man was simply too dense to realize the harder he squeezed the people, the sooner his demise would surface.

There was a certain point where people break. At first, it might seem like the bad things happened to the poor or disenfranchised, but it doesn't take people long to wake up to the reality it's happening to all of them. Kick some dogs, and they scurry away, kick the wrong one, and it attacks.

The scroll she was going to collect would give them the chance to stop hiding and provide an opportunity to fight back.

The resistance was small, and gaining a meaningful foothold had so far been impossible. They'd been working in groups of five or less since the failure of their last hideout. While such small forces cut down on what they could accomplish, there was a growing momentum in the populace that supported them. Men who had openly laughed in Khalid's face were now begging for his help. Neema was always impressed by how Khalid never held their previous behavior against them.

When a sheep is lost, it is the shepherd's job to guide them back to the flock.

He was a better man than people gave him credit for. It wasn't easy to welcome the people who abandoned you with the open arms of friendship, and yet he'd done it time and time again. Maybe it was his age that tempered his resolve. One day she hoped to have that same kind of silent courage, but for the time being her passions still drove her to make rash and hasty decisions. That might be why Khalid never let her go on a mission alone.

Until today.

When he came into her room and laid out his plan's details, she pointed out a few small tweaks and started to get ready. It would be nice not to be left behind like a pack mule when the others went on missions. She was tired of moving their crap from location to location. Today that would be someone else's job.

Her smile must have lit their neighborhood like the morning

sun when Khalid told her this was her task, and hers alone. All the nights she spent firing her bow with bloody fingers until her forearm was so bruised it stayed purple for a month had finally paid off. She was a warrior and a vital part of the resistance.

Everything I ever wanted.

Knowing that the future of the resistance rested in her hands felt good, but it also had her on edge. If any of Jabari's spies found out about the scroll, the entire mission would turn into a shit show. Making it out alive would certainly not be guaranteed. Obtaining the scroll with the location of a hidden oasis was worth risking her life for. Some things were more important than the life of a single person.

Like the fate of an entire nation.

It's just a simple task, Neema kept chanting to herself.

Any idiot could pick up a package and return it. She could go to the bazaar and find ten boys who would do it for a copper in less than a minute. While the task itself was easy, she still had butterflies in her stomach. The oasis would give them a real chance to fight back and a place to call home. This one little scroll could change their fates forever.

It was funny how quickly the tides were changing. It seemed the wealthy merchants didn't like having a foot on their neck any more than those who worked for them. Things had been wrong for so long most of the people finally felt backed into a corner. When that happened, a person only had two options.

Fight or submit.

Not everyone was a fighter. It took a certain kind of ruthless courage to go toe-to-toe with another person and kill them. However, there were all kinds of ways to fight back against corruption. Some people did it with steel while others did it with words. More simply contributed money, or supplies, even places to hide. As far as Neema was concerned, they were all part of the resistance.

She'd feel better about today once she had the scroll in hand

and was on her way back to Khalid. The man was more than just the resistance leader; he was like a father to her. Deep down he never would have wished this life for her, but after her mother's death in the jaws of the Pharaoh's monster, she had almost been alone. By the morning after their escape, Jabari had slaughtered her remaining family members.

At least she had someone in her life that cared about her. That was more than she could say for most of the orphans of Naroosh. Those poor children often died from hunger or were sold into lives that were worse than death. Neema always found it amazing how many people could walk by starving children without giving them a second glance.

A better life for the people is why they fought.

There was enough wealth in their land to make sure that every belly was full and that no children would die of starvation, and yet it happened daily. That was the very reason she begged Khalid to teach her the ways of the warrior and not force her into a life of submission. Someone had to tip the scales in favor of the little guy.

Neema wasn't a proud fighter. All that mattered in a battle was the outcome. If she lived and they died, then the Gods had smiled upon her. Anyone who felt differently was an idiot. There was no honor in battle, no mercy. She'd seen the Pharaoh's soldiers murder women and children on their knees and vowed to be just as cold and heartless as those monsters that called themselves men. For every innocent life the soldiers took, she promised to take ten of theirs.

An easy task since the Pharaohs' men swarmed over the desert like ants on pastry.

Her job today wasn't to extract her pound of flesh. Just like she forced herself to walk slowly, she stayed her hand when it would have been easy to kill. The scroll was the priority. She could settle her vendettas later.

The future was unfolding before her like a rose against the morning sun.

It was time for the resistance to move forward. They were done listening to the promises of a better tomorrow. They would make their future. A future where being born poor didn't determine a person's worth for their entire existence. *Caste systems were bullshit.* Everyone deserves the chance to rise or fail based on their own merits. Jabari thought of the people as inconsequential.

He was about to learn the price of his arrogance.

The temple was in the center of the city, and while it was nice to know that religion was still at the heart of their people, a drop-off at a cozy little temple along the outskirts of the city would have made her life vastly easier. It was easy to hide along the fringes of Naroosh, but the heart of the city swarmed with Jabari's men. The morning hour would lessen their presence but not eliminate it.

Every one of the hooded figures she passed could have been one of Jabari's spies.

Not many of the soldiers would have been able to see through her disguise. Some of them might not even recognize she was a woman except for the veil she wore to cover her nose and mouth. Some of the bastard's spymasters might be able to pick her out of the crowd by body type and uncovered eyes.

So while she had to move slowly, Neema also needed to be in and out of the temple like the wind. Then it was another slow walk out of the city before linking up with Matteo and the camels. The two of them would ride off into the morning sun like the famous bandit princess from their histories.

First, the scroll.

The temple came into view, and she couldn't help but marvel at its size despite being here many times before. Every time she came to pray at the building it filled her with a sense of wonder. Maybe it was the brilliantly colored tile pools or the incense wafting lazily through the air, but Neema always felt at home once she was standing inside the temple walls.

After stepping through the entrance, she immediately knew something was wrong. A feeling of panic had replaced the sense of calm serenity that normally greeted her. There should have been a guard by the door. Stealing from the temple was a death sentence and an affront to the gods, but desperation often forced people to be reckless. The guards were merely there to discourage such foolishness.

Yet, they aren't here now.

Neema drew her sword and picked up her pace. Having an open blade in the temple was sacrilege, but she had the feeling that someone had already broken that rule this morning. The last thing she wanted to do was die because she was more worried about being proper than she was about protecting herself. If she were overreacting, Neema would happily make a donation to show how seriously she repented for her callous actions.

All that mattered now was finding Yansesh and securing the scroll. The priest's quarters weren't too far from where she was now. Neema started to run, and soon she was sprinting through the temple's corridors like a woman possessed. Panic flooded her system. She couldn't be too late.

How could anyone know about their plans?

Neema skidded to a stop outside of Yansesh's room. Instead of kicking in the door and stumbling into trouble, she took a few moments to slow her breathing. It didn't pay to get into a fight when she could barely stand. Deep breaths in through her mouth and out through her nose. As soon as she stopped sounding like a bull in heat, she reached out for the door handle.

Patience had never been one of her better virtues, but she was slowly taking Khalid's lessons to heart. Sometimes it paid to be cautious, and other times a person had to be bold. The true warrior was the one who could read the situation and react faster than their opponent. Subtlety in battle was something she was still coming to terms with. It wasn't only the killing blow that mattered but how you got there.

Picking where and when to fight was as important as the battle itself.

Neema's left palm was sweaty as she reached for the door. Oddly enough, her right hand wrapped around the grip of her sword didn't seem to be sweaty at all. Part of her was happy to know when it came down to fighting her nerves could handle anything. It was the anticipation that was killing her now. She knew what she would find inside but desperately wanted to be wrong.

Khalid had a saying, *hope and the fool go hand in hand.*

Neema was no fool. She made her own destiny. No one handed her anything; she clawed and scraped and survived. Now she was thriving. THRIVING. If someone was waiting inside, they better have brought a fucking army.

Her training took over at the last second, and instead of jerking the door open and charging inside, she pulled it open slowly. Inching the door open took more willpower than it should have, but she was a work in progress.

Khalid liked to tell her that he wasn't the most skilled warrior in all the land, but he might have been the smartest. There were many fine warriors in the kingdom, but most of them were arrogant and overconfident. It was the fighters' boon and folly to believe they could always win. She had watched him fight more times than she could count, and it was always the same.

Khalid always played defense. It didn't matter if it was a grand champion or a boy with a broomstick. The old warrior would watch and learn. When Khalid had seen enough to gain their measure, he would pounce. Death for the champion, and a welt along with a fatherly pat on the head for the boy with the broomstick.

Fuck it.

Her patience burst like a damn as she flung the door the rest of the way open. There were two men inside facing the far wall. Neema could just make out Yansesh beyond their bulk. The priest had a cut on his arm and was pressing himself against the wall so hard it was as if he thought he might be able to will himself through it. His attackers looked startled at first, but now they were coming around.

Shit!

Neema had missed the early opening created by sneaking in through the door. Now both of her attackers were ready for her. If the men had any talent with a blade, she'd be in for one hell of a fight. She took a second to reflect on what went wrong so it wouldn't happen again, then squared her shoulders and set her feet for battle.

The time for reflection was over. Now it was time to fight.

Her sword went through the first man's ribs and up into his innards before he could even tell her to get the fuck out. The second man got his dagger up in time, but the lazy threat cost him his hand at the wrist. A look of pure horror spread across his face as the limb clattered to the floor still clutching the blade. The pain was about to hit, but before he could scream, she shoved her sword through his throat.

Both of Yansesh's assailants were down, and the priest was safe.

"Tell me you have the scroll?" Neema thrust out her arm, voice cracking with tension.

Yansesh couldn't meet her eyes as he hurriedly pleaded, "They killed the guards. They were going to kill me next. What else could I do?"

You could have died.

Neema knew that thought was unfair, but it didn't stop it from coming. Death was something that terrified most people and was one hell of a motivator if you were trying to force someone into doing something they didn't want to do. If it wasn't their death that scared them, Jabari had taught that there were always friends, family, a mistress, an illegitimate child that could be used for leverage. Everyone had something they cared about enough to give in. She'd watched Jabari's men use the tactic again and again.

She wasn't such a monster and would never actually harm the priest, but she also didn't have time for the man to come back to his senses. There was so much on the line, Neema had to act now, or the people of Naroosh would suffer.

Yansesh was no fighter, and his family didn't deserve to die for the resistance. The point of the whole fucking thing was to end the violence at some point. None of them wanted to end up being the next Jabari.

Neema couldn't waste another moment. The further behind the looter she fell, the smaller her chances at recovering their future was. She had to find the document before it disappeared forever. Before she tried to squeeze any more information from Yansesh, she needed to check the bodies.

Maybe she'd get lucky.

It was one thing to kill a man in battle and another to dig through their pockets after death. It was a distasteful task, but she'd been forced to do many blasphemous things since they started their fight against Jabari. This one wouldn't even keep her up at night.

On closer inspection, these men looked like simple thugs. They weren't well dressed or well-armed enough to be soldiers. Knowing the scroll most likely wasn't headed to the palace gave her hope. It was too bad she couldn't question the men.

Dead men tell no tales.

"Who was it? Where did they go?" Neema snarled.

She could make her amends for being rough on the priest later. She wouldn't let Khalid down, not on her very first mission. Her gaze hardened as she waited for the priest to find his resolve.

"I don't know," Yansesh blubbered.

Neema bent and grabbed the man by the front of his robes. Clearly, the thugs weren't going to leave the priest alive. So maybe one of them had loose lips. "You had to have heard something."

"They said something about a camp outside of the city, but I don't know where." Yansesh pulled away from her, trying to straighten his robes.

With a growl of frustration, Neema pushed the man back down to the floor. "You better have something more useful than that. It'd be just as easy for me to cut you down and say I got here a little too late."

She held her sword aloft.

Threatening to kill a priest was wrong on so many levels, but she wouldn't tell Khalid, and she could make peace with the gods later. Of course, she wouldn't harm the man even if he didn't know anything else. Killing should never become so comfortable that a person could do it without feeling it. Neema wanted to enter the next life with a clear conscience. Khalid would already be pissed that she put hands on the man let alone threatened him. It wasn't as if he wouldn't find out. Yansesh wasn't exactly known for his secret-keeping abilities.

"He said something about a golden bird, and he had a tattoo of Vitaria on his forearm." Yansesh held his hands over his head, tears leaking from his eyes. "I swear that's all I heard. Mostly I was trying not to die."

Neema put her sword away and slid the payment for the scroll into the man's hand. "A deal is a deal. See that this goes to something useful."

"It will, I swear it to you." Yansesh looked pleased. "I must go to the healers and call for the guards. You should disappear before they show up."

"That's a good idea." Without another word, Neema made her way from the temple.

She didn't know if the golden bird meant they were camping

by the monument to the god of flight and wind or if they were at the Smuggler's Grotto. Setting up camp by a well-traveled memorial seemed less likely, so she would be heading to find the smuggler and her scroll.

It was time to discover if the gods would lead her true or if they had only littered her trail with falsehoods.

CHAPTER TEN

Calling the Smuggler's Grotto infamous was an understatement of epic proportions.

There wasn't a single bit of crime happening in Naroosh that didn't move through their hideout in some way, shape, or form. The word on the streets was they paid an exorbitant amount of gold to Jabari for him to look the other way. Not a soul in Naroosh would have been surprised to find out the rumors were true. That was the kind of reputation Jabari had.

The payments must be the only reason the smugglers could still be in operation, that or Jabari ran them himself. It wasn't like their location was a secret. Three hills marked the edge of the valley, and after them, there was nothing but sand for hundreds of miles. From there it would be easy enough to assume that the caves closest to the river would be more convenient for smugglers, and a person was well on their way to finding Naroosh's den of iniquity. Not that anyone with half a brain would step foot inside the place.

Unless they were desperate.

Desperation and violence pretty much summed up the Grotto. There weren't many places people on the run from Jabari could disappear to and have a chance at survival. The desert was as unforgiving as their noble ruler and twice as merciless. No one lived out in the sands, so they went to the only place there was work outside the city.

Normally Neema would have been all for someone who needed a job finding employment, but the kind of work offered in the Grotto wasn't fit for a monster. Killing, murder, rape, all just the tip of the iceberg for these assholes. Slavers. Murderers. Monsters. She wished she could burn the entire place to the ground, but Jabari had to answer for his crimes first. Without a foundation of stability, they'd never be able to shift the tide.

Still, a girl couldn't right all the world's wrongs in a day. She had to prioritize.

Maybe once Jabari was dead the world would get lucky, and the smugglers would kill themselves off. It wasn't as far-fetched as it sounded when some new asshole was proclaiming himself king of the Grotto every few months. The smugglers spent as much time killing each other as they did killing others. There wasn't a man or woman amongst them that wasn't a seasoned fighter.

The Grotto wasn't the kind of place you could wander in and out of like the wind. Everyone there was suspicious of everyone. They never knew when a rat hid amongst the group, and no one was shy about making accusations. When it came to strangers, a person had to prove their worth. Khalid had done some business with the smugglers early in the resistance's infancy, but now they had less detestable ways of acquiring resources.

No one in the resistance believed that a man or woman should be bonded in slavery. Workers deserved to be paid for their time and treated with a modicum of respect. Did the slaves not bleed the same blood, hunger for the same opportunities, indulge in the same passions as the rest of them? It wasn't right for men to be whipped in the street like oxen and fed so little they died from starvation by the thousands.

Soon they would be able to end it.

Neema knew the only difference between her and one of the slaves was that Khalid saved her. By now Jabari would have grown tired of her, and she would have either been handed over to his men as a plaything and sold off or sent to the mines to labor until she died. It wasn't a life she would have picked for herself and one she didn't wish on any other.

Everyone deserved the chance to be free.

Spending too much time pondering the troubles of the world never did anyone any good. The real heroes were the ones out there doing things to fix it. Even in Naroosh, some people still believed in helping others. A heel of crusty bread might be trash to someone, but for the person who hadn't eaten in a week, the crust of bread looked as good as a feast put on at the palace.

So when it came down to talking about things or doing them, Neema wanted to be a doer.

The hills were drawing closer now, and Neema motioned for Matteo to fall back. The Grotto was no place for a boy, and she wouldn't have time to keep an eye on him. Going into the caverns alone wasn't high on her list of things to do, but right now she didn't have a choice. While she might not have any backup, it also didn't mean Neema had to play by the rules.

Smugglers had their secrets, but so did the resistance.

Khalid had a secret entrance into the caverns. Neema wasn't naïve enough to think no one else had found it over the years, but she hoped whatever wretched soul stumbled upon it didn't seal it off. Going up to the front door and asking for the scroll back wasn't an option, so she'd use the side door and hope for the best.

Gently steering her camel to the right, Neema followed a winding path up into the hills. So far she hadn't seen a soul, but smugglers weren't exactly known as morning people. In another ten minutes, she'd have to tie up her camel and proceed on foot. Khalid would have demanded she ditched her steed earlier, but time was of the essence, and patience wasn't really her thing.

Bold and in your face was more her speed.

It wasn't like the tattooed man was just going to hand over his prize. Her only chance was to intercept the scroll before he sold it off at the smuggler's bazaar. She pulled the camel up short and hopped off.

Do not fail.

She decided not to tie her camel down. Why waste time when there was no guarantee the camel would be there when she came back? There was no reason to risk someone finding it close to their hidey-hole and following her. Or worse, waiting for her when she came back out. It was a risk, but so was everything else in life.

A few minutes later she found the entrance to the caverns. Sand partially covered the opening, and it didn't look like anyone had been through the area in a while. After making sure all her gear was ready to go and her face covered, Neema ducked inside the entrance.

The place didn't smell any better than she remembered. Despite access to the river, bathing was still considered a luxury that most people couldn't afford. Who cared about taking a bath when any moment could be their last? Better to spend the coin on a strong drink. At least that was how she imagined the smugglers felt.

Personally, she loved bathing.

A warm bath was a luxury she didn't always have access to, but a daily dip in the river was something she never missed. It wasn't that she wanted to smell nice. She had scented oils for that purpose. Neema didn't like feeling scuzzy. Living in the desert was an opportunity to be covered in dust by ten in the morning whether a person stepped outside or not.

She wondered if there was a place in the world where it rained enough that the dirt didn't stick to everything all the time. What would it be like to live somewhere with green fields, or maybe mountains? One day Neema would love to find out, but she would never leave Naroosh until a new leader was in place and her people were free.

While the caverns had been relatively empty until now, as she drew closer to the market, there were more and more people walking the underground hallways. Neema made sure to keep her eyes up and to meet every challenging stare with one of her own. Showing an inch of weakness here would only invite an attack.

Several small clusters of men passed her, then a group of two men and a woman. Both of the men trailed behind the woman. As she passed Neema, her eyes almost seemed to smile.

The blow came from behind her on the left.

Despite the small warning, she hadn't been expecting the attack. At the last second, she turned slightly so she took the strike on her shoulder instead of the back of her head. The force of the club still sent her stumbling. The cavern wall almost smashed into her forehead, but Neema caught herself enough that the wall only made her see stars instead of knocking her out. Her legs wobbled a little, and one of the men saw an opening to grab her around the waist and haul her away.

What a fucking idiot.

The stupid bastard must have assumed she was unconscious. Not wanting to waste the advantage, Neema let the big idiot lift her onto his shoulder before stabbing him in the back. When his legs gave out, he tipped backward. Neema used the momentum to roll off his shoulder and come up on one knee with the dagger from his back ready to throw. Her wrist snapped forward, and the blade flew straight and true.

The second of the woman's guards stumbled back with Neema's knife in his stomach. He was out of the fight for the money, but a bigger question loomed right now.

Where was the woman?

Neema knew better than to stay in one place for too long. She kept the man with the stomach wound in front of her and the cavern wall at her back. A quick peek over her shoulder confirmed the first man she stabbed wouldn't get up ever again. That's why she stabbed him more than once, no reason to hope for the best when a few quick thrusts were bound to hit something vital.

Keeping the wall at her back, Neema pulled her sword free.

That greasy fucker with the knife in his gut wasn't faring much better than his dead friend. It would simply take him a little longer to get there. One thing almost no one in the Grotto had access to was a healer. Their value to the kingdom was worth too much for Jabari to waste one of their number here.

Neema shook her head to make sure her eyes weren't playing tricks on her. She still hadn't located the woman, but the man in front of her could be a problem if she showed up. There was no chance he'd live without a healer, and dying from a gut wound was a horrible way to go. His suffering ended with a slash from her sword.

The woman sprang out from behind her fallen comrade and tried to get around Neema. Letting her go wasn't an option. Neema couldn't risk having a group of smugglers trying to hunt her down. She used her sword to block the woman's escape.

Now that the two men were dead, the realization of what the woman tried to do to her hit like a truck. "What would you have let them do to me?" Neema snarled.

"Nothing you wouldn't have done to me given a chance."

Neema's sword slashed out before the woman finished speaking. She left a deep slash across the woman's right arm. "Consider it a gift."

In a place like this, she didn't have to strike the final blow. The next man walking down the hall would do it for her. Keeping the woman locked in place with the tip of her sword, Neema backed up until she found the first man's fallen club. It was time to give the bitch a taste of her own medicine.

A blow to the head sent the smuggler into oblivion.

Looting bodies wasn't her favorite thing to do, but she'd already done it once this morning so what was a few more times?

She got down on her hands and knees and rifled through the fallen's pockets.

The two men didn't have much on them—some worthless scraps that might have been called weapons in a pinch and a few copper coins. The woman on the other hand had a rather large pouch of silver on her, and one gold coin hidden in a pocket tucked under her shirt. With this kind of coin, it was no wonder she felt confident enough to strike. This woman worked for someone with power.

Going back to the boss without the silver wouldn't improve the bitch's day. Not that Neema should care at all, but part of her knew how quickly the radical could become commonplace. Even if the woman had tried to kidnap her, she wouldn't be so cruel as to leave her without a weapon. What was the point of fighting for a better future if she let herself become one of the monsters in the process?

It probably would have been safer to kill her, but Neema had her fill of blood for the moment. All she wanted now was the scroll, but her chances of finding it were as small as a drop of water in the ocean. The only way she stood a chance was if the Goddess Eternia smiled down upon her.

Still, she heard Khalid's words in her head over her own.

The goddess smiles on those who make their own luck.

Neema prayed and thought of where she could go that would put her somewhere where she could see the most people without anyone paying attention to her. The only place she could think of was where she was already heading. The market. If she found a quiet corner where she could sit and watch the people passing, she might get lucky enough to spot a Vitaria tattoo.

There was still a chance. Neema wouldn't fail.

CHAPTER ELEVEN

"Maria!" A woman screamed as she reached out from an overturned wagon for her daughter.

The woman's hands extended toward the girl, clutching violently at the air as if she could will her child back into them.

Tim noticed two things at once. Maria couldn't have been more than ten years old. She reminded him of his sister. There was no way in hell this girl would die now that they were there. The shock of seeing the young girl hiding in the woodpile was starting to fade, and his eyes moved from her terrified face to the creature hovering above her.

So that's what a harpy looks like.

He'd seen all kinds of harpies in different games. Some of them were sexy, and some of them were freaky. All of them were women. Imagine how awkward it would be to see all those male jiggly bits bounce around on screen every time they flapped their wings. He was sure there was some actual mythos as to why all harpies were female, but Tim preferred what he dubbed the bouncing ball theory. When he explained about the flapping wings and the floppy nether regions he always got a laugh.

Right now he didn't feel like laughing.

The harpy flapped her massive wings, sending a gust of wind toward them. They were still far enough away the blast didn't do damage, but the bitch's point was clear enough, don't come any closer or I'll fuck you up. The anger and the I'm-going-to-kill-you vibe certainly diminished how much he appreciated her naked torso.

That was another thing about developers.

They were suckers for luring young teen boys into games with super hot monsters. It was an age-old tradition. Why make all the monsters terrifying when some of them could be sexy and terrifying? It wasn't like they did it to honor the raging hormones of the male teen. There was a reason every man in the game had four-foot-wide shoulders and tiny waists. Not to mention a six-pack that would make Lenny Kravitz wonder why he still worked out so hard.

Now wasn't the time to nerd out about the validity of sexy monsters.

Tim ran forward and skidded to a halt next to Maria's mother. "I need you to go back and join the others."

"No, my daughter needs me!" She grabbed a handful of Tim's robes. "You have to help her."

Quest Received: Saving The Future

Scare away or defeat the harpy in battle while ensuring no harm comes to Maria.

Reward: Sometimes doing the right thing is its own reward.

Whole lotta quests without rewards going around right now.

Tim accepted it.

Sometimes the extra experience that came with a quest was worth the effort regardless of if it came with shiny loot or not. In this case, they would have helped without a quest. Tim didn't believe for one second that anyone in their guild would leave a little girl to die because the reward wasn't big enough.

It wasn't who they were.

Tim reached out, touched the woman's shoulder, and turned her so she faced him and away from her daughter. "We'll save her, but I need you to get to safety first." He held her gaze. "I can't be worried about you and Maria."

"I promise we'll bring her home to you." ShadowLily said the words like she was swearing an oath before Eternia herself.

Maria's mother glared at them. "If you don't, I will haunt you 'til the end of your days."

Without another word, the woman turned away from her daughter and sprinted back toward the farmhouse.

"Momma!" Maria cried.

She paused for a moment, and Tim's heart broke for her. When she looked back over her shoulder, he saw the wet stains on her cheek. It took all he had not to call her back, to let her watch as they saved her daughter, but the risk to all of them felt too great. Now his only job was to make sure they had a happy reunion as soon as possible.

The harpy lunged forward and struck the woodpile. Maria screamed as the wood shifted, and all of them instantly focused on what they needed to do. The young girl crawled farther back into the stacked rows, but they wouldn't be able to protect her forever.

Tim waved at Lorelei. "Might be a good time to introduce that feathery bitch to a few sharp and pointy objects."

"Getting her attention shouldn't be a problem." Lorelei nocked an arrow and let it fly almost instantaneously.

The arrowhead glittered in the bright afternoon sun like a silver missile. Tim watched as the arrow flew through the air, tracking its progress toward the munition's ultimate destination. The ranger's shot would be dead perfect, as always.

Right before the arrow would have plunged into the monster's chest, the harpy beat her wings again. The gust threw the bolt violently off course to the side. A single feather was impaled on the ground.

"Her wings have a lot of power," Lorelei called as she nocked another arrow.

Tim turned to Cassie. "Get in there and do your thing!"

"Like I was waiting for you to tell me." Cassie vaulted over the wagon. "Just didn't want to get shot in the back," she screamed back as she sprinted toward the harpy.

"As if," Lorelei huffed while letting another arrow fly.

This time the harpy used her wings earlier, and the arrow flew back toward Cassie, forcing her to dive out of the way.

"My bad," Lorelei shouted at Cassie's scowling face. The ranger shouldered her bow and pulled her knife free. "New plan."

The monster had been mostly ignoring them, seeing the girl as a much easier target. That was right up until Lorelei's first arrow pulled one of its feathers free. Now the bitch looked pissed. Not that Tim was entirely focused on her face. This was the first time he'd gotten an honest-to-God look at the creature, and he wasn't sure if he was disgusted or slightly turned on.

Did having feathers invalidate the power of boobs?

Sometimes he thought developers had fun seeing what they could pull off when it came to sexy repulsion. This harpy was no different. Feathers covered most of its fifteen-foot frame, but skin covered her other parts and was very, very distracting.

What was it with him being attracted to only the deadliest of women now?

There was a time when all he wanted was to find someone who wanted to hang out and game or watch movies. Now that he was with an assassin he saw how much he'd been missing out on. ShadowLily was as fierce in combat as she was in the bedroom, and while he was pretty sure he satisfied her regularly, if she turned into a fifteen-foot-tall killing machine his man parts might be woefully lacking. Maybe that's why harpies were so mad all the time. Had to suck not being able to get any nookie for the cookie.

Sometimes size mattered, and not just when you ordered fries.

Cassie was closing the distance quickly, but it would take her a few more seconds to get there. The harpy didn't dismiss the charging warrior as she had the ranger. Instead, she turned to face Cassie down. A tear in reality appeared in front of the creature, and Tim cringed backward expecting bolts of dark energy to rain down upon them. Instead, the harpy pulled a sword and shield from the opening. It closed, leaving nothing but a clear sky in its place.

With a sword and shield in her hands, the harpy almost looked like an avenging angel. Her fondness for murdering farmers and eating children precluded the angel argument, but it wouldn't have taken much persuasion to convince Tim the creature was a demon working for Vitaria.

Normal harpies didn't have weapons waiting for them in some kind of pocket dimension. In fact, most of the time they didn't even have arms. Only wings and the head and upper body of a woman, with taloned feet. This monster was all kinds of different and wouldn't be anywhere as easy to take down as a traditional harpy.

Tim scanned the boss now that they were closer, and the information only came back with a name, Helen.

Weird-ass name for a harpy.

The sneer on Helen's face as she waited for Cassie to close the distance between them was enough to snap Tim's thoughts back into focus. Looking in those hate-filled eyes reminded him of the first time he ever laid eyes on the scary mythical monster Mucklebones.

No one wanted to meet fucking Mucklebones.

Cassie slammed into the harpy's shield with enough force the monster flew back a few steps. All it took was one massive heave of the creature's wings, and she was back on the tank in an instant.

Shit.

Before sending his tank in to fight a monster they never faced before, Tim probably should have had his heals ready to go and his buffs cast. It wasn't like him to make such an amateur mistake. Watching Cassie almost getting cleaved in half reminded him always to be vigilant and quickly realigned his priorities.

Tim dropped into his Way of the Boulder stance to provide Cassie a boost, then quickly cast Curse of Giving on the boss. With a burst of healing directed at the tank, it gave him time to cast his buffs. Maybe he was having a case of the Mondays, but he always felt more prepared than this.

Wait, what day was it anyway?

Shaking his head to clear it, Tim tried to focus on the fight, but his heart wasn't in it. What in the fuck was wrong with him? Something didn't feel right. Then it dawned on him he might be suffering from some kind of status effect. His fingers moved slowly but eventually made their way through the Cleanse spell.

His thoughts cleared instantly.

It was a good thing they did because everyone was down, and the harpy was scratching at the woodpile with her talons like a fox at the hen house. Cassie was the closest to the mind-flaying bitch, and she was also the tank, which made her top priority. Tim cast Cleanse on her, followed by a Healing Orb.

He wasn't sure if he'd ever seen Cassie so pissed off. JaKobi could make her mad, but not like this. Their tank might as well have been a freight train of rage ready to deliver an economy-sized can of whoop-ass on the harpy. It was as though they had a little mini-Hulk.

The she-Hulk slammed her bō staff into the back of one of the harpy's wings, snapping the limb. Feathers filled the air like when a Randy Johnson fastball took out a dove on the way to the plate. Tim couldn't see a thing, and that meant trouble. Maybe this was the harpy's version of squid ink.

"Watch out!" Tim cried as he threw himself to the ground.

A screech pierced the air, and all the floating feathers blasted forward pushed by a gale-force wind. Most of them shot right over him, but one caught his cheek and left a razor-thin cut. If anyone on his team got hit by the blast full-on, it would have been devastating.

Tim jumped back to his feet, quickly checked his status bar, and met with an eyeful of depleted health bars. He preferred to keep his status window closed, but now and then he used it to get the complete picture in a second instead of having to look around. He almost felt like he was running with a group of players who decided it was time to do big DPS, and moving out of the giant red circles on the ground was optional instead of mandatory.

In this case, it wasn't his team's fault.

Who would have thought the harpy's feathers would have been razor-sharp? It wasn't like they wrote that shit in any of the storybooks. Tim had proven he could handle a few random hiccups during a battle without falling apart. A quick Healing Orb on Cassie would keep her up while he changed gears. Now he was finally able to test out some of his burst AOE healing.

He'd been working this option out in his head for a while and was excited to put his plan into practice finally. It was one of those things where he felt silly practicing his rotation over and over again until it became a part of him, but that was also what separated the cream of the crop from the masses.

All he had to do now was execute.

Who Needs a Shield was his opener for this gambit. It would give Cassie the boost she needed to survive before the rest of his healing kicked in. He quickly reapplied Curse of Giving and followed it by casting Healing Orb. As the orb splashed against the tank, Tim flipped his stance into Way of the River.

With his stance changed, the heals from his curses and any damage dealt should now spread to the party. With his curse pumping out healing to the entire group, it was time to kick things up a notch. Tim cast Behold My Power. The whole party staggered to their knees as though another blast of the harpy's power hit them, and not the recoil from Tim's spell.

Damaging his already wounded party wasn't exactly standard

healing protocol. Anyone watching his stream right now probably thought he was in trouble. At best, Tim held his team's health at about even, but in reality their health was slightly ticking down. Now seemed like the perfect time to put his mana pool to the test. How much healing could he pump out when he really needed it?

Looking at the heavens, Tim screamed the final words of Healing Storm. Fat droplets of rain fell onto his party, slowly healing all of them at once. It took everything he had to keep the spell channeled and their health moving up, but he only had to maintain it until his curse took hold, and everything would be right as the rain falling around them.

Seven seconds left.

One of the harpy's talons closed on Cassie's shoulder. The monster pulled its wings in tight, spinning fast in the air, then stopped at the same instant it let Cassie go. The tank flew across the farmyard like a doll tossed out of a car doing seventy on the freeway. She hit the ground with a heavy *thud*, bounced a few times, and crashed into the overturned wagon.

Cassie wasn't moving, but his status window also confirmed she wasn't dead.

It felt like the fight was spinning out of control. Maybe he had been too cocky walking into this battle without doing any research. Constantly winning had a way of making people take things for granted. Tim wasn't ready for another check-in with Barbara just yet, and he wouldn't have to see her if he could keep his mind focused on the little details.

He kept channeling Healing Storm, counting off the seconds until Behold My Power hit the harpy like a car thrown by King Kong. It was Tim's most powerful spell, and it was no joke. The bird-woman might not think anything was happening yet, but it would hit her soon enough.

When Cassie went down, JaKobi launched himself into the battle. A little healing rain wouldn't stop the power of his pyrotechnics. The flames didn't seem to be doing much damage to the harpy, but they kept her distracted enough for ShadowLily to rejoin the fight. Her blades ripped into the creature's lower legs as if they were tissue paper.

With a screech of pain, the harpy flew straight up until Tim almost couldn't see her anymore. They hadn't run into a boss-type monster that had made a run for it yet, so he got the feeling something bad was about to happen. If the developers didn't want monsters running off every time they got close to death, then the bird-woman wasn't fleeing. This was an attack.

Oh shit.

He could see the harpy now as it descended back toward the earth like a comet. There was some kind of magical energy wrapped around her like a shield. Tim might as well have been one of the dinosaurs watching the comet coming to wipe them all out. He stared at the falling harpy, a look of horror growing on his face at the inevitability of it all.

See you soon, Barbara.

He could see the harpy smiling as she plunged toward them. It wouldn't be long now since she was only forty feet above them.

Thirty.

Twenty.

The harpy's face twitched.

The world exploded in a cloud of dust, and Tim found himself sitting on his ass ten feet from where he'd been moments ago. Being a healer meant you didn't have the luxury of being injured until your entire party was good to go.

Nothing derailed a fight faster than losing a tank or a healer.

Continuing to inhale the dust was making him choke, and he still couldn't see shit. The cloud was getting on his nerves. He wasn't sure if he should cast Healing Storm again to try and knock the dirt from the air or if he should make sure Cassie was topped off. Their tank had been low on health before the harpy took a swan dive. She must be even worse off now. Tim pulled up his status bar to make sure she was alive and stared at it in shock.

Everyone's health was almost full.

"How in the fuck did that happen?" Tim mumbled to himself as he looked back at where he assumed the harpy's body was lying.

Behold My Power must have kicked in right before the creature hit the ground. That little twitch on her face must have been the spell taking hold. His team would have received a massive blast of healing right before she died. Still, why did she die? Tim thought about it for a moment and wondered if his spell broke her concentration. So instead of obliterating them all and flying away with Maria, the harpy hit the ground like a hotdog tossed off a skyscraper.

Getting rid of the dust quickly became his priority. He kind of felt like he was back at his house in the real world when the neighbor fired up his leaf blower and coated their entire back yard in dust. He'd always imagined being in his backyard during one of his neighbors' jaunts was like being trapped in a desert sandstorm.

Was there anything worse than dust?

Tim stretched his hands back toward the heavens and started to cast Healing Storm. He kept the spell channeled as he watched his mana drop in his combat log. It paid to know how long he could keep this up, even starting from a depleted mana pool. While he waited for the dust to clear, he also checked to see if the harpy was actually dead.

"Probably should have done that first," Tim groused.

Reviewing his log confirmed the harpy died from fall damage. Tim looked at where the bird-woman had smashed into the ground, and his jaw dropped when he saw more of the devastation. There was a giant crater in the dirt. It looked like a bomb had gone off, or maybe someone pulled a satellite from the sky and slammed into the earth for shits and giggles.

He didn't want to think about what the blast would have been like if the harpy hadn't lost concentration before hitting the ground. It almost felt like a kamikaze move. The kind of thing someone would do to try and shift the tide when the battle was all but lost. Not the sort of thing you'd expect from someone fighting alone.

The real question was quickly becoming, who was the harpy trying to protect?

The rest of his group stood and made their way over to the crater. Tim cast a quick Healing Orb on Cassie to top her off. She might not be a tank in the traditional sense, but no one would be able to tell by looking at her health pool. The tank gave him a quick nod as she moved past the crater toward the woodpile.

Maria!

After all this, how had he forgotten about the girl? Tim rushed to catch up with Cassie. Maria wasn't in their group, so he wasn't sure if the healing rain would have affected her or not. By the time he reached her, Cassie was already showing the girl how to hold a bō staff properly. Maria had few scratches here and there, but outside of remembering the attack, the little one would be fine.

One blast of Healing Orb fixed her right up but also earned him a look.

Cassie grinned. "I hate getting splashed with that stuff too, but you get used to it." She turned to Tim. "Why don't you go see what's left of that monster, and I'll keep training our newest warrior."

Maria giggled and swooshed the staff through the air.

Seeing the girl made Tim miss his sister a little more than he would have thought. A smile spread across his lips as he imagined how he could use saving his sister from a mythical beast against her. Maybe that could be their new bedtime tale, don't steal from your big brother's room, or he'll let the harpy eat you.

JaKobi looked at Tim and pointed into the depression. "You going in?"

"Might as well check to see if there's any loot." Tim hopped over the edge and made his way to the center.

At the crater's center was a very familiar-looking golden chest. Tim reached out and laid his hand on it. He didn't get a prompt to select an item so he pulled up his log to see what he received—a small amount of gold, a cracked ruby, and a note.

Well, this ought to be interesting.

Those damn farmers are getting too close to our operation. Make sure they stop digging into our business. Vitaria will have our heads if we lose the only foothold we have left in her sister's realm. Why the gods must continually shit on those of us dumb enough to work with them, I'll never know. Get the job done and hurry back.

Dr. Z

It looked like their problems in *The Etheric Coast* weren't over. Before they could go to Naroosh, they had to deal with this. Leaving an enemy at your flank was a big no-no. Tim might not have been a warrior, but he'd been destroyed by flankers enough times in PvP matches to know that when executed correctly, that style of play was extremely deadly.

Quest Received: Harpy's Got the Blues

The harpy in question might be dead, but that doesn't mean there isn't something to investigate. Find out what Dr. Z and Vitaria are up to and stop it.

Reward: The world doesn't end, oh, and a little extra gold for your trouble.

Tim accepted the quest and shared it with his group. A little extra pocket change never hurt anyone, and if the quest itself didn't have a large reward, that generally meant whatever bosses they had to kill would. He kind of preferred the rewards to come after killing a difficult foe. It gave the encounter a greater sense of accomplishment than being handed a weapon for going somewhere and collecting ten of something.

Although Tim was kind of getting used to picking his rewards when it suited him. Not having to decide right away if the item was an upgrade or not was nice. It gave him a chance to plan and look over his stats before committing to a new piece of gear.

One should never be too hasty.

Playing in *The Etheric Coast* was an amazing experience so far. It took what game developers had been doing with scaled difficulty and made it seamless. Every challenge felt like they had a chance to win and that a few missteps could easily send them all back to chat with their caseworkers. He didn't know if the game would always be balanced this way, but right now Tim felt pretty good about things.

Maria was riding on top of Cassie's shoulders now, and their tank was charging at random things the young one called so she could spear them with Cassie's bō staff. Tim laughed as he watched their antics. Things on the farm might not be perfect after the attack, but seeing Maria let him know that coming here had been the right thing to do.

The last thing he wanted to do was ruin the girl's happiness by telling her there were more monsters they had to deal with. If anyone in the group hadn't seen the letter, they could talk about it once they delivered their rambunctious package back into her mother's arms.

Tim shouted at Cassie, "Onward brave steed, we must return the princess to her castle!"

Cassie let out a bray and sprinted down the path back to the farmhouse.

ShadowLily nudged Tim. "You know, you're kinda good at that."

"Don't worry. My experience comes from having a little sister." Tim grinned. He knew full well she wasn't implying he had a child of his own.

The assassin winked at him. "Just saying, good with kids isn't exactly a turn-off." ShadowLily turned away and ran to catch up with Cassie.

"You stepped in it now." JaKobi smirked. "This is why I let Cassie think I'm not good at anything."

Lorelei smacked the fire mage on the back of the head. "That's why she's too good for you." She smiled at Tim as she dragged

JaKobi away. "My advice is to keep doing what you're doing, and don't listen to this guy."

Tim stood there for a moment thinking about how odd growing up could be. One day you were thinking about the future, and the next day you were living it.

CHAPTER TWELVE

The farmhouse was a hive of activity when they returned.

Maria's mother was the first to see them and sprinted across the open field toward her daughter. Cassie set the girl down, and all of them watched as she ran to her mom. A smile spread across Tim's face as he watched them embrace. This was the part of being a hero that was awesome.

Quest Complete: Saving The Future

You destroyed the harpy, but it was a close call. Imagine what would've happened if you failed. Being cursed by a grieving mother might have meant more than ill will. Rejoice in the fact you'll never have to find out.

Reward: Bonus experience has been delivered based on your participation in this quest.

System Message: You have gained a level.

"Nice!" Tim exclaimed as he looked over the text.

ShadowLily nodded next to him. "I wasn't expecting that."

"Do you think that means Maria's mother is a witch?" JaKobi whispered. "Maybe she can teach me something."

Cassie nudged the fire mage in the ribs. "Make sure you offer something for her time. We've already been paid for our quest."

"I would never use a lady's gratitude to earn free magic... oof...okay, I might have thought about it, but I can see how that would be wrong." JaKobi slowly moved away from Cassie while cradling his side.

Brother Colton, Maria's mother, and the girl herself met their party together.

Their rotund friend grinned. "I see you've met Priestess Shara and her daughter Maria."

Shara beamed at the group. "Thank you for bringing my little girl back."

Tim was going to say something, but Cassie spoke first. "It was our pleasure. She's one heck of a fighter. Another few minutes, and Maria would have handled the harpy on her own."

The tank lowered her gaze and winked at the girl.

"See, Mom? I told you I'm tough," Maria said with gumption reserved for a much older child.

Pride was etched all over Shara's face. Of course, she knew her daughter hadn't done those things, but for the first time since the attack, she was sure her daughter would recover. "Of course you are." She knelt to look into her eyes. "I need you to go over and protect all the other kids. Some of them aren't as brave as you are and need your help."

"With the babies. Ughh." Maria threw her hands up with the outrage that only younger children can muster when asked to take care of kids younger than themselves.

Shara waited for her daughter's tantrum to subside and held her gaze. "Wherever you're needed, that is the path we follow."

Still pouting but face full of resolve, Maria looked up into her mom's eyes. "Yes, Mother."

"Now go." Shara hugged Maria and pointed to where the others waited for her.

The little girl ran away, then stopped and sprinted back. Her small arms wrapped around Cassie's waist, and the tank hugged her back with as much ferocity. "Thank you for saving me."

Cassie bent so they were on the same level. "Anytime, kid." She grinned. "What do warriors do?"

Maria's face lit up. "Strike first, no mercy!" She lifted a fist and shook it.

Realizing that might not exactly be the path Shara wanted Maria to take, Cassie tried to make it better. "But not unless you check with your mother first."

Maria pushed Cassie over, blew the most vicious of raspberries, and ran away.

Laughing, Shara pulled Cassie back to her feet. "Don't worry, I've known for a long time Maria would walk a different path than mine. As long as she finds happiness and lives a life blessed by Eternia, who am I to judge?"

Brother Colton nodded before motioning them to follow him back to the farmhouse. "Is it safe for them to go back to work?"

"That seems a little harsh." Lorelei looked over the priest with an appraising eye.

The priest stopped and faced the ranger. "I only asked if it was safe for them to get back to normal. A lot of people count on the food we produce here."

Tim didn't want to hear an argument about people's safety versus profit. As far as he could tell, the temple gave the food away for free, and Brother Colton was concerned about the workers' safety. It seemed like the two sides had more in common than they did apart. It was funny how that worked sometimes.

Tim moved over to the priest and gently turned him away from Lorelei. "It looks like there might be a larger threat to the farm. I hoped to speak with you about it before we left to deal with it."

"A larger threat?" Brother Colton stammered.

Quickly regaining self-control, the priest moved to speak with his foreman Jim. "We need to keep everyone on lockdown. Can you handle it?"

Jim looked shocked that the priest was putting so much faith in him. "I'll round everyone up and get them into the stables. We can lock it down for a few days but not much longer. If we wait too long, some of the crops will go bad."

"Get everyone situated and join us inside the farmhouse. Once I have a better idea of what they discovered, we'll formulate a plan for how to proceed."

Jim gave Brother Colton a firm nod and moved into the crowd to get things organized.

The priest looked tired as he returned his gaze to Tim. "I'm not sure I should put so much faith in him after what happened today, but Eternia is a sucker for second chances." Brother Colton moved toward the house. "She doesn't like to give third ones though, so maybe a little time in the field for Jim will remind him what it's like to get dirty for a living."

"What do you know about getting dirty?" ShadowLily pulled the priest into a side hug and guided him into the dining room, which was now body-free.

A very roguelike smile appeared on Brother Colton's lips. "Oh, I've plowed a few fields and piped a few wells in my day."

"You naughty little thing!" ShadowLily exclaimed, enjoying the bright crimson patches on the priest's cheeks.

He held up a hand to stall any further inquiries. "In my youth. Now this humble man is simply a vessel for the goddess."

"That's what I used to call this guy." JaKobi held up his right hand. "Vessel for the godstick."

Cassie grunted. "Godstick might be going a little too far, don't you think?"

Tim wished Gaston and his crew of motley assassins was here. This was when they all would have gone *awwww, savage burn.* They'd been picking up slang from the other travelers and incorporating it into how they talked. The results were hilarious sometimes and often kept things from getting tense.

Tim's crew seemed to be doing well right now, despite their

near-death run-in with the harpy. If there was time to fit in a masturbation joke, things were either going great or about to spiral out of control. Since he didn't see a tornado on the horizon, Tim decided to feel pretty good about the day's accomplishments.

Everyone found a seat at the table and sat. When Jim and Shara joined them, they closed the doors to the dining room and took the two remaining seats. It didn't take Tim long to fill them in on what happened during the battle and the note they found afterward.

"This isn't good at all." Brother Colton shook his head. "We're going to need soldiers. I must go to see the High Priest at once."

He strode toward the door, then paused. "This goes without saying, but no one goes out in the fields until I come back and can personally guarantee their safety."

"Whatever you want," Jim replied as he stood. "But I'm not sure I should be in charge."

Shara smiled. "Eternia would say life is what we make with the chances we're given."

"Yes, she would." Brother Colton made the sign of Eternia over his chest. "Jim, you're in charge until I get back. If you need any advice, Shara is at your disposal."

Tim watched as the priest opened the doors and strode purposefully from the room. That left his team to decide whether they wanted to go track down Doctor Z now or if it made more sense to wait until the morning. Their chances of finding a secret lair in the dark weren't optimal, and they could all probably use a meal before heading back out.

"Jim, is there somewhere we can bunk down before heading out in the morning?" Tim looked at the foreman and hoped the answer wasn't outside somewhere.

Jim and Shara made their way to the door as he answered. "There are three bedrooms upstairs. You're welcome to any of them. I think it'd be best if I stayed with everyone else tonight since I'm sure they'll have a lot of questions for me to answer."

Shara gave their group one last smile and left the room with Jim.

"Looks like we have the place to ourselves." JaKobi grinned as he tilted his chair back and put his feet up on the table.

Cassie knocked his feet off. "Heathen." She pointed at the door. "Go upstairs and find a bedroom suitable for my station."

"Yes!" JaKobi ran from the room.

Strolling saucily after him, Cassie laughed. "Sometimes, it's just too easy."

Lorelei made a retching sound. "I think I'm going to stay down here for a bit."

"Probably a good idea." ShadowLily winked at her. "Let's see if we can wrangle up some grub."

Tim watched the two of them leave the room, but his mind was already drifting off to thoughts of how he could improve his rotation to eke a little more juice from his spells. The way he used Healing Storm today wasn't optimal. Getting flashy was fine and dandy for a fight the group knew, but for new encounters, he quickly decided defense was the better part of valor.

A little dust drifted down from the ceiling, followed by several thumping noises. Tim looked up, trying not to laugh out loud.

Maybe he should help the ladies with dinner.

CHAPTER THIRTEEN

Mornings sucked.

Still, they weren't all bad. Every momentous day throughout history started with a morning. Tim kinda wondered if George Washington hated mornings. Back then, the coffee—if they had any—was probably vile stuff. Imagine trying to win a revolution fueled by substandard coffee.

What a disgrace.

Tim kind of imagined George's coffee tasting a lot like the coffee he was forced to digest while interning in corporate America. He didn't know which bean countersigned on the coffee budget for the year, but they should've been brought up on charges. Maybe that was why insurance costs went up for his parents every year. Workers were being poisoned with cheap coffee all across America.

Thankfully inside *The Etheric Coast*, Tim had only run into decent cups of coffee. He was sure a bad one existed somewhere in the game. There weren't any cops here to take a drink and spit it out before glaring back at the coffee maker in disgust. If the coffee in corporate America was bad, the coffee in a police station was probably worse.

Why provide free coffee if it's undrinkable?

There was this scene in *Breaking Bad* that Tim loved. Walter White was in his underground meth lab with his assistant Glen. When Walter wanted some coffee, Glen walked over to this chemistry set where he'd perfected not only the bean-to-water ratio but the temperature and distillation of the perfect cup of joe. With coffee like that, who couldn't change the world?

Not that Tim would be firing up an RV anytime soon. Things didn't exactly work out well for Walter, and the Blue Dagger Society didn't have a crazy cool chemistry set. They did have a magic teapot.

Tim had been in love with the contraption ever since JaKobi brought it out. Coffee anywhere, anytime. He found if he used a coarse grind on the beans and placed them in a steel tea ball, the pot worked better than his coffee maker back home. His problem was he never remembered to bring the fucking beans.

Even Bayaz carried his own tea.

If Tim wanted good coffee, he would have to make a little more room in his inventory. Maybe now that no one was hunting him, he could ditch a few of the spare sets of clothes he kept with him. One or two changes outside of his gear should be enough. He could probably leave the extra stuff behind at the farmhouse. He was sure someone could use some practically new clothes.

Tim didn't get too many hand-me-downs while growing up unless they came from his father, but his little brother got all his old clothes. He always thought that must be the worst part of being a younger sibling. The best part was probably the little shit's ability to get away with anything.

After pulling the items he didn't want from his inventory, Tim folded the clothes so he could leave them in a nice orderly stack. He was pretty sure no one would want used clothes that he tossed around. It'd be like walking into Goodwill and having it look like a laundry basket exploded all over the floor.

It took him a few minutes to pull himself back from thoughts of his old life. He didn't have to do laundry inside the game, and his clothes repaired themselves, so he only had to buy new ones if he wanted them. One less worry for a cashed-strapped adventurer.

Not that I'm short on funds.

He wondered if the temple had a similar project to the farm in Promethia. It felt like there were still a lot of hungry people. In a world full of magic, it was hard to believe there wasn't a way to feed everyone at least a basic meal. How much could oatmeal and a little butter cost?

Starting a farm wasn't something he had time for, but investing in someone who wanted to start one was something he might have to look into. He was sure there were all kinds of players in this game who wanted to do normal things in a new environment. Maybe they could even breed new plants or magical ones.

Xander would have been all over cornering the magical marijuana market.

ShadowLily wasn't in the room so Tim decided it was time to get up and find something to do. He had an unfortunate habit of letting his mind wander off when he was alone. He'd crack a book for research, that would lead to a webpage, and somehow wind up with him in a chat group at 3:00 a.m. talking to people who really thought Abraham Lincoln was a vampire hunter.

A few moments later, Tim was dressed and heading down the stairs in search of coffee. He wouldn't have been surprised to find out that everyone else was already up and making plans for where to start their search. It was nice of them to let him always sleep in, but when the alternative was grumpy Tim, he understood why.

No one liked a grumpster.

Tim could already smell the coffee when he hit the bottom of the stairs, and it wasn't the cheap stuff. The scent led him to the kitchen like he was Snoopy or Toucan Sam. Either the farm had a stash of some legit coffee, or someone in the group had taken it upon themselves to look out for him.

He had the best friends a guy could ask for.

ShadowLily was in the kitchen, and she had a cute little apron wrapped around her tight leather pants. It was quite the contradiction in looks, and it was kind of making him hot. Not that they had time for any morning action. He could hear the rest of the group laughing at something in the dining room.

Maybe that's why people woke up early. Early bird gets the sex and all that.

"Something I can help you with?" ShadowLily smirked as Tim's eyes moved from her backside to her face.

A blush crept into his cheeks. Sure they were dating, but he felt weird getting caught checking her out so he tried to play it cool. "Just came looking for some coffee, didn't expect to run into such a hottie."

"The apron does it for you, huh?" ShadowLily's smirk stayed firmly in place as she poured him a cup of coffee. "Take this and go wait with the others."

Tim lifted the cup to his mouth and took a long sip of the delightful drink before extending it for a refill. "You know it's not the clothes, right? You do it for me. Without you, they're just clothes." He kissed her and accepted the top-off.

"Get ye gone, smooth-talker. There are a few things I need to wrap up in here before joining you." ShadowLily motioned for him to get out of the way so she could get back to work.

Tim didn't mind her asking him to leave. Truth be told, he was a complete disaster in the kitchen. His major contribution to most meals besides stuffing his face was either monetary or doing the dishes. Not a big deal because every chef in the world appreciated not having to clean up once in a while.

The dining room itself was more packed than Tim expected. Shara and Jim were back, and so was Brother Colton and another man in fighting gear. For the priest to have returned so quickly he must have ridden all night. It made Tim feel kind of guilty for not only getting a good night's sleep, but sleeping in while everyone was getting ready.

"Ah, just in time." Brother Colton flashed a warm smile. "The food should be coming soon."

Jim patted the seat between him and Shara. "We have a plan, and we'll be able to save the harvest."

"Eternia be praised." Shara grinned. "For the farm and those who protect it."

"As for protection," the fighter next to Brother Colton nearly growled. "My men have secured the fields and might have tracked down the source of the disturbance."

"Fantastic as always, Sam," Brother Colton exclaimed as he looked at the large map on the wall.

Sam pointed at the building they were in. "This is us." He tapped the map again. "This is where you slew the harpy." Moving his hand toward the edge of the map, Sam tapped another spot. "This is where we think you have to go."

Tim didn't bother to ask for Sam's credentials or why he was so sure this is where they should start looking for Doctor Z. The game had a way of moving players where they needed to be without making them struggle too much. It was fun to find a dungeon. It wasn't fun to spend three days searching the country-side to come up with bupkis.

"Thank you for all the hard work, Sam." Tim meant every word of it. They would have spent a good part of the day riding around looking for clues.

The warrior turned. "Don't mention it. As long as you don't screw up too badly, this will be a nice little training exercise for my men."

"We're not in the business of failing," Cassie shot back with the casual tone of someone discussing the weather.

Sam locked eyes with her. "My business exists because some-times heroes fail."

Before the two could square off for a good old fashioned show-down, ShadowLily and a group of men and women came in carrying trays of food. There were pancakes, eggs, potatoes, biscuits, and some kind of lemon cake that smelled like someone cut a slice out of heaven and served it on a plate.

JaKobi got Cassie back in her seat without incident. Tim smiled to himself. What was it with warriors? It was as if they always had to be the biggest thug in the room. Maybe that was why he didn't make such a good tank. He didn't have the right kind of killer instinct to be a front-line warrior.

As the dishes made their way around the room, everyone forgot about the business at hand and dug into the meal. The first five minutes passed in almost complete silence, as everyone ate like they hadn't seen food in a week. When people finished eating, conversations slowly filled the room. With most of the business already decided, the talk was of more light-hearted matters.

"I'm telling you, fire pong with spiced cider would totally be the best drinking game ever." JaKobi grinned.

A moment later, a flaming ball the size of a ping-pong ball appeared in his hand, and he tossed it into his water glass. Steam shot from the top of the cup and the flames went out with a wet *hiss*.

Lorelei winked. "I'm not saying the game wouldn't be cool, just that it has a very limited audience."

"What she means is not everyone can throw fire around like it's nothing," Cassie added with the air of a woman who's had this conversation a million times already and knows what's about to come next.

"If you could create something anyone could use, you might be onto something." Jim looked at JaKobi's glass of water. "That'd be just the thing for when we celebrate the fall harvest."

JaKobi's face lit up like he'd received a Red Ryder BB Gun for Christmas. "I'll see what I can come up with."

A groan escaped Cassie's lips, but outside of that single noise, she didn't try and rein him in. It was probably better that way. Some people needed to be allowed to create even when the idea wasn't perfect. As long as it was a hobby and all a person's money wasn't going into it, what was the harm? There was nothing wrong with having big dreams.

Even if other people found them a little silly.

Tim smiled as he watched them talk about adding flames to the cups' rims or maybe even hoops you could throw the balls through instead. His fourth cup of coffee had his mind lubricated just right, and he was ready to find out what kind of trouble they would run into today.

The harpy hadn't been an easy opponent, and he still felt lucky about coming away from that battle relatively unscathed. It wouldn't make sense to send your strongest monster into the field where it could be captured or killed. Typically, scouts were fast, lightly armored, and easier to kill. If the harpy was Doctor Z's first offering, they could probably expect much more challenging opponents going forward.

The thought of squaring off against something new and harder to beat was kind of exciting. At the same time, this meant they would have to tone things down a little. It was time to get back to basics. Just like in barbeque when the Pit Master said low and slow, their group would be taking things one step at a time today to avoid any major missteps.

He looked across the table and met ShadowLily's eyes. Tim could instantly tell that she was ready to get moving. Sitting in one place for too long made her antsy. It was kind of funny—in that regard, they were polar opposites. Tim was happy to stay in one place all day and do a whole lot of nothing. There was always a new game or a new restaurant a click away from making an appearance right where he was most comfortable.

At home.

The love of his life was an adventurous spirit. She liked to be on the move and never stayed in one place too long before being bored. It was funny how being opposites worked for them. ShadowLily could go off and run her assassination business while Tim ate at Joe's and tended to the healing shack. It let him have the right amount of laziness in his life while still being productive enough to feel like he was contributing. As much as he would have loved to enjoy a fifth cup of coffee, it was time to get the show on the road.

"Sam, I think it's time you have one of your men show us to our destination." Tim smiled as he moved his gaze away from his lady to the grizzled veteran.

The man stood and gave him a quarter bow. "Of course. I'm ready to leave when you are. I'll have a detachment of my men escort us to the perimeter."

Brother Colton moved from his chair to stand beside Sam. "Keep your men on the farm where they're needed. Let these folks do the work they're meant for."

The priest moved away from the warrior and headed for the door. "It seems as though we all have jobs to do. Might as well get started."

Shara gave Sam a very unpriestly wink. "I, for one, will feel better knowing that you're around."

"I'll have one of my men meet you outside," Sam stammered before he quickly followed Brother Colton from the room.

Jim rose from his chair not a moment later. "I'm going to join the crews for the harvest today." He looked over the group. "Thank you for coming." Without waiting for a response, he left the room.

Lorelei stood and stretched. "So what's the plan?"

"I think I can answer this one." ShadowLily gathered herself and scrunched up her face. "We're going to do things slow and cautious-like."

"Hey, I don't sound like that," Tim griped.

Cassie snorted. "Then tell us, oh wise leader, what were you going to say?"

"Only that there's nothing wrong with a little prudence," Tim spluttered.

ShadowLily's smile grew tenfold in size. "That's not what you said last night."

Everyone laughed, and Tim felt his cheeks getting redder by the instant. "Don't blame me when you die. The old 'Eternia magically resurrects someone' Hail Mary only works once."

"Don't worry about them, boss. I got your back." JaKobi hissed as he caught one of Cassie's elbows. "What...I'm just saying that I, for one, would like some heals in the upcoming battle."

Tim grinned. "Then you sir, will have them." He rose to his feet. "As for the rest of you, I'll be waiting here when you return from meeting your caseworkers."

"Hey!" the three women shouted at once.

Tim winked. "Please, like I'd ruin my reputation by letting you die."

The first biscuit took him by surprise, but by the time the third one was flying, he was fleeing from the room.

Everyone's a critic.

CHAPTER FOURTEEN

The weather was just about perfect.

Tim could see where that perfection ended, and the magic of the farm faded away. There wasn't even a small zone of weather change between the two spaces. On one side of the divide the weather was warm, and on the other, it looked downright chilly. If he wasn't mistaken, there was frost on the ground in a few places.

"We didn't explore much farther along the footpath since none of us came prepared for the cold," Lieutenant Greer stated as he pointed up into the hills and the forest beyond.

"I hate the cold," Cassie grumbled as she equipped a fur-lined coat.

JaKobi looked like he'd won the lottery. "I've been spending my free time in the library ever since we came to Tristholm, and I'm pretty sure I have a spell to help with the cold."

Tim didn't want to get his hopes up, but not being a fan of the cold himself, he was intrigued. He leaned forward like the co-host of a late-night infomercial. "Tell me more."

"It's nothing too special, only a small area of effect spell, but it should be able to handle a little cold. We run into a blizzard or something you better bundle up." JaKobi looked rather pleased with himself despite downplaying the spell's usefulness.

"Might as well go and test it out." ShadowLily pointed into the cold. "I don't like wearing bulky clothes since they restrict my movement."

It was hard for Tim not to be excited about ShadowLily's class choice. Who wouldn't like their sexy half-elf girlfriend running around in skin-tight leather outfits? If anything, he got the better end of the deal. While his body in the game was damn near flawless, he also spent almost all of his time in robes.

All this gorgeous and no one gets to see it.

Suppressing a smile as he poked a little fun at himself, Tim watched as JaKobi stepped out in the cold and cast his spell. The ground around the mage in a twenty-foot circle took on a slightly different shade, clearly defining his magic's boundaries. The fire mage turned and waved to let everyone know it was safe. Cassie kept her coat on, but the rest of them decided to trust in their fiery friend's ability.

Before stepping out of the farm's dome of influence, Tim turned to the lieutenant. "Thank you for your help."

"Not a problem. Now it's up to you to end the threat." Greer jumped back into his horse's saddle and headed back to the farm.

Tim stepped off the farm and into JaKobi's spell. There was a brief instant of being punched in the face by the cold. It reminded him of answering the door for a pizza during a winter storm. He'd shove the money at the startled driver, grab the box and slam the door. Hopefully, a little extra cash smoothed over the abruptness of the encounter. He hated the cold, but clearly not as much as Cassie.

Despite the warmth of JaKobi's spell, the little tank was still wrapped in her fur-lined cloak. Tim wasn't sure how she could stand it. If there was one thing he hated more than the cold, it was being too hot. At least in the cold you could pile on layers like it was nobody's business, but when it was hot out, there was basically zero you could do if the AC wasn't enough.

The realization that there wouldn't be air conditioning in the desert hit Tim like a ton of bricks. He decided it was time to stop complaining and be thankful he wasn't sweating his ass off and gave himself a little pep talk. A little cold never hurt anyone, challenges build character, rub a little dirt on it. He finished quoting useless one-liners and started walking. The last thing he wanted to do was fall behind and get left in the cold.

Following the path was simple enough. Tim noticed some new growth breaking through in places, indicating no one had used the trail in a while. Maybe some of the farmers used to hunt out here, or animals used the path before they realized the weather was perfect not so far away. Not knowing how the trail was created didn't stop him from being thankful for it.

The trees on either side of them grew denser. The large pines towered into the air, almost covering the group with their canopy. Tim looked up and realized that it was snowing. None of it reached their group because of JaKobi's spell and the trees' protection. Watching the white flakes fall out of the darkness of the canopy and melt as they hit JaKobi's shield was beautiful. It was almost like hitting the brights at night when driving in the snow. It made everything look like you were going warp speed.

When there was beauty in a game, there could also be a trap. Tim had to remind himself this wasn't simply a hike along a forest trail. The scenery and the warm bubble they were in made it easy to forget they were on their way to a confrontation. Until now, he'd assumed it would be a dungeon, but it could be a single boss encounter. It certainly wouldn't pay to stumble right into a boss fight unprepared.

Tim quickly cast his buffs and made sure he was in his Way of the Boulder stance. Not being prepared when they faced off against the harpy made him realize he'd grown a little overconfident. It was time to get back to basics and make sure they were ready if they ran into unexpected trouble.

"Be ready for anything. Any long-lasting buffs you have cast them now, and if it's a dungeon up ahead, we can reapply before we enter." Tim felt a little like he was gamesplaining to seasoned vets, but if he'd been caught up in the new scenery, maybe they had too.

JaKobi's hands moved through a quick spell. "Self-buffs are the best buffs."

Cassie snickered. "Sounds like someone who spent most of their life without a girlfriend."

"Gross." Lorelei tried to suppress a laugh.

The fire mage continued strutting forward. "Solved both of those problems at once then, haven't I?"

"Don't mistake problem-solving for luck." ShadowLily gave Cassie a high five before turning and sticking her tongue out at JaKobi. "Burn."

Before he could respond and dig the hole deeper, Tim reached out and put a hand on his shoulder. "You mind creating one of those light orbs for us and sending it out in front a little?"

A ball of perfect white light formed in JaKobi's palm. The sphere leapt from his palm and hovered in midair. With a small flick of his hand, the fire mage sent the ball out about thirty feet in front of them and set the light about fifteen feet off the ground. The orb gave off just enough glow to let them see if anything was lying in wait for them.

Tim let out a small sigh of relief when he saw what looked like a dungeon entrance in the distance. If they were this close to it without running into trouble, all the danger was probably inside. It was a nice change of pace from having to fight your way to a dungeon just to fight some more inside.

No one liked trash mobs.

Although the trash gave everyone time to chat and relax before the next big encounter. Sometimes it was a nice relief after the stress of raiding. So far in *The Etheric Coast,* Tim hadn't used the same methods to relax. Inside the game, he couldn't talk about sports or world events because he had no idea what was going on in the real world. At first, he kind of missed getting sports updates, but then he realized the benefits far outweighed the downsides.

There was no politics inside the game.

What he wouldn't have given not to open the news every day to hear one side or the other with some new crazy theory about how life in America was over as we knew it. Tim couldn't live his life dialed up to eleven. All he wanted was to graduate, get a job, and get rid of his debt as quickly as possible. So far, he was two out of three and moving in the right direction. On top of everything else he even got the girl.

If it weren't for my family, I'd probably never want to leave.

The group continued up the path. Cassie moved into the lead now that their destination was clear. Tim kept his eyes moving, trying to take in as much as he could. The trees peeled away from the path and created a wide clearing. It wasn't until they were in the open that he realized they were in a small valley, and the dungeon's entrance was in a large cliff face.

Trees did a damn good job of hiding the terrain change.

Outside the dungeon was the perfect place for an ambush. Providing a person got there first and secured the high ground. The good news for their group was that stuff like that only happened in *Braveheart* and *Vikings.*

Lorelei moved around the clearing and stopped at a little pedestal. It looked like the one that played the cinematic trailer to *The Hallow.* She looked at the group for confirmation and hit the button.

A holographic projection appeared in front of them.

The camera panned in from above, on a young doctor in his

thirties. Half of his shoulder-length hair was pure white, and the other half as black as midnight. There was no way to tell who or what was on the gurney as the doctor hunched over his patient.

Slowly, as if to draw the viewer's eyes across the dry blood on the floor and walls, the camera panned until it settled on a woman entering the room. Her nurse's outfit was tight in all the right places, but her face held the look of someone who was hired for their expertise and not merely because they were hot. Tim heard Lorelei suck in a sharp breath as the camera panned over the nurse's shoulder and followed her into the room from behind.

The nurse had a tail.

Not a little piggy tail, or something that might match her size like a dog or cat tail, no this woman had a full-on crocodile tail. It was thick enough that Tim wouldn't have wanted to get hit by it, and it looked sturdy enough she probably would never need to use a chair ever again.

He'd heard of stuff like this back in the real world. Of course, as science pushed the boundaries of what people thought was possible, there were always those willing to take the next step. Folks weren't only getting Lasik now; sometimes, they also had blue light filters or contacts inserted under the flap.

Many people didn't consider Lasik real surgery anymore. They could get it done at the strip mall, then grab a froyo. There were all kinds of body modifications going on. Once people started using plates under their skin to change their appearance, shit got real. This seemed like a natural evolution of the practice, but using magic instead of science.

In a hundred years, everyone might have a tail.

Tim let out a little snicker thinking of how fashion would change in his lifetime. It didn't matter how old you were. Something you owned would go in and out of style, maybe even more than once. People might have laughed at his Phish World Tour t-shirt, but in thirty years, some kid would find it at a vintage shop and think it was the coolest thing ever.

The nurse handed the doctor a medical instrument of some kind, and he used it to make a few final adjustments before stepping away from the table. Tim wasn't sure what he was looking at. Then it slowly dawned on him. There was a woman on the table, and she had a set of giant wings sprouting from her shoulder blades. The raw red around the base of the wings showed the wounds were fresh.

"Doctor Zacharias, how is she doing?" the nurse asked as she took the patient's vitals.

The doctor ran a hand through his hair, leaving a bloody streak through his pristine white locks. "The patient struggled with the changes I made to her skeletal system, but her body seems to have accepted the wings without issue. We won't know more until she wakes up."

The nurse bent so she could look into the woman's eyes. Taking one of the patient's hands in hers, she spoke. "Wake up, sister. Come back to me."

A groan escaped the patient's lips as she tried to push herself up from the table. Her eyes locked onto the nurse's. "Help me up, Jenna."

"Take it easy, Elenor." The nurse helped her into a sitting position.

Standing away from the two women, the doctor observed them impartially. He didn't look happy despite the fact the surgery had been successful. The two sisters continued to chat absentmindedly as the doctor cleaned his tools. The room darkened, and Tim expected the film to jump to the next scene, but it didn't. Instead, the doctor turned as white as a sheet while he waited to see what would emerge from the darkness.

An inky black blob formed in the air of the lab. The darkness expanded until it filled half the room. A woman stepped out of it, and it wrapped around her to form a dress.

Vitaria had joined their little party.

Doctor Zacharias immediately dropped to one knee. "Goddess, I am yours to command."

The goddess smiled. "So you have been successful yet again?" Her eyes moved over the two women.

"Only with your help. The intricacies of the magic used here are beyond my ability to comprehend." Zacharias moved to the table. "As you can see, perfection."

Vitaria turned away from them. "These simple constructs were merely a test of your abilities. What I desire is for you to create something exceptional."

Favoring the doctor by allowing him to meet her gaze, Vitaria moved forward as dark energy swirled around her hands. "Are you ready to receive my gift?"

The doctor's face couldn't have been any more split with emotion if it matched his hair. Part of him was clearly thrilled by what he'd accomplished, but there was also a look of disgust on his face. It was as though Zacharias finally realized that once you made a deal with the devil, there was no backing out.

Dropping to his knees, Zacharias lowered his head. "I am."

Vitaria reached out and clasped Doctor Zacharias' head in her hands. The dark energy coalescing around her fingers pulsed as she moved them around the doctor's skull. With each pulse, the darkness faded slightly, and Doctor Zacharias moaned. There was no way to know exactly what was happening, but it looked as if the goddess was infusing the doctor with magic.

"You have the blueprints for my creations. I expect to see progress when I return. Do not forget what rests in the balance." The smoky dress Vitaria wore started to pull apart.

Zacharias rose to his feet and held his arms in front of him as if he were begging. The hair on his head was almost entirely white now. A single streak of black ran across his scalp like a lightning bolt. "I don't have the resources for this kind of operation."

"You are resourceful. I trust you will find a way." Vitaria made a small gesture, and a chest full of golden coins appeared in the room. The rest of her dress pulled apart, and the goddess stepped back into the darkness and disappeared.

Elenor rose from the table and stretched her wings. "What do we have to do?"

Doctor Zacharias began speaking, and the camera slowly pulled away so Tim and company couldn't hear the words. The doctor and the women looked like they were having a massive argument about what would happen next.

Tim couldn't help but feel for the guy. Sometimes people let their ambitions run away with their better judgment. It was never a good idea to take the short road to success. Highly successful people were that way for a reason. Most of them worked with a relentless focus until achieving whatever goal they set for themselves.

Not always fun but highly effective.

"Anyone else not excited to find out what else Vitaria had him making in there?" Lorelei looked kind of creeped out.

JaKobi moved toward the door. "Are you kidding? I can't wait to get in there. This shit is so fucked up it's like walking into a horror movie."

"I guess if the guy protecting us from the cold is going in, I am too." Despite her words, ShadowLily also looked excited by the prospect of the dungeon.

Cassie pulled her cloak in. "It better be warm in there."

Tim put an arm around their tank's shoulders. "What do you say we go find out?"

Together they strode into the entrance of Doctor Zacharias' lair.

CHAPTER FIFTEEN

The market was a hive of activity.

Neema watched from her seat as she sipped a cup of tea. The price for a pot had been exorbitant, but they weren't going to let her sit here for free, and she'd recently come into some coins. The spot she picked kept her back to a wall and gave her a good view of the market's busiest intersection.

Keeping an eye on the foot traffic was testing her patience. It was like hoping to spot a grain of sand in the desert. She wanted to scream, shout, and cut every single one of these smugglers down until she had the scroll in her hand, but that wouldn't work any better. Asking for help was out of the question.

No one in the Grotto gave two shits about your problems.

It wasn't only the sitting that was getting to her. Neema was a creature who needed to be on the move. Sitting and hoping wasn't usually on her to-do list. Khalid would have told her that when her mind pulled in two different directions, the best thing to do was pray to the goddess for insight.

Praying wasn't really her thing.

She'd recently learned that a small amount of humility went a long way. It was why Khalid always played defense in a battle before going on the attack. Her leader's advice never steered her wrong, although she seemed determined to prove it for herself instead of taking his word for it. Everything up until this point had been instinct. Maybe it was time for a little divine intervention.

Eternia, Goddess of Light, please find it in your heart to point me to the scroll. I know I might not be worthy of your assistance, but Khalid is. All we want is to stop our city from falling further into darkness.

Neema waited with her eyes closed, hoping for some kind of response, but nothing came. Maybe all those nights she spent cursing the gods for her fate as a youth made today's pleas fall on deaf ears. That was fine. She'd spent her entire life relying on only one other person. If the scroll was gone, they would find a way.

She drank the last of her tea and set the cup down on the table. Reaching into the pouch tucked into her vest, Neema pulled out a few coppers and tossed them on the table for a tip. While the tea had been overpriced, she couldn't risk some disgruntled waiter following her back into the tunnels. It was time to get out of here. She'd pushed her luck as it was.

It took a few moments for the foot traffic to slow down enough she could leave the cafe. As she stepped out into the flow of bodies, a golden light splashed across her vision. Turning to search for the source, Neema homed in on a necklace a merchant was holding up to a torch. She was about to shout at the man to fuck off as so many of those around her were doing when she spied the tattoo she'd been looking for all morning.

Praise the fucking goddess.

Did the gods care if you swore when you honored them? There was no way to be certain until she died, but Neema was pretty sure emphatic praise counted as the best kind. Who wanted a worshipper quiet as a mouse when she was willing to shout it from the rooftops? Eternia was the most badass goddess around.

Although it might be prudent to keep the shouting to a minimum until after she secured the scroll.

The skeptical side of her mind told her that it could have been a coincidence that the man revealed himself right after she prayed, but sometimes it didn't pay to question things. If bad things happened for a reason, certainly good things could too.

Who couldn't use a little extra good luck?

Now she had to move. Standing still and staring at any person was an invitation for disaster. With what Neema hoped looked like casual disdain for those around her, she kept moving until she was about twenty feet behind the man. Then she peeled off to look at some worthless merchandise.

The man with Vitaria's tattoo argued with the merchant over the necklace's price. Neither man looked happy, and their exchange ended when her target spat on the ground and tossed the jewelry back to the vendor in the stall. The tattooed man moved away from the cursing merchant and continued into the market.

It didn't seem if any other items were catching his eye, and the man started working his way out of the market. The crowds were growing thinner now, and she couldn't risk him spotting her. Slowing down to let the man out of her sight was one of the hardest things Neema ever did. If the bastard called for help, she could end up dead. Or worse, someone else would kill him and take the scroll.

Never ask for help in the Grotto.

Casually moving with the crowd's speed to remain out of sight almost cost Neema the chance to see her prey make a sudden turn. She picked up her pace, knowing that if she lost him in the winding caverns the game was over. Eternia had given her this chance, and she kind of doubted that if she prayed real hard again a magical line would point her in the right direction.

The tunnel was long enough that she saw Vitaria's thug duck into the next passage. Now the chase was truly on. The thief either knew someone was following or was damned determined to make sure no one was. Neema tried to get her bearings as they ran, but with the endless turns, there was no way to be sure which direction was up let alone left or right.

The two of them spilled into a long, wide tunnel gasping for breath. There wasn't time to do things nicely. Dropping to a knee, Neema pulled her bow free and launched an arrow. Her eyes tracked the bolt as it closed the distance, and her prey hit the ground with a cry. It wasn't a perfect shot, but it didn't have to be. Any warrior could tell you that getting hit by an arrow hurt like hell no matter where it hit.

Some places were a little more sensitive than others.

Neema sprinted toward the man on the ground. He wasn't moving, but that was a gambit. The arrow had hit him right in the meat of the ass. Nothing vital there to worry about, so she pulled her sword free and approached the man with caution.

The sound of her sword scraping against the scabbard forced the fool into action. He rolled onto his side while holding his hands up in the most pathetic manner. "Please don't kill me."

"The scroll," Neema growled.

"Here, take it." He reached inside his cloak with one hand and tossed a sealed tube at her feet.

Before she could reach for it, a shadow fell across the man on the ground. The sound of a blade slicing through flesh reached her ears as she ignored the new attacker and lunged for the container. Her hand clasped around the hard tube. With it in hand, Neema tossed herself to the side and brought her sword up in a defensive position.

The attack she'd expected never came.

"It's a pleasure to see you here." The killer's words dripped with acid. "Dropping your head at Khalid's feet will feel better than a full belly on feasting day. I do enjoy seeing the man suffer."

Neema snorted. "No need to be so dramatic, Jalen. We both know you don't have the skill to beat me."

Laughter flowed from Jalen's lips. "A servant of Jabari never travels alone."

Fuck.

Without hesitation, Neema grasped her sword's hilt and threw it in an overhead motion like it was a gigantic hatchet. The blade moved through the air with a vicious *swoosh* but was so far off target that Jalen didn't have to move to avoid it. The man rushing past him to attack her wasn't so lucky.

As the body hit the ground, Neema had her bow back in her hands and was firing arrows as fast as she could grab them. The first three men who fell made the others hesitate before coming straight at her. She climbed to her feet and backed down the tunnel. The bastards knew as well as she did the longer she stayed down here, the easier it would be to surround her.

The Grotto wasn't going to instantly become a friendly place where Neema had friends to hide her. If she wanted to get out of this, she would have to do it on her own and do it quickly. When a warrior didn't have anything left in their bag of tricks, they did what cowards did at the start of a fight.

They ran.

Running was something Neema loved. She'd always fancied herself as a cheetah when sprinting around the yard as a child. Those days spent racing around had given her an endurance Khalid hadn't been able to keep up with for years. Neema found something special in that place between heartbeats and breaths that she couldn't get anywhere else.

All her training was serving her well now, but she needed some help. There wasn't enough room for her to get away clean. If the men followed her outside, she had no chance of making it back home alive. Running into the market with a gaggle of Jabari's thugs chasing after her would normally be suicide, but she had one advantage today she usually didn't have.

A pouch full of silver.

Neema reached inside her vest and pulled out the bag she'd taken off the woman who attacked her. It was the kind of money that would have been a game-changer for the resistance, but not in the way the scroll was. Sometimes it was worth sacrificing the needs of right now for the promise of the future.

After making sure the scroll was secure, Neema rounded the corner into the market. She threw the bag over the crowd of smugglers with one hand, then shot the flying pouch as it sailed high above them. The weight of the coins split the fabric wide open, and the silver pieces fell among the smugglers like rain.

Men and women fell to their knees grasping for the money. The smart ones grabbed a single coin and darted for cover while the bold reached for weapons and started shouting. Neema dodged through the crowd keeping her distance from anyone who looked too dangerous. Jalen's men didn't have that luxury as they barreled into the market like a pack of braying hyenas.

Not one to press her luck too far, Neema shot Jalen a parting glare and sprinted toward her freedom. A victory was a victory, and she wouldn't have to explain to Khalid how she failed because of her ego. She doubted Jabari would have anything kind to say about Jalen's failure here today.

The sounds of battle faded away as she continued down the caverns and back to the hidden entrance. Neema pictured Jalen already turning and calling for horses. He'd be scouring the sands for her soon enough, and in broad daylight, there wouldn't be anywhere for her to hide. It didn't matter how tired she was. Neema had to move faster.

It was funny how things often worked out. Her first mission was supposed to be a dull affair, something any child past ten summers could handle with ease. Instead, it had turned into quite the story. One Neema would be much happier to tell now that it had a happy ending.

Twenty minutes later, the hot desert air hit her in the face like a punch to the gut. There was something to be said for breathing in air that didn't make your mouth turn to dust in an instant. To her surprise, the camel she left behind was sitting outside the entrance.

Another instance of divine help, or simply a loyal camel not wanting to be left behind?

It never paid to look the gift camel in the mouth, so Neema did what anyone with a bit of sense would do. She praised the goddess for her help. "Eternia, see me home, and I will be in your debt."

The camel started toward Naroosh, and a smile spread across her lips.

She had done it. Neema wouldn't fail.

Khalid felt the laughter rumbling up from his gut and through his cracked lips.

They had been in the desert for two weeks following the directions on the scroll. While Neema cursed herself relentlessly, assuming she must have returned with a fake scroll potentially leading them out into the sands and their deaths, Khalid chose to believe Eternia would protect them and see them safely to their destination.

Then the water ran out.

It was easy to have faith when everything was going great. When you were trapped in the desert without water for two days, faith was a little harder to come by, and yet he had found enough hope to keep his.

This very morning as the sun rose on the horizon very well could have been his last in the world, but the growing light also brought with it a sight he'd been praying to see since they set out. Just over the hill, Khalid spied the tops of a palm tree. He rubbed his eyes and looked again. The treetops were still there. He reached out and shook Neema awake in her saddle.

"What?" She shoved his hand away, trying to go back to sleep.

"Neema, I see something." It could have been a mirage, but Khalid felt the small ember of hope he'd been holding onto flare into a fire.

The young warrior opened her eyes and glared at her mentor. "That's what happens when you run out of water. First, you get tired. Then you start to see things."

"If I'm going to die, let me do it in the shade of those trees." Khalid pointed in the direction they were going.

Neema snorted. "There aren't any trees…" Her words caught in her throat as she turned to follow Khalid's outstretched arm. There were trees and quite a few of them. "I see them too."

"Then let us go find out if Eternia has smiled upon us or if we have fallen victim to the trickster goddess." Khalid nudged his camel forward.

The camel didn't seem pleased at the notion of having to run but slowly picked up the pace. Khalid felt the weather change as they drew closer to the top of the hill. There was moisture in the air that hadn't been there before. If Vitaria was doing this to trick them, she had gone all-out. Two pitiful humans didn't warrant this kind of attention from the gods.

Cresting the top of the hill and seeing what lay below them almost made his heart stop. Khalid had never seen anything so beautiful in all his life. Nestled inside a wide circular valley was a giant lake surrounded by miles of shoreline. It was the kind of place they could build an army and finally fight back. Eternia had blessed them in a way he hadn't thought possible.

His camel had a mind of its own now that it had seen the water. The creature sprinted down the hill into the valley and straight toward the lake. Khalid almost cried out for the animal to stop for fear there could be a crocodile, but one of the river dragons would never survive the trek across the desert.

The camel hit the edge of the water, made it a few steps in, and tipped over as though the ground under its front feet disappeared. Khalid hit the water with a *splash* and found it was so deep that his feet didn't touch the bottom. His camel struggled for a moment but managed to find the edge and climb out. He would have been upset under normal circumstances, but after days of thirst, the water filled him with joy in a way nothing had for a long time.

Neema was laughing at him as he struggled to find the false edge of the oasis. He caught her eye as he finally gripped it and pulled himself free. Laughter bubbled out of him as he watched her. Once she had been a young girl, and now she was a fine woman and one hell of a warrior. He wasn't her father, but Khalid would have been proud to call her daughter.

The secret oasis was theirs and with it a chance for a better future for all their people. Khalid looked at the sky and praised Eternia.

Now the real battle could begin.

CHAPTER SIXTEEN

The inside of Doctor Zacharias' lair wasn't a clean-looking surgery room as shown in the video they watched outside the dungeon.

In reality, it looked like most of the dungeons he'd been inside during his time as a gamer. Although instead of rough cavern walls, these were as smooth as the stone countertops at the inn. Tim wasn't a stonemason so he had no idea if magic had shaped the walls or if thousands of very talented dwarfs had spent a thousand years making this cavern perfect. His money was on magic since he preferred that outcome over a thousand dead dwarves waiting for them.

That's why Cassie goes first.

"Far out." The tank reached out and brushed her hand against one smooth surface.

JaKobi tapped his staff against the same wall, and it sounded the same as when Tim used to knock his baseball bat against the curb outside his house.

The fire mage shrugged. "Sounds solid enough. We're also getting some ambient lighting, but I don't see any torches."

Tim thought about the darkness in the underground prison, and again when they fought the lizard rat that almost ate him. Things had a way of going pear-shaped when the lights went out, and now they had a very elegant solution to the problem. The group could laugh at him for being overly cautious, but there was a reason the turtle won the race.

While running headfirst into danger might not be his thing, Tim knew that sometimes you had to wing it. He was always reading how no plan survives first contact with the enemy. That was why he usually had more than one option. As the team continued to gel, he became more comfortable with giving up more control and might even do something downright hasty at some point and shock everyone.

This dungeon would be interesting, and he was looking forward to wrapping up his time in Tristholm and seeing what the desert held for them. First, they had to get there so it was time for him to stop worrying about other things and start locking in on what they needed to accomplish right now. They hadn't run into any trash mobs so far, but that might not last.

On top of the lack of monsters, there was no way to know what other kinds of magic Vitaria might have given Doctor Zacharias. All they knew now was that he could make animal-human hybrids. In essence, the dark goddess had created her very own Doctor Moreau. If he remembered correctly, none of the island's guests were thrilled with the outcome of their stay.

As much as Tim wanted to spend time looking at as much of the new dungeon as possible, he also wanted to get moving. Now wasn't the time for him to lay down his normal prep talk about caution and doing your best. Today, Tim wanted to give the crew something different so he dug down deep for one of his favorite preparation scenes in a movie. When it came down to preparing for things, there was no better role model than a space marine.

Tim channeled his inner badass and shouted at the startled

group, "Assholes and elbows, people. I want to see buffs cast and everyone in formation."

When no one moved, Tim growled, "Now!"

Cassie laughed. "*Aliens*? Really?"

"Just seemed to fit." Tim looked down at the ground and back up. "I guess I should be happy someone got the reference, and you all don't think I've turned into some kind of tyrant."

"Tyrant, nope." The fire mage snickered. "You'd have to be able to control any of the ladies for that."

Cassie spun and glared at JaKobi. He held up his hands in surrender. "Just saying."

Tim tried not to laugh. It was good to know that despite being their leader, he had about as much control over everyone as his fiery friend did. "I learned a long time ago that when it comes to love, you have to pick your battles."

Reaching out, Tim laid a hand on the fire mage's shoulder. "How about you toss one of those lights in the air for us before I tell Cassie what a bad boy you are?"

"You wouldn't." JaKobi looked shocked.

"Hey, what are you two talking about?" Cassie shouted back from the front of the group.

"Nothing." The fire mage tossed two of his lights in the air before looking back at Tim. "Bro code man, we gotta stick together."

Tim laughed, knowing he'd never throw his buddy under the wheels of the Cassie express. "Don't worry. I got you." He turned away from his friend and shouted to the front, "Cassie, I just wanted you to know what a good job your man is doing!"

"Fucker," JaKobi growled.

Trying to keep the smile out of his eyes, Tim recast his buffs and took his customary spot at the back of the group. It wasn't just that it was safer back here. It also let him get a better view of any potential battlefield. Cassie was upfront doing her tank thing, with ShadowLily trailing right behind her. Their two ranged DPS stuck out on the sides a little so they could use their skills without hitting the two melee characters. Tim liked to call it the Christmas tree formation.

Cassie kept her pace even and steady. For once, it seemed their tank was content to see what they were facing before pummeling creatures with her giant stick. With nothing jumping out at them he felt a little antsy, and maybe she did too. They kept moving forward, and he kept checking behind them, but there wasn't any sign of trouble. Something had to give.

When the tank stopped moving, the entire party froze as one.

In front of them, the hallway they were following ended in a giant room. Cassie probably stopped for everyone to catch up in case it was a boss room. Tim couldn't count the number of times he thought they were facing a simple puzzle only to be swarmed by monsters moments later.

Happened all the time in Star Wars: The Old Republic.

Any puzzle in that game might as well be a big sign that said, "huge ass monster about to be dropped on your head." That's why you never ran into a room and hit the big shiny buttons. So while the space in front of them looked innocent enough, looks could be deceiving. Developers always liked to keep a gamer on their toes, and Tim's were positively tingling.

Still standing outside the entrance, they all took in the scenery as JaKobi sent his lights flying over the space. The room was massive, and in the very center was a raised dais with a large stone panel on it. It looked like each wall had an enormous door built into it, so it was safe to assume the panel probably controlled the doors. All they would have to do was figure out how to get them open. This appeared to be the point of no return, a player's last chance to back out without dying.

Fuck that noise. He was ready to rumble.

Tim took the first step across the threshold into the room. "Let's check out the panel. Try not to touch anything until we get a sense of what it does."

Tim let Cassie move in front of him, but he hovered over her shoulder like that annoying person in line always trying to watch your phone. He hoped she could ignore his rudeness since he really liked solving puzzles in games. There were a few games where the mysteries seemed a little much, but so far they hadn't run into problems.

They moved up the small slope as one unit until they stood on the flat surface of the dais facing the panel. Small colored stones lined the panel's face, and Tim had no doubt about what that meant. They would have to figure out the proper pattern to open each door, and the clues were hidden around the room.

Finding the clues was his least favorite part of problem-solving. He liked figuring out the visual puzzles a lot better, but games weren't built only for him. There was also the question about whether it mattered which door opened first. Not every game did the order of importance, but in some, opening the wrong door triggered a trap.

Despite all his big talk, they would have to be careful. The panel in front of him clearly looked like a representation of the room. Etched into the surface for the one on the left was the image of a snake. The symbol in the center had worn away, and there was no way to tell what used to be there. A small button off to the panel's side looked like it would lock in any choice after they made it.

Right away, the risk-averse side of his brain said to skip the middle option. If there was a sure thing on the right and left sides of the room, they should probably start there. It always paid to have as much information as possible before a battle, and mysterious blank spots didn't help much when planning. In his experience, cats were less creepy than reptiles so he was leaning hard to figure out the cat side of the equation first. However, it was a choice for the group to make so if they found out how to open the snake lock first, then snakes it was.

"Let's spread out and look for clues. If you figure out how to open one of the doors, come back to the central panel and wait."

Tim descended into the room and hoped this part of the process would be quick.

JaKobi moved up to look at the panel, and his eyes raced across it for a second before he reached out and moved some of the tiles around. "I think I've got it." His hand moved up and then slammed down on the console's only button.

There was a loud *click*, and everyone turned to stare at him. "Aw shit guys, sorry about that." He held out his hands defensively. "The whole thing was so sparkly, and somehow I just knew how it fit together."

Tim wanted to be mad, but searching the room for clues was low on the fun totem pole. "At least tell me your sparkly little brain decided that we'd be fighting the cats first." He watched JaKobi intently, hoping for the best.

The fire mage looked back at the panel, then at Tim. The look on his face clearly said cats weren't on the menu. JaKobi slowly shook his head. "Sorry, boss."

"Cassie, I take it back. JaKobi is trouble, and you should dump him immediately." Tim shuddered as he thought about what they might be facing next.

The tank turned and looked at the fire mage, then grinned. "I don't know. He's kind of cute. I think I might keep him for a while."

"We all make bad choices," Tim grumbled as he stomped over to the ramp.

"Love you too, boss," JaKobi barked back as he descended to join him.

ShadowLily met Tim at the bottom and nuzzled into his shoulder. "Not a big fan of the creepy crawlies, huh?"

"Plus, who wants to kill kitties? What are you, some kind of monster?" Lorelei snapped.

Laughing, Tim pointed at the now open door. "Kitties, lizards, kitty-lizards, it's all the same to me." Sometimes a guy had to put on a brave face.

Lorelei huffed, clearly not buying it. "Just think happy thoughts."

Yeah right.

Cassie jumped from the dais to the floor to join the group. Warm, humid air poured through the entrance—the kind of environment snakes and crocs thrived in. The weather change didn't give Cassie any pause, but he noticed that her fur-lined cloak disappeared as she crossed the barrier. Once the entire group was inside, Cassie moved forward.

Reptiles were creepy.

Snakes were the worst of the bunch. What kind of person loved a snake anyway? It wasn't as if a snake loved its owner. They ate and plotted ways to escape. Kind of like cats, but at least the little fur demons showed some emotion. Yes, it was mostly when the little bastards wanted food or attention, but at least it was something.

JaKobi was pretty sure snakes didn't have feelings. Their id probably drove them just like a zombie. All they cared about was the next thing they wanted. Sleep, hunt, eat, sleep. While it was cool to watch a snake strike on a video, he was less than thrilled to think of himself as the meal. Nothing said unattractive like bruised, swollen, rotting flesh.

He wondered if Cassie would still feel the same way about him if he was all deformed. Then he realized it didn't really matter. Inside the game, he'd never be anything besides what he was right now. If he was ever hurt and couldn't be killed, a quick trip to Randy, his caseworker, and he'd be back to a hundred percent lickety-split.

The same was true for Cassie.

He watched her moving now and wondered how he'd gotten so lucky. It wasn't only her he was thankful for. The entirety of the

Blue Dagger Society made him feel like he had a family. As an only child, he didn't have any brothers or sisters to rely on. It was only him and the Ps. They were getting older now, and he was starting to wonder what it would be like when they were gone.

Did a person still have a family when he was the only one left?

Before he could dwell on it for long, JaKobi decided it was time to change his perspective. Shit, he knew plenty of people who hated their families, and he was lucky not to be one of them. He was trying to spend more time being thankful for the things he had in life instead of wanting what others had or being jealous of it. Some people needed a mansion. He just wanted to be happy.

Snakes weren't going to get him there.

Although it could be worse. At least the group wasn't facing a *Lake Placid* situation. He'd been to Florida exactly one time, and nothing in his life ever freaked him out as much as seeing those two eyes rise out of the water. There was something primal about seeing death staring back at you.

What big eyes you have.

Even as a teen, JaKobi had taken one look at those alligator eyes and knew what it felt like to be on the lower end of the food chain. It didn't matter that he was staying at a fancy hotel. The gator sure didn't seem to care how much his parents paid for the room. That bastard's room was free, and it came with snacks that paid for the privilege of being there.

So one look in those cold reptilian eyes, and he ran back to the room.

He'd spent a lot of time running since then. Part of him was always afraid. He liked to call it prudence, but he was really just scared shitless. Since then, JaKobi had been in awe of people who seemed fearless. Two of his heroes growing up were Matt Hoffman and Tony Hawk. Watching those guys sail through the air was something special. While what those guys did was dangerous, at least they weren't as crazy as those nutters who went swimming with the sharks.

Andy Casagrande has some big brass ones, that's for sure.

Since entering *The Etheric Coast,* JaKobi felt as though he was one of his fearless idols. While swimming with the sharks and flying through the air weren't on his to-do list, somewhere along the way he'd found his courage. Maybe it was the people he was with, or perhaps he'd found something within himself, but he was doing things he would never have thought possible. Not only was he involved in the fights, but he was also a big part of them.

Facing down a werewolf on his own certainly didn't hurt his confidence.

Plus, he finally had a girl. Sure, Cassie hit him a little more than was strictly proper, but that was the price you paid for being with a warrior. If you wanted soft around the edges, his girl wasn't the one, but JaKobi would take substance over niceties any day of the week.

The view from behind wasn't that bad either.

If he were able to pick a role for her, it wouldn't have been a tank. JaKobi hated watching her run headfirst into danger. It wasn't his choice though, and even if he didn't like seeing her get hurt, he'd always support her right to make her choices even if she got hurt.

That was the thing with tanks. None of them lived forever. He knew deep down that he would have to watch her die during one of these fights. He was going to lose his shit when that happened. Controlling the magic inside him was easy when his emotions were in check. When they weren't, the fire always wanted out. Fire was hungry, and the flames wanted to burn.

It was funny how they were so different. His entire class was based on self-control, and hers was about letting her fury loose. Somehow, despite their different personalities, whatever they had going on worked. He didn't know how long it would last. It wasn't as if he had a ton of relationship experience. One thing JaKobi knew for sure was that as long as their relationship lasted, he would enjoy the fuck out of it.

JaKobi looked up from his musing and realized the hallway they were walking down was quickly drawing to an end. There wasn't a door or anything, but the hallway widened into a large square room. Foggy glass holding cells lined two sides of the room. The lighting sputtered like an old-school horror flick, covering the cages in light one second and darkness the next. His additional lights took some of the creep-factor out of it, but certainly not all.

He stopped in front of the nearest glass cage and tapped the glass with his staff. JaKobi leaned forward, trying to get a good look inside. Something shot out of the darkness and hit the glass in front of him so hard it cracked.

He found himself sitting on the floor, not exactly sure how he got there. The cage was cracked, but the glass wasn't broken. He must have fallen on his ass when he saw the snake coming right at him. That was some scary shit. His instant reaction had been to get away when it should have been to cast his Flame Shield spell. No reason to run when you could let the threat incinerate itself.

Next time he'd be ready.

JaKobi stood and dusted off his robes. If the rest of the group was watching him, he had no idea. All he wanted was a better look at the snake in the cage. This time he approached the glass cautiously, trying not to disturb the creature within so he could get a better look at it.

Oh fuck, it's huge.

And the snake wasn't alone.

He stepped back from the glass, turned, and looked at the rest of the room. Cages lined the walls. There must have been hundreds of them. If they had this many snakes, who knew what Doctor Zacharias was up to?

He silently thanked Eternia that it wasn't worse. These snakes wouldn't crush boats in their coils like on late-night science fiction television although a person wouldn't stand much chance against one of them, at least not without some serious training. He was pretty sure their group could handle about twenty of these things at a time, but not if they got bigger or had human intelligence.

Cassie rounded the corner in front of them and made a gagging sound. "That's so disgusting."

Normally the sound of retching wouldn't make him eager to see what was around the corner of the last cage, but now he almost felt compelled to look. It was like watching a slasher movie. The scares were gross, but they were also the best part. Flames danced around his fingers in case trouble waited around the bend, but as he cleared the corner, the fire instantly snuffed out.

Cassie wasn't in danger, and disgusting was exactly the right word.

Human legs had been tossed around the room as though a toddler threw a tantrum at a doll shop. Men's, women's, long, short, black, white, there didn't seem to be any pattern at all. The only thing missing was children's legs, and for that he was grateful. You take any crime and do it to a child it's a million times worse. It seemed that despite the savagery of this place, Doctor Zacharias had some lines he wouldn't cross.

"What do you think this means?" ShadowLily held up a giant decapitated snakehead.

Tim's face lit up. He might have even been excited as he spoke. "Naga."

"Well, shit." JaKobi looked at the piles of body parts and couldn't help but agree with Tim's assessment.

Although these wouldn't be naga in the traditional sense. Normally the monsters remained mostly snake although they had arms like a human. These creatures would be more like driders or centaurs. He'd never seen a half-human half-snake before but couldn't wait to see what one looked like.

They would certainly have their hands full now. With the tops halves of these creatures being entirely human, they would be at least as smart as they were, with the advantage of being able to slither. Unless Doctor Zacharias had to do a few test runs, there might also be a lot of them. All the legs had to come from somewhere.

As he continued to look over the carnage, Tim stepped to the front of the group. "We have a pretty good idea of what's waiting for us on the other side of the door. Make sure to keep your wits about you and move as a group. We've got this."

Cassie watched Tim for a moment to make sure he'd finished his little pep talk, then moved toward the last door between them and a fight. Just in time, too. The flames were calling to JaKobi. They wanted to be set free.

The first naga that showed up would have a real crispy day.

CHAPTER SEVENTEEN

"Bigger than I expected." Cassie frowned as she ducked back around the corner.

Tim certainly didn't like the sound of that. Bigger than expected could mean a lot of things depending on your starting reference point. He'd kind of thought *The Etheric Coast's* version of nagas would be about the same height as an average person or maybe a foot or two larger due to their tails having to curve below them.

Clearly, he was naïve.

ShadowLily popped back into existence next to the tank and motioned to her. "I counted three of them." She pointed at the stone wall in three places. "Here, here, and here."

Cassie looked at where she pointed and poked her head back around the corner to look at the room again. "Got it."

Tim inched closer to the corner. When he reached the two women, he stopped. "Mind if I take a look?"

"He's going to freak." ShadowLily smirked at Cassie. "We probably shouldn't let him see."

Cassie grinned back at her best friend. "I mean we only keep him around because of his brain. We might as well let him use it."

"Here I thought it was for my magnetic smile," Tim quipped as he crept the last few feet to the edge.

There was always a chance they were playing a trick on him, but Tim prepared himself for the worst because statements like *bigger than expected* and *he's going to freak* didn't tend to ease a person's mind. No matter what, he was determined not to freak out just because they said he would. Whatever he saw, he would pretend it was what he'd expected.

He inched closer to the edge and leaned out around the corner.

After ducking back to safety, Tim pressed his back against the wall and drew a deep breath. He drew more deep breaths and repeated to himself, "I'm not freaking out."

Who was he kidding? He was totally freaking out.

Bigger than expected was right. Magic had altered the naga in more ways than simply being created. Vitaria's spell also increased the monster's size by double or triple what he'd expected. It was one thing to look around the corner to see a snake with the torso of a man, and another to see a fifteen-foot-tall monstrosity with a chest as wide as the Hulk's, and arms that looked like they could rip an oak tree in half with the ease Tim could smash a soda can.

The giant halberd resting casually on the naga's shoulder was all Tim needed to see to know they wouldn't be hashing out their differences over a cup of coffee. With a weapon almost as big as the naga itself, it could probably cut a person in half as easily as a chef cut a tomato.

Wait, did ShadowLily say there were three of them?

"I don't want to be a tomato," he blurted before he could stop himself.

ShadowLily's laughter was the deep kind that came from way down low in the belly. It was the kind of sound someone made when they couldn't help themself. "A tomato?"

Cassie snickered. "Okay, you were right. We shouldn't have let him look."

Tim wasn't scared. He just didn't like the thought of being chopped in half. All he remembered from his last death was that it hurt a good deal before it was over. *Hey, what's a few deaths between friends, right?* All new fights brought with them a bit of the unexpected. In other games, you got into a fight and repeatedly died until you figured things out. A person could probably do the same thing here, but it would slow their progress tremendously. When every death cost time, it was best to avoid them.

He'd rather spend the time leveling up than chatting with Barbara.

"Any chance we could take them one at a time?" Tim forced himself to look around the corner again.

"Let's find out." Lorelei dipped past him and let an arrow fly toward the naga.

Tim watched the arrow close the distance and sink into the creature's arm. The hallway in front of them filled with red light separating the group from the snake-beings in the room. A blocked-off hallway during a fight could only mean one thing.

Boss fight.

Oddly enough, knowing the three nagas were a boss encounter made him feel better about it. Having to wade through packs of giant monsters to get to the boss wasn't exactly fun. Sure, trash helped offset the cost of dying to bosses in other games, but Tim had always been of the mind that the fewer trash mobs, the better.

Sometimes trash was fun when it had a cool gimmick or set the stage for the boss, but too many of them was a bad thing. Spending twenty or thirty minutes between the bosses wasn't what he enjoyed. What he loved was the mechanics and working with a team. So in Tim's perfect game, there would be a lot of bosses and mini-bosses but not nearly as much trash.

He sighed in relief when he noticed Lorelei still stood outside the red film that cut them off from the bosses. If she had been inside the room when she shot the arrow, all of them would have had to watch her die without being able to do a damn thing about it. This almost felt like they got away with something, but he wasn't going to complain.

The arrow sticking out of the boss's arm melted away, and the wound healed completely. As soon as the boss was back at one hundred percent health, the red light blocking them from entering the room faded from view.

"So one at a time is out of the question." Tim tried not to look concerned about fighting three massive bosses at once.

Sometimes leadership was about projecting confidence even when you didn't feel the flow.

He stepped away from the wall so he didn't look like he was trying to hide. It didn't take much effort to stand a little straighter. His group was solid, and he had the ultimate confidence in their abilities. It wasn't like they were going to turn around now after coming all this way. What he needed to do was stop thinking and realize they didn't know shit about what was going to happen next.

They would have to wing it and hope for the win.

There was always a way to win the fight in games. You had to figure out the trick. A good developer hid it so it wouldn't be revealed until you were too wrapped up in the fight to notice. They would have to spot their opportunity, and if they missed it, he'd have to heal his ass off until they got it right.

"Cassie, you lead the way." Tim turned to look at everyone else. "Try and stay on her target unless you see something we need to address. With three bosses and only one tank, we can't afford to pull aggro."

Everyone nodded, and Cassie motioned for them all to step into the room. Once everyone was inside, she turned to look at the group. "Ready check."

"And willing," JaKobi replied with a chuckle.

Lorelei made a gagging sound. "Please start the fight before I puke."

ShadowLily disappeared.

"It's a go," Tim replied.

Cassie grunted. "I miss when people just said ready." She held up a fist and waited for them to get into a rough formation. Then she held up three fingers, then two, and finally one.

"Snakes suck eggs!" Cassie screamed as she ran into the room.

The naga turned to face the charging warrior and hissed, "Human cattle."

A *crack* echoed as the base of the halberd slammed onto the floor. Two screams filled the air as the other nagas slithered into view. Neither of the new monsters had weapons in their hands. While the creatures were strong enough to ruin their day without weapons, Tim had a suspicion something else was going on.

"Keep an eye on the ones in the back. They could be trouble." He hoped ShadowLily picked up on the hint and would try and take one of them out.

Cassie's bō staff disappeared as she pulled the hook and chain from her belt and tossed the hook at the boss in one fluid motion. The weapon wrapped around the naga's halberd, and she used it to pull herself forward. Tim could hear the crunch from her foot connecting with the boss's chest from twenty strides away. Then he had the pleasure of watching her use the momentum from her kick to backflip off the creature's chest and land perfectly on her feet with her staff in hand, and the chain wrapped neatly around her waist.

"That's my girl!" JaKobi screamed as he clapped and sent a Phoenix made of pure flames sailing at the bosses.

Lorelei's arrows fell among the creatures as Tim cast Curse of Giving. Being in the back gave him a good view of the room. The floor was kind of wet, but he didn't see any water that looked deep enough for something to lurk in. A few fallen trees dotted the room, and one live tree in the back left corner. Hidden under the sprawling willow tree at the back seemed to be rows of cells or cages built into the walls.

No way to tell if the cells were for aesthetics or if they would come into play later. Tim didn't put any level of craftiness past a developer. Sometimes it felt like they wanted to watch the players squirm. Part of him imagined all the game devs sitting around watching his stream and laughing about what was about to happen next.

Cassie had her hands full keeping the halberd from doing any major damage. The tiny tank dodged and twirled around like a master gymnast. He could have watched her move for hours and still never understood exactly how she did it. Tim was pretty sure Cassie bent in ways that weren't possible for anyone but a yogi.

While Cassie wasn't making any headway in the damage department, she also wasn't taking much damage. A quick check of the boss's status showed its health at one hundred percent. *That couldn't be right, could it?* The group had been fighting for a little while and should have made at least a small dent in the boss's health by now.

What in the fuck was going on?

Tim sent out a round of Healing Orb to make sure everyone was topped off and turned his attention to the three bosses working in unison. One of the females was using magic to create shields and deflect their attacks. She wasn't able to stop everything, but she didn't need to because the other female naga was a healer.

He wasn't exactly sure how to work his way out of this. If they tried to take out the shieldmaiden, the healer could handle it. Focusing on the warrior was already providing them with bupkis, so they had to change things up. He'd played enough PvP to know that whoever killed the healer first usually won.

In this case, taking out the healer wouldn't be easy. She basically had two tanks guarding her. It was one hell of a setup to mitigate damage. The nagas worked as a team to bleed away all their opponents' power and take them out. Tim's job was to figure out how to beat the system. If they couldn't do it by simply fighting, there was something in the room to help them. Tim turned from the bosses and scanned the room, wondering if there was anything he might have missed.

ShadowLily bursting from stealth stole his attention from the room before he got a decent chance to search for anything new— her daggers sank into the healer, cutting the naga's health in half. Everyone immediately switched their attacks to the wounded monster, but they weren't quick enough.

The warrior moved to block Lorelei's arrows. For the luxury of protecting the healer, the warrior also took a nasty blow from Cassie's staff. The massive naga shook off the damage like it was nothing, while the magic-user with the shields held ShadowLily at bay. The brief halt in their attacks was enough time for the healer to recover half of her lost health, then the bitch started healing her wounded party members.

What's the fucking trick?

Tim recast Curse of Giving to keep Cassie at full health and topped off ShadowLily with a Healing Orb. It felt like he could keep this up for hours, but what was the point if they never did any real damage? There had to be something else.

"Everyone get behind Cassie. Let's try and turn them so we can see more of the room," Tim shouted as he started to pivot to the left.

The tank rolled out of an attack and jumped off the naga's halberd before smashing him in the face with her bō staff. Cassie kicked off his chest to create some space and started to rotate in unison. "Good, I was starting to think you finally ran out of ideas."

"Help!" A voice called from the back of the room where the cells were built into the wall.

The sound of someone banging something against the bars started slowly, then echoed as more people joined the man asking for help. "Get us out of here!" a chorus of voices sounded.

Tim motioned for Cassie to keep moving until they were in a good location for him to get a look at the back of the room. When the tank had them in position, Tim topped off everyone's health and turned to examine the cells built into the cavern walls. There had to be a way to open them, or maybe that was the trick. Could they use the people in the cages as a distraction?

Would they even want to?

A player never knew what would happen when they let someone out of a cage. The people inside could turn on them as quickly as they did the naga. One thing Tim knew for sure was that being the bait or distraction never worked out well for anyone. So if setting the people free made them the distraction instead of his party, he was all for it. As a healer he might even be able to keep a few of them alive.

A very human arm extended through one of the cell doors, but he couldn't see past the bars to confirm if the rest was a person or not. "There is a switch over there."

Tim turned away from the cages and ran toward the button. There might not be power in *The Etheric Coast*, but there was magic, and sometimes the two things looked a lot alike. As he extended his hand to hit the button, he had a horrible thought. What if all the cages held smaller-sized Naga?

Fuck it.

Nothing else was working for them so it was time to take a risk. Tim smashed the button. The cell doors flew upward and crashed into the cavern wall hard enough to send down a shower of dust. People emerged through the haze in droves. The only thing missing was the sound of running feet.

Did I make a horrible mistake?

A man with a snake's lower half stopped in front of him. "Thanks for the assissssst," he hissed before going to join the others.

Tim didn't know what to say. He was speechless.

The guy seemed like a normal man, and yet he had the lower half of a snake and a definite hiss to his voice. Then Tim remembered what they had watched happen in the video. Most of the people here were kidnapped. They were the victims. If anyone had the right to be pissed at what was happening here, it was them. Imagine being a farmer one morning and a naga the next.

Not exactly the stuff dreams are made of.

Watching the man slither away filled him with rage. No one should have their essence changed without their consent. It was time for them to find a way to end this. Setting the smaller naga free couldn't be the only part of the trick. It didn't feel like their unarmed attacks would be much of a threat or a help.

There had to be something else he was missing.

There was more to this than what was happening now. There had to be. Players might stumble a few times before figuring out how to let out the prisoners, but eventually, they would figure it out. The key to the fight couldn't be that simple. Any developer worth a damn didn't only have one trick up their sleeve, and that meant more trouble was coming.

"Phase Two!" Tim screamed at the top of his lungs.

Shit! No one knew what in the fuck Phase Two was, including him.

All three bosses were taking heavy damage now. The healer was almost down to thirty percent, but something was starting to happen. He looked from the bosses to the floor and back at the fallen trees. The pieces began to come together.

"High ground! Get off the floor." He looked around for the nearest log and decided it was better to lead by example than to keep shouting random instructions.

Tim sprinted forward to cover the distance between himself and the nearest log. As he jumped in the air, he placed his staff in his inventory and slammed into the trunk with a *thud*. He didn't hit hard enough to knock the air out of him, but he'd have one hell of a bruise until he healed himself. Once he was secure on top of the trunk, he pulled his staff free and turned to scan the battlefield.

JaKobi and Lorelei continued to do damage as they moved toward downed trees. Tim quickly topped off their health before turning his attention to the tank and assassin. ShadowLily's face was a mask of pure joy as she slashed at the bosses with unbridled fury. The three naga's health was dropping at a steady clip, and Tim knew his girl was in the DPS zone.

"ShadowLily! Time to bail." Tim watched her take one last swipe before turning away.

The last hit put the healer's health at under twenty-five percent and triggered the next mechanic. Shields came down around the bosses, knocking their attackers away from them and to the floor. Tim watched as Cassie and ShadowLily struggled to climb back to their feet. The pair eventually succeeded but didn't seem to be able to move any further. They were stuck.

One look at the sly smiles on the boss's faces, and Tim instantly knew whatever was coming next wouldn't be good.

They'd never make it out of this fight without a tank, so Tim cast Cleanse on Cassie, leaving his girlfriend to struggle on her own for a little longer. His spell got the tank moving at half-speed, which he hoped would be enough for her to make it to safety before the boss's next attack hit. With Cassie on the move, he felt confident turning his attention to ShadowLily.

It wasn't often he got to play the hero in their relationship.

The assassin was in a ton of trouble. While Cassie had been knocked toward safety by the bosses, ShadowLily was behind them and had been pushed farther away. All Tim could do was focus on what he could accomplish now, and not what they might have done differently. He cast Cleanse on ShadowLily, and her legs started pumping furiously a moment later.

Without thinking about it, he cast Cleanse again and decided she might need some more protection and made sure she was covered by Who Needs a Shield. He wanted her to make it to safety, but it always paid to prepare for the worst while planning for the best. Tim watched her sprint across the room, willing her to go a little faster.

He knew she wasn't going to be fast enough.

It wasn't enjoyable watching someone you loved fight for their life and seeing the grim determination on their face as they struggled against a losing battle. ShadowLily might not think she would make it, but Tim would be damned if he was going to let her die.

That wasn't going to fucking happen!

The third of his Cleanse spells got her sprinting at full speed, but it wouldn't be enough. He couldn't watch anymore. Tim turned away from ShadowLily to see what the bosses were up to. As she fled for her life, the healer naga lifted her hands high in the air. Arcs of brilliant blue electrical energy flowed up and down the monster's arms.

A smile spread across the healer's lips, and she hissed, "Vitaria awaitssss you in the underworld."

The naga slowly reached out, and the electricity jumped from her hands to the shields surrounding the three boss monsters. Whips of electric energy slashed outward from the shields as the energy continued to build.

It wouldn't be too long now. They had to hurry.

Cassie made it to her tree trunk, but ShadowLily was still running. Tim switched all of his protective spells to the assassin and silently prayed for her feet to move just a little bit faster. He felt the release of power and turned to watch as the waves of electrical energy arced across the wet floor like a tidal wave of death.

Right before the deadly wave should have consumed her, ShadowLily jumped in the air like Carl Lewis. Tim watched as she glided through the air, hoping she would make it but knowing she would fall short. She hit the trunk on the side, her hands scrabbling against the surface but never finding any purchase.

Her descent was slow at first, but the harder ShadowLily fought against the inevitable, the faster she slid. If she hit the water, the assassin was dead. He couldn't watch, but he also couldn't look away. All the naga he'd released from the cells had already turned to ash. Tim knew this was only a game, but it didn't stop it from feeling real.

ShadowLily's feet were only a foot from the floor when she started screaming.

Her feet weren't moving toward insta-death anymore, but the assassin had three arrows sticking out of her, and her health was dropping fast. Tim guessed this probably wasn't an approved method of dodging the mechanic, but he wasn't going to say anything about it. A Healing Orb flew from his hands, and he cast Cleanse on her again in case Lorelei didn't have time to switch from poison arrows before saving the assassin's life.

It wasn't often a guy found himself thanking a person for shooting his girlfriend full of arrows, but today was that magical day. Tim turned to the ranger. "I hope I don't need you to do that to me sometime, but I'm happy knowing you would."

"You say that like this doesn't hurt like a motherfucker." ShadowLily grimaced as she tried to keep from moving.

Lorelei pointed at the floor. "Look what happened to the other guys." The ranger grinned and tried not to snicker. "And for the record, the next time I kabob you, there better be some better swearing. Motherfucker is downright pedestrian."

"I swear to Christ if you ever kabob me again, we're going to play a little game called 'it puts the apple on its head,'" ShadowLily shouted through gritted teeth.

Tim shrugged apologetically at the ranger. "Some of us are more grateful than others."

The electrical current running through the floor stopped, and it was time to get back to work. He didn't know if this phase repeated or if using the prisoners to trigger the electric event was a one-time opportunity they couldn't waste.

Tim was good and pissed now. ShadowLily had almost died, and the bosses smiled like they enjoyed what was about to happen. He didn't give two shits anymore. This was going to end now. Tim cast Behold My Power on the shield-bearer before calling to the rest of the group, "Get the healer."

Turning away from his first target, Tim cast Divine Light on the healer. He didn't know how long the bosses would stay stunned after the phase change, but he had a feeling it wouldn't be long. If they could get the healer down, the rest of the fight would be a cinch.

The healer's health plummeted as the group's attacks started landing with regularity. It didn't take much longer for the first of the trio to hit the floor dead. As soon as the healer's corpse hit the deck, the other two bosses broke from paralysis and looked for something to kill.

Cassie went to tangle with the warrior as Tim turned from the fight and ran for ShadowLily.

"This is going to hurt." He ripped the first arrow free from her arm.

The other two arrows looked to be sticking through more vital areas. He was hesitant to pull them out. It wasn't as if he were a doctor. One wrong yank and he might not be able to heal her in time.

ShadowLily growled through gritted teeth, "Just do it!"

Tim clasped the next arrow and ripped it free from her shoulder. A quick Healing Orb gave her enough health that he felt comfortable tearing the third arrow from her side. He yanked out the last shaft with a grunt of effort, and she fell to the floor. His heals washed over her fast enough that he knew she was alive, but she hadn't moved since landing.

With a cry of rage that would have made any ancient tribal warrior proud, ShadowLily sprang to her feet and charged back into the fray. Tim watched her run and finished topping off her health as she went. The scream she unleashed echoed off the walls in a wild blend of ruthlessness and pain that would have made anyone facing her have second thoughts about the validity of their decision.

Reminder to self—don't get on her bad side.

Tim hated to admit it, but seeing her dive into battle without a care for her safety was kind of hot. Not that he wanted to spend his days pulling arrows out of her, but there was something to be said about watching a hot woman kicking major ass. She was fury personified, and he loved it.

With the healer down, the remaining nagas changed their tactics. The magical shield caster kept an array of different-sized shields floating around them in concentric circles. The warrior used small gaps between the spinning shields to attack Cassie. Each time he lashed out, it left a small opening for the party to counter. It almost felt like they were back in a stalemate.

Right until ShadowLily went to work.

Tim didn't know how she did it, but somehow the assassin followed the warrior boss' halberd back through the shields. Once she was inside the barriers, the two remaining bosses never stood a chance. The shield-bearer went down, and they polished off the warrior with ease.

The boss's bodies swirled away in beautiful golden motes of light and in their place was a single golden chest.

CHAPTER EIGHTEEN

"Loot is why I wake up in the morning." Cassie grinned as she approached the chest.

Tim watched the tank move to the box as his smile formed. Loot in *The Etheric Coast* was a blessing for the group leader. He didn't have to worry about distributing the goods because the loot pools so far seemed to be individualized. A character placing their hand on the chest equaled shinies straight into their inventory. Not to mention all the coins and any other knick-knacks were randomly assigned when the first person opened the trunk.

One less thing to worry about.

At some point, Tim was sure the chests might start containing more crafting materials or something else they'd want to toss in the guild bank for when some of the others picked up crafting hobbies, but until then, looting was life on easy street for this guy. It didn't even matter who went first unless you were the superstitious sort.

Cassie stepped away looking pleased. "Shoulder Guards of the Dancing Bull."

"Sounds about right." Lorelei blew Cassie a little kiss as she stepped up to the chest. Laughter escaped the ranger's lips as she looked at her item's name. "Guess that's karma. I got something called Hood of the Screaming Squirrel."

"Probably has awesome stats." JaKobi laid his hand on the chest and frowned. "Didn't know that socks counted as loot." The fire mage took a moment to equip them, and his frown turned upside down. "Socks of the Meditating Bear. Increases my mana recharge rate outside combat by fifty percent."

Tim thought those socks would come in pretty handy in certain situations. The healing shack specifically came to mind. He wondered how much healing he could do when his mana pool was damn near infinite. JaKobi would probably use the item when he worked on his new spells. The guy was always trying something new or tinkering with something old to tweak it.

Looking over at Tim, ShadowLily turned and pointed at the chest. "You go first. I don't want to go after sock boy."

"Don't mind if I do." Tim wasn't too worried about the socks. In fact, he wouldn't mind a pair of his own.

Trinket of the Smiling Monkey

This item can be added to any piece of jewelry and will provide +1 to a random stat. Trinkets can be removed and reapplied to another item after twenty-four in-game hours.

Everyone was watching him expectantly. "Trinket of the Smiling Monkey."

"You do smile an awful lot." ShadowLily laughed as she stepped past him toward the chest.

Tim had to agree that he did find himself smiling more than ever. Why not? Things were going well. There was a lot in his life to be thankful for, and the future looked pretty bright. It didn't pay to focus on the negative moments in life when the fun ones were so much better.

"G-string of Ineptitude." The assassin met each of their gazes, daring them to laugh.

When no one had the courage to crack up at the item name

ShadowLily took pity on them and did it herself. "Seriously guys, it was a joke."

Instead of a G-string, ShadowLily pulled a dark green gem from one of her pockets. The stone was too dark to be considered an emerald, but Tim couldn't think of any other way to describe it. The stone was cut and polished. Someone had obviously taken great care when creating it.

ShadowLily tossed the stone into the air before catching it deftly with her other hand and tucking it back into her pocket. "Jewel of the Viper. Increases my chance to poison a target by one percent."

Tim stared at ShadowLily as though he'd never seen her before. "Deceptive, brilliant, scary, and funny. How did a guy get so lucky?"

Leaning in close, JaKobi spoke in a very fatherly tone. "You see when a viper meets a monkey...ughuff."

Cassie stepped past the fire mage rubbing her elbow. "I think what he meant to say was, let's head back to the other room and see what we can find."

"Exactly what I was trying to say," the fire mage wheezed.

Taking pity on JaKobi, Tim hit him with a Healing Orb. "I thought it was funny."

"That's what I'm saying." He put an arm around Tim's shoulders as they walked back to the main room. "So when a monkey and a viper..."

Cassie shouted over her shoulder, "What are you two talking about?"

"A man's work is never done." JaKobi dropped Tim a sly wink and ran to catch up with his lady.

Tim kind of hoped the fire mage would have another trick up his sleeve when it came to solving the next puzzle. While he liked doing the puzzles in some games, he had to be in the right mood unless they were interactive. Searching a room for clues was cool in the movies but not so cool when a person had to spend hours doing it themselves. A little mental work and a whole lot of fighting was just the right balance when it came to game time.

Can't heal when there isn't damage.

The next room they faced would be interesting. Tim understood how Vitaria could mix a person and a snake. That was kind of like a centaur. How did she blend a cat and a person? He didn't know exactly how it would work, but with the dark goddess involved, it would probably be horrific.

As the party entered the main room, JaKobi strode confidently up the ramp to the controls. He looked around at the others to make sure no one else wanted a chance to search the room or a stand at the console before he went to work on solving the puzzle.

After a few moments of moving the tiles around, the fire mage looked at Tim. "Care to do the honors?"

Lorelei stepped forward. "For God's sake." She smashed her hand down on the button. "Let's get a move on already."

Tim looked from the console to the doors as they opened and back at the console. He remembered the original pattern, and now looking at the new one he had no idea how JaKobi had made the adjustments. As far as he could tell there weren't any clues scattered around the room, and not being able to figure it out instantly like his friend was bugging the shit out of him.

Pointing at the command console, Tim demanded, "How?"

"I'm not exactly sure, I just kinda looked at the tiles, and they all made sense." JaKobi shrugged in an effortless way that implied he was going with the flow. "Happens to me all the time. I just kind of roll with it."

Tim felt like he'd had a few of those moments since coming into the game. When they happened, it was usually better not to question it and assume it was the goddess looking out for him. So instead of feeling a little worried like he normally would, Tim was kind of excited to see what came next.

Cat people. Who comes up with this stuff?

Cassie was waiting at the entrance to the next boss chamber

with her hands on her hips. She rolled her eyes as Tim approached. "Let me give this a try. Be careful, don't take chances, and try not to die."

Smiling despite the knock on his constant harping about attention to the details, Tim placed a fingertip alongside his nose. "Got it in one."

"All right then, let's get this party started." Cassie moved into the hallway.

The tank clearly didn't share his penchant for taking things slowly as she moved into the corridor at a jog. If this was a mirror of the last series of rooms, he understood her desire to get it over with. Cats in cages and human body parts on the ground, how scary could they be a second time around?

Tim didn't mind that there was a darkness to what was happening here. He always felt better about killing things when he knew he was smiting evil. It wasn't very heroic to go around smiting peasants, but vanquishing evil was another story altogether.

Cassie froze in place, and Tim realized maybe he'd spoken too soon.

This room indeed mirrored the other room, only this time some kind of large cats filled the cages. He wasn't a huge cat guy, but he was pretty sure they were leopards of some sort. Whatever breed they were, the things certainly looked deadly enough without modification. Maybe he'd been wrong all along. Cats were more sinister than snakes. Who hadn't seen a video where a cat knocked something perfectly good off the table just to see it go *splat*?

The leopards were kind of a paradox for the room. They weren't particularly scary in the cages, kind of like visiting the zoo. At the zoo, they didn't feed the cats human corpses. At least he hoped that the people had been dead when they were tossed inside. As far as he could tell none of the bodies had hands. Wouldn't be easy to fight for your life without fucking hands.

The only difference between this room and the gladiatorial arenas of Rome was the Romans didn't normally cut off the hands of the people they fed to the lions. Wasn't sporting enough, and all they cared about was putting on a good show. It was amazing how the world changed. One day there were giant arenas of people fighting to the death, and the next, football players filled them.

A pretty nice change considering getting tossed around and eaten by an animal was a horrible way to go. It didn't matter if it was in the wild or an arena. Being torn apart by a shark, lion, or bear had to hurt. There was a movie where a guy got mauled by a bear, and it was one of the most horrific things he'd ever seen. Maybe the images stuck with him because now and then on the news you heard about someone getting eaten while camping. The rub usually being that the victim was a huge nature person.

The animals didn't give a fuck.

Tim wasn't a nature guy. He was a city boy. While he had fun getting out of the city and fishing for a weekend with his dad, he would much rather be back at the house killing a few beers and going on a dungeon crawl or two. There was something to be said for the convenience of home and the delivery of pizza.

Oh man, he really missed pizza.

Joe was going to have some work to do when they got back. Tim would charge the man with making the perfect pizza. He could almost taste it now. One of the leopards screeched, drawing his attention back to the bodies, and his appetite died instantly.

The rest of his party was waiting outside the boss' room, and he hurried to catch up while pushing the images of the cats enjoying their daily meal out of his thoughts. The last thing he wanted to think of before going into a fight was ending up like one of the people in the cages so he focused on the task at hand.

Tim reached the group and decided to try a new approach to taking on a fight. "I trust you guys. Let's buff up and play it by ear."

"Really? I miss my normal 'take it slow, don't do anything stupid' pep talk," ShadowLily chided.

Tim motioned for them to get moving. "I don't remember seeing anything like the last fight before, so getting our eyes on the room and playing it safe isn't going to help much."

Turning slowly, he met each member of the party's eyes one at a time. "Plus, you never let me down. Why start worrying now?"

"I kind of like this new side of you." The assassin almost giggled. "You're going to have to keep it up if you want us to take you seriously."

Lorelei snickered. "Keep it up, God, you straight people are the worst."

ShadowLily blushed. "This time I wasn't trying for innuendo. I swear." She placed a hand over her heart but couldn't keep the grin from her face.

The ranger gave her a flirty wink. "I'm just jelly because I don't have anyone to talk shop with."

"What, are you kidding?" JaKobi stammered. "You want to talk about hot chicks? I'm all in."

"It's not quite the same, but I appreciate the effort." Lorelei checked the string on her bow. "I'll stick with the ladies even though they don't value the female body as much as I do."

Tim gave JaKobi a high five. "Boys night!"

"Yeah, buddy!" the fire mage exclaimed.

"Men." Cassie shook her head before pulling Lorelei into a hug. "We might not be into chicks, but don't let that stop you from talking about them with us. We're all in this together girl. We want you to be happy."

ShadowLily joined them. "For real, anything you need we've got your back."

The three of them broke apart, and Lorelei had the hint of a smile curling at the corner of her mouth. "I hope when we get back, there might be a farm girl or two that was grateful for our intervention."

"Everyone likes farmers. They even have their own app," JaKobi snarked from behind.

Before anyone could retort, Tim tried to intervene. "Lorelei can break the farmers' daughters' hearts after we take care of business. Until then, focus."

Cassie snorted. "Fine by me. The sooner we get out of here, the sooner I get a beer and a bath."

The tank's ready check went off without any fanfare this time, as the group dialed down the banter to focus on the upcoming fight. With no objections to starting the battle, Cassie led them into the boss' chamber. The air inside this room was as warm as the last, but the heat was dry where the other was humid and moist.

Tim didn't expect to see much water in this room. If he remembered correctly, most felines abhorred the stuff.

There wasn't a lot to see as they moved farther in. So far in the wide-open space, the only defining part of the landscape was a large swath of six-foot-tall grass in the center. That, and there appeared to be bars welded all over the chamber's sides and ceiling.

The big difference from the last room was the bars didn't look like they led to cells. It was more like they were monkey bars set about a foot off the ceilings and walls. They were the kind of thing you'd see in a monkey enclosure, but monkeys certainly weren't the only creatures that enjoyed climbing and jumping from things.

Cats loved to climb and jump. A room like this would be a paradise for them if they could grip the bars. Looking around the room didn't give him a ton of hints. In a space like this, attacks could come from anywhere. Above, behind, hidden in the grass. The Blue Dagger Society was in for one hell of a fight. The room wasn't the ideal spot for a battle, but the odds were never stacked in the player's favor anyway.

Cassie stopped moving forward and held up a closed fist for the others to stop and stay quiet. She lowered her arm and pointed at something moving through the grass, then it leaped onto the wall and climbed until it reached a hidden exit at the top of the room.

The cat had human fucking hands instead of paws, yet somehow also looked to have razor-sharp claws.

"That's not something you see every day," JaKobi whispered.

A second cat yowled as it ran from the grass to another hidden door on the floor of the room's right side. A cacophony of others answered its screech. The leopards were almost acting more like a pack of wolves to coordinate their attack.

Cassie squared her shoulders and screamed into the swaying grass, "Bring it!"

CHAPTER NINETEEN

A square platform rose from the grass in the center of the room.

"Everyone on the platform!" Tim screamed as he ran forward.

There was no way to be sure, but it felt like getting on was the right idea. Not having the strength or skill to jump super high, getting to the platform before it lifted out of reach was paramount to his dignity. The last thing he wanted was to ask two of the women to throw him on top of the damn thing.

So instead of asking for help like a civilized man, he ran.

Cassie looked surprised as Tim sprinted past her. *Yep, that's right. I'm breaking all the rules today.* He launched himself up, barely grabbing the edge and pulling himself onto the smooth surface before it clicked into place.

Success!

He turned and looked down on the others as they made their leaps. It was no surprise when ShadowLily and Lorelei flew through the air and landed gracefully on the platform. At least the viewers on his stream got to watch someone leap with style. His running belly flop probably wasn't the thing people tuned in for.

Thankfully healers weren't traditionally judged on their jumping prowess.

JaKobi skidded to a halt right before he needed to jump. He looked up at the platform. "It's not going to happen."

Cassie came up behind the fire mage and grabbed him by the robes. She pulled him roughly backward before chucking her boyfriend into the air like a farmer tossed a bale of hay onto the back of a truck.

"I'm flying," the fire mage squealed with glee before hitting the deck.

Cassie made sure JaKobi wasn't going to topple off the edge before taking a few steps back and preparing for her jump. Their tank took three bounding steps forward and leapt into the air without much grace but a ton of power. She landed in the super-hero pose in the center of the platform and slowly rose to her feet.

The tank faced the rest of the party. "Can you tell me why we're up here in the open instead of down there using the grass and the walls for protection?"

Tim looked around the room and thought of the creatures moving in and out of hidden openings. Then he made himself draw a deep breath and scanned the room again, looking for anything else that might have changed since they entered. Several smaller platforms had descended from the ceiling and were scattered around the room. They wouldn't be much help to him unless he learned how to fly, but it might give their enemies a space to rest or gather before attacking them.

This wasn't going to be a traditional boss fight. The cats weren't big enough to pose much of a problem alone, but coming from different directions in large enough numbers, they wouldn't be easy to deal with. If enough of them came at once, they might overwhelm the group. He didn't know about the others, but Tim felt painfully short on area of effect attacks. Most of his spells were geared toward damaging a single target.

"Get ready for anything, but my guess is we'll face some kind of wave attacks. Enough of those cats come at us, and it's going to be a problem." Tim wished he had a better handle on what was going to happen, but there was no way to be sure.

JaKobi ran to each edge of the platform checking to see if it would shift and how slippery the surface was. "Kind of reminds me of *Gauntlet*. This is going to be awesome."

"Without the maze, it's just another fight." ShadowLily pointed out.

Lorelei looked at all of their faces. "I have no idea what you're talking about. *Gauntlet* must have been before my time."

"Just get ready for a lot of cats." Tim looked around but didn't see a timer or a countdown clock anywhere. "My guess is a small number will come first, then more of them. That or they'll keep sending waves of the same number hoping we eventually make a mistake and die."

Cassie grunted. "So be ready for anything? Not super helpful."

"Shoot anything that moves, seems like a simple enough plan." Lorelei pulled her bow free and nocked an arrow.

Tim adjusted his stance into Way of the River. He'd switch back if Cassie started taking a shit ton of damage, but it felt like the entire party might need healing during this fight. The key for them would be finding a way to work together and ensuring that they weren't attacking the same targets.

Instead of asking them to keep clear lines of fire, Tim positioned each party member on one edge of the platform. He ensured that the two ranged specialists were on opposite ends and could help clear targets off from the broadest range possible. When everyone was in place, he stepped into the middle and tried to prepare himself for whatever came next.

"I'll try and make calls and help out where I can, but I'm counting on you guys for the DPS." Tim looked around the room trying to spot some kind of signal or a button to start the fight, but he didn't see anything.

One of the leopards yowled from somewhere inside the walls.

A handful of others answered the call. There was no way to tell if the leopards also had increased intelligence or only human hands for feet. The fact that they were signaling each other to coordinate an attack had him a little worried, but the team had undoubtedly faced tougher monsters.

A little nervousness was okay, as long as a person pulled it together. There wasn't a gamer in the world that didn't know the feeling of slaying a raid boss for the first time on the last pull of the night. So while Tim knew he couldn't get complacent, he also had enough faith in his group that he could draw a few deep breaths and relax.

Maybe not.

"Get ready!" Tim called as he spun in a slow circle looking for the first of the cats.

It didn't take long for the first of the monsters to dart into view. The thing was fucking fast considering it had human hands for feet. It didn't look like the leopards had any weapons or even the smarts to use them at this point. Granted, when a monster had a mouth full of four-inch-long teeth and razor-sharp nails on their hands, they didn't need any extra help being dangerous.

Lorelei's bow *twanged.* "Shit, I lost it in the grass. Didn't expect them to be that fast."

Two more cats appeared at the far end of the room and flew across the bars welded onto the ceiling. They moved to opposite sides of the room so fast it was hard for Tim to follow their bobbing progress. It was as if his eyes couldn't register the fact he was watching giant cats move like monkeys.

The three leopards coordinated their attack almost perfectly. One came in from the top right, another from the top left, and a rustle of grass from below indicated where the third would attack from. Tim heard the noise behind him and knew exactly where the third leopard was. He didn't turn to see if JaKobi could handle it. Instead, he fixated on Lorelei and Cassie.

Lorelei's bowstring *twanged,* and she cursed again. The cats were hard to pin down because they could change directions instantly by using their front hands instead of their back ones. It almost felt like their every movement was created to make it harder to shoot the creatures from range.

On his right side, Cassie watched another leopard as it swayed back and forth between a few bars. The monster was clearly sizing her up and trying to figure out the best way to attack. It didn't take long. With a hiss like an alley cat, the leopard sprang from the bars like a furry ball of death.

The resounding *crack* that came from Cassie's bō staff as it slammed into the leopard reminded him of the sound of someone hitting a home run with a wooden bat. Unlike a pro slugger, things didn't work out so well for the leopard. It turned out taking a staff to the head while doing a death from above maneuver was hazardous for a kitty's health.

Lorelei let out a triumphant cry so Tim turned to see how JaKobi and ShadowLily were doing. He might as well have not worried about them at all. The ashes falling gently to the floor told him all he needed to know about what happened to the last leopard. Now they had to get ready for more.

"Prepare for the next wave. Call out how many you see and if you need help." Tim made sure everyone's health was full and got back into position on the platform's center.

A solitary yowl was the only indication the group received that the fight was on.

ShadowLily spun her daggers in her hands. "I see three."

"We also have three," JaKobi replied as he clapped to send a burning phoenix flying at the leopards.

The flashy spell didn't hit any of the creatures, but it did force them to split apart. Tim cast Curse of Giving on one of them before pivoting and doing the same thing on Lorelei's side of the battlefield. A little passive damage and healing would only increase their chances of success.

Thankfully healing wasn't an issue yet.

Two of the leopards fell to Lorelei's arrows before getting close enough to jump for the platform. She was figuring out how they moved. It was great for their group and not good for the monsters they faced. Tim wasn't worried about the two of them taking out the last one so he turned to watch the other side of the battlefield.

JaKobi had ashed one of the cats, but the other two worked together in a new way. One of the leopards grabbed the other and used the bars to throw the first cat at the group like a cannonball while leaping in behind it. Tim hadn't expected the kamikaze move, but the fire mage took out the first cat, and ShadowLily used her throwing knives to get the last one before it reached the platform.

Last time, the number of leopards doubled.

Tim checked, and no one had taken any significant damage yet, or if they had his curse was enough to boost them back up. Healing might become a bigger part of this fight if they were about to face twelve of the cats. Maybe there was more he could do to help. His root spell was kind of weak, but it only needed to stagger one of the leopards. If they could keep the cats coming in smaller numbers, they had this fight in the bag.

"They're coming," Lorelei called as she let an arrow fly.

This time there hadn't been a warning so the cats were pretty damn smart. It was getting to the point where if all the leopards attacked at once they might be in real trouble. Tim hoped this was the last round, but he had a feeling there was at least one more. It didn't feel challenging enough yet, and deep down he knew the developers would never make things this easy.

"Ah, fuck." JaKobi grimaced as he watched what was about to happen.

All six of the cats on their side of the platform were about to do their kamikaze tactic again. Tim wasn't sure if the same thing was happening on the other side and didn't want to look. He could deal with whatever happened as long as they stopped one of the attacks.

ShadowLily pulled her daggers free. "Do what you can to their shield cats, and I'll handle the rest."

The leopards launched their shields at the platform and charged in behind them as before, only this time three of them came all at once from different angles. Tim decided JaKobi could handle two of the cannonballs by himself so he focused on the one farthest away.

Divine Light slammed into the leopard, throwing off its trajectory to the platform. Instead of landing on it and tearing them apart, it smashed into the side with a *thump*. The human hands clawed at the top of the platform, three-inch-long nails digging into the surface. It wouldn't be long before the other three were on them. He had to make sure they didn't have a fourth helper.

ShadowLily moved in to meet the charge of the three remaining leopards, and Tim screamed, "Jump!"

The assassin leapt into the air, and Tim's Flame Burst spell roared to life under her feet and knocked the last of the initial attackers loose. JaKobi dealt with one of the follow-up cats alone leaving two for ShadowLily to handle. If anyone could kill two of them without breaking a sweat, it was her.

Tim turned away from the fight on their side of the platform to see what he had to deal with on the opposite end. Lorelei had killed two of the leopards and Cassie a third, but now one of them had grabbed hold of the tank's staff and was making life difficult for both of them. At least the leopard wasn't doing much damage to her. Cassie was shaking her weapon back and forth so ferociously the cat was mostly hanging on for dear life.

The other two leopards were still a good distance away but were throwing some kind of ranged attack at Lorelei. Tim couldn't tell what the projectiles were, but he was pretty sure it wasn't shit. Maybe they had rocks, or it could be magic. There was no way to tell for sure right now.

Despite not being able to make any offensive progress, Lorelei didn't seem in danger of taking any major hits, so Tim was going to get the cat off his tank. His best single target spell that didn't take forever to activate was Divine Light, but he didn't want to risk hitting Cassie with a bolt of energy.

They couldn't afford to waste time if these were timed rounds since the next set of leopards could be coming soon. Tim dropped his staff to the platform and pulled his dagger free. He lunged forward and stabbed the leopard with five quick thrusts, and Cassie tossed it back into the grass below.

Tim made sure to retrieve his staff and tuck away his dagger before turning to help whoever needed it. JaKobi and ShadowLily had ended their fight, and Lorelei just finished off one of the cats from a distance. The last leopard was still focused on Cassie. She dodged one of the thrown projectiles and sent her hook and chain winging out at the leopard.

One quick yank was all it took, and the giant cat flew directly toward them. Cassie dropped the chain and pulled her staff free. The leopard never stood a chance. The bō staff cracked off the cat's skull, and it fell into the grass below.

"That had to be it right?" Cassie turned, looking rather triumphant.

Tim didn't see a golden chest anywhere, and the platform hadn't lowered. "I'd get ready for the next wave."

"This is going to be a real shit storm isn't it?" JaKobi replied as the top of his staff burst into brilliant purple flames.

There might have been a way to sugarcoat it, but the final wave of any battle was supposed to be hard. With potentially twenty-four of the cats coming at them, this would get crazy interesting real fast.

"Just try and stay calm." Tim drew a deep breath and prepared for what was coming next.

This felt like one of those moments where it all might come down to how long he could keep them alive.

"Five coming on our left," Lorelei called.

"Oh fuck, I have ten of them." JaKobi took a hesitant step back.

Tim reached out and gently shoved the fire mage back to the edge. "Then light the pussies on fire."

"We don't need no water…" The flames atop JaKobi's staff turned from purple to bright ruby red. "Let the motherfuckers burn."

Tim almost finished the lyrics with him, but if the fire mage had work to do so did he. He targeted a couple of the leopards farthest away with Curse of Giving to get some healing rolling in. They weren't taking a ton of damage yet, but it would come soon.

Sitting back in the center of the platform gave Tim a chance to see what the leopards were throwing. They appeared to be some kind of hardened leather balls, which is why he probably thought they were chunks of poop earlier. It was the kind of thing they'd call a non-lethal round back in the real world, but he'd refer to them as poop pellets.

No one wanted to get hit by poo, even if it was fake.

If enough of the hard pellets hit a player, they could easily fall off the platform, and it would be all teeth and claws until they died. Cassie wasn't even trying to play offense anymore. The tank used her staff like a stickball bat to keep the projectiles at bay, while Lorelei shot as many arrows into the cats as possible.

The group was taking some serious damage now, and Tim sent out a round of Healing Orb to add to the small amount of healing coming in from his curse. This part of healing he enjoyed most. It almost felt like his own mini-game. While the others worked hard to defeat the threat, he worked twice as hard to keep them alive.

Tim's view of the world around him shrank to the health bars of his companions. He didn't have to worry about too much in the middle of the platform unless the leopards upgraded their weapons of choice. All he had to do was move now and then so they couldn't lock in on his location. After that, it was one healing spell after another.

He didn't look up. He didn't even have time to breathe. Everyone was taking damage now. Sometimes it was one hit at a time. Other times his friends were getting hit two or three times in rapid succession. Tim wasn't sure if his Curse of Giving would do enough damage to kill any of the leopards but having a few up sure helped his healing.

Did everyone else feel as stressed as he did?

Spell after spell had his mana redlining. Tim fell to his knees, his fingers twitching through the motions of Healing Rain, and everything went fuzzy for a moment. He heard ShadowLily scream a warning, then one of the leopards sank its teeth into his arm.

It was easy to forget how much getting injured hurt in this game when it hadn't happened to him in a while. Being bitten by a leopard kind of felt like being stabbed ten times and having your arm crushed in a hydraulic press. The cat's eyes rolled back as someone severed its head from its body.

"That was the last of them." Cassie knelt and pried its jaws open, then tossed the head off the platform.

"Let's hope there isn't a mega knockout round." JaKobi grimaced as he looked around the room.

Tim climbed back up onto unsteady feet. He had to wait for a full minute before he could cast a Healing Orb on himself to stop the bleeding. Now he knew what LadyCat's group had felt like after their battle in the recruitment video. The fights were fun, but the aftermath took a moment to get over.

The platform lowered to the ground, and Tim thanked Eternia for the break. As the platform clicked back into place, a golden chest appeared by the door. He focused on topping off each person's health as they moved across the room. When everything was in order, Tim quickly unequipped and equipped his clothes. He had to admit it felt good to have fresh clothes on even if his skin was still a little grimy.

Cassie stopped in front of the chest. "Maybe I'm not a cat person after all."

Lorelei cut in front of her and laid a hand on the golden chest before the tank could. "I am."

"Armguards of the Leopard. Improved accuracy with ranged weapons, and plus four to dexterity and strength." The ranger's grin grew as she equipped the item.

"Not being a cat person and not wanting to go first are two different things." Cassie winked to let them all know it was a joke before reaching out and touching the chest. "No Pity for the Kitty. Add this adornment to any piece of armor to reduce damage by felines up to thirty percent."

JaKobi laughed as he moved forward. "Now that all the good stuff is gone, I might as well go." His mouth fell open as he saw what came into his inventory. "Nine Lives."

The fire mage paused as he read over the item description. "So I don't get to die nine times and live, but I do get reduced fall damage and will always land on my feet."

"Not exactly handy in all situations, but magical items don't have to be." Tim laid his hand on the chest.

Item Received: Wilbur's Fur-Lined Shoulder Guards

Wilbur was a famous member of the Desert Storm Defensive Unit. His battalion held off an attack by fearsome Sand Devils until help arrived. He was granted the shoulder guards in honor of his accomplishments.

+1 to Perception, Vitality, Revitalization, and Luck

"Dude, that's awesome." JaKobi gave Tim a high five.

ShadowLily went last as was her usual style. "Shoulders of the Four-Handed Thief. I get bonuses to Dexterity and a five percent boost to successfully steal an item while pickpocketing."

She equipped the shoulders. "I might never use the second part, but I'll take all the dexterity I can get."

Tim wrapped an arm around her newly bulked-out shoulders and pulled her in for a hug. "Let's go finish this thing."

"The same thought just crossed my mind." ShadowLily gave Tim a quick kiss and vanished.

JaKobi moved past the startled healer. "Better keep moving. She's liable to beat this dungeon without us."

Tim picked up the pace.

CHAPTER TWENTY

Dr. Zacharias leaned against the surgery table, panting with barely contained rage.

"All my work is gone!" He picked up a tray of random medical implements and threw it across the room.

Vitaria would never believe this wasn't his fault, and now his wife and daughter would never bask in Eternia's light again. It wasn't fair. Why now? When he was so fucking close to being done with this madness? All he wanted was to free their souls from damnation.

Was that too much to ask?

His grip tightened on the surgical table and the steel buckled beneath his fingers. "All I needed was a little more time."

A cry of pure agony escaped his lips, and the doctor spun while clutching his stomach. He fell to his knees, groaning in pain. The skin on his arms ripped and split as his muscles grew larger. The room filled with a series of loud *cracks* as the doctor's bones broke. The sound of his limbs snapping echoed in the small space like the sound of a gun being fired in a hallway.

The creature that rose from the floor wasn't so much a man

anymore as a monster. His arms were too long, and his hands rested well below his knees. The length wasn't nearly as intimidating as the lean ropy muscle that covered them or the claws extending from his hands instead of fingers.

There was no way to tell how tall the good doctor was now, but it was clear that he was bigger than before. Now his back hunched over, and his legs had bent with the weight of his torso. The only way anyone would have known this was the same man was the lightning bolt of black hair going down the center of a now bald skull. Although with the doctor's new size, the hair looked more like a series of jagged black stitches than a hip new hairstyle.

Slobber dripped from his mouth, and insanity burned in his eyes. He turned and scanned the room for any sign of the intruders. Not seeing anyone immediately, Doctor Zacharias leaned back and bellowed into the night. It was the kind of sound that would have made the villagers in a story shudder and bolt their doors and windows closed. It was the call of the creature Grendel in *Beowulf*. The scream was full of agony and longing, but the deep undertone of the man's desires was filled with murderous rage.

His family had been taken.

His hopes of seeing them again were gone.

All he had now was a hunger. A desire to make the living and loved feel as he felt, to hurt as he was hurting. Why should others get to be happy when his life was in ruins? A little magic to help his research was what the witch said. A small price to pay was all she requested. The price had been their lives and his servitude.

Now the world would pay. He would happily burn it all to the ground.

Grief and rage overtook him, and he screamed again before picking up the surgical table and throwing it through the wide double doors. Doctor Zacharias stomped after the table and ripped one of the doors from its hinges when it refused to swing.

Now that he was out of the lab, his feet moved with purpose. The doctor was starting to get a feel for his new body. He felt like he could do anything, that no one could stop him now. At least he wouldn't have to wait much longer. The fools were coming to him and in Vitaria's sacrificial chamber no less. There could be magic in suffering, beauty in death. He would be their deliverer to the underworld, the executioner of their fate.

This time when the scream escaped his lips, the good doctor almost felt happy.

CHAPTER TWENTY-ONE

"Did you hear that?" JaKobi looked around the puzzle room, searching for the source of the sound.

Cassie gave him a gentle nudge. "Just do your little magic thing to open the door." She wiggled her fingers at the console. "If we get back soon enough I might do that thing you like later."

"With the honey and the feather?" JaKobi grinned from ear to ear as Cassie nodded in response.

Tim watched their exchange and wondered if he was as foolish. It was kind of amazing what women could get men to do with the thought of a little sex or even a little debauchery added to the regular old routine. He tried to think of a time he would have passed on sex to get his way, and he really couldn't think of one.

He looked down at his waistline. More thinking with the big brain little guy.

Maybe it wasn't normal for him to talk to his dick, but if he wasn't going to do it, who was? Tim wouldn't be a slave to his desires. He was a man of substance, a man of high moral character.

ShadowLily bent over and brushed some dirt off her boots, and his eyes went straight to her ass in those tight leather pants.

I'm going straight to hell.

"But the view is good," he mumbled to himself.

The assassin turned with a little smile pulling up the corner of her mouth. It was the kind of look that said yeah, I still got it. "What was that?"

Trying not to blush, Tim waved in the panel's general direction. "Oh, I was saying I hope this doesn't take too long."

"You know, just because this looks easy doesn't mean it is." JaKobi glanced from the puzzle to Tim, looking slightly frazzled. "Plus, you ruined my daydream. You'll never guess how sticky honey can get."

Lorelei stepped up and hovered her hand over the button on the console. "My daydream is to get the door open so we can get back to the farm for a party. Not every farmer's daughter is into boys, you know."

"The question is, are they into...oof," JaKobi stammered as Cassie hit him in the ribs. "Of course it doesn't matter what they're into." He coughed nervously into his hand.

"Exactly." Cassie pointed at the console. "Now, work your magic."

It took JaKobi about ten seconds to get the tiles in the right position. When they were all set, he nodded at Lorelei, and she slammed her hand down on the button. The large central doors opened, and there was a noise. Tim didn't know how to describe it other than it sounded like the most forlorn creature in the world.

They couldn't worry too much about the twisted soul they would face. Their job was to find Doctor Zacharias and put an end to this madness. How many lives had the man ruined to play with some new magic? New spells were great, but there had to be a line a person wouldn't cross.

That was always the moral quandary.

It was easy to do what was right when nothing was on the line. Tim could wax poetic for hours about treating people better, but the second someone cut him off in traffic he would lay on the horn as if he was doing a twenty-hour stress test. That was a far cry from taking a life, but it was the same issue. How far would he go to get everything he ever wanted?

Right up to the edge, or over it?

Thankfully for him, he didn't have to answer that question. Right now he had everything he ever wanted and then some. It was hard to imagine things getting any better than they were, so he was saving like a miser. There wasn't anything wrong with planning for a little downturn in a person's good fortunes as long as they remembered to enjoy the good times along the way. The only thing that could fuck up his life now was if he lost ShadowLily.

That wasn't going to happen.

It was weird. Right up until the moment he met her, Tim had always kind of thought the stories about true love were a little ridiculous. How could you meet a person and just know? Then it happened to him, and now their relationship had reached the point where he couldn't imagine his life without her.

Another cry escaped the open doors in front of them, and it made him feel like every happy thought he had was gone. It was like watching a TV drama where everyone died in the end and left the viewer feeling exhausted.

A quick once-over of the party showed everyone felt about the same. Tim gave Cassie a firm nod. "Let's go end this."

"On it." Cassie pulled her bō staff from her inventory and walked down the stairs on the other side of the door.

The rest of their group followed the tank, spreading out in their standard formation. This place was starting to bring Tim down, and he was ready to put it behind him. He couldn't wait to get to the deserts of Naroosh and start exploring. It would be nice to shake things up for a while.

They moved down the wide hallways until they stopped outside a small wooden door. On the other side, they would face Doctor Zacharias and whatever evil creations he had left. More naga, maybe some leopards, or even the woman with alligator tail. Everything was in play, so they had to be ready.

Tim opened the door for Cassie. "After you."

"I kinda wish you weren't only a gentleman when you wanted me to rush headfirst into danger," Cassie huffed as she moved through the now open entryway.

"That's the only time I know how," Tim quipped as he followed the others inside.

The room in front of them wasn't anything like what he expected. He was almost a hundred percent sure the boss would be waiting for them in a surgical suite or something similar. Instead, they were in a wide circular room. Columns lined the interior, making a small outer walkway and a wide-open central space.

An altar of obsidian stone awaited them in the room's center. It kind of reminded him of when the White Queen killed Aslan, except this altar was solid black and not quite so reminiscent of Stonehenge.

No one had a dark altar for shits and giggles.

There didn't seem to be a way to trigger the fight except to step out into the open. Cassie watched him to see if it was okay to proceed. Not seeing any other immediate solution, Tim nodded. As their party stepped into the center of the room, the wailing sound came from above them.

Tim looked up and was surprised to see the room opened above them like a cavern. Jumping from one wall to another was one of the largest men he'd ever seen. That was if you could call him a man. The creature moving toward their party was so misshapen it could have started as a man, or an orc, maybe even an ogre.

Being deformed didn't appear to make the boss any less deadly as it made the final leap to the center of the room and landed on the altar. The extra-long arms made its claws as good as any weapon, and the fucker had range. Not to mention being athletic.

Moving into the room the way the boss did wasn't something just anyone could do.

"When I found this room, I thought it would change everything." Dr. Zacharias held his arms out wide, indicating the space they were in. "In a way, I guess it did." The weird moaning cry issued from his lips but this time it trailed off in bouts of laughter.

It dawned on Tim that things hadn't gone well for the good doctor since they'd seen him in the opening cinematic. Part of him still couldn't believe that the monster in front of them now was the same man. He went so far as to turn on the boss's nameplate for a moment to confirm it. Whatever knowledge Vitaria gifted him with had twisted the doctor into a representation of the man he'd allowed himself to become.

"The way is opening, and she will have such sights to show you." Doctor Zacharias grinned as the madness overtook him. "The darkness can be beautiful if you're willing to embrace it."

Cassie set her feet, ready to charge in. "I've heard about enough of this shit." She twirled her staff around with a flourish. "Just shut up and die already."

The tank charged forward without saying anything else, and ShadowLily disappeared. Tim made sure to switch his stance back to Way of The Boulder and cast Curse of Giving on the boss. With his primary responsibilities taken care of, he looked around the room for any clues as to what might happen next.

A scan of the room didn't reveal bupkis.

JaKobi wasn't jumping up and down and pointing at anything so his magical spider senses must not have highlighted anything worthwhile for him to bring to the group's attention. Outside of the altar and the ring of columns, there wasn't much to see. Zacharias could always summon help from above or make a special attack that forced them to hide behind the pillars, but that all seemed too simple for the final fight.

Despite dodging around most of Zacharias's attacks, Cassie was taking a good deal of damage. Tim quickly cast Healing Orb and wondered if this fight might be dramatically different than what they faced so far. It'd been a while since they'd been in a straight-up slugfest. The real question was could they bring the boss' health to zero before he couldn't keep up with the healing?

Things seemed to be going to plan for the most part. The health bars of most of the group were full, minus Cassie who needed constant monitoring. Tim quickly checked his status sheet to make sure she wasn't suffering from any negative status effects, but she seemed clear of any detrimental debuffs.

Was this really going to be a tank and spank?

Cassie was moving the boss around the room with ease, and his health was dropping at a pretty steady clip. Now and again ShadowLily took some additional damage but nothing significant enough to make him worry. As the boss hit seventy percent, Tim cast Behold My Power.

Might as well get it out of the way early.

The small amount of feedback damage the party received from his spell hit like a truck. That wasn't normal, and he didn't have any way to stop it. He'd never had one of his spells used against him in such a way, and the worst part was the feedback would hit all of them again, and soon.

Tim recast the Curse of Giving and followed up with a small burst of Healing Storm. As the group's health slowly ticked up, he blasted each of them with a Healing Orb and waited for the next wave to crash into them.

This time the pain wasn't nearly as bad. The healing over time aspect of his spells kept the group on their feet, despite the fact they were suffering near-constant damage. If Tim could keep their bars close to full, the DPS wouldn't stop fighting. The boss's health hit fifty-one percent right as Behold My Power triggered.

Doctor Zacharias let out a wail of grief and ran back to the altar. When he climbed on the stones, his health started to trickle back up. They had to get him off the altar but they couldn't fucking move. It took Tim a moment to stop panicking and focus on Cassie. If he could get her mobile, she might be able to knock the doctor off the altar and prevent the healing while he freed the rest of them.

Focusing on his hands with the intensity of someone with psychokinesis trying to blow up a pineapple, Tim clearly pictured what he wanted to do. His hands twitched through the Cleanse spell, and Cassie was on the move. She had her hook out and wrapped around the boss' leg before he could shout instructions.

Tim freed himself next, then the ranged DPS. ShadowLily shot him a withering glare as she waited for her turn to be set free. He understood she wanted to be back in the fight first, but the ranged DPS would make a bigger impact while she still had to close the distance to the boss. In hindsight, he would have set her free first to avoid the death stare, or maybe it was that her look promised no sex for an indefinite amount of time, and he was willing to do anything to avoid such a harsh punishment.

Bad little brain, bad.

Cassie pulled Doctor Zacharias free from the altar, and the rest of the party was already attacking him again. The boss' health had only climbed back to just above fifty percent, so they'd stopped the mechanic before it slowed the fight too much. Despite the small uptick in his health, the boss looked a little ragged. His breath came out in snorts like a bull's. Tim didn't know if the boss was going to charge or give up.

It turned out it was neither.

When the doctor's health hit forty percent, he started to run around the room using the columns as steps. Tim had never seen anyone move so fast. To keep himself off the floor must have taken amazing strength or a lot of magic. Tim wasn't exactly sure what would happen next, but he wanted to be ready for anything.

A faint blue light enveloped JaKobi. The fire mage looked help- lessly around at the rest of the party. "Not again."

Tim didn't know how he knew what to do next except to call it a spark of divine intervention. There were normally two tactics developers used when the boss singled somebody out, and they boiled down to doing two very opposite things. Either get the fuck away from the target as fast as possible or run to them to share the damage.

This felt like an all-in situation.

"Stack on JaKobi!" Tim cried as he ran toward the mage.

Tim ran into JaKobi and wrapped his arms around him as though he was a life preserver. With a thought, he sent a Healing Storm down on the group as the rest of them followed his example. Tim closed his eyes and started a countdown in his head. Three. Two. One.

This was going to fucking hurt.

Doctor Zacharias sprang from the circle of columns and slammed into the party, sending them flying apart like bowling pins. Tim didn't bother to stand as he sent out the next wave of healing. All that mattered now was killing the boss before he could hit them with another of his massive attacks.

As the boss's health approached twenty-five percent, Tim called to the group, "Give it everything you've got. Don't stop until he's dead."

"Easy for you to say," Cassie snarled as she took a slash from Doctor Zacharias' claws across her shoulder.

Tim tried not to laugh at her pain. He knew how much being hit hurt, but he also knew he could make that pain go away damn near instantly. "I don't hear you complaining about the free beer you get for being the damage sponge."

"It's like death by a thousand papercuts." Cassie grimaced. "That shit stings."

He wasn't going to laugh this time. Instead, Tim focused on getting Cassie back to full health. Behold My Power wasn't active to cast again, and using Divine Light seemed like an expensive treat when everyone wasn't nearly close to full health. Healing Storm took the edge off the worst of the damage, but he felt like he was falling behind.

What the fuck is happening?

Doctor Zacharias' health dipped under twenty percent, and he let out another of his pitiful cries. The damage the party was taking increased again. Tim looked around for the source as he cast a quick round of Healing Orb on everyone.

"This is getting ridiculous." Tim cursed as his eyes moved from person to person.

What was causing all the damage?

The realization hit him like a meat tenderizer to the knee. The boss reflected a percentage of their damage at them, and as his health got lower, the feedback received was worse. Tim was tempted to tell everyone to stagger their DPS to make his job easier, but he also didn't want them to get hit by another round of what he called the Column Smash.

Keeping up with the healing at fifteen percent was pretty easy, but his mana was depleting rather quickly so he started to conserve it where he could. Tim reapplied Curse of Giving and cast Who Needs a Shield on Cassie for the final push. Right before they hit ten percent, he used Healing Storm to top everyone off.

A bubble of dark purple energy surrounded Doctor Zacharias as he moved back toward the altar for healing. The amount of damage the party was taking doubled again.

"Don't kill yourself by being too aggressive," Tim shouted as he sent out the next round of healing.

It felt like his every moment was dedicated to healing now. There wasn't time to think. All he could do was fire off the next spell to stay ahead of the spikes. It was too bad his cleansing spell wouldn't work on the boss.

Wait. Would it work on the boss?

Tim didn't remember the spell specifically saying anything about it working only on allies, and in some games taking buffs off a boss was a mandatory part of a fight. It might be worth a shot if one extra cast wouldn't kill anyone.

He sent out the next round of Healing Orb, then cast Cleanse on the boss before reapplying Curse of Giving. Tim watched to see if his spell did anything but the dark energy around Doctor Zacharias didn't appear to fade in any significant way.

It was worth a chance, but now they had to really push it.

"Finish him!" Tim shouted in his best Mortal Kombat voice.

The boss hit five percent, and Tim fell to his knees and lifted his hands to the heavens. Healing Storm took effect, and he pushed all his remaining mana into channeling the rain. The group's health slowly ticked down, but the doctor's went down faster.

Cassie used her chain and hook to pull one of the doctor's legs forward while ShadowLily slashed at the other from behind. Zacharias stumbled and dropped to one knee. Lorelei rushed forward, dodging a swipe of the boss' razor-sharp claws before flipping into the air. Somehow she pulled the doctor's head backward, exposing his throat. Tim knew this was it. ShadowLily was going to end it.

"Nooooo!" Doctor Zacharias thundered.

Maybe Tim shouldn't have been surprised when JaKobi ran toward the boss to end the fight, but he was. His friend had grown a lot since the first day they met him, and he was proud of him. Seeing him fly through the air and slam a ball of flames down into Doctor Zacharias' mouth was the latest highlight in their adventures together.

The rest of the group backed away from the boss, and Tim was about to tell them to keep going when a light went off inside the boss's stomach. Before he could duck out of the way, the doctor's midsection exploded.

The fight was over, but Tim's mouth was full of Zacharias.

The boss tasted about as good as one would expect an exploded person to taste. In short, it was easily the most disgusting thing he ever ate in his life. *Even worse than kale juice.* Tim would have gladly slurped down nothing but kale for the rest of his days if he never had to taste exploded Zacharias again. He spat out what he could, used his robes to wipe off the worst of the mess, and placed them in his inventory.

When Tim pulled his robes out and equipped them, they were spotless, and he felt better for having something clean on. When they got back to the farm, he would drink as much beer as he could find to wash the taste out and hopefully pass out early. Food felt like something that might be a no go until he could forget about the horrible aftertaste.

The rest of the party was covered in goo but not nearly as bad as himself. It didn't look like any of the others had been forced to enjoy the Zacharias sampler so he was a little bitter about it. All he wanted now was to get the loot and find something to wash his mouth out with properly.

The body disappeared in a brilliant flash of swirling golden motes, and as they faded a golden chest appeared.

"I think Timibal Lector should go first." Lorelei snorted with laughter.

Tim grinned as he approached the chest. "You don't know. Doctor Zacharias could have been delicious."

Just saying delicious almost made him barf.

Screw that guy, he was dead, and there was loot to be had. The glittering chest in front of him consumed all his attention now. Tim rested his hand on the chest and stepped back to see what he received.

Item Received: Spell book of Disturbance

Do your enemies have buffs you wish they didn't? Then the Spell of Disturbance is just what you need. Remove one friendly or beneficial spell from an enemy. Not all buffs or spells can be removed.

"Sweet! I got a spell that can remove buffs from enemies." Tim almost couldn't believe his good luck.

"Dude, that's awesome." JaKobi clapped him on the back before placing his hand on the chest.

A new hat appeared on JaKobi's head. "Wizard's Hat of the

Unquenchable Flame. The item adds duration to my damage over time spells."

"Don't hog all the good stuff." Cassie laid her hand on the chest. "Seriously, Bootlaces of Recklessness?" The tank glared at JaKobi. "You're lucky I like all the benefits."

"I like them too." JaKobi gave her a sly grin.

Lorelei stepped between them on her way to the chest. "Can't let you two have all the fun."

A lopsided grin spread across the ranger's face. "Quiver of Poisonous Intent. Gives my arrows a small bonus to any piercing damage done. It's pretty freaking awesome."

Cassie mouthed to JaKobi while holding up two strings, "Bootlaces."

Last to step up to the chest was ShadowLily. She reached out and laid her hand on the chest before stepping back. "Trinket of the Leaping Leopard. Apparently, I get a bonus for jumping and damage while airborne. If you see me jumping around during fights you know why."

Lorelei jumped from spot to spot on her way to the door. "Don't worry, guys. I'm doing a lot of damage, I swear."

"Be happy I'm not jumping on you," ShadowLily quipped with playful menace.

The ranger laughed as she turned to wink at her. "Better ask your man first because I might kinda like that."

Tim moved forward and slung an arm around Lorelei's shoulders. "Maybe we can work something out."

"Fuck off," Lorelei and ShadowLily said in unison.

He couldn't help but grin as the two women chastised him. Tim held up his hands defensively. "Okay, okay, farmgirl for Lorelei, and the bestest most wonderfulest woman I know for me."

"Bestest most wonderfulest is kind of weak, don't you think?" Lorelei smirked.

ShadowLily removed Tim's arm from the ranger's shoulders and replaced it with hers. "And what if I wanted the farm girl?"

"You really stepped in it now," JaKobi chided as he passed the stunned healer.

Cassie picked Tim up and tossed him over one shoulder. "Don't worry. I've always wanted brother-bands."

"Is that like sister-wives, but for chicks?" JaKobi sounded appalled.

Cassie slapped her hand down on Tim's ass so hard he squawked. "Looks like it's you and me then, big guy."

Tim jumped off Cassie's shoulder and sprinted toward ShadowLily. "Save me! I don't want to be a bro-band."

JaKobi jumped and landed over Cassie's shoulder with a grin spreading across his face. "Some guys don't know how to be grateful. Carry me to bed, woman."

Tim didn't see JaKobi land on his ass, but he heard it just fine as they kept walking. He loved his friends so much he couldn't imagine his life without them. It was time for them to start a new adventure in a new land. He didn't know what awaited them in the desert, but he was dying to find out.

CHAPTER TWENTY-TWO

The party going on downstairs was in full effect, but as usual, Tim was late.

Everyone downstairs would have to be content to wait a while because he'd been covered in boss and wasn't getting out of the tub until he was one hundred percent sure he was clean. Getting bathed in blood really made a person rethink how many baths were appropriate to take in a day.

While he didn't enjoy baths nearly as much as showers, he had to admit they were kind of relaxing. They were also the perfect place to go over his stats. Tim had a couple of pending quests to turn in, and he hoped they'd be enough to give him his next level. Then he would have two skill points to spend.

There was no time like the present to determine if he earned enough experience, so Tim selected the first quest he wanted to turn in.

Quest Complete: Harpy's Got the Blues

Reward: Five gold coins

You received an item from every single boss. You should be happy to get anything from this quest besides experience.

It was true that he'd picked up some great new gear and a ton of experience in the dungeon. Not every quest had to be for the most epic piece of loot. Sometimes the small upgrades and experience were even more valuable. Right now, Tim wanted to hit level twenty. He was getting so close to his next class change he could taste it.

His next quest also wouldn't offer any additional rewards, but the smile on Jessi's face when they told her she was right about the harpy was worth all the gold in the world. The young acolyte was excited enough to be correct, but she was over the moon when Brother Colton promoted her.

Not a bad result for the young lady considering the look on Brother Colton's face when he saw Jessi sprinting toward their party. Their rotund friend had been so concerned that Tim had thought the young woman was trying to attack them. It was funny how a chance encounter ended up with them saving a farm and helping a lot of hungry people.

Questing always felt rewarding when there was good loot, and they got to help someone. It was time to turn in his next quest and see if it was enough to get to his next level. Then Tim could review his skills and join the party downstairs. A beer sounded pretty good, and if he didn't get out of the tub soon, he would have prune hands for the rest of the night.

Quest Complete: Farm to Table

You slew the harpy and saved the farm. Not only that, but you uncovered a much larger threat to the kingdom and handled it as well. You've earned the respect of Brother Colton and Jessi and increased your group's reputation in _The Etheric Coast_. As a bonus, you have been rewarded with five gold coins.

System Message: You have gained a level.

Sweet!

Tim was level sixteen now, and he could almost taste his level twenty class change quest coming up. Getting the next boost in skills and power was going to be awesome. He'd been lucky enough to get to skip over all the work the others had to put into their class change missions the first time so it was a pretty good bet he'd have to go through it this time around.

Nothing worth having came without hard work.

That was one of the things his parents always ingrained in him. They reminded him ever so gently that you could blame the world for where you started or how hard your life was, or you could work to better yourself and those around you every day. It was a lesson that wouldn't have meant much if he hadn't seen how hard they worked. Watching his parents get up with the sun and go to bed long after it was down every day without complaint was what got him to college.

Then I got a job and a girlfriend.

It was funny how life had a way of changing when you didn't expect it. He'd always wanted to be a famous singer but had a voice even autotune couldn't correct. He could hold his own when it came to sports, but making it big was a pipe dream. Sadly, there wasn't a future in smoking weed and playing video games so he picked business.

Numbers always made sense to him in a way that words didn't. Kinda funny how his love affair with numbers found him living inside a game instead of placing market orders for a brokerage firm. Not that entering the game was exactly risk-free, but it was better than being trapped in a cube. It boggled his mind why these companies kept huge offices when many people could do the same job from home.

Whatever. Even working from home sucked when the other option was slaying monsters for a living. Especially when there was a new land on the horizon, one filled with new possibilities and rewards, it was time to stop stalling and get to the desert.

Sadly, they wouldn't carry him there in the tub so he had to move things along himself.

Tim pulled up his status menu and quickly allocated his two unassigned skill points into intelligence, bringing his total to thirty-five. There was a moment where he debated putting them into endurance to get closer to the twenty percent threshold, but the mana regeneration supplied by his intelligence was key to his success. As soon as he got his secondary stat over forty, he'd make sure to hit twenty endurance next before building his wisdom again.

The fights wouldn't last long if he couldn't survive a single hit.

With his stat points out of the way, Tim turned his attention to his skill sheet. It was amazing how many notifications one could let pile up when they didn't look at them for a long time. At least he didn't have to acknowledge the messages to receive the benefits from his upgraded skills, but he liked to read them anyway to make sure he didn't miss any new developments. Plus, the game's AI put a little snark into the comments so it almost felt rude not to read them.

Skill Increased: Behold My Power

Rank: Apprentice level four

You really like using this spell to kill things. Now that you've reached the apprentice ranks, the spell's cooldown has been decreased by a small amount. This reduction doesn't come without a cost. The spell will now take 1.15% of your group's health every second for ten seconds before delivering the total damage to the boss and applying the debuff.

Debuff: Powershock

Powershock increases the damage the target takes from all sources by five percent for ten seconds.

It was nice to get this skill into the apprentice ranks finally. The only thing that had been holding Tim back from using it more often was the cooldown. Right now the spell was normally only good for once a fight unless everything went perfect. Now he'd have to see if he could use it to increase the DPS' opening burst and again to close out the fight. There still might not be enough time, but he'd never know if he didn't try.

The trick would be making sure he had enough mana to heal

through the damage the spell caused to the party while they were taking additional damage from the fight. It wasn't impossible but using this spell was always heavily situational.

Skill Increased: Small Blades

Rank: Apprentice level seven

When in doubt, grab a knife and start stabbing. That's exactly what you did, and it helped your group. Continue introducing others to the sharp end of a small blade to increase this skill.

Tim didn't get a chance to use his daggers nearly as much as he liked to. That was the rub when he picked a support class. Not being a damage-dealer didn't mean that he couldn't get stabby. It just meant he had to pick the right moment to do it. Plus, it was nice not always getting blood on his hands.

Skill Increased: Dodge

Rank: Apprentice level five

It's funny how getting hit by things doesn't feel good. Fortunately, you seem to have a knack for avoiding damage, even if it feels more like luck than skill sometimes. Keep dodging attacks to increase this skill.

Tim wanted to be offended, but the update was pretty accurate. He didn't dodge things as much as run away and hope they didn't hit him. If he kept his dexterity stat up and flying objects kept missing him he might start to dodge things on purpose someday.

Skill Increased: Flame Burst

Rank: Apprentice level five

When you call upon them, the flames will burst from your hands and incinerate your enemies, or the spell would if you used the skill a little more often. Hopefully a good singeing is all you need it for.

Hey, that was a little unfair.

Tim might not be the best at using this spell, but at least he could use it for more than a distraction now. Who knew? This might be more of his go-to at the next rank, but for now Divine

Light packed a little more of a punch although the mana cost was higher.

Skill Increased: Healing Storm

Rank: Apprentice level five

Channeling this spell for extended periods isn't the most effective use for it, but it sure boosted your rank rather quickly. Keep using this spell in new ways to see what it can accomplish.

The AI was right. Channeling this spell during the harpy fight almost cost them the battle. It sure healed a shit ton of damage, but it obliterated his mana. Tim would make sure that he used this spell more judiciously in the future because he could always switch stances and use his curses to heal the entire party as a backup option.

Skill Increased: Who Needs a Shield

Rank: Apprentice level five

Sometimes taking damage is unavoidable, and for those situations, this is the perfect spell. This curse reduces the target's damage by 11% and increases your entire party's dodge chance by 2%.

The cooldown on this spell was damn near as long as Behold My Power, but it was easily as useful. Whenever Cassie or someone else was going to take a huge hit this spell always saved their ass. When healing alone wouldn't cut it, Who Needs a Shield was the difference-maker.

Skill Increased: Curse of Giving

Rank: Apprentice level eight

Taking, taking, taking. You really enjoy taking your enemies' health and using it to heal your group. There's a certain kind of person who relishes hurting others to help themselves, just saying.

Curse of Giving now returns 15% of the damage done as health.

That wasn't very nice.

Tim thought the game might be a little judgy with this one. He was using the mechanics available to his class to heal. It didn't mean he liked hurting others. Sometimes he got the feeling the game threw one or two of these explanations at him every time to gauge his reaction. *Hope the AI liked what it saw.*

Skill Increased: Cleanse

Rank: Apprentice level nine

Negative status effects are becoming a thing of the past. The more you use this spell, the stronger it will become and the more effects it can dispel. Keep using Cleanse to find out what it can accomplish for your group.

That was much nicer.

It was funny how many more flies you caught with honey. Being nice to people didn't have to be a scam. There was something to be said about treating the people you disliked as well as the ones you cared for. It took a special kind of person to pull it off. Tim was trying to be better at that, but sometimes he liked to scream fuck you as loud as the next guy. Not that screaming at anyone resolved a problem faster. In fact, in most cases, it slowed down the eventual resolution a great deal.

Unless it was an order from an officer in the military. Then screaming worked just fine to get things moving double-quick.

Skill Increased: Healing Orb

Rank: Journeyman level six

Splashing people with water must give you a certain amount of satisfaction. This is your favorite spell, and you use it with great effect. There isn't a lot to be said about good old reliable.

Healing Orb hasn't increased in potency or effectiveness, but if you achieve the Master ranks there could be a special bonus.

Tim didn't mind if his favorite spell didn't get a big boost for the last few levels. He knew it was strong enough, and it helped with his cleansing duties if they fought lower level trash. Healing Orb was the best spell he had by far for healing output versus mana consumption, and he didn't expect that to change anytime soon.

One thing he hated in games was when developers did a patch and decided now was the time they wanted some other skill to shine, so they nerfed a player's favorite skill into oblivion. So far, *The Etheric Coast* had a gentle touch when it came to balancing, and he really appreciated it. No one wanted to wake up after being top of the charts the day before to find out they were struggling to clear basic content with the same rotation.

Tim needed to read faster, or ShadowLily would be pissed at him for taking so long. The bath was nice, but he wanted to go downstairs and have fun and not a fight about why he took longer to get ready than she did.

It didn't take too long for him to find the plug in the bottom of the tub. Then a quick pitcher of water over the head to make sure he was completely clean, and it was time to get out. Sadly, he didn't have a spell to dry off instantly so Tim still had to use a towel like everyone else.

While Tim was drying off, he continued reading the rest of his notifications.

Stances

Skill Increased: Way of the River

Rank: Apprentice level four

While stances don't provide huge incremental increases, they do get nice bonuses at higher levels. Keep using the selected stance at opportune times to continue leveling the skill.

Tim kind of expected as much. His stances were vehicles for his curses. The real power increase would come when he upgraded his class and learned new curses. If he could cast two or three curses on an enemy at once, the heals would flow like a river.

Skill Increased: Way of the Boulder

Rank: Apprentice level seven

You must be happy you're not the one on the other side of all

those attacks. Keep using this stance when you have a single target in need of protection. You're doing the right things. You just need more practice.

Messages like this almost made Tim feel like he was about to get hit with some bad news. There was a chance he was a little too pessimistic at times. It felt like too much good news or if he received too many compliments that the other shoe would drop, and something bad would happen. So far the game had never led him astray, and there was no reason to believe it would start setting him up to take the fall now.

Buffs

Skill Increased: Armor of Eternia

Rank: Apprentice level six

Reduces the damage of all dark magic attacks by 6%, and the effect to weakness by the same amount. This effect now lasts for eight hours.

While it was a small increase in potency, the buff received a massive bonus in duration. It would be awesome not having to re-buff between every encounter. While it would pay to take a second and make sure his buffs were still active, he wouldn't have to waste time recasting them and reminding everyone else to do the same. As far as he was concerned, this was a major quality of life improvement.

Skill Increased: Attacks of the Faithful

Rank: Apprentice level six

This buff converts fifty percent of normal damage into holy damage. Some creatures in the world of Eternia will take increased damage while against others it will have no effect. In the case of fighting a monster with holy attributes, this spell will weaken your attacks so be aware of the creatures you're fighting.

Thankfully most of Tim's fights had been against creatures of evil or tainted by evil. He imagined if he ever got the chance to fight Cardinal Jepsom this spell would have been a detriment.

Thankfully the Cardinal had been murdered by wraiths, and Tim got to save the day by raining down destruction on his killers with Divine Light. He made a mental note to be more careful about using this buff around creatures that might have a holy influence.

Now that he was dry, Tim re-equipped his clothes and headed downstairs to join the party. The second he hit the stairwell, the sound of music from outside and the smell of food from the dining room hit him all at once. It reminded him of the holidays. Good food, light music, and a whole lot of fun.

JaKobi pressed a glass of beer into his hand the second his feet touched the ground floor. He sipped, savoring the dark flavor. After a long day, nothing took the edge off like a nice cold beer. He sipped again before clapping the fire mage on the back.

"Thank you, I needed that." Tim took another healthy swallow and wondered which direction he'd have to go for a refill.

JaKobi grinned. "Sure thing, boss. If you need Cassie or me, we'll be outside. Fire pong is totally catching on."

"Nice." Time gave him a high five and moved toward the dining room.

His next surprise was as pleasant as the beer, but it came in the form of pure happiness for another person. It seemed Lorelei had found herself not one farm girl to spend the night with but two. He could just make out the three ladies canoodling in the parlor. It wouldn't be much longer before they disappeared upstairs by the looks of things. When Lorelei looked up and caught his eye, he winked and turned to look at what was for dinner.

It turned out even a mouthful of Zacharias couldn't tame his belly for long.

When he'd loaded his plate with two pieces of fried chicken, two biscuits, and a mountain of mashed potatoes smothered in a river of gravy, he made his way outside. It was a feast fit for a king, and one Tim greatly looked forward to. So far there was only one thing he was missing to make his night perfect.

Not seeing the woman of his dreams anywhere on the way to

the door, Tim continued outside and found an open table under some fairy lights to dig in. A full glass of beer replaced his dwindling one, and he looked up to see ShadowLily smiling down at him. She kissed him on the forehead, avoiding his gravy-soaked mouth, and sat. They watched JaKobi and Cassie play fire pong with the farmers as he finished his meal.

"This is kind of perfect, isn't it?" ShadowLily looked out over the farm as she nursed her beer.

Tim pushed his plate away, feeling full and hating himself for still wanting desert. He settled for wiping his mouth with a napkin and sipping his beer. He leaned back in his chair, enjoying the moment. "It really is."

List of Tim's Current Stats and Skills

"Tim" level sixteen Battlesworn
    Primary Stats
    Strength: 13
    Endurance: 14
    Dexterity: 20
    Intelligence: 35
    Wisdom: 46
    Perception: 6
    Vitality: 4
    Revitalization: 4
    Luck: 7

Notable Gear
    Weapons
    Simple Dagger of Dexterity, +1 (X2)
    Staff of Divine Retribution, +4 Intelligence +5 Wisdom

. . .

Armor

Tarnished Circlet of Divine Wisdom, +1 Intelligence +3 Wisdom

Wilbur's Fur-lined Shoulder Guards, +1 to Perception Vitality, Revitalization, and Luck

Battlesworn Robes of Justice, +4 Intelligence +6 Wisdom

Jerkin of Unmeasurable Delight, +1 to all base stats

Paul's Gloves of Mending, +4 Wisdom +7 Intelligence

Belt of Wisdom, +2

Pants of Recovery, Increases mana regeneration

Boots of Swift Regeneration, Increase base movement speed and mana regeneration by 1%

Jewelry and Accessories

Leather Wraps of Divergent Health, 10% chance for single target healing spell to jump targets and heal the secondary recipient for 50% of the value.

Wristband of the Goddess, 10% damage reduction to dark based attacks

Ring of Marginal Transcendence, +2 Wisdom

Necklace of Unshakable Will, +3 Wisdom +1 Intelligence

Trinket of the Smiling Monkey, +1 to a random stat

Skills

Appeal to the Goddess: Novice rank one

Disturbance: Novice rank one

Infiltrator: Novice rank three

Quick Feet: Novice rank four

Night Vision: Novice: rank six

Backstab: Novice rank seven

Throwing Knives: Apprentice rank two

Sneak: Apprentice rank three

Behold My Power: Apprentice rank four
Dodge: Apprentice rank five
Flame Burst: Apprentice rank five
Healing Storm: Apprentice rank five
Who Needs a Shield: Apprentice rank five
Small Blades: Apprentice rank seven
Curse of Giving: Apprentice rank eight
Weaken Undead: Apprentice rank eight
Cleanse: Apprentice rank nine
Divine Light: Apprentice rank nine
Healing Orb: Journeyman rank six

Stances
Way of the Boulder: Apprentice rank seven
Way of the River: Apprentice rank four

Buffs
Armor of Eternia: Apprentice rank six
Attacks of the Faithful: Apprentice rank six

Open Quests
The Deserts of Naroosh

"Neema, get to the gates!" Khalid roared as he fired a bow nearly as tall as he was.

No shit.

Wanting to get to the gates and actually getting to them were two different things entirely. A battle raged all around her, and it made going from Point A to Point B a little more difficult than she initially expected. They didn't bring enough men for a sustained incursion. This was supposed to be an in-and-out type of deal. All their intelligence said the fort should have been nearly empty.

"Yansesh. I'm going to kill that little shit," Neema grumbled as she dove behind an overturned cart.

The priest's information was about as reliable as the man himself. How the squirmy little weasel got the job masquerading as a priest, she'd never know. It wasn't like the resistance had a plethora of choices when it came to having sources close enough to Jabari to gain any useful intelligence. So they took what they could get when they could get it.

This little tidbit of information appeared to be a trap that they paid handsomely to be in.

Five years ago, the resistance found the secret oasis and was finally able to establish a foothold in the region. With a base, Khalid made bolstering their numbers his top priority. Today the resistance was bolstered by thousands of fighters and ten times as many supporters. Their numbers were growing, but Jabari and the Pharaoh had resources that made their dwindling supplies look like table scraps left for the dogs.

Every member of the resistance was facing an opponent in better armor with better weapons and twice as many men.

The odds were never in their favor.

This job was supposed to be the score that kept the resistance alive for the next six months. They couldn't afford to turn back now. Men couldn't fight when their families were starving. There was food inside the fort, and they were going to get it. Without the supplies here, the resistance wouldn't make it another month. She'd rather die than see the resistance they fought so hard to create turn to ash on the wind.

"Archers!" Khalid cried from somewhere behind her.

She knew what was coming next, and this would be her only chance to make a run for it. Sometimes being the fastest runner in the resistance sucked, and today was that day. They didn't have the manpower to throw numbers at problems. The resistance had to come up with innovative solutions. Those solutions didn't include sending men to storm the fort walls with ladders. The age-old strategy cost too many lives and never won the day against an organized opposition.

So they made a bomb.

The nice thing about the explosive was that it only required one man or woman to use it. That sucked for the person who drew the short straw, but at the end of the day losing one life was better than losing hundreds. Not that Neema planned on dying. The witch had promised them the fuse would last for two minutes, and that was just enough time to get things done if everything went perfectly.

Neema spent the last two days training for this moment, and she still only succeeded on one out of every three attempts. Today she had to get it right on the first attempt because there wouldn't be a second chance. A few deep breaths to steady herself, and she pulled the flint free from her vest. The call would come soon, and she had to be ready for it.

"Fire!" Khalid screamed with relish as he let his bow sing the song of death.

The archers on the parapet would have to duck for a few seconds to avoid the volley fired by the resistance. That was her window to make it to the gate. Neema had to run now before the men could stand back up and pick off an easy target. The small flint smashed against the stone, and the sparks flew straight to the fuse as if by magic. Sparks bubbled from the end, and Neema started running.

When Neema sprinted across the sands, she was so light on her feet she might as well have been flying. Little puffs of dust erupted behind her as her legs pumped in a furious rhythm. All she could do now was put every ounce of strength she had into charging the gate. Her legs burned as she drove them for everything they were worth.

Running was normally her happy place, but the energy she felt right now was more frenetic. The fuse snapped and crackled as she ran, reminding her every moment that she held utter destruction in her hand. If she moved any faster, she would have left the earth. Her breath came in ragged gasps from her mouth, and snot flew from her nose. Not the kind of thing that was very attractive, but sometimes living required putting such vanities aside. There was only room for thought now.

Go. Go. Go.

Neema looked up at the gate and realized she wasn't going to make it, at least not with time to get away. Throwing the package was something the witch told them not even to attempt, but it wasn't like she could set that shit down in front of the gate with a cocky smile and a wave. While Khalid's archers might be able to keep the men on the walls occupied, the ones hiding above the gatehouse's fortification wouldn't be worried about arrows at all.

The men at the gate would be waiting for an idiot dumb enough to get close with hot tar or rocks. So while she swore up and down to Khalid before they started that she wouldn't dream of throwing their precious little bomb, that was exactly what Neema planned to do.

Arrows snapped past her, and she cursed under her breath. Khalid's archers better up their game, or throwing the bomb wasn't going to happen. She'd go splat in a spot between the gatehouse and the desert. What a fucking waste. The arrows *did* serve as a friendly reminder that slowing down wasn't an option, so she ran like the very hounds of the underworld were nipping at her heels.

Sliding to a stop ten feet from the gate, Neema lobbed the bomb forward as gently as she could. The dusty container hit the ground just short of the barrier, bounced once, and rolled to a stop against the wooden timbers. The fuse was still shooting off sparks, and that was all she had to see before turning and running back the other way.

"Fire!" Khalid's voice roared over the chaos.

Knowing the job was done gave Neema's legs enough energy to keep going. Running back to their forces was a much friendlier sight. It was nice to watch the arrows flying toward her enemies instead of having death staring her in the face. The archers were staggering their attacks now, not letting the men on the parapets get off any shots without significant risk of injury or death.

Neema's thundering heart slowed enough she could finally hear her breathing. It felt like the return trip to Khalid took twice as long as before, but it must have been fast because the explosion hadn't happened yet. Her breaths were still coming in great heaves as she turned to see if the bomb would explode the way the witch promised.

As she watched the gate, Neema couldn't help but think this was what a fish must feel like when it was plucked from the river. Air was a luxury. Her vision swam with little black spots. Then the world turned brilliant orange.

The thunderclap rolled over the resistance like a wave, sending several men staggering backward as though someone punched them. When the witch talked about an explosion to remember, Neema had been pretty sure she was full of shit. If anything, the blast was much bigger than she'd ever dreamed it could be. If the bomb had gone off when she threw it the resistance would have been down one freedom fighter.

The stone blocks and wooden boards that made up the gate were raining down from the heavens like the gods had decided regular rain was too bloody boring to be good fun. The men on the parapets were all screaming, but none of them were shooting. Now was the time to move. Neema looked at Khalid and nodded. This wasn't supposed to be a prolonged fight. They needed to get the supplies and get the hell out of there.

"Charge!" Khalid roared at the top of his lugs.

Sometimes Neema wondered how he could even speak after a battle, not that she was doing any less.

Neema felt the scream tearing from her lips as she charged forward with the rest of the resistance. She moved slower now, making sure that when she reached the destruction at the gates, she still had enough energy to fight. That didn't mean she couldn't enjoy the moment with everyone else, even if she let them through the entrance first.

The resistance stormed through the new opening. Two groups of men went for the food and water while another headed for the armory. Their carts were making their way inside now, and as soon as they were loaded, they'd head back into the sands of the desert, bound for home.

All the rest had to do was buy them some time.

Neema flowed through the courtyard, taking lives as easily as the summer heat. Her blade rose and fell with impunity. Anyone inside the gates was a soldier working for Jabari, and therefore their lives were forfeit. Even fifteen years after her family was slain, revenge burned in her heart as bright as the sun. The hardest part for her was knowing when to block out the sun.

Today wasn't that day.

The tide of the battle shifted dramatically in their favor with the explosion. It felt as though the fight was firmly in their hands now, but when everything felt like it was under control, there was always one more surprise. Emerging from the fort's largest building was a man she never wanted to see. Dracon had to turn his massive shoulders sideways to fit through the door the rest of his soldiers sprinted through with ease. It was said that he'd once thrown a camel nearly twenty feet.

Neema couldn't even tip one over.

The two-handed sword on Dracon's back was as famous as the man himself. The blade was named Splitter. The tales said that the weapon got its name when the warrior had split a man in two as neatly as if he were cutting a cord of wood. She wouldn't have been surprised if the sword weighed twice as much as she did. Neema scoffed at the idea when she'd heard it the first time, but seeing the weapon in person, she believed it.

If Dracon was here, this fort was more than a supply depot.

They needed to get out of here, but someone would have to buy them the time they needed to retreat. Neema ran to Khalid's side. "Dracon is here. Signal the retreat."

"We don't have enough—" Khalid started to protest.

Neema placed a hand over his heart. "What we have will be enough. Get them out of here."

"What will you do?" Khalid watched her levelly, hoping she wasn't up to something foolish.

"What I must." Neema turned and ran toward Dracon.

Khalid watched her go. "So must we all."

"That's it! We're done here. Take what's in your arms and go," Khalid roared from behind her.

Knowing that Khalid believed in her was enough to restore most of her flagging energy. She would need all the strength she could muster to face Dracon. The big bastard was all power and rage, and she needed to be swift and light. Neema left her sword in its place and pulled her daggers free.

Light as a feather.

"Dracon!" Neema screamed, drawing the mighty warrior's attention to herself.

The large warrior stopped shouting orders, his eyes going wide at the sight of her. She pointed at the ugly bastard while thinking of all the good men and women he'd killed. "Your time has come."

Better for him to think I'm overconfident.

"The Desert Wolf. I should have known you'd be the only one dumb enough to come here." Dracon sneered across the space between them as he pulled Splitter free from the scabbard on his back.

He held the sword as easily in one hand as she did one of her daggers.

"Let us see who the gods favor today." Dracon looked down at his servant and gave him a final order before squaring his shoulders and stomping forward.

It was funny to hear him speak of gods when they all knew the Pharaoh's followers only served one of them. Vitaria's influence had consumed this land like a plague of locusts. Once there had been prosperity for anyone willing to work. Now only a few reaped the benefits of the many.

That would change.

"This is going to be fun." Neema moved.

It was interesting how time seemed to slow as the fighting started. Once she had a weapon in hand and someone to kill, everything quietly fell into place. While others were good at hunting, fishing, or building, she was good at killing. Neema had spent the last fifteen years honing her deadly craft from sunup to sundown.

There wasn't a deadlier bitch in the desert.

Dracon's sword came at her as though she was sparring with a fencer and not someone wielding a small house. Neema wouldn't have been surprised if the weapon was three feet longer than she was tall. The man wielding it had short stubby arms, but the blade gave him plenty of reach.

There was no way she could compete from a distance, and getting in close was risky business. Thankfully for her, all she had to do was keep him busy unless the opportunity for more presented itself. Taking out one of Jabari's top generals would be a huge bonus for the resistance, but getting everyone out with the supplies was more important.

So far Neema was able to stay out of reach. She was mostly dodging his attacks. While her daggers might not break if she tried to block Splitter, her arms might. Not being able to shift the weapon with her blades made this fight much harder than it needed to be.

Splitter moved through the air with so much force it left turbulence in its wake.

After rolling inside the next strike, Neema grinned. She was pretty sure she had the man's measure now, and it was time to get to work. Twisting, turning, slashing, laughing—her world was a whirl of madness and blades as she danced around the much larger man. Dracon was bleeding from several slashes now, and his exhales came out as growls of frustration.

There was a chance she might get to kill the fucker.

Neema understood why he had a fearsome reputation. On the battlefield against swaths of other heavily armored men, Dracon would have been a nightmare to fight. Against one quick woman, he wasn't quite up to the task.

Khalid's horn sounded, and she knew that meant most of their forces were clear, and he was signaling to the stragglers they would be left behind if they didn't hurry up. Neema was fully into the flow of the battle and didn't want to leave. She was sure with only a few more minutes of effort that Jabari would be short one general. It was the thing they needed to boost morale after a long summer of getting their asses kicked.

Everyone loved a big win.

It was easy enough to slip inside Dracon's guard. That should have told her all she needed to know about what would happen next, but Neema missed the signs in her haste to land a killing blow. The general twisted away from her attack at the last second, taking one of her daggers across his armored chest while the next bounced harmlessly off his shoulder.

The general reversed his grip on the sword so the tip pointed down at the ground. Instead of making a massive slash upward that Neema could have easily avoided, Dracon gently pushed the blade outward like a shield. With his strength, it didn't take much movement for the sharpened edge to tear through her armor as though it was made from tissue paper.

Neema screamed as the sword cut into her chest and shoulder. The dagger in her right hand fell to the ground as the muscles in her arm went limp. She threw her entire body backward, missing the slice she'd been expecting in the first place by a hair's breadth. As soon as her back hit the ground, she flipped back to her feet and dove through the bastard's legs. That was about all of the acrobatics she had left in her. After running for the gate and getting wounded, she was out of energy.

If this was her time to go, she would meet Eternia with a smile on her face. Her left arm still worked, and that was all she needed to land a blow to his inner thigh. Neema twisted the blade while screaming in defiance. Her entire life had been like this, one insane fight to the next. Her existence always teetered on the verge of falling apart. Most people were scared of death. For her, it would be a vacation.

Dracon took the blow to his leg without flinching. He brought his foot up, smashing his armored boot into her chest. Now that she was on her back again, Splitter rose high into the air, ready to add another victim to its epic legend.

"So dies the little wolf." The general's shoulders muscles tensed as he swung.

The sword came down in a violent arc, but right before it hit the blade changed direction. An arrow bounced off Splitter's tip. Or did Dracon change his attack mid-swing to cut the bolt in half? Either way, the results were the same. It spared her life, and Dracon lost an eye. It took her a moment to put it all together, but when he deflected the arrow, it must have bounced into his face.

Rotten luck for Dracon and the chance she needed to escape.

The general was lying on his back and screaming in pain as his men dragged him away.

A hand clamped down on her shoulder, making her jump.

"Time to go." Khalid helped her to her feet. Then they were running.

The battle was over, and the day was theirs.

Hopefully, they had someone at camp who could tend to her arm. The last thing she wanted to do was become a bean counter for the resistance. There wasn't exactly an army of one-armed warriors out there making their names as heroes, and she refused to be anything but.

Neema pushed the thoughts of her arm away. That was a worry for another day. Today they were victorious, and they should celebrate. When they made it back to the oasis, she would find a jug of wine and a beautiful lady to ease her pain.

The world didn't have to be perfect when you could find joy in the little moments.

CHAPTER TWENTY-FOUR

Why did every day start with a morning?

Couldn't they as a society just make a law that it was illegal to leave your house before ten a.m. and to work past five at night? Tim laughed to himself for making a big deal out of mornings when he never had to wake up early unless ShadowLily told him he absolutely had to. Thankfully for their relationship's sake, she liked having the mornings to do whatever she wanted while he slept in as long as possible.

Today was one of those rare exceptions to him being tired until he drank three cups of coffee. It might as well have been Christmas morning as far as Tim was concerned. They were heading back to Tristholm this morning, and from there it was a hop, skip, and a portal ride to Elmore's Hallow and the desert beyond.

Tim wasn't sure exactly what they would find there, but he knew it would be different. Games tended to have different continents or maps. Shit, sometimes even zones on the same map felt totally different because of the monster a player faced. One second, players would be in the frozen highlands, and the next, a player wished they didn't see snow again for the rest of their lives.

That was how the developers kept them moving.

The desert certainly would provide the Blue Dagger Society with a change of view, and Cassie would be happy she wouldn't have to deal with the cold for a while. For Tim, it was wondering how their story would continue to unfold. Plus there was a chance there could be pyramids, and who didn't love the thought of looking for treasure in an actual tomb? Tim was kind of a sucker for all things Egypt.

What kind of person didn't like the thrill of adventure that came with a treasure hunt? Saving the old monuments to preserve a nation's history or stopping a mummy from taking over the world was a job for heroes, and they were just the bunch. The desert should be a land rich in booby traps, death, and mystery.

They were going to be some of the first people in *The Etheric Coast* to see it.

Tim hopped out of bed with a little more gusto than usual. He wasn't even mad that he didn't have a cup of coffee waiting for him. The fact that he could drink all night, use Cleanse and wake up feeling refreshed was the best thing ever. Hangovers were for suckers, and he didn't like to think of himself as a person who could be taken advantage of. Not that most people had a choice. Without a healer to take away their problems, they were SOL.

Overindulgence usually carried a steep price.

His bath the day before left him feeling clean enough, so Tim used some water and a cloth to wash himself off before equipping his gear. Now that he was locked and loaded it was time to find the others and track down a cup of coffee. A human should only be required to wait so much time after waking up until being caffeinated.

Tim made it downstairs and into the dining room in a flash. He was surprised to see that it was only his team waiting for him there and not some of the important members of the farm with them.

"Brother Colton left this morning, and Shara is out praying

over the new crop," ShadowLily informed him as she walked across the room to hand him a cup of coffee.

"Ughh." Lorelei groaned from somewhere on the floor. "Try to keep it down. My world is spinning enough without noise."

Tim almost laughed at her condition, but he'd been there one too many times himself. College was a place for learning, but it was also a place to see how much a person could drink before passing out. The great students mastered the art of both partying and studying while a certain few only mastered the art of becoming seven-year seniors. Xander, his best friend and college roommate, was the perfect example of too much party, and whoever the valedictorian was probably studied a little more than they should have. On the other hand, Tim had a pretty well-rounded experience and walked out the door with the same degree as everyone else.

Tim sent Cleanse to the downed ranger with a flick of his wrist. It wasn't her fault she'd been too busy relieving some stress to find him before passing out. Tim was pretty sure if he didn't have ShadowLily and found himself in Lorelei's situation, he would have suffered the hangover for the chance at a night with two farm girls. Shit, there was probably an entire series of movies called *Double Farm Girls* that kept teenage boys busy for days at a time.

Lorelei's head popped up over the edge of the table. "I feel wonderful, thank you."

"One of the many small blessings associated with being my friend." Tim beamed before sipping his coffee.

The ranger piled food on her plate. "Now I can eat. You know, if you could bottle that spell as an elixir you'd be the richest man in the world."

Tim's brain started wondering if he could do that. He'd have to talk with JaKobi and find out if they had any knowledge on bottling spells at the Mage's College. If he could do that, it would be another revenue stream for their guild. Coffee sloshing into his cup for a top-off distracted him enough to pay attention to the others again.

"Don't even get those big wheels turning. We have other plans for today." ShadowLily pointed at the table. "Sit. Eat."

Cassie tossed her fork onto her plate and leaned back with a satisfied expression on her face. "If you eat fast enough we could be back in Tristholm by midday and in Naroosh by nightfall."

"Just let me get my grub on, and we can go." Tim smirked over at Lorelei. "My guess is the horses aren't exactly prepped for our return trip yet."

Lorelei snorted. "Give me a break. Up until five minutes ago, you would have been lucky if we were leaving before tomorrow."

Three biscuits and a container of honey disappeared in a blink. "I'll see what I can do."

"I'm pretty sure one of her guests from last night works in the stables. We might want to give her a minute." JaKobi smiled as if he were indulging in a little farm girl fantasy of his own.

Cassie gave the fire mage a look that said, your days of rubbing one out to Double D Farm Girls are over. "It'll take me at least that long to wipe that stupid grin off your big ugly face."

The wistful expression on the fire mage's face faded instantly.

Tim chuckled. "That didn't take nearly as long as you thought."

"Remind me if I'm wrong Cassie, but I believe it was you who said all the farm boys should have to walk around with their shirts off, so we could get a look at their rocking bods," ShadowLily said with a grin that implied she caught the tank being a mega-hypocrite and loved pointing it out.

"I might have said something to that effect," Cassie waffled.

JaKobi poured himself a glass of rumpleberry juice and tried not to enjoy the moment too much. "As long as this shirtless paradise goes both ways, I'm all for it."

"Totally not the same thing." Cassie looked horrified.

Tim topped off his coffee again and speared a sausage with his fork. "Why? Because you ogle them in a less-sexual way?"

"Please, that girl wants to lick champagne off their abs and take a ride on the farm boy express." ShadowLily winked at her friend. "I'm just saying that there might be a small double standard we take advantage of."

Cassie looked shocked. "I'd never sleep with someone who called sex 'riding the farm boy express.' Nothing wrong with admiring the hardware though."

"Or daydreaming about it," JaKobi prodded.

"Fine! Just try not to drool all over yourself." Cassie looked down at her plate of food.

JaKobi reached out and gently turned her head so she was looking at him. "Baby, I only drool when I'm looking at you."

"Sappy," ShadowLily quipped.

"But delivered at the right time with the right inflection." Tim was grinning from ear to ear.

JaKobi looked into Cassie's eyes, then his robes disappeared, and some rough-spun hemp pants and a flannel shirt that was open down the middle replaced them. A shovel rested on one shoulder. "Wanna ride the farm boy express?"

The tank's eyes rested somewhere between excited amusement and exasperation. She stood, and her outfit changed into a tied-off crop top and short shorts. "I do declare that I think there is a field ready for plowing."

Cassie ran for the stairs with JaKobi chasing after her at full speed.

"For the sake of my sanity, I'm going to pretend that didn't just happen." Tim blinked once and sipped his coffee.

ShadowLily smirked at him. "You didn't think it was so silly when you had the same idea last night."

Tim coughed into his fist. "Or when I lent him the shovel this morning."

"You sly dog." ShadowLily was beaming from ear to ear. "I'll have to keep my eye on you."

He pushed his plate away, stood, and stretched. "All I'm saying is that the appropriate time to break out said shovel isn't at breakfast."

"Oh, I don't know about that. You never know when it's a good time for shoveling." ShadowLily sipped her coffee as they moved out to the porch and sat on the swing.

Tim sat next to her, wondering if this wasn't the best view in all of *The Etheric Coast*. It was so easy to relax in this game. It was as if all his worries disappeared. He was surrounded by great people that liked to have fun and didn't mind poking a little harmless fun at each other along the way.

He reached out and took ShadowLily's hand in his, and they rocked on the swing together while watching the morning idle past.

———

Lorelei showed up with the horses about an hour later.

The ranger wore an ear-to-ear grin. Last night and this morning had done her a world of good. It was nice to see her happy. She walked toward the farmhouse almost as if she were floating on air with the horses trailing behind her.

Tim saw Sadie and rushed down the stairs to say hello. He rubbed her nose the way the horse liked it and leaned in to whisper in her ear, "I have a little snack for you when we get back to Tristholm. Don't tell the others."

Sadie whinnied and stomped her front hooves.

"All right." Tim reached inside his robes and pulled out one of the two apples he'd taken from inside and fed it to the horse. "You got me."

Sadie almost seemed to be laughing. If the horse could talk, she clearly would have been telling him that horses were smarter than people.

It seemed kind of rude to jump on someone's back when they

were trying to enjoy a snack, so Tim waited for Sadie to finish before he mounted.

"Back in the saddle again." Tim hoped that wasn't too corny.

Lorelei laughed. "Keep the nineties where they belong."

"It's the music of a generation," JaKobi casually replied as he and Cassie walked out in time to hear their comments. "Be happy he's not into the eighties or spandex."

"You got me there." Lorelei looked at Tim, clearly imagining him wearing a skin-tight spandex suit and trying not to giggle. "Everyone ready to go?"

When four yesses came back, Lorelei led them onto the path. They would be back in Tristholm in a few hours. Then it was through the portal and into the desert beyond. Tim was so excited he wanted to gallop back, but it would be nice to take their time so they had the energy to fight on the other side if they had to. Once they went through the portal, Tim didn't expect they'd be getting a whole lot of rest.

The trip back to Tristholm was a lazy affair.

It almost felt odd not being accosted by someone with another task the second they set out to fulfill their quest. Not that Tim was complaining. Without Jessi's little side quest, they would have missed out on a couple of levels and a whole lot of loot. When it came down to the feast or famine equation, Tim knew he wanted to land on the feast side of the fence.

Sure he could have been worried that he only had one active quest left, but why sweat it? One thing he knew about games was that whenever a player went to a new zone, they were overloaded with new quests. Then the feasting would begin anew. He wouldn't be surprised if all of them hit level twenty soon.

Probably right before getting hit with the whammy.

There tended to be a big jump in difficulty when a player

crossed certain level thresholds. The bosses either hit harder or had new mechanics. Sometimes it was getting used to new skills that took a while. One thing he knew for sure was that his class would change, and with those changes, he'd have to be flexible. It never paid to get too comfortable while leveling. Today's top skill could be in tomorrow's forgotten bin.

Normally he'd take a useless skill off his action bar, but inside *The Etheric Coast*, there weren't action bars to put your skills on. So in this case, he'd have to avoid using a skill if he didn't think it pulled its weight anymore. Everything he'd learned so far was pretty useful in the right situations but not always applicable. He doubted the developers tried to make useless skills, but for every player that thought their ability was great there was a player on the other end screaming for a nerf.

Fuck nerfs.

Tim always felt that a better solution would be to create a new baseline for the other classes with a few tiny increases than to wipe out a group of players that were happy with how things were. If players started destroying bosses, it was equally simple to fix— tweak the bosses' resistances or health to make the fights challenging again. Of course, it all sounded simple when he wasn't the one doing the work.

Or paying the bills.

When it came right down to it, whoever paid the bills called the shots. They wanted nerfs because it was more cost-effective than tweaking other classes? Then by God, there would be nerfs all around. So far he hadn't run into the heavy-handed approach in *The Etheric Coast*, and it was nice not to have to worry about what rotation would be viable from week to week.

Tristholm came into view, and he was as relieved to see the walls as he was on their first trip to the city. Not having werewolves chasing them was a bonus, but his excitement was no smaller today. It was merely a different kind.

When they reached the stables, Tim slid off his horse and made sure that Sadie didn't have a bit in her mouth before retrieving the last apple from his inventory. He rubbed her nose gently as she feasted on the tasty treat. White foam burst from the horse's mouth as she crushed the apple in her jaws like a press. It was amazing how strong a horse's jaws were—damn crocodiles of the plains.

"Next time we're back in the city, I'll bring you an apple even if I don't have to go anywhere." Tim grinned as she nudged him in the chest with her head. "Okay, okay, two apples."

Sadie whinnied in response and turned to head inside the barn.

"You made a friend there." Lorelei turned away from her horse and checked her gear to make sure it was ready for the journey ahead.

Tim didn't know if he had to check his gear. After equipping everything, he assumed it was always fine. "My parents weren't into pets. There was no chance in the world I was getting a horse, but I would have loved to have a dog."

"Maybe we can find you one, and we can take it on adventures with us," ShadowLily replied as she strolled past him.

Cassie pushed Tim toward the portal. "Worry about Fido and the horse later. Let's go do desert things."

"I'm with her." JaKobi grinned.

Tim mouthed "Traitor" at him, then reached out and touched Cassie's earlobe. "Is that honey?"

He'd never seen Cassie blush before. It looked a lot like her angry face but with a hint of embarrassment instead of the usual rage.

"Fuck off. That's not where the honey goes." She walked faster.

JaKobi looked as though he wanted to tell Tim exactly where the honey went but decided not to at the last second. With Cassie's penchant for hitting him, it was probably a good idea. Not to mention the fact that Tim didn't need to know. It wasn't that hard to make an educated guess. Anything else put images in his head he could do without ever seeing.

Tim almost started laughing again but stopped himself.

The last thing he needed was to give anyone any crap about what they did in the bedroom. If she wanted to, ShadowLily could tell some tales that he might never hear the end of once they made it out into the public. So he buttoned his lip and tried not to think about exactly where the honey went.

<h1 style="text-align:center">CHAPTER TWENTY-FIVE</h1>

Khalid knew that Neema was still bristling from their conversation.

It was a warrior's pride that made them want to take on every challenge themselves. Trying to fix the world's problems on one's own was as pure folly as waiting for snow in the desert. Even with an army of like-minded individuals, creating real change in the world was hard.

Who knew that more than him?

There was a time when he had a wife and a daughter. While he had never remarried, Khalid still had a daughter in a way. Neema might not have been his flesh and blood, but she was his daughter in every way that mattered, and she was also his partner in the resistance. Not to mention the fact she was their best warrior, devoted much of her time to others, and never backed down from a fight when the cause was righteous.

Even when the cause wasn't quite noble, Neema would rather settle a dispute with her fists than with her words. Not everyone was cut out for flashy wordsmithing. Some people led their lives by doing and showing others through their actions. No one cared as much about the resistance as she did. Neema just showed it differently.

Despite his constant teachings, her fighting style remained wild and erratic. It gave her an edge in combat, but it also made her vulnerable. There was no way to know if the arrow he'd fired at Dracon would have killed him since the giant bastard cut the thing in half.

How was that even possible?

It seemed unfair that one man could be so strong and fast at the same time, with reflexes that seemed so near god-like they couldn't be matched. Khalid had spent a summer trying to knock padded arrows out of the air like the storybook heroes, and all he ended up with was bruises. The fact Dracon had stopped one while wounded made him a formidable foe and one that probably shouldn't be faced alone.

As with problems, some fights couldn't be won alone. What they needed was a group of champions. People to take on the hardest battles so they could deploy their resources more efficiently. Of course, Neema wanted to be the one to bring those targets to their knees.

Hence the tense set of her shoulders as she rode in front of him.

It wasn't his place to tell her not to fret, that she wouldn't be stuck counting grains of wheat with the old maids at the oasis. Khalid knew her value, and it was tenfold with a sword in her hand rather than an abacus. Her talents wouldn't be wasted with a useless death, not if Eternia was right.

After the fight with Dracon, Khalid had prayed to the goddess. They had a base, they had the numbers, but outside of Neema and himself, they lacked seasoned warriors. Yes, they could train them, but that would take years, and securing supplies for their growing numbers was becoming harder with each passing sunrise. So instead of asking the goddess for more help when she had already given so much, Khalid simply asked her what she wanted him to do next.

The vision came to him in a dream.

Eternia pointed the way across the sands to a cavern. He'd heard rumors of such a place being the gateway between realms, but no one who entered the caverns was ever heard from again. It was one of those places only the foolish would enter, and yet that was where the goddess was sending them.

Eternia wasn't exactly one to explain herself, but she had also never tricked him or led him astray in any way. She either helped or didn't answer his call. Oftentimes she appeared to him when she wanted something done. So when the goddess told him to go somewhere, he went. He did it without question or hesitation. Why worry about problems that might come to pass when he already had enough worries to fill a hundred lifetimes?

They would find an answer to their immediate problems in the caverns.

"Neema, what do you see?" Khalid called to the young warrior.

As much as it pained him to say it, he was older now, and his eyesight was starting to fade. There was no shame in it. At least he didn't let his pride overwhelm his good sense when there was a resource riding in front of him with eyes sharper than any falcon.

"There is a cave up ahead." Neema sat straighter in her saddle as she went on alert. "I don't see anything else yet."

Khalid watched her as she scanned the sands around them for trouble. He on the other hand gave his horse a good rub on the neck before kicking him into a trot. There wasn't any trouble for them waiting ahead, only answers, and he was desperate to seek them.

"Race you there," he called as his horse took off past her at a gallop.

Neema urged her horse to run faster. "Cheater."

"Winners never cheat," Khalid cried as his horse tore through the desert sands like a fish through water.

Five minutes later they were standing outside of the cavern opening, grinning at each other like idiots as their horses drank from a hidden trough built into the cavern's wall. He was pretty sure Neema had won the race, but it had been a matter of inches and the best he'd done in years.

He was old and deserved a bigger head start.

Neema dunked her head in the trough right next to the horse to cool off. "By the gods, it's hot today."

"The oasis has made us soft." Khalid smiled as he dunked his head in the water. "That doesn't mean one shouldn't take what is given."

"Like these warriors of yours," Neema spat.

Khalid held his hands palm outward. "We need an edge to shift the tide. Eternia has provided it for us."

Neema turned to look at the portal. "That remains to be seen."

Blue energy filled the empty space, and a moment later the portal was active. They both pulled their bows free and waited to see what was going to come out. Khalid might have believed in the goddess with his entire heart, but he also believed in prudence. All it took was one of the other gods to take offense, and their boon could turn into a pile of camel shit in an instant.

A man in a bright red robe flew through the portal and landed on his stomach. "I said I wanted to fly, not get tossed through the portal like a piece of luggage."

"Hey, you could have flown. The only way to be sure it wouldn't work was to try it," a short woman with a bō staff across her back replied as she emerged from the portal.

Next came a woman garbed from head to toe in black leather with fearsome daggers strapped to her hips. She looked light on her feet. Not the kind of person Khalid would want to get in a tangle with unless he had help. Behind her came a man in solid black robes. The robes were an odd color choice since he was clearly a healer. The last person to step out of the electric blue light was a woman with a bow.

The bow user was the only one who spotted them. She pulled her weapon free as Khalid put his away. These weren't the kind of warriors he'd expected, but if they were good enough for Eternia, who was he to judge them differently?

"Neema, put your bow down." Khalid motioned for her to aim the weapon at the sands as he slowly walked forward.

The excitement at finding something and right when they arrived had him almost tingling with anticipation. This was what he'd been waiting for since the resistance started, the next big thing to shift the tide. If they could remove Jabari's generals, they might finally be able to take the fight to the man himself.

"Guys, we've got company." The bow user kept her weapon ready but lowered it as she assessed their threat level.

The man in the black robes glanced up, looking slightly sick. His fingers twitched through a spell, and his complexion cleared up almost instantly. "One of these days, I'm going to get through the portals without wanting to puke."

"The price you pay for fast travel." The man in the bright red snickered as he turned to watch them approach.

Khalid held up a hand in greeting. "Eternia promised that I would find the answer to my problems in this very spot, and who should appear as we approached but five brave adventurers."

There was no reason to start on the wrong foot. Khalid wouldn't force anyone to help him. That was what Jabari did. He was all about letting people make their own choices and dealing with the consequences of them. With all his heart, he hoped they agreed to work for the resistance.

Neema didn't look very impressed with their five visitors. "I'm not so sure these are the ones we're waiting for."

The one in the black robes extended his hand. "Hi, I'm Tim. This is ShadowLily, Lorelei, Cassie, and JaKobi." He pointed at each of his companions in turn.

Khalid grabbed his hand and gave it a firm shake. "Khalid, and Neema."

Cassie stepped forward. "Now that the introductions are out of the way let's get down to business."

Neema cracked a grin. "I take it back. I kinda like this one."

Khalid snorted despite himself. Of course, she'd like the impudent one. "Maybe you're right though, Neema. It wouldn't hurt to give them a task to accomplish before we bring them into the fold."

"What did you have in mind?" Neema tried not to smile. Khalid had assigned her more than a few of his special tasks, and they were never easy.

"I thought they might be the right ones to finish off Dracon." He smiled.

Killing two birds with one stone was always a bonus. If Eternia's warriors proved true, they would have new allies, and Dracon would be dead. If they weren't up to the task, they would be dead, and he was out nothing but some of his time. It was a cruel truth, as harsh as the heat of the desert.

Neema's smile turned into a frown. "Are you sure?"

"They look like they could handle it." They didn't, but Khalid needed to know what Eternia gave him to work with.

"You're the boss." Neema looked a little worried, but she wouldn't try and stop him from sending them to face one of Jabari's generals.

Khalid turned toward Tim. "I have a task for you, should you choose to accept it."

Tim gave a slight bow. "We'd be delighted to help, as long as the price is right."

"Ah, as with all things it always comes down to money." Khalid grinned and sent him the quest.

Quest Received: Taking Dracon's Head

Dracon is one of Jabari's three generals and a significant threat to the future of the resistance. Bring his head to the

point indicated on your map for a reward and further opportunities within the resistance.

Reward: Doesn't it feel good working for the little guys for a change? Sure, they have less gold, but fighting for a noble cause is half the reward. This quest starts a chain, and the reward for Step One is ten gold coins.

The young man named Tim held out his hand. "You've got a deal."

Khalid was starting to wonder if he'd given them a little more than they were ready for. Eternia had sent him a gift, and he didn't want to squander it on the first day. Their group certainly looked eager to walk into the unknown, but it wasn't his place to judge them, only to direct them as he saw fit.

Eternia would guide them to victory, or she wouldn't.

He signaled to Neema that it was time to go. Before leaving, he touched Tim on the forehead to give him the coordinates to Dracon's location. "You have three days. Don't let us down."

It looked as if the healer was about to respond, but then the one in all-leather cut him off. "We'll see you later today. We didn't come to play around."

Neema huffed as she climbed into her saddle. "I like this one too."

It was true.

These adventurers might not be from their land or share their customs, but the five of them seemed to be a decent sort. That counted for a lot in his book. The last thing he wanted to do was send them into the fight completely unprepared for the encounter's difficulty. Maybe he should give them a little tip.

"Don't take Dracon lightly." Khalid paused for a moment. "Three days." He held up three fingers, then turned and mounted his horse.

They rode out into the sands, and he couldn't help but think of how life was never what you expected it to be. He wasn't sure what they would find at the caverns, but five young adventurers from another land certainly weren't it. Eternia was never wrong, so the fighters she sent were the right ones for the job. All he had to do was have faith, and the goddess would always provide.

Faith in the desert was as hard to come by as water, but his faith was as deep as the oasis.

CHAPTER TWENTY-SIX

There sure was a lot of sand in the desert.

Tim looked out over the horizon and didn't see anything else. There wasn't a tree, or a bush, even a fucking lizard. There was only the sand and the heat. He was reconsidering his stance on the cold. A little cold seemed a lot less daunting than this never-ending heat.

Even the wind was no relief.

In fact, it only made things worse. It was like walking headfirst into a blow dryer. Any hint of moisture a person had cooling them off was gone instantly. He thought he knew about the heat, but dry heat was a different kind of monster.

"Whooohoooo!" Cassie shouted as she hit something that looked suspiciously like a beachball to JaKobi.

It turned out not everyone hated the weather.

Cassie was like a new woman. Gone was all of her heavily padded leather armor, and in their place was a tank top and shorts. Where she found the time to go shopping for a tank and shorts, he'd never know. Shopping was something he hadn't done in a while. Outside of a few initial purchases so he could blend in with the locals, Tim hadn't spent time in the markets. The benefit of wearing his big cushy robe was that no one could see what he wore underneath.

Or lack thereof.

Everyone seemed to be enjoying themselves but him so instead of wallowing in his thoughts, Tim decided to indulge in his friends' happiness. He put a big smile on his face, hit the beach ball back to Cassie, and dared the world to say he wasn't having fun.

"How much further, do you think?" JaKobi asked as he walked next to Tim.

It took Tim a second to pull up his interface, and then he laid the map over it with the location Khalid had given them. "A few more miles."

"Damn, is playtime over?" Cassie switched out of her casual clothes and back into her standard gear. "We should probably take things slow, never know what's hiding in the sand."

Lorelei frowned. "I hope there's something in the sand. Since we came out of the portal there hasn't been anything but sand. We might as well be walking in front of a green screen."

The ranger frowned at the sun on the horizon. "The only way I know we're going in the right direction is because my map says so."

"I mean there aren't even hills. It's just flat open nothingness." ShadowLily held a hand up to shade her eyes. "It's like we're in the loading program again."

Tim splashed himself with a Healing Orb to cool off for a second. "Yea, but the loading screen had perfect weather."

"Shh," Lorelei whispered. "I see something."

There was something in front of them. It wasn't much but a small dip in the sands. Down in the gully was a small fort made of stone. Not the kind of place a military man would typically build a stronghold. If this was supposed to be a hidden location, it did the job just fine, but being down in a hole with enemies up above was a recipe for disaster.

If the attackers brought a few catapults the fight would have been over before lunch.

Tim knelt, trying to keep his profile as low as possible. It would be easy for someone down below to see them silhouetted against the skyline. Whatever they were going to do, they couldn't stand here and wait to be seen.

"Do you see anything else?" Tim's eyes weren't nearly as sharp as the ranger's.

Lorelei shook her head. "The fort looks like it has two main buildings at one end and a stable at the other." A small snort escaped her before she could stop it. "All told it's not the kind of place that makes a very impressive first impression."

"I hate the 'let's test them out' easy thing," Cassie grumbled.

Tim grinned. "I don't. I love it. It's much better than the 'this boss stomps your face into a million pieces' version."

"There is always that." JaKobi spun in a slow circle and stopped to gaze down into the fort for a moment. "Why are all of you kneeling?"

Lorelei stood to her full height. "As much as I'd like to tell Cassie to drag him down into the sand with the rest of us, I still don't see anyone. I think we're safe to get closer without any issues."

"Let's do it." Tim pointed at Cassie. "You're up."

The tank moved to the front of the group. "Stay behind me, and try to keep up. Whatever you do, don't die. It'd besmirch my record, and we can't have that."

Cassie took off at a light jog, and the rest of them followed her. They weren't in their usual formation right now, but a single file line. As they got closer to the fort, Tim could make out some of the details that he hadn't been able to see before. Lorelei was right. The place was nothing special.

A building on the far left looked like a warehouse, and one closer to the center on the left side could have been housing. The horse eating hay on the right indicated their ranger was correct again, and the entire right side of the fortress was dedicated as a stable. There was no way they could learn more without going inside each of the buildings, but it looked like they wouldn't have to.

A giant of a man walked out of the central building covered from head to toe in black plate mail. The warrior didn't have a helmet on, and Tim couldn't help but wonder if it was because of his missing eye. A helmet could have blinded him completely if it slipped, making that piece of armor more of a hindrance than a boon. That or the guy knew the scar across his cheek leading to his eye only made him look ten times more intimidating.

While the armor was impressive, it was the giant bastard of a sword they were all staring at. Tim started to get the sense Khalid was a real funny guy sending them out here to die. Not exactly the introduction he'd been expecting to the new zone.

Dracon opened the gate to the fort and stepped through the giant double doors. "I'm so happy you're here. I've been so bored. It was nice of Khalid to send me a gift to keep me entertained."

"I see there's no one else here to close the gate," Cassie chided.

Dracon shrugged and favored them with a smile that would have wilted flowers. "There might have been a small issue with my last assignment. As you can see Jabari decided to station me somewhere befitting my contributions to the Pharaoh's great empire."

Jabari was a name they had heard before. The emissary sent to dissuade them from entering the desert came from Jabari. If this man also worked for him, and by proxy the Pharaoh, then killing him would put them firmly on the bad side of the people in charge of this land. Was that something they wanted to do?

Life was always easier when you worked for the winners.

It didn't take long for him to come to the same conclusion the rest of his group already reached. If the Pharaoh worked for Vitaria, then anyone working for him was the enemy. Khalid might not have made the best first impression, but he was clearly on the right side of this fight. Trust was probably hard to come by, and the Blue Dagger Society didn't mind proving they were worth it.

"I'd love to tell you that we aren't here to kill you, but we both know I'd be lying." Tim pulled his staff free and cast his buffs. "Is there any final message you have for Khalid?"

"Fuck that bastard and the lot of you." Dracon pulled his sword free and twirled the giant weapon around as if it were made out of cardboard instead of steel. "If you think I'm going to lay down and die just because you said so, then you're about as bright as the shit I just took."

Tim turned and looked over at ShadowLily. "I always thought I looked kind of smart. Do I not look smart?"

"You look very smart, honey," ShadowLily said before disappearing.

Dracon laughed. "She didn't sound very confident."

Cassie pounded her staff on the ground, the sand robbing the gesture of the dramatic effect it was supposed to have. "You sound like a dump truck of fucks."

Tim looked at JaKobi, and the fire mage mouthed, "Just go with it."

"I just checked, and my staff also works as a giant can opener, so buckle up big fella, I'm about to crack you open." Cassie roared with rage, and the fight began in earnest as she charged into the fray.

Dracon dropped into a fighting stance and prepared for the little warrior.

It was impressive the way the general moved with all his armor on. Not to mention how he sliced the giant blade around like a six-year-old with a sword full of bubbles. Tim wasn't even sure if he could lift the boss's weapon let alone swing it, but he was pretty sure Dracon could make a living in Vegas cutting VWs in half with a single strike.

Cassie wasn't nearly as impressed as Tim. The tiny tank flew at the boss with utter disregard for his size or the weapon. She smashed her staff against his armor, earning the resounding *thud* she'd been robbed of when thumping it into the sand. Dracon laughed as the blows struck his chest piece. The general ignored her attacks completely to focus on his offense.

This fight wouldn't be easy. The only part of Dracon not covered in thick, impenetrable armor was his head. Unless Cassie, Lorelei, or ShadowLily got lucky with a headshot, they were basically out of this fight. Most of their DPS would have to come from magical sources. JaKobi would have to handle the boss mostly solo unless they found a way to get creative.

Tim quickly cast Curse of Giving and Behold My Power. It was time to see if the reduced cooldown would have any real effect in battle. Not wanting to miss out on the chance to use his new spell, Tim also cast Disturbance. He wasn't sure if it did anything, but he would have to get used to working it into his rotation when it would be useful.

Surely the game wouldn't have given him the spell if there weren't enemies to use it on.

The battle was going well, but the three women were basically held at a standstill while JaKobi did the heavy lifting. There didn't seem to be a ton of healing needed right now, minus what Cassie was absorbing from the boss and the feedback from Tim's spell. Since everyone was taking damage, and Cassie wasn't getting destroyed by the boss, he switched into his Way of The River stance and fired off a Divine Light burst.

Dracon wobbled when Divine Light hit him and fell to a knee as Behold My Power rocked his world. Cassie cracked her staff off his dome, and the general roared in rage. Rising to his feet, he whipped the great sword around him in a deadly whirlwind.

They'd seen that move before, and Cassie and ShadowLily were able to scramble away from the attack without taking too much additional damage. A Healing Orb on each of them, and they were almost back to full health. Tim reapplied Curse of Giving and fired another blast of Divine Light.

While they were making a small amount of progress on the boss' health, the fight wasn't moving along at the pace he was used to. What kind of boss had impenetrable armor? That didn't seem fair considering how small his head was compared to the rest of him. Tim didn't see anything outside the fort that would be useful in cracking open the giant tin can of a man, but the general did leave the door to the fort open.

There was always a chance he was wrong, but this wasn't working, and they needed to change things up.

"Get inside the fort!" Tim screamed as loudly as he could to be heard over the loud *clanks* coming from in front of him.

Lorelei was in melee range now, her bow proving ineffective against Dracon's armored body. "Are you crazy? We don't know what's in there."

"Then go check it out. It's not like you're doing any damage out here." Tim looked at Dracon's health sitting at ninety percent and tried not to get frazzled.

Lorelei snapped, "That's cold."

"Don't worry. It's not only you." ShadowLily peeled away from the fight, grabbed Lorelei's arm, and dragged her toward the fort. "Let's go."

There had to be a way to get his armor off or something that weakened the boss so they could do more damage. Otherwise, he knew why Khalid avoided this fight. It felt like they were attacking a tank, and all they had were toothpicks instead of that cool-ass sticky bomb from *Saving Private Ryan*. Something had to give, and with nothing outside the fort and the door purposely left open, it was probably inside.

It could be a trap, but he didn't think so.

"Cassie, rotate that big boy so we can back into the fort nice and slow," Tim shouted.

Lorelei and ShadowLily had almost made it inside, and they would know soon enough if he'd been a fool or not. If they all died, all he could do was apologize and not send them into the fort the next time they tried to kill Dracon. Tim motioned to JaKobi to join him behind the tank as he kept up his relentless assault on the boss.

Tim moved behind the fire mage to give him a clear line of fire and grabbed his robe to guide him back into the fort. With a thought, he flipped his stance back into Way of the Boulder to protect Cassie before reapplying Curse of Giving to Dracon. There weren't any screams of terror coming from behind him so he didn't turn to see what was in the fort just yet. For now, he was focused on keeping Cassie alive and JaKobi from falling as they moved into position.

"Are you sure that's a good idea?" Dracon mocked them. "Haven't you ever heard the term never enter the dragon's lair?"

If the boss didn't want them inside, there was a good chance Tim was right about his assumption that they needed to get inside sooner rather than later. Hopefully, Lorelei and ShadowLily found something that would help them inside. Otherwise, the fight would continue as slowly in a different location.

No one wanted to take part in three-hour fights, and at the pace they were going it would take about that long. If they didn't move fast enough there was always the chance Dracon would hit an enrage-timer and send them all back to meet their caseworkers. Tim fired a blast of Divine Light to try and speed things along before checking Dracon's health. The boss was still at eighty-seven percent.

His armor must provide some pretty superior magical protection as well as stopping nearly all their physical attacks.

The self-proclaimed dragon felt a little more like a raid boss right now than one made for a group of five players. Tim would have suspected they stumbled into a fight above their level if Khalid didn't send them directly into it. The general's damage output also wasn't off the charts, so they were probably in the right place. They merely needed to figure out the trick. It had to be inside the fort so the group was right where they were supposed to be.

"We found what you were looking for," Lorelei called from somewhere high above them.

Tim turned to look at where she was and felt a huge grin form on his face. *They found the trick all right.* Lorelei and ShadowLily were sitting in large ballistae mounted inside the fort's walls and pointed down at the gate. The large crossbow-like weapons nestled into small stone-covered alcoves, explaining why they hadn't seen them from outside the fort.

Cassie took a nasty hit from Dracon's sword, and Tim fired a Healing Orb to get her health moving back in the right direction. A couple more hits like that and this fight would quickly shift in the general's favor.

Tim waved his hands in the air. "What are you waiting for?"

"Fire in the hole!" Lorelei screamed as she fired the first giant weapon.

A huge bolt shot out of the ballista and slammed into Dracon's arm. A second bolt hit his other arm a split-second later. The boss let out a cry of rage as he fought against the shafts that penetrated the plates on his arms. That was when Tim noticed the chains dangling from the backs of the bolts.

The chains held Dracon in place, but that wouldn't do them a whole lot of good. The boss could still wiggle around enough to defend himself from their attacks aimed at his head. Tim looked around, trying to think of what they were missing because outside of hitting pause, not a lot else was fucking happening.

He sent another burst of healing at Cassie and racked his brain for the answer to their problem. It was so simple he could have kicked himself for not thinking of it sooner. If there were chains, there was a way to pull the bolts back to the bow. This fort wasn't big enough for teams of men to turn giant cranks so there was probably a magical solution.

He merely had to find it.

Along the back wall between the two buildings on the left was a lever. Tim would have ignored it as unimportant, but it was almost dead center between the ballistae. It might not mean anything, but it could also be the solution they were looking for. With Dracon still tied up with Cassie, he decided the best way to find out was by pulling the damn thing and praying for the best.

He sprinted across the stone courtyard and lunged for the lever.

Dracon screamed in rage as the armor on his arms ripped away. The chains rattled as they pulled the bolts back toward the ballistae, and the general's armored plating fell to the ground as the bolts clattered up the fortress walls.

The attack exposed the boss' arms, and that put them in a better spot than they started the fight in, but it was still far from ideal. To do some serious damage, they needed to find a way to get Dracon's breastplate off. The real question they needed to answer next was, did they have to try and pry his legs off first, or could they go straight for the kill shot?

It would be just the kind of trick developers would use to thwart the eager beavers. Taking a shot at the wrong section would be a waste and maybe even trigger a special attack from the boss. It didn't feel worth the risk, when if they continued at their same pace the fight was well in hand. They were in a new zone facing new challenges. Tim's vote was on playing it safe.

"Do the legs next!" Tim shouted up to the women on the ballistae.

Lorelei wore a cocky expression that said, *why can't my bow be this big as this one* as she scanned the courtyard. "We have a one-minute cooldown on these things."

Fuck.

"Cassie, you're going to have to keep him busy," Tim called as he sent out his next round of healing.

The tank rolled out of Dracon's next attack and looked back at

Tim with an expression that would have made JaKobi cringe. "What do you think I've been doing?"

She had a fair point, and the last thing he needed to do was distract her. Dodging Dracon's massive sword would have been hard enough without someone yammering in her ear all the time. JaKobi was still doing his part to bring down the boss's health so there weren't any further instructions he needed to give.

Tim drew a deep breath and tried to relax.

Their fight against the boss was going fine right now. All Tim had to do was keep Cassie's health topped off and wait for Behold My Power to be castable again. He stayed put where he was by the lever knowing he'd have to pull it at least one more time. A devil sat on his shoulder shouting for him to do more DPS, but the practical part of his brain told him to save his mana in case all hell broke loose, or the boss was out of his armor and ready for a solid beating.

"Ten seconds," Lorelei shouted from above.

Tim looked at the ballistae and back at the tank. With her in the way and being so short that she came up to Dracon's codpiece, it wouldn't be an easy shot for either of the women. While he was pretty sure both of them were talented enough to make it, why risk it?

"Cassie, get above his legs!" Tim hoped he gave her enough time to jump or roll out of the way.

Dracon heard Tim's warning shout and changed tactics, trying to crowd Cassie so she couldn't get enough clearance to jump clear. Every time Cassie tried to dodge to the side or roll away, the general stayed damn near locked to her. He knew where the weapons that stripped his armor away were located and was doing his best to make it impossible for them to take the next shot. If the boss wasn't going to play nice, then Cassie would have to get creative.

Tim wondered if she'd go up or under.

Cassie feinted to the side as though making a run for it, then cut back and charged straight for the boss. Tim felt his chest tighten as she flipped over Dracon's sword as if she was entering *The Matrix* and used her staff like a pole vaulter to flip over his head. She landed as nimbly as a cat on the general's other side with a big shit-eating grin on her face.

Cassie *thunked* Dracon on the head, forcing him to turn and face her and exposing his back to the ballistae behind. "Objects in the mirror are closer than they appear, asshole."

JaKobi turned to look at Tim as the ballistae fired. "She's trying out some new things."

"It would have been perfect if there was a mirror involved in the fight." Tim was trying not to laugh as the large arrows pierced the boss' leg armor.

Cassie walked casually around the pinned boss, then marched toward Tim. "Did you see that shit I just did?" She used her fingers to mimic someone running and jumping on the other hand. "It was fucking incredible. I didn't have time to come up with the perfect line while I was bouncing all around dodging a sword bigger than me. Okay?"

"What would you have said?" JaKobi grinned as he looked at Tim. "I would have gone with 'let me introduce you to my little friend.'"

ShadowLily shouted down at them, "That's weaksauce."

"Pull the damn lever," Lorelei screamed. "We can debate the validity of her one-liners after we kill this guy."

Cassie stomped her foot. "So?"

He had to think for a second, and it wasn't that great a line. It wasn't the kind of thing that would have passed muster if he'd had more time to think about it, but for having to come up with something on the spot with an angry tank in his face, Tim had to admit it wasn't half-bad. "Batter up?"

"Better, but not quite up to your standards." ShadowLily laughed from above. "You better pull the lever before Lorelei comes down there and does it for you."

Tim pulled the lever.

As before, the chains pulled the large bolts back to the ballistae, and the armor on Dracon's legs was gone. Now the warrior kind of looked like one of the Bowser bosses straight out of *Mario Brothers*. The hulking black armor pieces still covered his chest and groin area, but his arms and legs looked smaller because they were no longer carrying the extra mass.

Lorelei looked at something on her ballista and called down to the group. "Two-minute cooldown this time."

Cassie giggled. "You're telling me we have to look at turtle boy for two whole minutes? I might not be able to contain myself."

Dracon let out a roar that shook the fort's walls and stripped off his chest piece. He threw it off to the side and glared daggers at the tank. "You dare to mock me? Let me show you what The Dragon of the Desert is capable of."

The boss' skin took on a slightly red sheen, and Tim instantly knew he was enraged. There was no more time to waste. They needed to bring the general down now. "Hit him with everything you've got!"

It wasn't often in a fight where the boss hit the enrage timer at seventy-five percent health. Not unless a bunch of people died or the group completely missed a mechanic. He didn't think they missed anything as big as an actual mechanic, but maybe there was something he could do that no one else in his party could.

Tim cast Disturbance.

The red glow around Dracon stopped increasing in strength, but it didn't go away. He wasn't sure if Disturbance stopped the General's transformation or if it was something else, but for now, he wasn't getting any stronger. This was it, crunch time. They were about to find out who had the mojo over the last three-quarters of Dracon's health.

Tim topped off Cassie's HP as he watched the tank take control of the fight. Control might have been too kind of a word. She wasn't exactly dominating the situation, but she kept up with enough of Dracon's attacks that Tim wouldn't be overwhelmed by his healing duties.

The boss' health was dropping quickly now that his armor was gone, but they had a shit ton of it to burn through. Tim looked at his mana and back at the general's health. If they were going to win this fight, they needed to go faster. With a quick thought, Tim reapplied his Curse of Giving and cast Divine Light again before turning to keep up with the heals.

ShadowLily entered the fight again with a backstab that seemed to stun Dracon. Lorelei didn't hesitate to take advantage of the opportunity to fill the slow-moving boss with arrows. His health was down to seventeen percent now and falling quickly.

Dracon used his sword to create room and leapt backward so his back was to the wall. Tim thought he was moving into a better position so they couldn't surround him, but he was wrong. The general lifted his sword above his head and slammed the blade into the stones of the courtyard so hard they shattered.

"Shockwave!" Tim didn't know if he was right or if there would be an earthquake, but he knew they had to get away.

There wasn't anything to jump on as the power from Dracon's sword rippled forward, shattering the stones as the energy came toward them. Then the power washed over the group like the shockwave from a bomb, knocked all of them to the ground, and stunned them in place for a second.

ShadowLily was the first back on her feet, and she paid for that honor by taking one of Dracon's massive shoulders to the gut. She flew through the air like a stuffed animal tossed aside by a child in the fits of an epic tantrum. The assassin crashed into the wall twenty feet behind them and went down in a heap.

Tim rushed toward ShadowLily's side, only stopping to heal Lorelei from a dagger wound to the gut.

When had Dracon started throwing daggers?

JaKobi was up now and doing damage. He was trying to draw the boss off the rest of them while Cassic got into position. Their tank had been the closest to the shockwave and was only now climbing back to her feet. Tim cast Cleanse on her, but it didn't seem to have any effect.

Dracon didn't seem too bothered by JaKobi's efforts, not when the general saw the chance to take one of them to the underworld with him. Cassie still looked a little wobbly as the boss shifted direction and ran toward her. Tim didn't have many immediate options, but he might be able to buy her a few seconds by casting Snare.

The spell made Dracon stumble for a step, and that was enough time for Tim to cast Healing Orb on Lorelei and toss a microburst of Healing Storm into the air. Seeing people's health pools moving in the right direction again made him feel good, but the ten percent left on the boss' health meter had him worried.

They needed a bigger push, but could he risk it?

Tim cast Curse of Giving and Behold My Power. Outside of using all his mana to keep healing, his contributions to the fight were pretty much over. He knew who needed to end this fight and had a good idea for signaling him to take drastic action.

"Fire it up! Fire it up!" Tim chanted as though he was one of the criminals from Devil's Night in *The Crow*.

JaKobi was putting everything he had into ending this fight. The fire mage knew what was at stake and used every spell in his arsenal to find the right combo that would finally end Dracon. The boss' health pool was up to the task, and JaKobi's violent efforts weren't going to be enough to save Cassie's life.

With five percent of his health left, Dracon's sword slammed into Cassie's stomach like a rifle round fired from close range. Splitter's tip ripped out through Cassie's back in a shower of blood and guts that would have made George Romero blush.

Tim hit all of his "oh shit" buttons at once. They were so low-level he didn't have anything that was an instant cure for such a devastating blow, but he could fire off his heals repeatedly to try and keep up with the intense damage.

Cassie's life hung in the balance as Behold My Power took effect. Dracon dropped to the ground dead, but that only increased Tim's problems. The boss swirled away in beautiful golden motes, and so did his sword. It left Cassie with a gaping hole in her midsection that Tim was ill-equipped to handle.

JaKobi knelt next to Cassie, grabbing her hand and clutching it tightly. "Fight it, baby. Tim's going to heal you right up."

His mana bordered on nonexistent, but they were out of combat now so it was also recovering at a much faster rate. His every thought, every movement went into keeping her alive. The skin on her belly started knitting together, and Tim placed his hands on it, pushing every last ounce of his energy into the wound.

Cassie gasped, and her body went limp.

Everyone looked at each other, but no one said a thing. Was she dead? Tim looked down at his bloody hands still pressed against her stomach and felt it move. Then it started to shake as laughter bubbled up from the tank's lips.

"If you wanted to feel me up there are better ways to do it." Cassie kept laughing.

Tim pulled his hands from her stomach and looked over at ShadowLily with an "I'd never" expression.

"How's that for a one-liner, bitch?" Cassie wheezed out between giggles.

Tim felt his heart start beating again. "That was pretty good."

CHAPTER TWENTY-SEVEN

They'd defeated the boss, but how would they get his head?

Tim looked at where the body used to be, and there was a golden chest waiting for them. Would Khalid take their word for it that they killed Dracon, or would he send them on another test? He wasn't exactly sure how they would come to terms on the kill, but Tim knew they would find a way to work it out.

The boss was dead, they killed him, job done.

Cassie's drying blood still covered his hands. So when the tank gave him a questioning look, silently asking if he wanted to loot the chest first, all he could do was shrug. "Be my guest."

"Almost getting split in half certainly has its privileges." Cassie swaggered up to the chest.

Lorelei watched her go. "When I saw that sword tear through her, I thought she was dead for sure."

ShadowLily put an arm around the ranger and gave her a gentle squeeze. "I think we all did."

"If it happened to anyone but us I would have said it was badass. As it stands, I almost had a heart attack." JaKobi kept his eyes locked on Cassie. "I know she'd come back to life, but it still feels pretty real."

Cassie grunted. "You guys act as if I didn't have that big bastard right where I wanted him all along."

The tank reached out and laid her hand on the chest. "Leather Pants of the Wounded Bear." Cassie frowned. "I'm not a fucking Bear. Cheesehead for life."

Tim gagged reflexively. "Only way I like my cheese is grated."

"Just be thankful we don't have the NFL in *The Etheric Coast*, or you'd have to watch your team keep getting their asses kicked." Cassie poked him in the ribs as she walked past. "Oh, and I have something else for you."

When Tim turned to find out what she was going on about, he stared at Dracon's severed head. "Where in the fuck did you get that?

"Must have given it to me when I opened the chest." Cassie thrust the head at him. "Here you go."

Tim glanced at the boss' severed head once more and made a shooing motion. "Why don't you hold onto it?"

The head disappeared, and Cassie hugged him. "Thanks for saving my ass."

A smile spread across his lips, and Tim returned the hug while trying not to get his bloody hands on her. "It's kind of my job." When she looked up at him, he gave her a quick wink that made them both laugh.

The members of his party weren't only his friends anymore. The people in the Blue Dagger Society were his family. Tim would gladly die to save any one of them, and not only because it was his job, but because he loved them all in their way. Life wouldn't be the same without any of them. At least in this world, they didn't die for good. They would always come back.

Saving a life made him number two in the loot pool, so Tim reached out and touched the chest. All he could think of as he looked at his hands was that he really wanted some water. While it was easy to clean his clothes, he couldn't do the inventory trick on his skin, and getting dried blood off sucked. Not to mention that being drenched in his friend's blood probably didn't do much for his look as a healer. It made him look more like the psycho killer from a low-budget horror film.

Item Received: Hermit's Pants for Special Guests

These pants belonged to the Holy Priest Schooler, who after saving the life of a royal, renounced his vows to the temple and decided to spend the rest of his days in seclusion. It wasn't often he wore pants, but when he did, it was only his special ones and only for certain visitors.

+2 Endurance, +2 Intelligence

Special Ability: Wearing these pants boosts your ability to have stimulating conversations with yourself.

It turned out not every magical ability was useful.

At least he'd always be entertained while wearing the pants and the stats were better than what he currently had equipped so he was pleased with the reward. Tim was also relieved to find out he didn't receive a copy of Dracon's head. It turned out Cassie was honored with that job exclusively, and he was more than okay with that.

Lorelei moved past him to claim her reward. "Recurve Bow of the Viper. The stats on this thing are amazing. I take back everything I said about the desert. I love this place."

JaKobi looked at ShadowLily and realized now wasn't the time to try and beat her streak of opening the chest last. He moved forward to claim his share of the loot. "Bracelet of the Burning Eye. Increase critical chance with fire-based spells."

"That's pretty nice." ShadowLily moved toward the chest and laid her hand on it. "Hairpin of Brutality."

Everyone watched to see if she was kidding.

A solid white hairpin appeared in ShadowLily's raven black hair. "Increase damage from slashing and stabbing. Not exactly the cutest thing but highly effective."

"Right, it'd sure be nice if we could customize our look a little. Why do the devs always think players enjoy looking like they were dressed by the colorblind at a rainbow festival?" JaKobi rattled off.

Tim chuckled. Anyone who played any of the older online games felt the pain of not having a customizations tab. When the best pieces of gear came from different sources, people's characters often ended up looking quite ridiculous. While *The Etheric Coast* didn't have a customizations tab, he didn't see anyone getting anything out of place yet. Plus, all the gear they were getting now would probably only be around for a few levels at most, then it would be replaced by something better.

"Don't be such a snob. Put on your new shinies, and let's get out of here." Tim moved toward the stables and noted they were full of horses. "At least we have a ride to the meeting spot."

Cassie looked down at her bloody midriff and to the trough of water outside the stables. "And some water to clean up with."

Lorelei followed them. "I'll get the horses ready. Hopefully, wherever we're going has a pool."

"I'd be down with that. Or a beach. Beers by the water sound fantastic." JaKobi grinned. "When do we get to take a vacation?"

"When you've earned it," Tim grumbled, playing the hardass.

ShadowLily wrapped an arm around JaKobi's waist and dragged him toward the stables. "Which will be never, so I hope you enjoy what you do."

"Damn, that was cold." Tim couldn't keep from cracking up. "You can vacation whenever you want, as long as Cassie approves it first."

JaKobi pouted. "I'm a strong independent man. I can make decisions on my own."

"Let me know how well that works out for you." Tim dipped his hands into the trough and started washing the blood off.

"I'll have you know Cassie respects me." JaKobi sounded appalled that anyone would suspect otherwise.

"I respect that ass," Cassie shouted back.

JaKobi turned red and whispered to Tim, "I think she meant mind, my sexy mind."

"I'm sure she did." Tim snickered.

Khalid's meeting place turned out to be a cluster of tents in the middle of nowhere.

While Cassie loved the change in weather, she wasn't a big fan of the relentless nothingness of the desert. At least there were trees and animals in the forest. Out here, there was nothing but sand.

Sand was great at the beach or when you had access to a shower. Riding out in the endless ocean of silty grains she had neither of those things. Right now she would have given up her quest reward for an ice-cold beer. Fuck, an ice-cold anything. The only good news was that she couldn't get any dirtier than she was now. It would take her a year to get all the damn sand out of her hair.

At least it wasn't cold.

The cold was her nemesis. Cassie hated how it dried out her skin, and her nipples were always getting chafed. If she had to wear more than two layers of clothes, she didn't want to go out. That was why she was a West Coast girl. She could cheer on the Packers from the warmth of her covered patio. So while she was a little grumpy at the sand coating her arms, she realized the alternative could be worse.

The icy wasteland of Naroosh.

So while she hated being covered in grit, with enough sand in her ears to start an ant farm, Cassie decided bitching about the alternative was worse, and it was time to start counting her blessings. She found a man she really liked. Sure, JaKobi wasn't the type of guy she'd normally go for, but those guys always ended up being assholes so she took a shot in the dark.

Best decision I ever made.

Her little ball of fire was a quirky guy. JaKobi liked reading over movies, but he still watched a lot of them. He preferred a night in over a night out on the town, and his taste in music left a lot to be desired. Still, there was something about him that made her feel special. Cassie knew that he'd never hurt her because when it came right down to it, he cared more about her than he did about himself.

She was starting to feel the same way.

Movement from inside the tent cluster's center brought her attention back into the moment, and Cassie scanned the area for threats. Nothing jumped out as being dangerous. The tents were arranged in a tight semicircle to block the wind. Sitting in front of the tents playing a game with stones and dice at a small table was Khalid and a group of warriors.

One of the men looked up after what must have been a shitty toss of the dice and shouted as he spotted their group. He stood and reached for a weapon leaning against the tent behind him when Khalid reached out and grabbed his arm. She couldn't hear what the older man said to the warrior, but he sat without his sword.

Khalid must have known they were approaching although he kept playing the game, never once looking in their direction. He was a cagey bastard, the kind of person it paid to keep an eye on. Not everyone could master the trick of appearing to be less than they were, but he'd done it so well she almost missed it.

Not trusting the casual display, she scanned the sands around them with a more scrutinizing eye and found two hidden warriors. *Nope, it was three.* The last guy was pretty decent at staying hidden, but she could make out the whites of his eyes as he laid under a sand-covered tarp.

"Not to alarm you, but we're basically surrounded," Cassie whispered to Tim.

The healer and leader of their little group didn't look worried, which was odd for him. Tim always thought three steps ahead, and while it made him the butt of a few of their jokes, it also saved their asses. If he wasn't worried, there probably wasn't anything to worry about.

"Not much we can do about it now." Tim kept a smile on his face as he watched Khalid. "Lorelei is keeping an eye on things."

Cassie wasn't exactly sure how to play this situation. She wasn't the kind of girl to hide behind flowery words. She wanted to know the truth and hear it always. Being honest wasn't the kind of atti-tude that got someone ahead in many situations, but it was who she was. If people didn't like her, then they could fuck right the fuck off.

"How do you want to play this?" Cassie wanted to know when she should pull out the head and wave it around.

Tim's gaze left Khalid for a moment to look her directly in the eyes. "Shock and awe."

"I can do that." Cassie tried to hide her smile.

She might be little, but she packed a hell of a punch in that tiny package. Shock and awe was kind of her specialty. Not to mention Khalid had been a little rude to them earlier, so she would enjoy rubbing this kill in his face. He gave them three days, and they'd finished in one. Less than one really, considering they didn't start until well after mid-day and spent thirty times as long traveling between destinations as they did fighting.

Wiping the cocky grins off his men's faces would feel nice. They obviously hadn't been able to beat Dracon on their own. The Blue Dagger Society had handled their problem so quickly their heads were going to spin. One would have expected the people solving your problems would be treated with respect, but so far the warriors appeared to be okay with slightly hostile indifference.

"Did you find the task so unappealing you gave up already?" Khalid sat back with a knowing smile.

The men around him laughed as if he'd told the funniest joke in the world.

Cassie pulled the head from her inventory and tossed it on the table. Dracon's decapitated head plowed through their game, tipping over cups of wine before stopping in front of Khalid with his one remaining eye staring accusingly. The general seemed to be saying, do you see what they did to me?

"Truth be told, he wasn't much of a challenge," Cassie lied through her teeth. "I'd think about adopting a more respectful tone before the same thing happens to you."

Laughter rumbled from Khalid's belly as his warriors bristled around him. "Fair enough, and as for my respect, you've earned it."

Khalid stood, plucked Dracon's head from the table, and tossed it out into the sands. "It will take a few moments for my men to pack up. Then we ride."

"Where are we going?" Tim sounded more excited than worried.

Wiggling his finger back and forth, Khalid grinned like a merchant about to score the deal of the century. "To the home of the resistance. There are many things we need to discuss."

"Is Neema going to be there?" Lorelei asked in a hopeful tone.

Khalid appraised the ranger with a knowing eye. "She will join us for our planning session."

The warriors were already busy breaking down the tents, putting out the cooking fire, and readying the horses. They worked together like a well-oiled machine. It was amazing to see what a group of people could accomplish when they worked together as a single unit with a united focus. They'd broken down the camp and loaded their horses in a matter of minutes.

The wind would blow the sand over this spot, and within hours it would be like they were never there.

Khalid mounted his horse and motioned for their group to join him at the front. "I will send my men ahead with word of our impending arrival. I think when we reach our home, you will be pleasantly surprised."

"I'd settle for a bath and no more surprises," Cassie grumbled as they started to move.

Khalid looked her over and seemed to be pleased with what he saw. "Neema is much like you. The sand grates on her as if it were an enemy nipping at her heels."

"Well then, she probably knows the best way to get the fucking stuff off. I hate being covered in dirt with a passion." Cassie brushed off her arm, but there was no hope of getting clean without a bath.

"We have a saying in the desert. 'The sands are as unstoppable as time.'" Khalid looked out over the wide-open expanse.

Cassie snorted. "I guess a little dirt on my arms is no big deal then."

"Now you see the light." Khalid's smile lit up like the setting sun. "Why worry about what can never be changed when there are already a million small things you can do to make the world a better place?"

The old warrior leaned back in his saddle. "Neema would say that I talk too much of change and hope, but I see a brighter future for all the people of our land."

"Then let us go, and talk about the future." Cassie patted herself on the back. Maybe she wasn't too bad at this politics thing after all.

They rode off into the setting sun on their way to find out what Khalid and the resistance had in store for them.

CHAPTER TWENTY-EIGHT

JaKobi ran off the edge of the building, body covered in flames. "Cannonball!"

The fire mage flew through the air and splashed down into the oasis water as everyone cheered him on. It turned out that once you were part of the crew, Khalid threw one hell of a party. It was impossible not to have fun when everyone around them was so happy.

This was the kind of welcome they'd hoped for when they came through the portal. Although, Tim wasn't sure why he expected so much. Early on in most games, the NPCs regarded players with a hefty amount of skepticism. Why wouldn't they when the other would-be heroes they'd run into never came back from their quests?

While the Blue Dagger Society earned a fair amount of fame on the coast, the desert people had no idea who they were. It wouldn't have done Khalid any good to lead just anyone back to his secret oasis. Once enough people knew about something, it wasn't exactly a secret anymore.

Dracon's death was cause for great celebration among the

people of the resistance. It seemed all of them had suffered at the hands of the warrior in one way or another. Tim watched as JaKobi and Cassie fought against Neema and Lorelei in a game of chicken and wondered how much a person had to drink before they played that game. Then he turned and saw ShadowLily silhouetted against the firelight and realized how happy he was.

Tim nursed the strong desert wine as he watched the others play for a while, then turned to find Khalid standing on his left. He tilted his glass to the warrior. "This is truly a magnificent place."

Khalid beamed with pride as he looked out on the oasis and the people gathered there. "It's one of the very few places the resistance can truly call home. The oasis was a gift from the Goddess Eternia herself in a roundabout way."

Tim looked out over the deep waters and thought about how special this place was. Having access to water made the oasis damn near priceless. Back in the real world, this location would have probably been a posh resort that cost ten thousand dollars a night, instead of a base housing an army.

Not that the resistance was big enough to be called an army. There simply weren't enough of them. They must be great fighters if Dracon was the least of their worries. That wasn't exactly an easy boss fight for them, and if this was the baseline for battles, then the next bosses they faced would be a cut above what they'd seen so far. While Tim knew a great deal about fighting single enemies, he didn't know a lot about war.

The good guys weren't the only ones to win wars, and they weren't always the ones with the best fighters. Most of the time it felt like the side with the best logistics won. Never underestimate how important it was for a soldier to be clean and well-fed. It couldn't be easy keeping an army supplied with everything they needed to keep fighting. Shit, he couldn't even keep up with buying enough socks.

How was it he always lost so many?

He almost couldn't wrap his mind around how much effort it

would take to keep an army and their families fed, clothed, and in good physical condition. Keeping the oasis afloat must have taken a large group of people to coordinate multiple tasks. It was a nightmare of a job, and one he was happy not to have.

Khalid's biggest worry might have been that he didn't have an army to worry about. Instead, he had about a thousand men and twice as many hangers-on. The family members of the resistance fighters were mostly a burden when it came to supplies, but a lot of them must have contributed in other ways. There were animals to attend to, weapons, and armor that needed repairs, but if they couldn't fight, their contribution was limited.

And expensive.

"Not many people have the courage to stand against Jabari and his forces, and for those who do, this is the best I can give them." Khalid sighed and gestured for Tim to sit. "It's a constant struggle to keep our hopes alive."

Tim wasn't sure how to respond to that. It was one thing in movies when they talked about the resistance's lack of resources and another when dealing with it yourself. He almost felt as if they were about to be a Viking raiding party pillaging the countryside for the supplies they needed before storming the capital to seize the day.

ShadowLily sipped her wine as she joined them. "Tell us what we can do to help."

The old warrior looked shocked, but a grin showed on his lips as he made the sign of Eternia over his chest and looked at the heavens. "The Goddess always provides, does she not?"

"She does have a way about her," Tim agreed with a smile of his own.

He didn't know if anyone else in his party had spoken with the goddess directly as he had, but it was always an experience. Eternia didn't show up often, but when she did, things generally changed in a big way. The fact that Khalid's faith rested with a goddess Tim already knew made him feel better about which side of the battle they'd chosen to support.

ShadowLily set her glass down. "It sounds to me like we need to come to terms."

"Terms?" Khalid feigned innocence.

"Yes." ShadowLily's eyes locked onto the older warrior's like a falcon. "What's in it for us?"

Khalid rose from his seat, the bones in his knees cracking as they took the full weight of his body. "We all have mouths to feed, is what we tend to say in these parts. Let me think about our conversation for a while, and come up with acceptable terms for your service."

Tim felt the weight of the moment as he stood and offered Khalid his hand. "I'm sure whatever you come up with will be acceptable." He ignored ShadowLily's groan. "Now tell me that you have something better to drink than this piss."

Laughter rumbled from the older warrior's belly. "I might be able to scrounge something up as long as the two of you can keep a secret."

After tossing the remaining wine in her glass out onto the sand, ShadowLily rose from where she sat and joined them. "Now, you have my attention."

Khalid produced a jug from inside his light cloak. It never dawned on Tim that the NPCs had inventories as well, but there was no way he'd hidden that big-ass jug under his arm this entire time.

I mean, the guy didn't even have any pockets.

"This is something I've been saving for a special occasion, but the moment feels right. Thank you for your assistance with Dracon." Khalid handed ShadowLily the jug of wine. "I will see you again in the morning."

"Thank you," Tim called to the old warrior as he walked away, then faced ShadowLily. "We have a private tent and a jug of wine. You know what I'm thinking?"

"That we need to find someone who can move two bathtubs into the tent so we can spend the rest of the night reading and drinking this fantastic jug of wine by candlelight?" ShadowLily winked at him.

Tim laughed. "I was going to say get fucked up and do things to each other, but I'm not knocking the bath idea."

"Maybe we can save the bath for after we accomplish the task you've set out for us." She took his hand and led him down the path to their tent.

The morning came and with it the heat.

It was one thing for it to be ninety degrees in the middle of the day, and another thing entirely to wake up and already have the heat as a constant partner. If it was this hot now, it would only get hotter. Tim needed to get a hat to keep the sun off his face, or maybe a turban.

Turbans were practical, and if Harrison Ford could pull it off, so could he.

There was at least one nice thing about the morning heat. It robbed him of his normal inclination to crawl back under the covers and sleep in. When it was cold out, Tim never wanted to get out of bed. All he wanted to do was stay curled up in the warmth forever.

He prayed for the day he could afford heated tiles, or maybe plumbing that didn't shoot out icicles for the first three minutes of the morning.

And what Tim wouldn't give for a little air conditioning.

His battle right now was one of deciding if his robe was too hot to wear for their meeting with Khalid. If he chose not to, what in the fuck was he going to wear? ShadowLily appeared as if out of nowhere and tossed a pile of clothes on their bed.

It didn't matter where they were or what they were doing. He couldn't keep his eyes off her. That was how he knew this was the real deal and not a silly infatuation. When that feeling he had every time he saw her never went away it had to mean something. It didn't matter to him if she was all dressed up for a fancy night out on the town or her armor for kicking ass. ShadowLily was always the most beautiful woman in the world to him.

Plus she always brought him presents.

"I picked these up from their supply shed." She frowned at Tim's expression. "With Neema's permission, of course. I'm an assassin, not a thief."

Tim let out a nervous laugh. "Good. For a second there, I was picturing Khalid's face when I walked into our meeting wearing stolen clothes."

"Maybe I can stop Neema from telling him first because I'd pay to see that." ShadowLily pointed at the clothes. "Put those on and get to the big tent for our meeting."

She turned and walked out of their tent. "If you hurry, there might even be coffee left."

Left, as in it might almost be gone.

Tim exited the tent a step behind her with his new clothes in place. He was a lot of things, but a guy who didn't get coffee wasn't one of them. "So what do you think of our hosts?"

"Good people with a hell of a fight on their hands." ShadowLily paused and scanned the oasis. "I don't see how we couldn't help them."

Tim thought the same thing. "And last night?"

"My dad always told me if you're good at something, never do it for free." ShadowLily looked pleased as she recalled the memory. "It sounds harsh, but he didn't mean it in a don't help your friends, family, and neighbors kind of way. What he was really saying is know your value and don't let people take advantage of you."

"Solid advice as long as you can honestly assess your value." Tim laughed, thinking about several people back in the real world who couldn't even get close to doing an honest self-assessment about whether they owned too many clothes, let alone an actual personality defect. "Most people tend to have an overinflated sense of worth."

ShadowLily laughed. "The wise man knows that he knows nothing at all."

As they walked toward the larger tent, Tim thought about the context of that quote. It wasn't that Socrates was saying that he didn't know anything. He was acknowledging that he didn't know everything. When he wanted advice on the law, he went to a lawyer. If he needed to know how to build a boat, he saw a ship-builder. In short, he was saying don't go to a politician and ask them how to build a ship.

You'd get a shitty boat.

It was the kind of thing people could do more of today. Everyone thought they were an expert on everything because they could Google it and watch a video on it. There was a huge difference between seeing someone do something and doing it yourself. If there wasn't, Tim was pretty sure he'd be a guitar-playing god. Instead, he was a video game junkie with a business degree.

When they made it inside the command tent, the smell of food hit him right away. Tim looked over the spread and had no idea what anything was, but it all smelled fantastic. At least there wasn't a giant snake that when cut open had baby snakes inside or monkey brains. Everything here looked slightly familiar, just not what he would normally eat for breakfast.

Tim gave the others a half-hearted wave as he moved away from the food and beelined for the coffee. If his favorite morning refreshment was in limited supply, he would make sure he got his fill before any of these other hooligans could snatch any of his delicious liquid away from him. Coffee was his thing. They would have to find their own way to caffeinate.

"My preccioussss." He rubbed the top of the coffee pot.

JaKobi waved him over. "Get over here, Gollum. We have things to discuss."

Cassie speared a sausage on her fork. "Khalid was telling us he has a plan."

ShadowLily grinned at the old warrior like the Cheshire cat. "And some gold."

"When the thanks of a people just aren't enough," Neema mumbled.

The assassin turned on her so fast that Tim saw Khalid reach for the grip of his sword. "Can't support myself on your well-wishes, and it's never polite to ask people to work for free."

Khalid tossed a fat pouch of coins on the table. "Gold we have, it's capability and finesse that we lack."

ShadowLily picked up the hefty sack and tossed it back to the warrior. "Then let's talk shop."

While moving toward a map hanging against one wall, Khalid pulled a knife from his belt and pointed at a spot. "I have two more targets for you to handle."

He tapped another point on the map. "Killing Jabari's remaining generals should be enough to throw the rest of his men into disarray. If you accomplish these two quests, we can move to Phase Two of the plan."

"What's Phase Two?" JaKobi asked as he tossed a small ball of flames between his hands.

Khalid slipped the dagger back into his belt and turned his full attention to the fire mage. "It's something we talk about after Phase One is complete." He noted the young man's frown and continued, "It's not that I don't trust you, but we have to be careful even here."

"Operational security. Got it." JaKobi extinguished the flames and offered his hand to the warrior. "No offense given, and none received."

"Well said." Khalid shook his hand and pulled JaKobi into a hug, clapping him warmly on the back. After he released the fire mage, he turned to face ShadowLily. "Now we bargain."

She tossed him the empty jug of wine from the night before.

"I'm sure whatever you offer will be sufficient." The assassin smiled in a way that said she'd be as happy slitting your throat as carrying out the job. "Providing that bag of gold was as big as I think it was."

"I will leave that for you to decide." Khalid placed the empty jug on the table and sent the quest information.

Tim always loved getting quest updates.

Quest Received: Slaying the Zerker

Helix the Mad was tossed into the fighting pits to die. What emerged a week later wasn't a man anymore. Jabari had enough men, but he needed a monster, and now he had one. Slay the Zerker, and save the people from his ruthless insanity.

Reward: Ten gold coins

The reward wasn't the greatest, but it was double what they were getting before coming to the desert, and the bosses would have loot. Sometimes the chance for a new piece of armor or a weapon made all the difference when deciding to accept a quest or not. That and the extra experience questing provided. Questing was always the fastest way to gain levels.

Tim was pretty sure between the experience, potential loot, and gold Khalid offered, ShadowLily would be satisfied.

Quest Received: Dancing with the Daughters

Did you really think you'd get to dance? Seriously?

The dancing daughters were named because their blades weave a tapestry of death so succinctly it almost represents a dance. A dance of death. May you find success where so many others have failed.

Reward: Ten gold coins

"I'd start with the Zerker, but you know your business." Khalid pulled a fresh jug of wine from a cabinet under the map.

Tim glanced at ShadowLily to make sure the compensation was fair enough, and she gave him a slight nod. They'd never tried to haggle on the price of a quest before, and they hadn't here either. It was interesting to know that they could. It seemed like a small difference from other games, but it made the situation much more realistic. It was almost like a choose your own adventure story. Would the player choose to squeeze the resistance for every last coin, or would they help for a smaller fee to see them succeed?

This was a whole new world, and he had to remember while this was a game, it wasn't like any other he'd ever played before. Tim had to throw all the old rules out the window. Bargaining for increased quest rewards when necessary, maybe even turning them down in certain situations could become beneficial. He would have to spend more time minding his actions outside of combat if he wanted to take things to the next level.

He accepted the quests. "If you think starting with the Zerker is the way to go, then that's what we'll do. This is your land. While in it, I humbly defer to your judgment."

Khalid handed Tim a glass of wine. "Then spend the morning relaxing. We leave this afternoon."

Neema whispered something in Khalid's ear, and he swore. He shoved the jug of wine into the woman's chest and stomped out of the tent.

"We have a small internal issue to handle, but when you're ready to leave, I will be waiting for you at the stables." Neema sipped from her glass of wine. "I'll escort you out to our staging area in the desert. It's not as nice as this, but it will give us a safe place to rest between encounters."

Neema polished off her glass of wine and exited the tent in the same direction Khalid left.

"Never a dull moment." Cassie clinked her glass against JaKobi's.

The fire mage lifted his drink in cheers and polished it off like it was a shot. "So what's the plan, boss?"

Tim didn't have to think about it for long. They would all be busy going forward so they needed to take the time off where they could. He looked at the in-game clock and decided they could all use some time to themselves. If they met at the stables by three that would give them most of the day to get to the staging area Neema mentioned.

"Everyone has the day off until three. Be at the stables right on time. No excuses, no bullshit." Tim looked around the room. "And try not to get into any trouble before then."

ShadowLily stood and started to leave. "I'm going back to bed."

"I was going to see if they had a forge, but bed sounds better." Tim took ShadowLily's hand, and they walked out of the tent together.

A moment later, he ran back into the tent and stuck his head inside the flap. "That's three! Don't be late."

"Fuck off, Dad." Lorelei winked and followed him out of the tent. "If you guys need me, I'll be at the armory or the range."

Tim thought about reminding her of the time to meet, but no one liked "that" guy. At some point, you had to trust people to do what they were supposed to, then respond to the outcome. Lorelei wasn't a flake. She'd be there at three, no questions asked. On the other side of things, he'd better send someone to find JaKobi a half-hour before the deadline just to make sure.

The fire mage was great with research but shit with time management.

ShadowLily tugged at his hand and pulled Tim toward their tent. "Stop that big brain of yours from working right now, or you'll never fall back asleep."

CHAPTER TWENTY-NINE

Tim was surprised to find out the stables were an actual set of buildings and not merely horses tied up under a hemp cloth for cover. It was funny to think that the animals had better lodging than the humans, but the tent had been oddly comfortable. It was almost like a cabin with soft walls. He wondered if it could be called a tent once so much stuff filled it.

Comfortable, soft, cozy stuff.

It seemed that even way out in the hidden oasis, there was a little luxury available. Their tent had been amazing, the food delicious, and the people welcoming. After a rough start to their life in the desert, Tim had started to feel at home here. Well, as much at home as he felt anywhere that wasn't his old room at his parents' house.

Neema waved them over as they approached. "Lorelei is in the stables right now picking out the best mounts for you."

ShadowLily reached out and pulled Neema into a quick hug, shocking the warrior. "She has a way with animals."

"People too," Tim chimed in before he could stop himself.

The assassin laughed, easing some of the awkwardness out of

his comment. "As you can see, some of our party has more charm than the others."

Lorelei walked out of the stable and tied a horse to the rail before disappearing back inside to get another one.

"Oh, I don't know. I kind of like what I've seen so far." Neema pulled her gaze away from the stable doorway with some effort. "We have a long ride ahead of us. Are you up to it?"

Tim went over to say hello to the first horse Lorelei selected. "I'd rather be able to fly there, but seeing as we don't have any flying carpets…" Tim watched her hopefully, but it didn't look like she was going to make his dreams come true. "Well then, these incredibly beautiful and strong-looking horses will be just fine."

The horse he stood next to pawed the ground with one front hoof in agreement.

"So is there anything you can tell us about this Zerker?" ShadowLily deftly changed the subject as Lorelei tied the next horse to the rail.

Neema took a moment to consider their question in earnest before responding. "He's dangerous and quick, with no self-regard for his welfare. Sadly, all of what I'm telling you is based on reputation alone. I've never seen the man fight."

"What are the fighting pits?" JaKobi asked as he and Cassie made an appearance.

The look on Neema's face said she didn't like the question but would answer it anyway. "The pits are fights held for the wealthy's enjoyment. When a slave or someone arrested by Jabari's thugs is deemed dangerous, they throw them into the pits. There is no food and no way out. Only one rule exists. Survive."

"And the Zerker survived?" Cassie asked in a hushed whisper.

Tim couldn't imagine being tossed into a pit full of cannibals to fend for himself. The strength of will it would have taken not only to fight them off but to take a bite of the forbidden meat himself was incredible. Of course, killing and eating people had probably twisted the Zerker into an insane freak. He wanted to feel sorry for what happened to the man, but all he could do was think of him as a problem that needed to be solved.

"He not only survived, but he thrived. Helix the Mad lasted for three years in the Pits of Naroosh. Ten times as long as any other fighter." Neema shook her head in disgust. "I heard Jabari lost thirty men just getting the bastard in a cage."

"That's horrific." JaKobi said the words with awe.

Neema nodded, not catching his tone. "No one knows what happened to Helix until he reemerged as Zerker. With such a ferocious monster working for Jabari, the people were too scared to challenge him."

"I'm not even going to ask about the Daughters then." Tim looked at the rest of the group, hoping they felt the same.

Neema jumped into her horse's saddle. "It's best that you don't. Their story is even worse."

"Worse than a cannibalistic pit of despair? I've gotta hear this shit." JaKobi was grinning. "Come on, tell me we can hear it." He looked at Tim with pleading eyes.

Tim tried not to laugh as he waved for JaKobi to calm down. "Let's deal with the Zerker first. Then you can ask Neema if she wants to fill us in on the details."

"Neema, don't let me down." JaKobi turned his goofy and enigmatic smile on the warrior. "I'm counting on you."

The Desert Wolf nodded her head in acquiescence. "If you take care of the Zerker, I will gladly tell you all I know about the Daughters."

"Fuck yeah!" JaKobi exclaimed as he jumped into his saddle.

ShadowLily tried not to look exasperated as she slid onto her horse as effortlessly as she would sit in a chair. "Let's get going. The desert calls to me."

"That's rather poetic of you, babe." Tim climbed into his saddle with a small struggle. "I almost feel like we should sing *Rawhide*."

Cassie found her mount. "Wrong people of the desert, dumbass."

"I know, but it's not like I know any Egyptian songs," Tim pleaded his case.

Cassie rode past him. "Then maybe singing should be off the table."

"And it's not like you have the best voice," JaKobi snarked as he joined his girlfriend at the front of the group.

Lorelei on the other hand took pity on him. "Move 'em on, head 'em up, Rawhideeeeeee!"

"Now that's what I'm talking about!" Tim grinned from ear to ear. "I'm on a mission from the goddess."

"Damn straight you are." ShadowLily pointed at the others riding out of the oasis. "Now, let's go prove it."

Eight hours later, the desert had a few sparse shrubberies.

Tim thought of all the times he bitched about having to run between cities in older games. He hated it then. It felt like such a waste of time when he wanted to be out slashing, cutting, killing. Ugh, and being a healer back then meant leveling at a snail's pace unless the player had a dedicated group. In most games today, things were much simpler.

Not in *The Etheric Coast*.

Traveling in Eternia took some time unless they were zipping through portals. Their access to the portal network made the journey between cities instantaneous, but from there they were just like everyone else. At least now that they'd made friends they had access to horses. Walking was for suckers. Plus, the long rides gave him a chance to think, and that was one of his favorite things to do.

With his new pants having a conversation with himself was easier than ever before.

He knew the others were taking the time to update their skills or work on side projects while they rode, but not all of them. Not unless flirting was considered a skill. If it was, Tim judged Lorelei to be in the master ranks already. He might not be a lesbian, but he knew when he saw the chemistry train pulling into the station. So while the others worked or tinkered and Lorelei flirted, he handled some of the business matters he'd been putting off.

Tim sent a letter to Mr. Applebottom to check on the status of their projects and to find out if he needed access to any additional funds, or if they had enough in their reserves to start any of his more eccentric ventures. When he'd done that, he sent a letter to Judy and asked if there was anything he could get her to make her life easier. The woman would be considered a saint back in the real world. It took a special kind of person to dedicate their life to others. When he got back to Promethia, maybe he could do something special for her, like buy her a new house.

No one deserved it more than Judy.

Thanks to Tim's efforts to revitalize the slums, real estate there was getting harder to come by. He'd been able to secure a large percentage of the land with Mr. Applebottom's help. Right up until they put in the market kiosk, the slums had been a buyer's market. Now people wanted in, and he was lucky enough to be in the position of deciding who got the golden tickets. It was his job to rent to businesses that would thrive.

When the merchants made money so did he.

Rent from the new buildings was coming in at a steady flow. He kept ten percent of the proceeds in his personal account and reinvested the rest into his projects. It was an aggressive strategy but one that kept him ahead of the other investors trying to profit off the work he'd accomplished by cobbling the street and refurbishing the buildings. While the money he was making was important, he was surprised by the joy he felt in helping others find success.

Sometimes all it took was a small nudge to get a person going in the right direction. A clean place to live, a safe place to sleep, and a belly full of food didn't have to be a luxury. It was amazing how much more productive people were when they didn't have to worry about the details all the time. People talked down to the poor, but some of them were the hardest-working people he knew.

His parents worked their asses off to give him a chance.

The older he got, the more he appreciated their sacrifice. The fact they didn't consider dedicating all of themselves to their children as a sacrifice said all you needed to say about how much his parents loved their children. Every choice his parents made was to make sure he and his siblings had the chance to succeed, and now in a small way, he was able to offer the same opportunity to others.

Even if they were only ones and zeros.

Tim pulled up his interface and looked around. He didn't spend nearly as much time going through the system as he should, but he knew there was a way to check his bank account remotely. He'd have to find it. A few minutes later, he found the right tab and was able to verify just how much was coming from his little ventures and why Mr. Applebottom hadn't asked him for anything additional yet. His eyes settled on the figure, and he closed them, sure he'd seen the number wrong, then drew a deep breath.

They'd been adventuring for a long time, and he hadn't needed gold for anything except for crafting materials and food, so he hardly ever looked at his stash let alone his bank account. So the shock at seeing the number of coins listed was astonishing, to say the least. The fact that this was only ten percent of his earnings and would continue to grow was an even more mind-blowing thought.

Tim looked at the number three thousand a few more times before finally believing the truth. He was rich. Shit, if the slums kept trucking along he'd probably never have to adventure again if he didn't want to. Right now he was having way too much fun to give it up, and he was dying to find out how the story would unfold.

There was no way to know the exact real-world value of the gold without going to the currency exchange, but it was probably close to sixty thousand dollars. He'd have to sell some of this off and pocket the earnings before the market devalued. The longer players played, the less currency was worth. A gold today might be worth a copper a year from now. There was no way to know if Mr. Applebottom could handle that for him too, but it was worth a shot so he sent him a quick message about what he wanted to do.

Tim had learned the importance of taking care of the people you cared about as a child. Sometimes you did that by being there, and other times you did it by helping out financially. He'd never met a person in life who didn't hit a rough patch or another from time to time. The one constant was that when a person offered to help they always did it with love. Today he was going to share some of the love with his favorite people in the world.

Tim filled out a transfer request for three hundred gold coins and sent it to each member of his party, and put an extra three hundred in the guild bank for a rainy day. He wouldn't be in the position he was in to make this kind of coin without his guild. Sometimes saying thank you didn't feel like a big enough gesture. What was the fun in being rich if you couldn't share it with the people who got you there?

"What the fuck?" JaKobi looked around in confusion. "Bossman, I think there's been a big mistake."

"Did you get the same alert I did?" Cassie looked at her boyfriend, searching for confirmation.

They whispered to each other for a moment and broke apart. "Explain," they demanded in unison.

Tim felt pretty good right now. The sun was down, and all his friends were smiling. When life was good, it paid to celebrate a little. "I had a few investments come through with my projects and thought I'd share." He gave them all a stern look. "Don't get used to it."

Who was he kidding? If the money kept coming in like it was now, he'd be happy to continue sharing it once he cashed out some additional money for his parents. Everyone in the guild worked hard to be the best at what they did. It wasn't their fault that Lady Briarthorn and the High Priest had given him a huge leg up in the game with an early quest chain. Without the generous gift, he wouldn't be in the position he was in now. It was a good spot of luck.

Or maybe it was fate.

"Probably should have saved this for after the fight. I can already see Cassie trying to decide what to buy at the auction house." JaKobi laughed when she scowled at him. "That girl really loves her shopping."

Cassie snorted. "I'm not shopping right now. You can't buy anything away from a kiosk. What I'm doing right now is called window shopping."

"Ah, the old look and don't buy trick." ShadowLily giggled. "I've never been very good at that myself."

Tim grinned from ear to ear. It was nice to see everyone happy after spending the entire afternoon and evening riding to their destination. The only person who looked slightly confused was Neema. She hadn't gotten an alert and probably thought that the heat made them all lose their damn minds.

The sparse bits of shrubbery scattered around the landscape were becoming more frequent. Tim didn't see another oasis anywhere, but there had to be some kind of water source nearby. This was the most life they'd seen in the desert outside of the oasis itself.

There were a few shapes Tim couldn't quite make out in front of them, but Neema didn't seem concerned. A few minutes later their guide stopped at a railing and dismounted from her horse. She tied her reins around the rail and moved to get something from her saddlebags.

Neema lit her torch with a spark from the flint she carried around her neck. The Desert Wolf didn't wait for them to dismount before she walked off into the darkness alone. As Tim tied his horse to the railing, several other torches lit in an ever-growing circle. Inside it was a cluster of tents and a fire pit.

It looked like a great place to catch a few winks.

"Welcome to Shangri-la." Neema held her hands out with a flourish and cracked up.

"This place might not look like much after visiting the oasis, but it puts us about halfway between our two targets. After your fight with the Zerker, you can wait out the heat of the day here before taking on the Daughters."

Neema moved toward one of the tents and tossed her stuff inside. "I'll be here when you get back. I might even have dinner ready and waiting if you don't take too long." She shrugged. "Or breakfast if you get lost on your way back."

JaKobi rubbed his back. "So straight to the next fight, huh?" He looked at the tents with a longing expression.

"I vote we take down the Zerker and get some solid Z's," Lorelei stated. "You know me. I don't like wasting time."

ShadowLily looked at Neema's tent. "No, you don't."

"Shut it," Lorelei snapped, but with a grin on her face that said, you might have busted me, but I don't care. "I can't help that I'm gifted with the ladies."

Tim felt a small chuckle escape his lips but cut it off as the two women rounded on him. He held up his hands in surrender before pointing back at the horses. "So is it Zerker time?"

Cassie decided for all of them. "Let's go get this fucker." She jumped back into the saddle and turned in the direction of the Zerker's encampment.

"Couldn't have said it better myself." Tim hopped into his saddle and followed their tank into the dark desert night.

CHAPTER THIRTY

The skulls on spikes were a nice touch.

As if the creepy wavering torchlight wasn't enough, nothing said stay the fuck off my lawn like the decapitated heads of your visitors. Not that the Zerker had a lawn. The front of his fort was a long dirty trail of blood and regrets. Anyone dumb enough to come here probably had their heads on one of the spikes, or maybe a body part hanging from the fort's wall.

Tim wasn't going to try and count the skulls. He would probably have more luck with the bodies hanging from the gates or maybe assuming it was a greater number than he'd like to think possible. His general feel of the place was, this was exactly what hell looked like. He imagined the perfect torture for the worst of the worst would be getting sent here, to be killed and consumed on repeat forever.

That was the kind of thing that would make a person reexamine their life choices.

For the people who died here, this very well might have been hell on earth, but at least they wouldn't have to repeat the experience in the afterlife. Once Tim and his friends killed the Zerker he hoped it brought some justice to their souls.

If nothing else, burning this fort to the ground when they left would improve the smell of the place. The stench of rotting flesh was bad enough, but throwing it under the giant heat lamp in the sky made it a million times worse. The buzzing flies almost drowned out the reek. Most animals had the good sense not to leave corpses around where they slept. Not even the fiercest of creatures wanted to be annoyed by flies in the middle of the night.

As they drew closer to the gates, Tim realized he could make out bite marks on some of the limbs lying in the sand. Even one or two of the heads fresh enough to have skin looked like they'd had their cheeks gnawed on. It was one thing to see something like this on the big screen, but experiencing it in person was something else.

Part of him was fascinated by movies and shows about cannibalism. It was one of the most depraved acts a human could do. Sure it looked insane when you saw it happen in a movie like *Green Inferno*, but when Hannibal did it on the TV show, there was an entirely new twist.

He made food that looked delicious.

That was the worst part of the show. The food looked so good that the viewers wanted to eat it, but also knew he made that meal out of the gardener. It was like watching *Iron Chef*. Only, the secret ingredient was people. Until it wasn't. Having dinner at Doctor Lector's was like rolling the dice.

People or animals, his guests never knew.

One thing they never showed in the movies or the shows was how people would have reacted. Imagine climbing into bed and turning on the local news for a minute only to see the man you had dinner with last week being arrested as a cannibal. How badly would that freak a person out?

What a mindfuck.

None of that psychotic finesse was on display here. The Zerker was pure animal. He took what he wanted at the time and tossed the rest away as if it was a slice of tomato that fell from his sandwich instead of a person.

Just looking around this place disgusted Tim to the point he wished he could nuke it from orbit and be done with it.

"JaKobi, any chance you're strong enough to pull a meteor down on this place?" Tim turned away from the gruesome displays left by the Zerker to look at his new best bud.

The fire mage thrust his arms into the air, then brought them down with a dramatic flourish. He looked around as though he expected a meteor to have come down and was surprised not to see one.

JaKobi looked at Tim and winked. "I was this close." He held his fingers about an inch apart. "I swear."

"I think a simple 'no' would have sufficed." Tim probably would have laughed at JaKobi's antics, but the vibe of this place had him down. "When we leave I want you to burn all of this to the ground."

JaKobi's eyes pulsed with an orange glow. "It would be my pleasure."

A scream coming from the fort made all of them turn and focus on the gates.

A woman in ripped and bloody clothes sprinted out the open door. She kept glancing over her shoulder as she raced forward.

A limping man appeared next. "Run, Fria!"

He made it three more steps before an ax slammed into his back. The man crashed to the ground, and his hands clawed at the sand as he tried to pull himself forward. Fria turned to see where he was and skidded to a halt. Before Tim could call a warning, she ran back to the wounded man.

Zerker exited the fort next with a casual swagger. It was the kind of walk that said, I'm not in any kind of a hurry because there's nowhere to go. He wasn't what Tim expected. Most of the bosses they faced were gigantic, but Zerker couldn't have been over seven feet tall. He also wasn't a walking tank like Dracon. The man was thin to the point of starvation, but thick, lean muscle covered his body.

Fria tried to drag the man with her while he screamed for her to drop him and run. The Zerker ripped his tomahawk-like ax free from the man's back with methodical precision, flipped the grip in his hand, and brought the sharp pointy end down on Fria's skull like it was a pickaxe. She dropped dead at his feet, and he pulled the weapon free with a grunt sending a shower of blood and skull across his legs.

"What in the actual fuck?" Lorelei whispered.

At the sound of her voice, the Zerker looked up and saw them for the first time. "Have you come to feed the beast?"

"Feed you deez nuts!" JaKobi grabbed himself in a way that would have made the men who filmed *Braveheart* proud.

"Crunchy, but not my favorite part." The Zerker pulled a matching hatchet free from his belt. "With you, I think I'll start with the tongue."

Cassie spat on the ground. "You want a piece of my man's sweet ass you gotta go through me."

"Little, kind of sour. Probably have to tenderize the shit out of her to get anything worth snacking on." The Zerker spoke to himself as if he forgot they were there.

Laughter bubbled from the general's lips with the insanity of an imprisoned Renfield. "No one ever comes to play anymore. I'm so tired of the screaming. It's so tiresome when all they do is beg, and all I want is a fight."

The Zerker smiled at them, revealing teeth that he'd filed to points. "You did come to play, didn't you?"

"I've heard about enough of this shit. Go and hit him with your stick." Not the most elegant command Tim had ever given to start a fight, but it would do. He made a shooing motion toward Cassie. "Go get 'em."

With just the right amount of attitude for a tank, Cassie flipped

Tim the bird and ran toward the boss. "Let's see if we can work on that oral hygiene."

Tim watched Cassie wind back as though she was going to use her bō staff as a bat. The blow was aimed right at the boss's head, but he didn't even try to move. Right before the staff would have caved in half of the Zerker's skull, the tomahawk came up and blocked the attack.

Cassie was too stunned by the sudden change in the outcome to recover, and the Zerker slashed her across the belly with his hatchet.

Who Needs a Shield was the first thing Tim cast. Yes, he needed to heal her, but the damage resistance and buff to Cassie's already outrageous dodge chance felt paramount. Next on the list was a blast of Healing Orb to take the edge off the tank's immediate needs. His opening rotation wouldn't have been complete without also casting Curse of Giving on the boss.

This fight already felt like it was spinning out of control, and it just started.

Cassie was moving at full speed now, her single staff a disadvantage against the two axes. She seemed to have found her rhythm though and was moving just enough to stay relatively damage-free. With the tank now having firm control of the boss, it was time for the DPS to get to work.

Flames washed across the Zerker's skin, and his left leg had an arrow sticking out of it. ShadowLily's appearance forced him to turn away from Cassie and deal with the assassin head-on. The daggers and axes sparked off each other with every hit. Shadow-Lily wasn't doing a single bit of damage, but the boss's back was unprotected and facing most of the group now.

Before they could take advantage of the situation, the Zerker pulled a rotting arm from the bag on his hip and tossed it on the ground at Cassie's feet. "Tasty sweet, soo good to eat," he singsonged as a buzzing sound filled the air.

A swarm of flies descended on their party.

It was more like a cloud of gas coming at them than a swarm of bugs. Gas probably would have been better than the buzzing wall of gross that surrounded them. Tim was afraid to take a breath, and he certainly had no idea where the Zerker was. Ducking his head into the arm of his robe as the flies hit, he shouted, "Bring the fire!"

He didn't look up or try and see if JaKobi was acting on his instructions. He just kept his head buried in the crook of his arm. The insects were swarming all over him now, trying to get in his ears and mouth. Tim hated every second of this but didn't have a single spell that would work against a bunch of bugs. Having a couple of flies buzz around the living room back home was enough to drive him batshit. This was the stuff of nightmares.

The swarm was the kind of thing that would create the perfect distraction before a devastating attack happened.

Tim already pulled the trigger on his only big bonus for the party's dodge chance at the beginning of the fight, so he cast Behold my Power and a round of healing orbs to help mitigate the spell's damage while he waited for JaKobi to take care of their fly problem.

"We're in business," JaKobi cried with glee. He lifted a hand and snapped his fingers.

All of the flies erupted in tiny fluffs of smoke and fell to the ground as their wings burned off. "Don't ask me how I did that shit. Just be happy it worked."

Tim turned to thank JaKobi and noticed that the boss was crouched behind his friend, waiting to pounce. His eyes must have gone wide because he watched the fire mage frown and mouth the words "not again" as the Zerker's ax rose into the air. The weapon started its descent to the back of the mage's skull when an arrow slammed into the boss's arm.

Zerker's arm didn't move a fraction of an inch as the arrow pierced it.

ShadowLily slammed into the boss like a WWE wrestler on

prime time TV. Her wild shoulder charge wasn't enough to send the boss flying, but it did move him to the side enough that the blade slammed into JaKobi's shoulder instead of his head. The mage went down in a heap, screaming in pain. Tim started healing him as Cassie tried to pick up the boss again.

The tank snapped her bō staff in half and went toe-to-toe with the Zerker's twin weapons as Tim tried to get JaKobi back on his feet.

As he healed, Tim was surprised to see that instead of looking like he wanted to run, JaKobi looked ready to fight. He'd grown into kind of a badass since they met. Back on that first day, the fire mage would have run away from just about anything. He'd never actually seen the man get angry before, and it was rather scary.

Lorelei and ShadowLily were doing their best to help Cassie, but she was taking a beating. Tim cast Healing Storm and channeled it for a moment before following it up with a round of Healing Orb. JaKobi was on his feet now and lurching forward to rejoin the fight. The fire mage needed more heals, and Tim had just enough mana to give them to him.

JaKobi's limp disappeared, and his arm went from hanging limply to casting a spell. Flames erupted over his robes as if someone had doused him in gas and lit the match, but the mage wasn't screaming. Instead, his walk evened out as he closed into melee range.

Whips of bright orange flames appeared in his hands and slashed outward with magical speed. The lashes tightened around the Zerker's arms as he howled in rage. Tim felt Behold My Power hit, and their opponent dropped to his knees. Lorelei ran forward and plunged her knife straight into the man's chest.

A black cloud of energy erupted from the Zerker, sending them all stumbling backward. Lorelei's dagger fell out of his chest, and the boss's health reset to ten percent. A gentle red light surrounded him, indicating he was enraged and his attacks would come faster and hit harder.

This burn phase was going to be intense.

JaKobi shot a blast of fire into the boss that jettisoned the mage back twenty feet. The retreat must have been intentional because his health was still full-ish. Lorelei was firing arrows as she retreated to safety. Cassie was trying desperately to get the fucker's attention, but the Zerker only had eyes for the ranger.

Stabbing him in the heart was a big mistake.

ShadowLily was behind the boss, and her throwing knives were going up his spine as neat as buttons. He didn't slow down, but his health was plummeting rapidly. The Zerker sprinted forward like a freight train of inevitability. Spittle splattered from his mouth in his insane rush to make sure he took at least one of their group with him.

Watching the boss' health wasn't doing Tim any good. They'd cut it down to five percent, but they weren't going to be fast enough. The Zerker's twin tomahawks were above his head, ready to split Lorelei open.

Tim felt helpless but then realized there was something he could do. The words to Snare tumbled from his lips. The Zerker's right foot slipped. It only slowed him for a fraction of a second, but it was enough time for Lorelei to get her bow up in some semblance of a shield. The boss' attack failed to obliterate the ranger.

The Zerker missed his chance.

Cassie slammed into the boss from behind, sending him stumbling over the ranger before he could strike again. Zerker turned with a scream of rage, tomahawks driving Cassie backward almost faster than she could move. The tank was at full health so Tim did what any healer should do in that situation. He started trying to earn his one percent share of the DPS.

Divine Light flew from Tim's staff and slammed into the boss repeatedly. He could heal the rest of the party after the fight. All that mattered right now was making sure they got out of this alive enough to need healing.

Tim's mana plummeted faster than when he channeled Healing Storm, but the damage he was doing would be enough to bring the Zerker down before he had to worry about it.

Tim couldn't see through the flames being cast by the fire mage, but he knew when the fight ended by the beautiful golden motes swirling high above the blaze. "Kill the fire."

The flames dispelled, and all that remained of the infamous boss was a glittering golden chest.

CHAPTER THIRTY-ONE

"JaKobi, why don't you go first, then get to burning." Tim wearily pushed the fire mage toward the chest.

The fights certainly felt like they were getting harder. They almost lost someone in both of their recent ones, and that hadn't happened in a while. It felt like they might have been brute-forcing a few of their encounters recently, but that luxury was rapidly disappearing. Khalid also mentioned that this was the easier of the two fights so they were going to have to up their game.

At least the next location wouldn't be covered in dead body parts. The developers tried hard not to repeat the same thing too close to one another. If body parts always covered everything, they started to lose their meaning.

"Sure thing." JaKobi rubbed his shoulder as if it still pained him as he moved toward the chest.

Tim cast a quick Healing Orb on the man, not sure if he had a phantom itch from being nearly cut in half or if he was still injured in some way. It sure felt like they were all injured after that fight.

Something about the battle had been very visceral and draining. It was the kind of fight you only wanted to do once.

"Cinch of the Wanderer." JaKobi paused as he looked over the item stats. "Bonuses in all the right places and makes it easier for me to cast on the move."

The fire mage turned in a slow circle. "I hate this place, but I love this item. Three stars."

Developers probably loved the fact there wasn't an instant feedback system after fights. If groups died repeatedly, the one-star reviews would be catastrophic. Nothing tanked someone's spirit like talking to their manager about a bad score. Tim probably would have given the encounter a four, and he hadn't even seen his share of the loot yet.

Lorelei sauntered past them and placed her hand on the chest. "Come on. It wasn't that bad."

The ranger brushed a bit of gunk off her shoulder that might have been skin. "Okay, it might be a little much, but I'm giving it five stars."

Lorelei pulled her new bow out of her inventory, and it looked as good as new. Now she also had a matching quiver. "I'll scout ahead and make sure the fort is empty before he burns it down."

"Didn't even think of that. Thank you, Lorelei." Tim walked toward the chest.

Cassie cut him off. "Uh-uh, buster. I want in on this loot parade."

Tim gave her a tiny bow. "After you, milady."

"Yes!" She did a happy dance. "I got a new bō staff."

Her happy dance turned into more of a skipping shuffle that included a bunch of vigorous hip thrusts. "Ups my defense in all kinds of ways, and watch this." Her staff broke into two parts with a chain between them and went back together as if it had always been a single staff.

"That's pretty badass, like the world's biggest nunchucks."

ShadowLily imitated Cassie's shuffle as she moved toward the chest.

"Bitch." Cassie grinned. She was too excited about her new toy to be mad at anyone.

ShadowLily placed her hand on the chest. She turned and smiled at Tim. "Hope we didn't take all the good stuff, but I'm not complaining about this new set of throwing knives."

The assassin pulled a flat obsidian blade from her bandolier, tested the balance for a moment, and let it fly. One of the skulls twenty feet away shattered into pieces. "Nice."

This was one of those moments where he was excited for everyone else and nervous to see what he would get. Sure he'd be happy with anything, but after the rest of his group got such great stuff, Tim didn't want to get Goat Herder Boots of the Shit Stained or something equally as awful. He reached out and said a prayer to Eternia as he put his hand on the chest.

Item Received: Orb of Concentration

This is an off-hand weapon.

Helix the Mad first used the Orb of Concentration to increase his ability to regenerate mana. No one knows what happened to him in the pits, but when he came out, the orb was something he used to entertain himself between slayings or feedings, mostly because he thought it was shiny.

+4 Wisdom, +5 Intelligence. The orb decreases the chance of spells being interrupted and increases mana regeneration in combat by a small amount.

Can be used in conjunction with a two-handed weapon.

It must be called Orb of Concentration because you can use it with another weapon. Not exactly an easy feat when his other weapon was a giant staff. Tim would have to try it out in their next fight and decide if using the orb was worth the extra effort. The item sure had all the intangibles he looked for, but sometimes great-looking drops fucked up the rotation.

He'd only keep using the orb if it made him better.

Lorelei walked out of the fort backward, guiding JaKobi through the doors as he continuously sprayed the interior with flames. Something about burning the place down felt right. Some evil was so vile it had to be cleansed from the earth, and this location was one of them.

"JaKobi, let's wrap it up. I've had about enough of this place," Tim shouted over the roaring fire.

ShadowLily grabbed Tim's hand and dragged him back to the horses. "Let's get out of here. I could use some cuddles."

"After what we saw here, I think we all could." Lorelei looked in their camp's direction.

Tim pulled the ranger close with his free arm. "Listen, if things don't work out with Neema, you can always hang out with us."

"I'll keep that in mind, but you might have noticed my problem isn't with getting the ladies. It's with keeping them." Lorelei watched them with a sly grin. "So don't expect company."

Cassie wrapped an arm around JaKobi's waist as they walked back to the horses. "Normally I'd say I wanted a drink, but I'm in more of a cocoa mood. I wonder if that even exists in this game."

"I'm sure we can find you something, but maybe not until we get back to civilization." JaKobi looked around, noting the fact this place was far from civilized. "The only problem with helping the little guys is that you miss out on all the perks of the city."

Tim snorted. "If this place is considered a perk, I'm good with wine over cocoa."

"Touché." JaKobi slid into his horse's saddle. "But you're picking up what I'm putting down."

ShadowLily poked JaKobi in the ribs before climbing onto her mount. "Yes, the bad guys probably have roofs and beds. Not to mention food and whores."

"I know that wistful look on your face is because you're hungry," Cassie snapped at JaKobi. "Not because of the whores."

The fire mage spurred his horse into a trot. "We ate so well last night that I wasn't dreaming of food."

"Asshole!" The tank spurred her horse forward to chase after him.

The three of them remaining behind laughed at their antics. Tim couldn't help but think that was a bold move for his friend. If she caught him before she calmed down, he was a dead man.

Neema had a surprise for them when they reached their staging area.

He hadn't expected much for dinner. Tim thought of her as a fierce warrior and not a cook, but it should have been no great surprise that people could be more than one thing.

Tim looked over the food selection as he walked closer to the fire Neema built and noticed that all of it was vegetable and fruit-based. Just the kinds of things they needed after that fight. The last thing he wanted to see right now was any kind of meat.

"Come sit. You've had a long day." Neema waved them all over to the fire. "Eat and relax, and when you finish dinner, try some of the honeyed tea."

Tim noticed the smaller pot sitting on a nest of coals off to the side. "Tea?"

"It's a luxury for us, but the honeyed tea is a gift from the goddess herself." Neema made Eternia's sign over her chest.

JaKobi looked at the container. "She actually made it herself?"

"It's an expression, dumbass." Cassie whacked JaKobi in the stomach. "Now eat your veggies and drink the tea."

Tim tried to add a little humor to the moment. Anything he could do to bail out his boy. "Okay, Mom."

"You have to drink the tea too." ShadowLily nudged him closer to the coals.

"Me?" Tim looked around like a startled rabbit. How did this become about him?

ShadowLily moved toward the pot and filled two cups. "It'd be rude not to. Our host has gone through all the trouble of making it."

Neema looked like she was about to interject when Lorelei put a finger over her lips and led her away from the others.

Shit!

Tim accepted the tea, realizing that he was out of any other viable option. He slowly raised the glass to his lips. The sweet taste of honey and lemons washed over his tongue. Despite his deep hatred of leaf water, this was pretty good. Not the kind of thing he'd ever replace coffee with, but as an after-dinner sip, well, he could probably get used to it.

Tim looked up and realized everyone was watching him. He sipped again and smacked his lips a few times. "It's not half bad."

"The look on his face when he had to drink the tea was priceless." JaKobi grinned at him. "Happy it worked out, bro."

Cassie nudged her man in the ribs. "Be nice, or I'll make you eat that." She pointed at something that looked like a cross between an octopus and kale.

Tim moved over to inspect the fruit spread. Something that caught his attention, but he couldn't make out what it was. Some kind of cantaloupe cross? The fruit had a slimy exterior with four long dangly legs, but the center was a bright orange color with seeds in the middle.

He poked it with a finger. "Definitely fruit."

In a burst of motion, Tim scooped up the slimy fruit and tossed it at JaKobi. The mage gave an unseemly squeak as he tried to dodge out of the way. Instead, the fruit hit him in the face and fell to the ground.

"Tastes like fruit punch." JaKobi motioned t Tim. "Toss me the other half." He caught it after a few bobbles and pulled Cassie toward their tent. "Come on. You have to try this."

Cassie grinned. "A woman's work is never done."

"Tell me about it." ShadowLily poured another glass of tea and handed it to Tim. "See? Tea doesn't have to be the devil."

It might not be the devil, but it certainly wasn't angelic.

The heat of the day hit faster than he expected.

Tim had kicked off half of the sheets by eight a.m., and by ten, he was sweating. He didn't know how people could live outside in such warm places. Back in the real world, he wouldn't be caught dead without an air conditioning unit. Sleep was something that required cool air and big cushy blankets.

People like to brag about modern amenities but having sewer access, air conditioning, and heating was amazing. If a person made enough money, they could keep their house set at an ideal temperature year-round. Now they even had solar panels and batteries for homes that didn't cost more than a car. More people were making the switch to clean renewable energy, and that was cool as fuck.

There was probably a magical solution to the heat issue, but he had no idea what it was. He climbed out of bed, trying not to wake ShadowLily, and used a washcloth to clean off his sweaty body. When he felt clean enough, Tim donned his robe and stepped outside. It wasn't often he was the first one awake.

Funny, all they had to do to wake him up on time was have JaKobi heat up the room.

Tim sat at the firepit. There were a few stray wisps of smoke coming off the embers, but for the most part, it had burned out while they slept. Their meal from last night was there and looked untouched. He pulled out his magic teapot and filled it with coffee grounds and water before placing it on the warm coals.

He might be in the middle of the desert, and it was easily a hundred degrees, but coffee was a way of life. Not a choice.

The smell of roasting coffee brought the others out of their tents as though it was a Folgers commercial, and they gathered around the fire waiting for the sweet roast to finish.

Neema looked at the pot. "What is that smell?"

Tim grinned. "This is how the other half lives."

"Don't let him fool you. Without sugar and cream, coffee is just bitter." Lorelei extended her cup for some and winked at Neema's frown. "It's an acquired taste is all I'm saying."

Tim filled up a mug halfway and handed it across to the warrior. She sniffed the liquid, wrinkled her nose, and tried a sip.

Neema gagged. "It's disgusting."

"A dagger to the heart!" Tim sipped from his cup, then took Neema's and dumped the liquid from hers into his mug to top it off. "On the plus side, more for me."

Neema looked like she was kicking herself for talking shit about their drink, but she didn't apologize. "Last night, you were successful in fulfilling your quest. If you turn it in now, I will tell you the story of the Daughters."

Tim rose from his seat and walked over to where the honeyed tea was. He quickly placed Neema's mug in his inventory and retrieved the clean cup. Once he filled it with honeyed tea, he handed it to her. "You're going to need your voice to tell a good story."

Tim hoped she realized this was his way of letting her know he wasn't offended by what she said about the world's most perfect beverage. When he sat, he turned in his quest.

Quest Complete: Slaying the Zerker

Let's be honest. You did *The Etheric Coast* and the people of Naroosh a great service. One of Jabari's most intimidating generals is now off the board. With each victory, the resistance claims more of the land back for the people.

Reward: Ten gold coins and increased reputation with the resistance.

Neema smiled as she tossed small bags of coins around to each member of the group. "You've lived up to your end of the bargain. Now let me live up to mine." She looked out over the fire as if recalling a memory or a dream. "The tale of the Daughters started long ago…"

Sabrina and Savine were the twin daughters of the legendary swordsmith Gerald Halvelston. He knew early on that his sons would inherit the forge and all the wealth that came with it so he promised to give his daughters a different skill set. Surely if his sons could make the swords, his daughters could use them.

Not being a man to do anything by half measures, Gerald devised a plan for his daughters' training. What he expected from them was perfection, and what he expected of himself was to get them there. What was the point in doing a thing if a person didn't put their all into it? Every task, no matter how small, had a purpose. This was as true at the forge as it was in life.

Any thug could swing a sword, but a master was a symphony of destruction.

So when it was traditionally time for the young women of their city to go to finishing school, Gerald put his plan in motion. He'd be damned if his daughters would be trained to cook and clean and dote on some man who didn't respect them. They were born to walk a different path. This swordsmith's daughters would not be women of the court or things to be shown off on men's arms. They would control their destiny.

First, they needed to train, and before they could train properly, the two girls needed to get in shape. They said a warrior was only as good as her sword. Gerald believed the sword only served to enhance the arm behind it, and so the girls trained. They needed to build strength so they lifted different sized bars of steel in the forge's front yard. Their stamina was abysmal, so he made them run three miles a day and swim to the other side of the lake and back.

His daughters were exhausted and cranky, but in Gerald's

mind, if they were tired enough to be irritable, they weren't training hard enough.

So he pushed them harder.

It wasn't long before some of the townsfolk asked after the girls. When the responses Gerald gave in town weren't good enough, they came out to the forge inquiring after the young ladies' well-being. The two young women were in fine health, but their hair had been chopped off at the shoulders, and they wore men's pants. It wasn't exactly proper, but the town could hardly afford to lose the swordsmith so when he told them where to shove their expectations for his daughters' future, they didn't say a word. His daughters were busy becoming something, not becoming something for someone else.

Summer turned to fall. Then the new year was on them.

The difference in Gerald's daughters from when they started their training was as different as the seasons. Each morning they ran a nine-mile circuit around the city, followed by three laps in the lake. It was only right for a father to be proud of his girls for working so hard, but when the girls saw his smile their spirits wilted. It was an expression that said this was the easy part, and they were about to work harder than they ever had in their lives.

The two daughters were right.

Now that they'd stripped any useless fat off their bodies and strengthened their muscles to the point Gerald knew they could handle the stress, he gave them their most challenging task yet. Building muscle was the easy part. Training it into something useful was work. Harnessing the potential of a warrior's body also had to be based on flexibility and fluidity of motion. His girls wouldn't be fighting in fancy metal plates. They had to be able to move.

Now when they finished their morning exercise, instead of lifting the heavy steel bars, his daughters worked on a series of stretches. Gerald had bartered a sword with the monks of The Etheric Mountain to gain access to their training methods, and now he passed them on to Sabrina and Savine. When the women complained that their muscles hurt in ways they never felt before, he did what any father would do.

He made them train harder.

A year had passed from when the girls should have first learned to balance a book on their heads for posture. Instead, they could now balance on a heavy beam for hours at a time, as easily on one foot as the other. Their balance was superior, and their dedication unwavering. His girls had done everything he ever asked of them, and it was time to reward them for their efforts.

Were their spirits crushed when he revealed their training blades? Maybe a little, but they were learning the why behind his madness. He didn't need to explain to them that they had to earn the right to use real steel. Gerald could see in their eyes that they understood the lessons he had been teaching them since their training started.

Nothing was ever handed to you. If you wanted something, you had to earn it.

Gerald spent the next year teaching his daughters everything he knew about basic swordsmanship. When his daughters could easily best him and all of his sons in combat, he brought in an instructor. A year later he brought in another, and the process repeated until the girls could learn nothing new from a teacher.

It was time to let them go.

While his daughters had been busy training, he'd spent the last three years painstakingly crafting them the perfect weapons. The blades were forged from the ground up with Sabrina and Savine in mind. He made the steel lighter than he would have for a man but folded it on itself hundreds of times over, making it stronger than any blade he'd ever forged. The swords were the final masterpieces of a career spent pushing the limits of what swords and magic could do.

Gerald presented the blades to his daughters, and this time their smiles weren't ones of trepidation. Together they had fought through the endless hours of training, and now they were ready to fight. He looked over the two girls, handed each of them a bag of golden coins, and told them to come back when they found what they wanted out of life, and he would support them in whatever they would do.

Together the two daughters created their fighting style. It was said they moved together so well it was like fighting a single person with two blades. Their movements were too smooth to be called anything as barbaric as swordplay. It was more like they wove a deadly tapestry of death.

It might not have been what Gerald envisioned, but he was proud of them.

So Sabrina and Savine left the safety of the smithy to find their glory.

It didn't take long for the Two Daughters to make a name for themselves as mercenaries, then bounty hunters, and finally assassins. Their father's training prepared them to fight, but not for the fallibility of men. Noble causes turned into treacherous ones, and eventually, the reason itself didn't matter, only the coin.

The daughters' names became the thing of nightmares. Don't fuck up this job or the Two Daughters will come for you. Just like any person of ill repute, Sabrina and Savine also gained a certain amount of attention and adoration. Almost all of the top assassins in the world were men, but none of them had the class, the looks, and the perfect record that the Two Daughters did.

So Jabari's scouts found them and offered them enough gold to pique their interest. Once The Daughters made it to the desert, their real work began. Jabari showered wealth upon them as they'd never seen before, but it was more than riches he gave them. He filled the role of the father they'd been missing since leaving home. He cared for them, and they protected him as if their lives meant nothing.

With the Two Daughters by his side, Jabari accomplished more in a year than he did in the previous ten. Whenever one of the outlying villages disputed the Pharaoh's taxes or wanted to cause trouble, he would offer them a choice. All-out war, or their two finest warriors against his. Then he would point at Sabrina and Savine, and the men would laugh.

They never laughed for very long.

Once his power in the kingdom was secure, he turned the Daughters loose to run his raiding parties into other realms. They brought back with them countless riches, which he used to bolster his wealth and the palace's defenses. There was always the threat of rebellion on the horizon, but Sabrina and Savine could quell any uprising.

"Now, with half the world under the Pharaoh's control, the Two Daughters are waiting for a new fight." Neema sipped her tea and looked around the circle.

The Desert Wolf shuddered as if remembering something horrible. "I saw them once, walking through the market. It was only for a few moments, but I damn near shit myself."

Standing from her spot by the fire, Neema moved to pour another glass of honeyed tea. "They didn't look like much, just two women walking in front of Jabari. But when a man came out of the crowd and started yelling, they cut through him so quickly that as his body slid apart, Jabari walked through the gap without even breaking stride."

"Fucking A," JaKobi breathed.

Tim wasn't so worried. Cassie had the perfect weapon to fight against the Daughters.

Things might not be perfect, but he wouldn't let a good story throw him off his game. If all someone needed to be dangerous was a good story, there would be many more dangerous people in the world. If the Daughters were looking for a challenge, the Blue Dagger Society would give them one.

CHAPTER THIRTY-TWO

Lorelei and Neema said their goodbyes as the others got the horses ready to go.

When the horses were ready and their gear secured, they all met back around the fire. Neema took the lead. "I have a few things to do tonight, so I might not be back here before you."

The warrior pointed at an area off to the side of the camp. "There is firewood in there if you need it, and I will be bringing food back with me. It will be something we can eat on the move. I'd like to be back to the oasis by the morning if possible."

Tim was one hundred percent on board with that. The oasis had to be twenty degrees cooler than the rest of the desert. He could have sworn when they woke up today it was already in the nineties. *The fucking nineties!* What kind of madness was this, where the lows for the day were in the nineties? In a lot of normal places, those temps would be the worst heat of the summer. If it only got hotter from there, when would it stop? One hundred, one hundred and twenty? It was pure madness.

Bitching about the weather wouldn't make him a very respectful guest. It wasn't like Neema could wave her arms in the air and turn the temperatures down for him. The weather was the weather and as unchangeable as the sun rising in the east.

"Thank you for all your help, Neema." Tim gave her a warm smile. "Our journey here wouldn't have been nearly as direct without your guidance."

Neema moved to the edge of camp and jumped into her saddle. "Take care of the Two Daughters, and I'll be in your debt."

"I like the sound of that." Lorelei grinned as she watched the warrior ride off.

Tim turned her way. "The sooner we get done, the faster you can return to your lady in waiting."

"Then let's go kill these bitches," Lorelei quipped as she walked toward the horses. "They're seriously slowing my roll."

Nothing else needed to be said. They got on their horses and rode.

Riding through the desert gave Tim time to think, and right now his mind turned to Phase Two. Whatever the hell that was. Khalid wasn't so great with sharing information yet. Tim guessed they hadn't earned enough of the man's trust to be included in other plans. Holding the resistance together couldn't be easy, and openly sharing with people they hadn't vetted would be a mistake.

Tim got it. He just didn't like it.

There was also part of him that was in awe of the man. It was a pretty big achievement to get a large group of people together and keep them together. Let alone get them to accomplish anything meaningful as a single unit. Tim had been a part of more than one guild that imploded, and it happened for all different kinds of reasons from petty to flat-out insurrection. If it was that hard to keep twenty-five people together and motivated, he had no idea how Khalid could manage to do it with thousands.

The fact the man wasn't getting pulled apart by so many demands on his time was an impressive feat.

The only thing Tim could use to compare his time management skills to Khalid's was his first year in college. There was so much going on. Sure there were classes, but then there were also clubs and groups that demanded a lot of extra time. Not to mention all the girls, beer, and a part-time job begging for more of his attention. With so many things going on it was amazing more people didn't fail out of college their first go around.

He'd quickly learned how to balance things around what mattered most. He wasn't going into debt so he could do keg stands and miss class. Tim went to school because his parents gave up everything to get him there. Flushing all their work down the toilet for a few beers seemed rather disrespectful. All he wanted to do was make them happy, and spend some time finding out what was next for himself.

Tim was a simple guy.

All he needed to have a good time was his laptop, a beer, and a really good game. Now that he was living in one, it was hard not to think of himself as the luckiest man in the world. His girlfriend was amazing. He had a group of friends that a guy couldn't live without. It was as if every single one of his fantasies had come to life.

All he needed now was a bank account with at least six zeros after the first number, and he might as well be in heaven. He'd get there one day. Having the financial security to find something he was passionate about and pursue it for the rest of his life would be amazing. It was so close to becoming a reality he could taste it.

Maybe not the millionaire thing, but Tim could probably swing becoming a debt-free college graduate relatively quickly.

Their ride into the desert was going better than yesterday's adventure, and by that, Tim simply meant that random body parts and trails of dried blood didn't cover the road to their destination. In fact, the sands almost seemed to be receding a little, making way for a more luscious environment. If the path they were on wasn't made of stone, he would have felt like they were making their way down a country lane instead of being smack dab in the middle of the desert.

Tim reminded himself of why they were there, and it wasn't to take in the sights.

"Let's buff up." Tim cast his buffs and checked his status to make sure everyone else had done the same.

JaKobi reined his horse to a stop. "Maybe we should let Lorelei go first. She might be able to sweet-talk these bitches into giving up."

"These bitches?" Cassie lifted one eyebrow and waited for an explanation.

Tim wasn't sure his friend could wiggle out of this. It was one of those unspoken rules that women could call other women bitches, but when men did, it was derogatory. The social etiquette code didn't have to make sense to him. It was just how things were. A little sheen of sweat appeared on the fire mage's forehead.

"You know, the Dementor twins," JaKobi stammered.

It wasn't a perfect gambit, but he didn't plead ignorance so much as completely ignore the situation and try to steer it in a much more JaKobi-friendly direction. Tim was pretty impressed. Not many men lived to tell the tale of how they escaped using the dreaded word, but in the end, it might not have been his retort that saved him, but simply the fact Lorelei had called them bitches first.

"Dementor Twins is acceptable." Cassie turned to look at ShadowLily. "Training them is the hardest, isn't it?"

The assassin grinned. "Just wait. It's when they start training you that's the problem."

ShadowLily took in the expression of disbelief on Cassie's face and decided to explain further. "My mom hated sports, but she watched all the games with my Dad. Eventually, she cheered louder than he did."

"That's just good loving," Tim replied. "You don't have to like the same stuff, but it's nice to recognize how much the other person enjoys their thing. Sometimes you might find happiness enjoying something new through their eyes."

ShadowLily didn't talk about her mom much. Tim had the

feeling she died, and it was one of those things that made her sad. Losing a parent at a young age could be devastating. At least when they were older, you knew it was coming. Not that it made it feel any better. He knew there was a day when his parents wouldn't be around anymore, and the thought terrified him. His parents were his rock, his anchor in the world. Without them, he didn't know who he was.

At least she still had Joe, and he was someone they were all thankful for.

Lorelei looked from ShadowLily to Tim. "Kind of like how she likes tea, and you like coffee."

Tim's head whipped around. "Don't expect me to start cheering for tea anytime soon." He paused for a moment, not wanting to admit it but also wanting to be honest. "Although, I could drink some more of that honeyed tea."

He clapped a hand over his mouth, realizing what he'd said out loud. "But only at night, and only on special occasions."

"Someone call Eternia, we just witnessed a miracle." Cassie roared with laughter.

JaKobi grinned. "Hell must have frozen over because I never thought I'd hear you say any cup of tea was good enough for seconds."

Had he said that?

"Let me clarify." Tim lifted one finger in the air and puffed himself up with the air of a man about to issue a proclamation of the finest order. "There is one kind of tea I find acceptable to drink for pleasure. It will in no way, shape, or form, ever be better than coffee."

Lorelei pointed off in the distance. "Let the caffeine snob have his way. We're almost there."

Her eyes must have been much better than his because right now all Tim saw in the distance was a little squiggle on the horizon. It could have been a house, but it also could have been a mirage. Tim had noticed on their rides that sometimes he thought he saw trees or water in the distance only for them to reach that point to find nothing there.

Lorelei wouldn't make something up, so it was time to stop dicking around and get serious.

Tim wasn't sure of their best course of action yet so the longer it took them to approach, the better. He reined his horse to a stop. "Let's leave the horses here and approach on foot."

"Maybe I can assassinate one of them." ShadowLily leapt off her horse and pulled her hood over her head.

JaKobi made a less graceful dismount. "Wrong game."

"Nothing is ever that easy." ShadowLily pulled her hood back down. "But it was a nice thought."

Cassie made her way to the front of the group. "Just get behind me, and get ready to kill things."

The group got into their standard formation and checked their buffs. Tim kept his eyes moving from side to side looking for threats as they walked toward their destination. This place was the opposite of the Zerker's in about every way possible. Where the Zerker decided that heads on spikes were the height of exterior home designs, the Daughters seemed to prefer flowers.

It was crazy to think that anyone would waste water on flowers out here. Water in the desert was as priceless as gold, and yet they had more flowers than many of the homes he'd seen by the coast. Not that it was his place to judge how rich folks spent their money. They earned it and could spend it on what they wanted, even if he thought it was stupid. The Daughters wanted flowers and could afford them, so they had them in a place where no one else did.

Seeing what he'd thought was a home was instead a small fort was a relief. There was something about going up to a cottage and slaying the inhabitants that felt wrong even if they were monsters. Attacking a military installation covered in flowers was a little easier to swallow.

Dracon's fort had been the kind of building one would expect to find a ruthless general lurking in, even if he ended up being a disgraced one. The place was as unforgiving as the man himself. Zerker's little palace was easily the most disgusting thing Tim ever had the misfortune to smell. Nothing said turn around and never come back like human body parts scattered across the yard like garbage.

So the fort in front of them was an upgrade. The doors were a rich, warm wood. The bricks on the walls had been covered with plaster and painted white. Flowers and ivy covered just about everything in sight. Tim had to pinch himself to make sure he wasn't walking into a fantasy or being drugged.

Wait, was something drugging them?

Tim cast Cleanse on himself, and nothing looked different. For a moment he was afraid that when he cast Cleanse, the pretty scenery would have faded and he would be standing in Hell itself. Relieved that Hell would have to wait for another day, Tim continued looking over the fort. It was the nicest thing they'd seen since coming to the desert.

Too bad it belonged to some cold-blooded killers.

It would have been nice to come to a spot like this and swap stories about recipes and gardening, but they were here to end two of Jabari's generals. Taking the Daughters off the playing field was the last thing they needed to accomplish before Khalid revealed Phase Two of the resistance's plan. Everything they were doing now was to free a nation from the clutches of tyranny.

Tim was all about freedom.

People needed to be free to make their choices, even when they were bad ones. Such as when he went to a party and drank so much he spent the next day puking his guts out, or taking that certain someone home when sleeping with the ex was a recipe for disaster. Learning how to deal with one's mistakes so they didn't repeat them was part of the process of being human. At the end of the day, his philosophy on life was simple. If you weren't hurting others, then it was none of his business what people did.

The Daughters liked hurting people, so they had to go.

"This place is beautiful," Lorelei commented as a butterfly flew down and landed on the tip of her arrow.

ShadowLily looked around. "I could retire in a place like this."

"If we could all be so lucky." Tim couldn't help but think this was damn near paradise.

A woman appeared at the fort's entrance. Her crimson red leather outfit stood out as a stark contrast to the white walls of their surroundings. The woman almost seemed like a mirage, but Tim knew it was the start of the encounter.

The woman standing in front of them appeared to shimmer with the heat, then two of them stood side by side. These were the Daughters, Sabrina and Savine in the flesh.

Each of the swordmaker's daughters held a single blade in their right hand. Their left arms were covered in dark heavy plates from the shoulder down to the elbow, and tight black leather bindings wrapped their forearms. The two shared a look and took a few steps forward.

"What do we have here, Savine?" Sabrina looked at her sister with mock surprise.

Savine stopped and made a show of counting them. "Five on two is hardly fair, but we get so few challengers these days. Even Jabari hardly needs us."

"Don't pout, dearest one. The world is full of people to kill." Sabrina grinned at her sister. "We need only to leave the desert to find new opportunities for glory."

Sweet laughter tumbled from Savine's lips. "Today, Vitaria provides. We didn't even have to leave the house."

The two women stopped about fifty feet away from them. "Tell me, adventurers, who has sent you here to die?" Sabrina cooed.

"Tell us the name so we can go after them next. Only a coward doesn't fight their own battles." Savine stared at them coolly as if daring them to disagree.

Tim had about enough of these two already.

They spoke with flowery tones and sounded reasonable

enough, but they were snakes in the grass. These two women might as well have been the Professors Umbridge of the desert. Evil was easy to face when it was something like the Zerker, but when it was all wrapped up in flowers and sweetness, it wasn't always as easy to tell which side was the right one.

"We come on behalf of the Goddess Eternia, via her humble servant Khalid," Tim called.

He would never hide who he was fighting for. Every opportunity he was blessed with since entering the game had come at Eternia's hand or the people who worked for her. The Goddess set the wheels in motion. He just worked his ass off to make the dream come true. A person never knew in life when they would get their chance, but everyone had a moment that defined them. Tim hoped he continued to make the most of his as they came along.

"The desert rat." The Daughters laughed together.

Sabrina thrust her sword at them. "He would have made a fine challenge in his youth."

"If we can't have his blood, we'll have yours." Savine lifted her blade in challenge. "Try and die well."

"I do get so tired of the screams," Sabrina chided as they moved forward.

Cassie snarled. "Normally I like it when a woman has a big old set of brass lady balls, but these two rub me the wrong way."

"She said they rub her the wrong way." JaKobi was laughing with maniacal glee as he sent the first blast of fire heading toward the Daughters.

Tim cast Curse of Giving on each of the bosses. The double healing provided to Cassie should allow him a little flexibility when it came to approaching how to handle the rest of the battle. As the tank and the Daughters clashed, he found himself holding his breath until the initial confrontation was over.

Cassie had split her staff in two and was using it to fend off their blades. A few of their strikes were getting through, but his curses took care of most of the damage. Tim looked over every-one's health to make sure he wasn't missing anything and cast Healing Orb on the tank to bring her back to full health.

The Daughters moved together so fluidly that whenever one was attacking the other was defending. Their blades knocked arrows out of the air and swept magical attacks aside as if they were nothing. Even ShadowLily joining the battle didn't do much to increase their DPS. It added a little extra to the amount of healing he had to put out.

He hoped this wasn't another fight where they'd be at a stale-mate until there was some kind of mechanic to bail them out. What he wanted right now was a straight-up knuckle-busting slugfest—their swords against his team's wit. Whoever desired the win the most would come out on top. His group was giving it everything they had, but right now, their progress had stalled.

The Daughters shimmered again and suddenly became one woman twice the size, with a single sword to match. Cassie took a nasty cut to the leg before she snapped her staff back into a single piece to fight against the new threat.

Tim had his hands full topping off the tank's health while simultaneously keeping his jaw from dropping. Neema said they fought as one, not that they became one actual person. He wasn't ready for it, and neither was Cassie, and it almost cost them every-thing. The tank's health was close to full, but his mana had taken a beating in the process.

Everyone else seemed to have only minor nicks so Tim sent out a quick round of Healing Orb before focusing on Cassie again. Casting Behold My Power next was risky, but if he didn't do it now, he might not get to use it at all. Having the spell off cooldown was one thing. Having the mana to heal everyone on top of casting it late in the fight was something else entirely.

The first wave of damage feedback staggered the group for a moment. He hoped when he reached the spell's next tier the stagger effect would be lessened or removed altogether. He could handle the damage with a round of Healing Orb, but the seconds he lost casting them might be better used doing something else.

The Daughters were all power in their new form. Speed was a thing of the past. Each one of their strikes was lethal. Cassie was being pushed back farther with each attack and taking a ton of damage. The Daughters weren't faring much better. Focusing on the tank exposed them to a lot of extra damage.

When the Daughter's health hit eighty percent, they split back into two.

Sabrina and Savine moved so quickly he couldn't follow their motions. All Tim knew as it happened was that normal people couldn't move that fast, and his team was in a shitload of trouble. When the sword appeared in his stomach a second later, his suspicions were confirmed. Luckily for him, Sabrina had picked a different target or he'd be walking into Barbara's office already.

JaKobi had a look on his face that said, "why is it always me?" as Sabrina pulled her sword free. The fire mage grimaced as he fell to his knees. "Now, can I call them bitches?"

Cassie flew into the battle and pulled Sabrina off her man. "You have my permission to call them whatever you want."

Blood bubbled from his lips as he tried to stand up. "Time to smack a bitch up."

Tim was trying to laugh, but it was hard when you had a sword shoved through your guts. He didn't have the quick one-liners down like JaKobi, but the mage had bought him some time to think of something. All it took for Tim's smile to slip was Savine pulling the sword back out of his stomach.

He might have even cried a little.

Savine looked down at Tim as she prepared to finish him off. "What, nothing smart to say?"

While he might not have been thinking straight when the opportunity presented itself, Tim didn't miss his moment. "Look out behind you."

The warning didn't give Savine enough time to defend herself from the backstab.

When she screamed in pain, all Tim could think about was when his torment would end. He tried to cast Healing Orb, but his health was draining too quickly. Tim's mind was starting to get a little fuzzy. Blood loss was a real downer. If he couldn't heal, maybe he had one last trick in his bag.

Tim switched into his Way of the River stance. Cassie let out a little squawk as some of her defensive protections failed. The tank could be pissed off at him after they all lived, but his plan would have to work first. Behold My Power hit them again, and his health plunged to just under fifteen percent. JaKobi wasn't doing much better. It would all be over soon, one way or another. The next wave of his spell dropped them to five percent health.

Then Behold My Power worked its magic.

Tim was instantly back up to sixty percent health. A moment later, he switched back into his Way of the Boulder stance to help Cassie out and cast Healing Storm. He didn't have enough mana to channel the spell as long as he would have liked, but it took the worst of the edge off. A few more heals and everything would be back to the status quo for the time being.

He looked over his stats and those of the party and realized they could probably survive one more round like the last one before he was totally spent. As he thought about what was coming next, the Daughters shifted forms back into the single warrior. The boss' health still showed the two separate bars although they were one woman now. Sabrina's health was at fifty-five percent, and Savine's at sixty percent.

Tim didn't know if this was one of those situations where they had to keep the boss' health close or the other one would get a buff, but it seemed to be happening pretty naturally so he decided not to cause a fuss about it. All they had to do was keep their health moving down. If they survived one more split, they would have enough DPS to end the fight easily.

That was when the red circles appeared on the ground.

Red was one of the universal colors that meant a player needed to run because something bad was about to go down. There was a reason they used the color on stop signs and for stoplights. One thing any gamer worth his salt knew was that you never stood in the red circles if you wanted to live.

So instead of insulting the team by shouting out a red is dead warning, Tim simply called, "Watch your feet!"

Cassie started to turn the boss to give them the most room to maneuver, and the DPS followed her out of the red circles with time to spare. Tim kept up the healing and reapplied Curse of Giving as they settled into their new position.

Two pots flew out of the fort and landed on the ground. As the containers shattered, they filled the red circles with flames. The burning pitch looked like it would last for hours, more than long enough for them to run out of space if they weren't careful. Now things were getting tricky, and Cassie would have to watch her placement of the boss to minimize their chance of taking fire damage. They also needed to cluster in two groups so if the pots targeted random people they could still control the placement.

"ShadowLily, get up front with Cassie." He turned toward the others. "I want you guys stuck on my ass like the creeper at the club who won't catch a hint."

JaKobi grinned. "Bro, you're not supposed to use cross-sexualized metaphors, but I'd give the system all the gold in my account right now if some guy appeared and started grinding on your ass."

"Just kill the boss. We can talk about my hot ass later." Tim sent out his next round of healing.

Two more red circles appeared, and this time they were in predictable spots under the players' feet. Cassie was able to rotate the boss, and they all got to safety with time to spare. That was when the Daughters split again.

Tim cast Who Needs A Shield on himself as a precaution. If he got hit again, he needed to be able to cast.

Sabrina's blade tore into ShadowLily. "Payback's a bitch, hon."

"Funny, we were just saying the same thing about you," ShadowLily ground out between jagged gasps for air.

Savine came straight for Tim, and he realized this was when being a healer sucked.

Getting stabbed once in a day was enough, but twice, fuck that noise. Tim was ready to see these two go down. Stab me twice, shame on you, stab me thrice shame on me.

The Daughters continued their relentless assault as he worked to get off a Healing Orb. The spell took effect, and he healed the others before the damage could get any worse. Tim was so impressed by their group. It didn't matter what happened. Someone was always ready to pick up the slack. They worked so well together that it was probably the best group he'd ever been a part of in his life.

Sabrina's health was at fifteen percent while Savine's was at twenty.

The bosses looked like they had enough health to get off a third round of the splits before his team would be able to kill them both, and that meant one of their group would probably die based on the amount of mana he had left. A quick look around and Tim could see they all knew it.

Fuck it, he didn't come here to lose, and he was going to fight until the end.

"Give them hell!" Tim roared, hoping to inspire his friends.

The Daughters laughed as they formed back into a single woman. The red circles appeared, and Cassie started to move them. Their strategy was perfect, but they were still going to lose. They didn't quite have the DPS to kill them, and he didn't have the healing to keep them alive through a third round of the boss' most devastating attack.

It was so frustrating when it felt like they were doing everything right and were still going to lose.

He hated this shit. There had to be a way for them to win.

Was there something he was missing, something that would give them the edge they needed to pull out a victory? Tim tried to think of the one thing he was missing. His new spell. *Holy shit.* After he'd used Disturbance on the Zerker with no effect, he'd tabled it for later experimentation. The Daughters clearly had some kind of buff on them. If he could remove it, maybe it would stop them from splitting.

Tim felt like this was the moment they'd pull the fight from the clutches of defeat as he mouthed the words to Disturbance.

Sabrina and Savine fell apart and landed on their knees.

The spell removing their buff worked out better than he expected. Not only did it stop them from doing damage on the split, but it also stunned them. Why hadn't he thought of this earlier? The bastard developers gave him so much to worry about that he almost missed the trick. Tim didn't know if he should be impressed they made him work so hard or pissed at himself for nearly missing it.

The bosses never got the chance to come out of their stunned state. They died in each other's arms and disappeared in a swirl of beautiful golden motes. Resting in the Two Daughters' place was a golden chest.

CHAPTER THIRTY-THREE

Loot was such a wonderful thing.

Getting stabbed, beaten, bruised, and killed by magic was all worth it because of the golden chest at the end. Cassie didn't get into tanking because she liked getting the crap kicked out of her. She did it for respect. When people had a good tank in their group, everyone knew it made life infinitely easier.

If you want to be in high demand, play an in-demand role.

No disrespect to healing, but who wanted to stand in the back of the fight and only fire off spells? That wasn't adventure. Adventure was getting down in the muck and fighting toe-to-toe against the biggest badasses the world had ever seen. Being stabbed was a badge of honor, and singed flesh was another day at the office.

There was nothing quite like the rush she got charging into the fight while everyone else hung back. For a moment, it always made her feel as if she was saving the day by herself, and that feeling was worth coming back for.

Even when it hurt.

The Zerker was angry, but she didn't take the brunt of that rage. Even here, when the Daughters split they hadn't come after her, so she avoided the hardest-hitting attacks of several fights by omission. For each of the devasting attacks her party took, Cassie was hit, bruised, beaten, and cut at least a hundred times.

Being stabbed and feeling her flesh knit itself back together as she made her next attack was the weirdest feeling. What it taught her was never to slow down. The pain she felt was only momentary as long as she kept moving. Sure each little attack made Cassie question the sanity of her decision to tank, but at the end of the day, she kind of liked being the center of attention.

Without a tank, the fight was over.

Cassie liked to think of her going first on loot as the tank tax. Plus, it never hurt anyone because the system automated the haul, and as far as she could tell whatever position a player picked didn't matter as far as returns went. While she liked the random loot from bosses because it was a little more powerful, she also kinda missed the quests where she got to pick her own. Filling in the gaps in her gear was so much easier when a girl didn't have to rely on drops.

As much as she wanted to go first, getting stabbed twice was the kind of thing that moved a person to the front of the line. Plus, he was a healer and probably didn't get the small benefit of reduced pain receptors as she did. Getting a sword through the stomach would have slowed her down. For him, it had been completely paralyzing.

She stopped in front of the chest, then turned and motioned for Tim to come forward. "You go first. You earned it."

The healer stepped forward still looking a little pale from the fight. He hadn't done the inventory trick on his robes yet, and his dried, crusty blood covered them.

"Maybe heal yourself again, and switch out the robes. You look like the final girl in a serial killer flick." Cassie stepped back from the chest, giving Tim room to take care of business.

Lorelei snickered. "He was the one trying to show everyone his ass."

Tim's robes disappeared for a moment and instantly replaced themselves. He gritted his teeth in exhaustion or pain, but when he slammed his staff against the ground, a light mist fell over the party. Any discomfort Cassie felt went right out the window as the cool, wet drops fell around her.

Healing in the game was something else.

The color returned to Tim's skin, and he stopped casting the spell. He closed the three steps to the chest with a much sturdier gait and placed his hand on it. "Boots of Tranquility. I lose my movement speed bonus, but I pick up some additional dexterity and endurance."

"Not too shabby." Cassie started to move forward, but Lorelei cut her off.

The ranger laid her hand on the chest. "A new hunting knife." She blew a raspberry at Cassie. "See ya, wouldn't wanna be ya."

"If I didn't love you so damn much, I'd beat you fucking silly." Cassie drew a deep breath to calm herself.

This was the kind of thing she was working on. Most of the time, she did this to herself by always insisting on being first. With a little self-evaluation, it was easy to see how that might come off the wrong way. Not that she'd admit it to anyone.

"Would anyone else like to go?" See, she could be as magnanimous as anyone else.

JaKobi walked forward as if he didn't have a care in the world and missed all the subtlety of her tone. That's why she was falling in love with the big oblivious jerk, though. While no one else on the planet, or any planet, could put up with her shit, he did it with a smile. Instead of having a mini freak out about being shoved down to fourth on the loot list, she smiled as he placed his hand against the chest.

"Wristbands of the Wandering Warrior." JaKobi looked a little perplexed. "Doesn't exactly feel like it was made for me, but my secondary stats are weak. Maybe the game's trying to give me a hint."

Cassie slowly turned toward ShadowLily, but her friend only waved her toward the chest. "Go ahead. I can see it's killing you."

It really was.

She was like a kid at Christmas every time one of these little golden present droppers appeared. She didn't even have to leave out milk and cookies. In fact, Tim covered the tab on her beer and gave her a hefty bonus so there was nothing to be upset about, even if she did get something bad or have to go almost last. When she thought about it, everything was coming up Cassie.

Placing her hand on the chest was the icing on the cake.

Item Received: Pants of the Dancing Piranha

James Silverman was a man of many eccentricities, among them the belief that his pants gave him the ability to dodge almost any attack. Desperate to prove this point to the world, James set out to cross the River of Teeth on foot. Sadly, Mr. Silverman didn't complete his journey that day, but his pants were found four days later completely unscathed.

+5 Endurance +4 Dexterity

Special Ability: Attacks aimed at the pants have a greater chance of being dodged.

Hopefully, the pants worked out better for her than they did for James.

Cassie equipped the pants, checked out her butt to make sure they didn't make her look like she was stuffing a couple of bowling balls back there, and let out a contented sigh. It wasn't every day she got something useful that also made her look good. She knew the game's AI probably didn't care, but the pants made her feel appreciated.

ShadowLily moved up to the chest. "Vest of the Daughters."

The assassin turned to face the group, her face molded in a look of pure shock. "Guys, this is my first piece of epic gear."

"Yeah, the piece sounds awesome, but is it really epic?" JaKobi looked down at his outfit. "I mean come on, I look pretty epic."

ShadowLily smacked him on the back of the head. "Not that it looks epic, it has a tag that says epic. None of my other gear has that."

"That might be the first epic drop for the entire group." Tim looked pumped. "That means we all have a shot at getting something special from now on."

Cassie hugged ShadowLily. She might have been a little jealous but her item, despite the name, was rather badass. Tim was also right. This opened the door for all of them, and what kind of friend wouldn't be happy when their bestie scored an awesome item? It was only going to make life easier on all of them if the bosses died faster.

"Let's get back to camp. I want a chance to get cleaned up before Neema comes back." Lorelei walked toward where they'd left the horses. "Or better yet maybe she's waiting for us, and we can go right back to the oasis."

Tim and ShadowLily followed her.

"One less day in the heat. I'm all for it," the healer grumbled as they walked.

JaKobi gave Cassie that goofy little grin she couldn't get enough of, and she pulled him in for a kiss. "Thanks for putting up with me."

"You? Good God woman, have you looked at me? I'm a mess without you."

Cassie slapped his ass. "If you need instructions, there's a horse. Jump on it."

"Lucky I don't jump on you." The fire mage grinned at her and made a heart out of flames in the air.

"Get the fuck out of here," is what she said, but what Cassie really meant was, I love you.

***

Khalid beamed as the group returned to the oasis.

The adventurers were returning in triumph, and it did his heart well to see it. With Jabari's three most fearsome generals out of the way, they could plan attacks of their own. He had a few targets already selected, and it looked like he picked the right group of adventurers to carry them out.

Phase Two would start tomorrow.

Tonight they would feast and drink. Tomorrow the resistance would plan, and three days from now they would deal Jabari a blow he'd never be able to recover from. The future looked bright for the people of the desert. He wondered if any of the people would remember what freedom felt like.

It had been so long since a person could be anything they wanted. Would they know how? For the last twenty-five years, all of them had all been subject to every whim and desire of a mad bastard, and now he would be the one to feel the squeeze. Things would only get tougher for Jabari going forward, and the stress would make him more ruthless.

In the short term, the people would pay.

There would be time for him to worry about their fate when Jabari was dead. Until then, he would act without worry and trust in Eternia's holy light to guide him.

Tim splashed his feet in the bath.

Yeah, it was a little childish, but he'd earned it. They'd been working their asses off since coming to the desert, and there was no Joe's to feed his burning desire for pancakes. Maybe it was weird that the thing he missed most since they left Tristholm was always having his favorite comfort foods at his fingertips. There would be time for more Joe's after they finished the task set out for them by Eternia.

Sooner if he could find a messenger with portal access.

Until then, he'd keep drinking the warm honeyed tea as he looked over his stats. He'd made some real progress since coming into the desert. Not only with new gear, but he'd passed the next ten-point threshold for both intelligence and wisdom. If he gained another level or two, he might even be able to get his endurance over twenty.

Tim's intelligence now provided increased mana regeneration and a small bonus to his overall mana pool. Every little bit helped. He looked at his wisdom and smiled at the bonuses he received to healing and damage output. Crossing over the fifty threshold gave him a decent reward. He wondered how big the increases would grow the closer he got to one hundred. He bet some of the bonuses started to look a little ridiculous.

Something to look forward to later.

Before he looked over his skill increases, Tim decided to turn in their latest completed quest. He was pretty sure the rewards would be enough to give him his next level. Every single quest inched him closer to twenty. He was so excited about finding out what his class could do next. Level twenty felt like the time when it finally started to take shape.

Quest Completed: Dancing with The Daughters

It didn't end up so much of a dance as you being brutally stabbed through the stomach more than once. Most healers try and avoid taking that kind of damage. You should probably do the same thing in the future. In the end, you overcame their deadly dance. Good for you.

Reward: Ten Gold Coins

The gold was a nice bonus considering the kind of drops they were getting from the bosses. Some of the best gear he had came from their early adventures in the desert. The experience they were earning was higher, and the fights were more difficult. Tim tried not to get too giddy, but he had to admit that he was enjoying himself.

I get paid to do this?

Yes, yes he did.

System Message: You have obtained level seventeen and have one skill point to distribute.

Tim had been trying to get his intelligence over forty, but the orb accomplished that for him. Now that his intelligence was right where he wanted it, he needed to focus on getting his endurance up. These new bosses hit harder, and he needed to soak up more damage on the off chance he had to take a few more of those nasty hits or had the misfortune of being selected by an unblockable boss mechanic. He couldn't risk being the only one without enough health to survive.

There was being a glass cannon, and there was playing recklessly.

Tim dumped his free skill point into endurance, bringing his total to eighteen. In two more points, he'd hit the next threshold and pick up a small bonus. Those little bonuses added up once a player had enough of them. With his latest point allocated it was time to look over his skill increases.

Skill Increased: Disturbance

Rank: Novice level two

Look at you. You just got this skill, and you're already using it the right way. Well really, it's two for one, but it's early on, and we're sure you'll figure out how to use this spell when needed. Disturbance only receives minor changes at higher levels.

Tim didn't think the spell had to do more. Knowing he could remove a beneficial buff from a boss was enough. He'd have to tinker around to figure out which buffs he could and couldn't remove, but it was a damn useful spell and probably saved their lives.

Skill Increased: Snare

Rank: Novice level six

When you need to buy some time to save yourself or someone else, this is the spell to buy you half a step. Keep using

it to increase the spell's effectiveness in combat. Maybe one day you'll be able to do something more than making a boss trip.

Sometimes a trip was all you needed.

Tim thought about all the times he used Snare. They weren't exactly memorable, but he lived through every encounter so it got the job done when he needed it. Of course, the spell would be better if it was a little stronger, but he was working on it. He didn't need the game to keep reminding him to use it. Snare wasn't as important to his skill set as some of his other spells, so it didn't see as much time in his rotation.

Skill Increased: Flame Burst

Rank: Apprentice level six

There is a certain sense of satisfaction that comes with lighting something on fire. Sure the living things make some noise, but they're also trying to kill you. Keep lighting things on fire in new and interesting ways to develop this skill further.

Tim wasn't exactly sure how to light things on fire in new and interesting ways, but he would try to find some. He usually pulled out Flame Burst when everything else failed, and he didn't have the mana to cast Divine Light effectively. Although he had to admit that Flame Burst saved his ass on more than one occasion, and he should probably get it to the journeyman ranks sooner rather than later.

Skill Increased: Behold My Power

Rank: Apprentice level seven

Wham, bam, thank you ma'am. This spell packs a punch, and you use it with great effect. Keep doing what you're doing, and everything will be fine.

Tim loved it when the skill increase messages were uplifting. It was nice to know the system thought he was doing something right once in a while. Sometimes when he got the updates they felt like a slap in the face, but not today. Today the system was smiling at him because even in this new land they were kicking some major ass.

Skill Increased: Healing Storm

Rank: Apprentice level seven

And Eternia said, let there be rain from the heavens and may its drops heal all the people. She might have said it, or maybe it was a poet who made it up in her honor. Either way, the spell makes healing water fall from the sky, and that's pretty cool.

Healing Storm was his only AOE heal unless he changed stances. It cost a shit ton of mana to use for extended periods, but the healing it put out was second to none if more than three people were injured. If three people were hurt, they were already in trouble, and using up his mana became less of an issue until later in the fight. He hadn't run out of mana yet, but he'd been damn close more than he'd like to admit.

Skill Increased: Who Needs a Shield

Rank: Apprentice level seven

When the tank goes boom, someone's gotta be there to help them out. In this case, it's you. Thankfully this spell also provides a small bonus to your entire party's dodge chance for those extra tricky situations. You've used this spell quite well but need to use it more often to take advantage of all its applications.

Who Needs a Shield saved all their asses on more than one occasion. It was the only panic button spell he had. If everything was turning to shit, this is what Tim used to clean the drain. About to eat a cleave attack, the entire group was taking massive damage, or he needed to recharge some mana? Who Needs a Shield was the only spell he had that would accomplish all three.

Maybe it was time to find out if he could cast it more than once per fight.

Skill Increased: Cleanse

Rank: Journeyman level one

Look at you, look at you. To think it all started with you curing a hangover, and now you're the big man on campus. Not

everyone can remove negative effects from themselves, let alone others.

Your Cleanse skill has reached the journeyman ranks and can now remove two minor effects or one medium-tier effect per cast. Some effects may still take multiple casts to remove.

Tim loved using his Cleanse spell.

When in doubt, cleanse it out, was his motto when it came to casting Cleanse. If it looked bad, it was worth giving Cleanse a shot. The spell worked on everything from poison to curing diarrhea and was one of the handiest tools in a healer's rotation. If they ever got in a fight with stacking debuffs, being able to remove multiple stacks in one cast would be a huge bonus. This spell kept getting better and better.

Skill Increased: Curse of Giving

Rank: Journeyman level one

Curse, curse, curse, shake your booty.

Welcome to the Journeyman ranks with your first curse. While this one only provides modest damage, it returns ten percent of that damage to the target or targets of your stance as healing. At this level, Curse of Giving receives a new benefit. All targets affected by the healing effect of this curse also receive a one percent reduction in damage for the duration of the effect.

Tim had to reread the description to make sure he saw it correctly. This would be a nice benefit for Cassie. What kind of tank wouldn't be thrilled about taking less damage, even if it was only one percent? Not to mention that if he flipped stances to Way of the River, then everyone would get reduced damage. The future was bright for this spell, and the master ranks would provide another twist.

He couldn't wait to see what it was.

It was so cool how this game provided him with an incentive to keep grinding. If a player liked a particular skill or spell, all they had to do was keep using it to gain increases. They couldn't simply cast the damn thing at a wall for hours, but finding something to fight in *The Etheric Coast* wasn't exactly difficult, and he was sure there were plenty of groups recruiting. When all the best content in the game required a group, you could damn sure bet people were looking to recruit and be recruited.

On the whole, they were pretty damn lucky not to have to worry about searching for new players. They'd locked in their group the second Lorelei showed up. While he missed Gaston's antics, their time with the assassin had always been borrowed. His replacement ended up being just what they needed at the time and continued to be an amazing fit. The ranger had made herself irre-placeable.

Skill Increased: Divine Light

Rank: Journeyman level one

Look at you. It's Billy Badass with three skills in the Jour-neyman ranks. You know it only gets harder from here, right? Wait until you see what it takes to become a Master or a Grand-master. It's like climbing up a mountain while carrying a pig, but you better do it quickly or Madam Zaroni will put a curse on you.

Divine Light does what it's always done. It burns holes of holy fire in your enemies. While moving to the Apprentice ranks provided a ten percent damage over time effect, moving into the Journeyman ranks provides splash damage from the initial target. Now, all enemies standing within five yards of the initial target will receive one percent of the initial cast's damage as splash damage. This damage can't be ignored or dodged.

Whoa!

All his skills that reached the Journeyman rank received some great benefits, but this was the one he liked the most. His healing numbers were always going to be awesome, but the more he could contribute on the DPS side of things, the more it eased the burden on the entire party. While casting curses was a hundred percent more cost-effective on Tim's mana, he only had two of them, and one of those had a ridiculously long cooldown. Now if they had to fight a group of enemies, he could hit more than one.

Skill Increased: Healing Orb

Rank: Journeyman level eight

Good old Healing Orb. This is your number one spell and has been for some time. Normally we'd tweak it just to change things up, but it seems to be working within normal parameters. You've obviously found something you enjoy using, and you use it well. Keep it up, and you'll be a master in no time.

Well, maybe not no time.

It was true. Tim used the shit out of this spell. When it was cost-effective, gave a burst heal, and had a heal over time effect, why wouldn't he use it all the time? Having a Healing Orb on anyone who was taking damage was a creed to live by.

It seemed crazy that he might make it into the Master ranks soon. That seemed almost too good to be true considering he hadn't hit level twenty yet. Although each time he leveled this skill, it took a dramatic uptick in usage to make any headway. Moving from where he was now to Master rank one might take him as long as it took to get to Journeyman level eight. If working through Master ranks took him two or three times as long as it did going through Journeyman, he wouldn't be sniffing Grandmaster status anytime soon.

Stances

Skill Increased: Way of the River

Rank: Apprentice rank six

When everyone's in trouble, why not just heal everyone? You use this skill when it's appropriate but try not to get into the position where everyone in your party needs heals too often. Eventually, they'll start dying.

Tim wished he could use this skill more. Where this ability would shine was in a raid situation. If he wasn't the healer assigned to the tank he could switch into Way of the River and heal large DPS groups to keep them in the fight. He didn't know if this game had raids at the end, but getting into a twenty-man fight in *The Etheric Coast* would take some serious planning. Coordinating one group was hard enough. Getting four separate groups on the same page would be a logistical nightmare.

Skill Increased: Way of The Boulder

Rank: Apprentice rank nine

When someone needs to be a rock, you make them a fucking rock. Yes, I can swear, I'm an advanced intelligence system, not a grade-schooler. You know what you're doing with this stance. When you reach the Journeyman ranks, it may obtain an additional benefit.

That was pretty straightforward. Tim tried to keep his stance directed at whoever would be taking the most damage. Normally that was only Cassie, but he'd switched to other people in the group a few times to save them from big hits. He would have to pay more attention to try and get the most out of stances as he could.

Buffs

Skill Increased: Armor of Eternia

Rank: Apprentice rank eight

Divine protection is your shield against the darkness. While this buff might not seem powerful on the surface, a five percent reduction in damage can be the difference between life and death.

Every single member of their party had come close to dying, and he had died. It wasn't so bad. Last time he died, Tim got a streaming contract. If it happened again, they might offer him a house in the Hamptons and an actual salary. Okay, nobody would be giving him a mansion or millions of dollars anytime soon, but he felt too good about all these increases not to be overly optimistic about his chances.

Skill Increased: Attacks of the Faithful

Rank: Apprentice rank eight

You hit things, and the people in your group hit things. As long as they aren't divine in nature, this is exactly the buff you need to use. Eventually, you'll run into some nasties that take additional damage from this skill, so keep using it.

Tim liked having a buff to his attacks for the group and also not having to worry about his buffs too much. In some games, managing them felt like its own mini-game. He wanted to cast them and forget about them. Which he could pretty much do now they lasted eight hours.

With all his skills finally updated, Tim dismissed his interface and looked around the room. A trail of tealight candles led from the bathtub to their bed. Waiting in bed was the most beautiful woman he'd ever seen.

How had ShadowLily set this up without him noticing?

Sure, she could go into stealth, but Tim was pretty sure her ability didn't extend to candles. Sometimes he was something else. Tim had been so absorbed in his updates that he missed her coming into the room, and now that he knew she was there he was overthinking things.

What he needed to do was jump out of the tub and rush straight toward the bed. So that was what he did. Tim leapt out of the tub with a flourish, hit the rug, and fell onto his ass with his towel fluttering down over him. He tried to stifle the groan that escaped his lips, but there was no way to hide it.

From the position he was in there were three things a person could do. Turn and run. That wouldn't work for him. She was his girlfriend, and there was nowhere to run. Next on the list was to jump to his feet and exclaim loudly, "Nailed it," and try to pass off the disaster as what any perfectly reasonable person leaping from a tub would have done. The third option was much simpler and exactly what he did.

Tim laid on his back, kicking his feet in the air like a turtle while he dried himself as quickly as possible. His exit from the tub might not have been as graceful as he would have liked, but the whole point of this was to get in bed with the love of his life, not to worry about who looked the coolest drying off.

He tossed the towel aside and ran toward the bed, ignoring the fact the towel landed in the tub. Four feet from the bed, Tim launched himself in the air and bounced onto the mattress next to his future.

"You don't need fancy lights to get me in bed." Tim smiled at her.

She grinned. "I know. They're for him." She pointed at the tent flap. "Antonio likes it when a girl sets the mood."

A giant of a man stepped into the open flap wearing only a loincloth. "I have come for the smoochie-smoochie."

Tim felt all the color wash from his face.

Antonio smiled from ear to ear and looked from Tim to ShadowLily while giving her a big thumbs up. "Did I say it right?"

She tossed the man a gold coin. "You did, but kind of ruined the effect when you asked how it went."

He nodded solemnly and backed out of the tent. "Enjoy your night."

Tim looked at the closed tent flap and back at the assassin. She'd totally set him up because he was taking too long in the bath. There was only one thing he could do. "Such a betrayal of trust can only be rectified by one thing." He jumped on top of her. "Tickles!"

"NOOOOOOOOOOOOO!" ShadowLily screamed between peals of laughter.

CHAPTER THIRTY-FOUR

Tim awoke to the smell of coffee.

Just like that, everything was right in the world. Sometimes it really was the little things in life that made all the difference. Some players wanted to own fancy estates or castles. All he cared about was some good coffee and even better company. Maybe a cookie or two if anyone had the time to pick some up.

Ugh, now all he could think about was cookies. What was it about a night of furious lovemaking that left him feeling so damned hungry in the morning? This was the kind of hunger that couldn't be fixed by coffee alone. It felt like he hadn't eaten in days.

Did he eat last night?

He couldn't remember.

From the second he got out of the bath until the moment he passed out, everything had been a whirlwind. Now it was morning, and there was coffee, so things must have gone reasonably well. No one stormed into their tent demanding help, and if they did, Tim hadn't noticed them.

After a quick trip to the chamber pot, Tim equipped his clothes and followed his nose to the sweet, sweet smell of coffee. Sitting at the table with her cup was the woman of his dreams, and luckily enough for him, she was also his girlfriend.

ShadowLily's hair looked slightly disheveled, which only made her look cuter. "It awakens."

"Here I was, thinking all these lovely thoughts about you, and I get called *it*." Tim poured a cup of coffee and sat. "I've never been more insulted in all my life."

She stared at him over the rim of her cup, her expression impassive. "Aren't we a bit of a diva this morning."

Tim was about to sip his coffee and stopped at the last moment. It was a good thing too because hot coffee coming out of a person's nose feels about as good as you'd think. A little chuckle escaped his lips. She'd called his bluff as usual. "Every morning, until at least three cups of coffee have been consumed."

"Try and tighten it up. We have a meeting to attend." Shadow-Lily stood and refilled both their cups. "Khalid is waiting for us."

Cassie and JaKobi joined them on their way to the command tent. Lorelei was nowhere in sight, but that wasn't unusual for the ranger. She always turned up on time for the important stuff, and that was all that mattered to him.

Khalid's tent might as well have not been touched since their last visit. The only change in the room Tim noticed was that the stack of papers on the man's desk had grown exponentially. It seemed even in games no one liked doing their paperwork. Tim was sure there was some poor soul in the army who'd dedicated their entire life to making sure the right forms got to the right places. It sounded like being stuck in hell, like that feeling of being trapped in traffic behind two slow-moving cars.

For eternity.

The tent flap on the far side of the room rustled, and Neema and Lorelei entered together.

Khalid turned to look at the two of them, a smile growing on his face before he turned to address the others. "Now that we're all here, it's time to get started on Phase Two."

He slowly moved his gaze between each person in the room. "I have a task for each of you to carry out independently, and you must accomplish them today. With Jabari's generals down, this is our chance to take the offensive for once."

Tim wasn't a super big fan of solo quests, not when most of his DPS came from his friends. "Are you sure you need us to split up? We're more effective together."

Khalid nodded as he looked at the giant map before touching five spots. "If we can secure these five locations, we might finally be able to move on Jabari's palace."

The old warrior looked at Neema with tears in his eyes. "If the Pharaoh loses Naroosh, his hold on the kingdom crumbles. We are so close to being able to take the fight straight to him."

Neema's smile said she'd like to introduce the Pharaoh to one of her arrows sooner rather than later. "If the Pharaoh dies, our people will be free."

Tim knew what it felt like to be on the verge of something you've hungered after for a long time. He'd spent the summer of his junior year of high school working two jobs so he could buy a new gaming console. The feeling when he powered that baby up was incredible.

He wondered what it would feel like to free a nation.

"All right, tell us what you need us to do." Tim probably should have made sure the others were on board before pledging their services, but it was too late now.

Khalid moved to an old wooden box on his desk. Once the lid was open, he pulled out a stack of sealed envelopes and passed them out. "You each have a job to do. May Eternia's light shine down upon you."

The old warrior left the tent without another word. He wasn't much for goodbyes or sharing, but Khalid had a presence and a sense of honor that were undeniable. All things being said, Tim felt good knowing he was working for the good guys. If Khalid thought they could accomplish these tasks alone, then they should probably be able to.

Neema took Lorelei's hand and led her from the tent. "Come on. Our horses are ready."

A very girlish giggle escaped Lorelei's mouth before she could stop it. "See you back here tonight?"

Tim waved her away. "Go, and have fun."

The two women left the tent together, and he couldn't be happier about it. If anyone deserved a few good breaks, it was Lorelei. Tim didn't know much about her life outside the game, but she'd been worked over pretty hard by the love train since coming into *The Etheric Coast*. If this was her chance to find a little love, then she should enjoy every moment of it.

JaKobi extended his arm to Cassie. "Care to grab some lunch before we go?"

"Don't mind if I do." She linked her arm through his, and they left.

Tim stood and glanced around the tent before looking at Shadow-Lily. "If they're going to eat and we leave now, there's a good chance we'll be back before everyone else and have this place to ourselves."

"After last night, I'm surprised you have the energy." Shadow-Lily let out a small yawn.

A smile quirked the corner of his lips. "It's cute you thought I was talking about sex. I want to get a nap in before any celebrations start."

ShadowLily stood and kissed him. "This is why I love you. We want the same thing."

"Can't help that I'm perfect." Tim downplayed the comment with a little nonchalance.

"Just get those buns back here, or I'm going to sleep without you." ShadowLily disappeared with a *pop*.

Tim squawked as she pinched his ass. "That was uncalled for," he shouted as the tent flap moved apart on its own.

Part of him wondered what it would be like to have sex with an invisible woman, but he liked looking at her so much he almost hoped they never got to try it. Tim walked toward the tent flap as he tried to pull his mind out of the gutter. There were more important things than getting busy, although his body tried to forget that fact at the sight of his girlfriend the instant she walked into or out of a room.

While he had the tent to himself, he might as well find out what he'd gotten himself into. He looked down at the envelope Khalid had given him and slit it open. Inside was a card with a single golden hieroglyphic on it. When Tim ran his finger across the golden symbol, a quest popped up.

Quest Received: Healing The People

There are members of the resistance in dire need of healing. I've marked a location on your map. Go there and find out why our warriors aren't returning to the battlefield as quickly as they should.

Reward: Ten gold coins

The quest wasn't as straightforward as go here and heal everyone, which was nice, and also a little concerning. Tim liked the fact that his healing powers weren't in question, and it showed that Khalid valued him more than to send him somewhere to heal X number of people for a reward. The part of the quest that had him concerned was that the wounded weren't returning in a timely manner. From what Tim knew about magical healing, they should be returning the same day, if not sooner.

Something about this stunk.

"I guess that's why he's sending me." Tim stepped out into the sunshine and walked toward the stables.

If he was going to get back before everyone else, he'd better leave now. There was no telling what kinds of quests the others received, and he wanted to sleep before they partied tonight. If anyone deserved a nap it was him, but first, he had to figure out what was going on.

Tim hopped into the saddle of his camel and started in the direction indicated on his map. He'd never ridden a camel before, but he was in the desert now, and by God, he was going to start doing desert things before a quest forced him into another climate where they didn't have camels to ride. When in Rome, and all that.

His camel spat into the wind, and the droplets splattered against them both.

"Maybe I should have stuck with horses."

The village of Har-Han was three concentric circles of dusty huts built around a central courtyard with a well. Telling which of the massive thatched huts was the medical building wouldn't be a problem since the line of wounded waiting outside marked it clearly enough. It was a mockery of everything he'd tried to accomplish in Promethia, and worse yet, Khalid was paying these jackals.

Maybe the healer who was working here wasn't very experienced.

That was the only real excuse for this, that or there wasn't a healer at all. If someone here were accepting money from Khalid and not healing the wounded, it would end now. The easiest way Tim knew how to hustle a hustler was to take away their hustle. In this case, if he healed everyone, the healer in Har-Han would be out of a job. That or it would force the idiot to make an appearance, and Tim could deal with him.

Before he got crazy, it was probably best to get the lay of the land. He didn't have any bloody clothes handy to blend in with the others, but he could make some if he were gritty enough. Tim pulled his dagger free and slashed his left arm.

"Son of a rat sucking donkey fucker, that hurts!" Tim gritted his teeth against the pain as he put his dagger away.

His next thought was to heal the wound quickly. Once he'd

done that, he pulled a spare shirt free and used it to bind his now-healed arm. With all the wet blood over the strips of his shirt, he fit right in with the rest of the resistance fighters.

Tossing a little limp into his giddy-up, Tim proceeded closer to the men in line. He stopped next to the first man he saw. "What's the holdup?"

"New, huh?" The man snickered and coughed a little bubble of blood at the corner of his mouth. "They get paid the same if we live or die. They don't seem to be in much of a hurry to help."

Tim frowned. "But Khalid does pay them?" He let the statement trail out there as a question, hoping the man might fill in the blanks.

"He does, but Jabari sends them whores and spirits. Who has time to heal when they could be drinking and fucking?"

Well, that explained a few things.

Jabari's gifts had corrupted the healers here. Tim wished that he could say he was surprised, but men had sold their honor for a lot less. A famous one even betrayed someone for thirty pieces of silver. He wanted to be sad these men would let others suffer while they delighted themselves, but in the end, he was mostly angry. How many men died while these healers indulged in Jabari's pleasures?

"Can you do me a favor?" Tim splashed the man with a Healing Orb and tried not to grin at the expression of astonishment on the man's face. "Do you think it would be possible to round up the worst of the wounded in one location for me? Get some of the others to help you, and tell them I'll make sure they're taken care of."

The man pulled his arm from a sling and tested it before extending his hand to Tim. "Josh is my name, and I'll get it done."

It looked like Josh wanted to say more but thought better of it. He turned away from Tim and walked into the crowd, selecting a handful of men and women to help him round up the worst of the wounded. Tim loved working with seasoned fighters. You didn't need to ask them to do something a thousand times. They did what needed doing without complaint.

They saved the complaining for their own time.

The people of Har-Han were probably getting tense, having so many injured warriors in their small village. There had to be a couple of hundred resistance fighters milling around, and there was no way their water well had been built to support that many thirsty mouths. Besides the living, there was a growing pile of corpses. No one seemed to know what to do with the bodies so they rotted under the sun with only a sheet hiding their decomposing bodies from view.

A single guard stood outside the door to the healer's building. The sounds of music and laughter slipped from under it. *So the men inside weren't afraid that everyone knew what they were doing.* Knowing what they were busy doing while the men and women of the resistance died turned Tim's stomach.

This had to end.

The guard at the door held up a hand. "Healings are done for today. Go back and wait with the others."

"I don't think I will." Tim wondered what this man would do. He was all alone and looked to only have a stout wooden club as a weapon.

The guard moved forward while lifting the club. "Being smart ain't going to get that arm healed any faster, friend."

"And what, you'll give me something to go with my hurt arm if I don't comply?" Tim knew what he was saying, but all he heard coming from his mouth was an unintelligible growl.

Cruel laughter bubbled from the guard's lips. "I won't have to. In a few days when that arm starts to smell, you'll do anything I want to get in the door."

Tim was starting to understand why they needed a man like Khalid in the desert. Someone with honor had to get this rabble under control. This was the kind of behavior he'd expect from murders and thieves, not the people who others counted on to help them in their time of need.

Tim had seen enough.

He cast Behold My Power without another thought. The guard's face twisted for a moment as if he knew something was wrong, but he didn't know what. It was nice to see the man squirm a little, his calm confidence shattered. Tim noticed that it didn't take much to make an arrogant man uncomfortable. All a person had to do was attack their sense of self-worth.

Or in this case, curse the fuck out of them.

"What did you do?" Spittle flew from the guard's lips as he screamed in fear.

A younger version of himself would have laughed at the man's panic after he caused the same feeling in so many others, but instead, he felt tired. How some people lost sight of what was important in life was so damn draining. Tim cast Snare and followed it up with a blast of Divine Light. He quickly healed the damage he'd taken from his curse and waited for it to finish off the guard.

Death was damn near instantaneous for the man, and it was a good deal better than he deserved. Now that the lone guard was out of the way Tim could go back and heal the others before dealing with the wayward healers in the temple. It had been a while since he'd been able to use his assassin skills, but now was the perfect time to dust them off.

Josh was true to his word and assembled the worst of the wounded off to one side. Tim clapped him warmly on the back. "Once I get these men healed, can you handle getting them back to wherever they need to be?"

"I can, but shouldn't we do something about..." Josh pointed at the temple. "Them."

Tim pulled a dagger free, flashing it in the sunlight before tucking it away again. "Don't worry. I've got a plan."

"About time someone set them straight," one of Josh's helpers replied from behind them.

Tim hit the man with Healing Orb and sent a quick burst of the spell out to anyone standing nearby. With a few of Josh's helpers taken care of, he moved to start taking care of the worst of the worst. These were the people who needed immediate healing just to get stabilized before they could be Cleansed and brought back to full health. Keeping them off death's door was the only thing that mattered now.

Thrusting his hands in the air, Tim let Eternia's healing waters wash over the dying.

It felt good to be helping people who really needed it again. The Healing Shack was his baby, and while Tim didn't get to go there as much as he liked anymore, the High Priest promised him that someone would always man it in his absence. This was his chance to do some of the good he was missing out on back home.

When Tim finished healing, Josh moved in and organized the healed, getting them back to where they were needed most. Tim moved through the crowds, healing everyone he could while trying to keep an eye on the healer's building for any sign of trouble. It would take him several hours, but he'd feel better carrying out the next part of his plan after all these people were healed and gone.

It wouldn't do a lot of good for his reputation as a healer to get caught assassinating a bunch of other healers, even if they were pieces of shit. Tim had to do this right. Once everyone was gone, he'd sneak in and off the bastards. When he got back to the oasis, he would tell Khalid he needed to find a new group of healers.

These weren't worth redeeming.

Tim moved from cluster to cluster as he healed all of Khalid's injured warriors. There were several hundred people here. It was the type of opportunity he needed to work on his Tarnished Circlet of Wisdom. He loved it when a quest served more than one purpose. Knocking out skill upgrades, item updates, and a quest all at once was the kind of thing that kept their guild ahead of the others.

Healing Storm took care of large groups of the lightly wounded, and Healing Orb took care of anything more serious. He moved from cluster to cluster with a purpose, only resting when he completely depleted his mana. What he really wanted now was a pair of those socks JaKobi won. It seemed like such a trivial boost, but he could use it right now. Maybe when this was over, he could search the auction house for something similar.

This was one of those situations where he didn't ask for money or thanks. These men had already paid to be healed and didn't receive the service. All he wanted to do was get them back in the fight and finish his quest.

Oh, and a nap. He *really* wanted that fucking nap.

It wasn't too long ago he hesitated and struggled with the thought of killing people in the game. Even bad people. He'd gotten over that little bit of hesitation although it still felt weird to him. Tim imagined that stabbing someone in *The Etheric Coast* felt exactly like it would in real life. The sensation added a sense of realism to the fights he wasn't exactly ready for, but now he was contemplating violence as the easy solution instead of the last resort.

Josh appeared after Tim finished healing the last of the wounded. "A few of us are going to stay and make sure you don't receive any interference from the other villagers."

He looked around at the empty courtyard. "Most of them were too afraid to come out when this place was full of the walking dead, but I don't know how long they'll stay in now that we've mostly cleared out. My guess is you'll want some room to work."

Tim thought about it for a few moments. If this town's entire existence was based on the healers and he wiped them out, there would be a lot of unhappy people here, and he might need help getting out. He also didn't want anyone to see him do what he was about to do. There was a reason assassins worked in the shadows.

"Keep the courtyard clear." Tim looked around at the empty area, wondering if he truly needed the help. "I'll be back as soon as I can."

"You got it," Josh shouted commands to a few of the men. "If any other wounded show up, I'll have them separated by severity and ready for you."

Tim hadn't considered that other wounded might continue to come for healing. Maybe he shouldn't kill the healers but give them the scare of a lifetime. His decision still up in the air, he walked toward the door. He'd make the call on what to do once he was inside. Looking at the sheet-covered corpses of people who didn't receive healing in time only bolstered his resolve.

Stealth would be his best bet going forward so Tim activated his and hoped the bonus from his Infiltrate skill would help him get eyes on the room and any potential targets before the fighting started. In a one-on-one battle, he might be okay. If there happened to be three or four of them inside, he could be in real trouble. Taking out as many as possible before being noticed would be crucial to his survival.

If he missed his nap because he died, Tim was going to be so fucking pissed.

Not to mention the shit he'd get from ShadowLily for missing their together time. She'd be worried, and he'd never hear the end of it. The last thing he wanted to do was have her fight all his battles for him, but if he couldn't handle this, she'd probably never let him out of her sight. He needed to show her that he was a grown man and fully capable of handling a little trouble on his own.

The real key here would be making it past the door. If he could slip inside unnoticed, then everything else would fall into place. He closed in on the door and reached out for the handle. Holding the handle down, Tim slid the door open a fraction of an inch. When no one called an alert, he pushed it open all the way.

Laughter spilled out into the courtyard.

"At least no one's going to hear me," Tim mumbled to himself as he slipped through the door and closed it behind him.

The building in front of him was one long hallway from back to front with rooms on each side. For now, the hallway was wide open, which was good because he could see the entire space and bad because there was nowhere to hide. Trying not to freak out about his escape options should things go awry, Tim focused on the details he could control.

Three rooms on each side, but only three lights on.

Tim looked at the lights. The first and third one on the left side were lit, and the middle one on the right-hand side. His initial feeling was to go toward the single light, but single didn't have to mean alone. Any of the rooms could have more than one person inside. By the sounds of the women's voices coming from the building, there was a very good chance he might run into additional complications.

Maybe murder wasn't the answer.

All he needed to do was make an example so the priests wouldn't accept Jabari's bribes until after they finished their healing for the day. Then Tim checked himself. People had died while these men indulged their needs. It was one thing to be a dick when you weren't hurting anyone, but this was some next-level indifference. It wasn't as if the wounded were half a world away. They were literally dying right outside the door.

Screw it. He wasn't going to get anything done by bitching about it.

Tim moved into the hallway and decided to check the unlit entry on his right before moving to the first room on the left. The longer he could keep things quiet the better, and it didn't pay to ignore a room because it was dark. His decision made, Tim moved to the door and grabbed the knob. He was pleased to notice that his fingers weren't sweaty.

JaKobi wasn't the only one who made strides since coming into the game.

It felt good to have a dagger back in his hand. Tim would have to buy himself a nice little upgrade if he planned to keep skulking in the shadows from time to time. The last thing he wanted was for his assassin's gear to fall so far behind it was almost useless. At this point he wasn't even bothering with changing his outfit. No one was going to tell an assassin they couldn't wear a robe if that's what made them happy.

The door inched open, and he stepped inside then closed the door quietly behind him. It was a good thing Tim decided to check this room first because there was a man passed out on the floor in the middle of the room. The only other thing of note that he could see was a large keg of wine in the corner.

"Maybe this guy had a personal stash." Tim looked around the room, but if everyone came in here for their wine, killing this man could potentially put him at risk if one of the other healers found him. Even if everyone was drunk, Tim was pretty sure they'd notice a dead body in the center of the floor.

Still, he was here now, and his Dad always told him never to leave a task unfinished. He almost laughed at the thought of his Dad's face if he saw how Tim was applying his life lessons. It was funny how some of the good ones applied to more than one situation.

If he were ShadowLily, Tim would probably have a cool skill to kill the man by stabbing him through the heart. Despite his cross-training, Tim wasn't a real assassin so he'd have to settle for something a little more practical. Like slitting the guy's throat. Last time he tried to kill a sleeping man he'd almost completely botched the job. This time he would do better.

It took a fraction of a second for him to unequip his boots. It left his feet vulnerable, but it also made him as silent as a person could be. He thought about ditching the robe to cut down on the rustling noises, but being called the naked assassin wasn't one of the things he wanted to discuss with people when he finally left *The Etheric Coast.*

The man didn't move as Tim pressed his dagger against his neck. He ran the blade through, making sure to go deep enough to hit the bone. It took more effort than he'd remembered, but at least he didn't screw it up.

Tim wasn't exactly proud of himself at the moment, but he also wasn't worried about this guy waking up and joining the fight later. If he wanted to get out of here and back to the oasis, he would have to be methodical but move with a speed that would leave *Agent 47*'s head spinning.

The best thing to do would be to check the other rooms with the lights off, then venture into more complicated territory. That plan only worked if he checked the other rooms quickly. Tim dropped back into stealth and moved into the hallway. Two rooms with lights on sandwiched the next room with the light off. Thankfully the walls weren't paper-thin or see-through, so he shouldn't have to worry about anyone seeing him unless the rooms were connected internally.

He moved to the door and stepped inside. The second room was empty.

Tim quickly double-checked the space to make sure he hadn't missed anything and exited. The sounds coming from the lit rooms were slowly losing vivacity, but the music was still jubilant enough to cover any stray sounds he might make. Without further delay, he moved into the hallway and toward the last entrance without a light on.

As he reached for the handle, the door opened.

Tim didn't look at who was in front of him. He put his free hand over their mouth and stabbed them repeatedly with his dagger as he pushed them back into the room. They hit the far wall with a *thud*, and Tim drove his knife home a few more times as the body slid down the wall and slumped on the floor.

The music hadn't skipped a beat so maybe he wasn't as loud as he thought. Every one of his senses was a jangled mess of information. His ears strained to pick up any sound, while his eyes watched the light coming in from the hallway for any signs of trouble. Tim tried to take a deep breath and realized he'd been holding his this entire time. He exhaled and then slowly backed away from the body.

While killing had become easier it turned out he still didn't enjoy it nearly as much when it was a person as he had to kill instead of a boss. Tim re-equipped his boots, and headed back out into the hallway. Dropping into stealth wasn't going to be much of a bonus for him, but he might get some extra damage in so it was worth a try. Any little bonus to his DPS was worth it right now.

He moved to the lit room directly across from him, and opened the door.

As soon as Tim walked into the room, he immediately wished he hadn't. Why was it whenever he walked in on people having sex it was always the worst two people in the world? Just once, he'd love to walk into a room and find two super sexy people throwing down. It just never worked out that way. Still, killing people while they were having sex was about as easy to do as when they were sleeping.

Not even bothering to try and hide, Tim rushed forward and stabbed the man on the bottom. Jabari's bribed healer looked at him with stunned eyes while Tim turned his to the woman on top of him.

After pulling a gold coin from his inventory, he handed it to her. "Stay quiet. This will all be over soon."

The woman nodded in shocked silence. She hadn't moved from where she straddled the man. If someone died on a person mid-coitus, did that make them a necrophiliac or merely someone with extremely bad luck? If that ever happened to him, he'd probably never have sex again. The last thing he wanted was for death to ruin sex for him. It was already hard enough to deal with.

Two rooms, two vacancies.

Since his good friend Norman wasn't here to help him create a few extra vacancies, it was time to make them himself. He had a woman to get back to and a nap to take. So he'd hit the last two rooms in order and get the hell out of Dodge.

Tim rushed into the next room, not wanting to stand in the doorway watching any more ugly hanky-panky and almost blundered into a woman. She squealed and dove to the floor, where she lay quivering in silence. The man on the bed looked from the woman back to Tim, his manhood going limp as he realized fun time was over.

"What is the meaning of this!" the healer shouted.

Tim ran across the room, clearing the distance before the asshole could do more than try and cover his shriveled cock. His knife found its way into the man's throat and ripped free.

"Silence is golden."

That one would give JaKobi a run for his money. What could he say? When the line fit, it just fit. Now they needed Cassie to up her game. The last one she used was pretty good, but he was starting to wonder if she liked yelling weird shit at people.

The man dropped dead, and the woman screamed.

So much for silence.

He'd been so close to being able to stealth his way through the building, but that was over now. Tim had to get to the last room and find out if it was empty before someone could escape and raise the alarm. He tossed a gold coin to the screaming woman, which shut her up instantly.

They said money couldn't buy happiness.

Tim darted back into the hallway, only this time he wasn't alone. A beast of a man ran toward him. As the man barreled into him all Tim could think was, *at least he had the decency to put on pants.*

Tim's back collided with the wall, and he heard something snap. He hoped it was the wall, but his adrenaline was pumping so hard it could as easily have been his ribs. His back hurt, but Tim had one advantage over the other healer. He had a knife. It didn't take much effort to drive the blade down into the healer's back, and that got his attention pretty quick.

The bastard let Tim go and tried to grab the knife. He always wondered why people did that. It was as though they forgot that pulling the knife out might be what killed them. In this case, it was the distraction he needed to attack. As the man in front of him tried to pull the knife from his back, Tim stabbed him in the guts four times with his other blade before spinning around the dying man and plucking his other blade free. He didn't even break stride as he sheathed the daggers and stepped out into the sun.

Is this what ShadowLily feels like all the time?

Tim did the inventory trick to clean off his gear. The last thing he wanted was for the people outside to see him covered in blood. It felt good to have been able to handle this quest on his own after all. Maybe he was a little more resourceful than he gave himself credit for. ShadowLily would be so proud of him.

Now if he could track down that camel, he could get the hell out there.

CHAPTER THIRTY-FIVE

The only thing JaKobi was missing was some phat beats.

That was the one thing he missed in *The Etheric Coast.* Music would have set the mood while he was doing research in the library. Sure, he could go somewhere where they had music playing, but it wasn't exactly easy to concentrate inside a tavern. Plus, then he'd have to be around a bunch of people, and his potential for getting anything accomplished with others around greatly diminished.

Instead of music, he swayed gently from side to side as his camel kept them moving toward their destination. The others might have hated these long rides across the empty desert, but he loved them. It was the perfect place to get some work done. His mom worked on her commute for years. No reason to waste her good example by being lazy.

Not that he was having any luck figuring out this latest spell. When the mage trainer handed him the book with a smirk, he thought it was just a "you're going to have to work hard for this" kind of thing, but it was more of a "you'll never solve this and your days of increasing your skills as a mage are over" kind of problem. Fucking puzzles. They were great—right up until they weren't.

JaKobi took one last look at symbols in the book and put it away. Staring at the pages and hoping something clicked wasn't going to do him any good. A quick thought brought up a map of the area, and the little dot he was heading toward was close enough he should probably crack open Khalid's quest and figure out what was in store for him.

Quest Received: Burning the Resources

Normally the resistance would prefer to capture the enemy's resources and use them, but the time for such tactics has ended. The battle must now be won in other ways, and the fewer resources Jabari's men have access to, the better. Go to the location on the map and make sure that none of the supplies are usable.

Reward: Ten gold coins

"Well, this should be easy. Burning is what I do." JaKobi whistled a little tune to himself as the camel continued slowly onward.

This would have been the perfect time for a line from his favorite book. *The man in black fled across the desert, and the gunslinger followed.* The only thing missing to make this little moment perfect was the man in black, because JaKobi was clearly the gunslinger. Ever since he'd read the book he wanted to make a kill shot and scream, "I kill with my heart, MOTHERFUCKER!" There probably wasn't a character more badass than Roland Deschain, and the fact that *Wizard and Glass* wasn't made into a standalone movie was simply ridiculous.

JaKobi loved the heroes from his favorite stories and was starting to think of himself as one of them.

Honorable. Well, of course, he was. Anyone would say so. Loyal. Only to his friends and family, which was an admittedly small list. Respect. He was probably a little too respectful, but the fire inside him wanted to burn, and he couldn't let it out for any little thing. Friendship. For the first time in his life, JaKobi had actual friends who cared about him, not just people that used him to get better grades in class.

And Cassie was the most amazing woman on the planet.

Sure, she hit him a little more often than he'd like, but she also made it up to him in ways he never experienced before. It was an amazing feeling to be with a woman who cared about him. Being with Cassie was all he'd ever wanted out of a relationship, and the best part was she also made him happy.

Head over heels, stupid in love, happy.

It was as if he didn't know what love was until it fell in his lap. While having time to work on his quest for a new spell was nice, he was ready to get back to Cassie. These quests were building to something, and their alone time together might become limited once the ass-kicking started.

It made sense, but he didn't have to like it.

JaKobi's camel decided that was the right time to spit. The sound made him look up and realize he was almost to his destination. He'd pretty much played it by ear since the beginning of this quest, and he was going to keep winging it. Tim probably would have a stroke if he knew JaKobi didn't plan out his fights at all.

He liked to let the battle come to him. It was the kind of thing he couldn't explain. Once the fighting started he just kind of felt the flow. There wasn't much to think about when the answer to the problem could be solved by throwing giant balls of fire at it.

"If you wanted to be a secret agent man, you gotta roll like a secret agent man," JaKobi whispered, trying to psych himself up for whatever came next.

If he told himself the truth, he'd much rather be doing this with his group, but sometimes a person had to find a way to succeed on their own. He reached deep, found the courage he had buried there, and rode his camel toward the fort's doors as if he didn't have a care in the world.

"Halt!" The two guards at the gate cried in unison.

JaKobi slowed his camel to a walk, then a stop. He studied the two men with an appraising eye. Both of them looked supremely confident. A scan of the ramparts above showed they didn't have much in the way of backup.

Did he look so meek that they weren't worried? Maybe he could use that to his advantage. He thought about it for a moment and tossed the idea away. This was his time away from the group, a time where he could cut loose.

"I say, my good fellows, you wouldn't happen to know where we are, would you?" JaKobi hopped off the camel and walked forward.

The two guards lowered their spears but seeing JaKobi unarmed gave them pause. They should have attacked him. It wasn't as if Jabari wanted everyone to know where his secret storage warehouse was. Just seeing this place should have been a death sentence so why they even hesitated was beyond him.

He wasn't going to make the same mistake.

JaKobi clapped his hands over his head, sending a burning Phoenix in between the guards and into the gate. The wooden gate burst into flames, and both men scrambled away from the heat, forgetting their spears in their haste not to catch on fire. He had something that could remedy that problem for them.

With a thought, he cast Flame Spear.

It always amazed him when a spear made of solid flames appeared in his hand and didn't burn him. Something about seeing the shock on someone's face right before he threw it at them was immensely satisfying. The two guards were no exception. The first one went down with a single spear. The second guard dodged fast enough to take only a glancing blow to the leg.

Then he disappeared as a fireball turned him to ash.

JaKobi was starting to feel it now. There was so much wood here, so many things to burn. He sent a fireball through the gate's wreckage before stepping into the fort itself. This would have made a fantastic scene in a movie, the hero blowing the gate up and walking through the fire to face the stunned soldier beyond. As much as he hated to admit it, he felt like a pretty big badass right now.

The soldiers inside must have thought so too because they fired arrows at him as soon as they saw him. A wall of flames took care of the projectiles. Then it was merely a matter of picking them off one at a time with controlled bursts of fire as they tried to reload. That was going a little too smoothly, and he was starting to feel like something big was about to happen.

Or maybe Jabari was spread so thin that he couldn't do any better?

The last soldier met his end, and JaKobi spun in a slow circle, taking in the fort's entirety and trying to decide what to burn next. It didn't matter since this was like a clearance sale at Crazy Mike's —everything must go. When it came to making things disappear, was there ever a better choice than fire?

Hot, beautiful, amazing FIRE.

While JaKobi couldn't melt through stone with any of his spells yet, he could burn most of the fort to ashes. Other than the walls and one building at the far end of the courtyard, everything was wood. Including the doors to the storerooms. The dry materials inside wouldn't take much persuasion to ignite so he only needed to pick a building and get started. Never one to waste time, he chose a door and cast a fireball.

The ball of fire disappeared halfway to its target as a woman's laughter filled the air.

"You arrived while I was indisposed. Kind of rude, don't you think?" The nameplate under the woman's feet labeled her as Vizerene.

This was when he got to play bad guy to the actual bad guy. How fucking cool was that? "Oh, I don't know. Kind of feels like I showed up at the right time."

"Maybe to kill some worthless filth, but not to deal with me." Water rippled down Vizerene's arms.

A water mage.

That explained her confidence. At best, their spells would even each other out. At worst, he might be at a slight disadvantage. The thing JaKobi needed to remember was he didn't need to kill her. All he had to do was burn the place to the ground. That put Vizerene at a distinct disadvantage because she couldn't just fight him. She also had to protect the fort's supplies.

If he could get her mad, JaKobi might be able to throw her off her game plan. "You can't be worth much to Jabari if he stationed you out here in the ass-end of nowhere."

It was kind of fun playing the villain. "And I have some dinner plans I can't miss."

Vizerene loosed a blast of water with a scream of rage. It was easy enough for JaKobi to throw up a wall of fire and use her distraction to ignite another of the storage rooms. Only three more and he could get out of here.

The same trick worked again to bring the remaining storage rooms down to two, but now she was onto his tactics and blocked all his attacks. They were at a stalemate for now, so maybe he would have to kill her anyway. He had a few tricks up his sleeve no one had seen yet, and it would sound so much cooler if he could say that no one alive had seen them yet.

It only then occurred to him that Vizerene might be trying to stall him until backup could arrive. She didn't have to beat him in a straight-up fight either to win. All she had to do was stop him from destroying the last two storage rooms. If she stalled him long enough, more of Jabari's soldiers would show up, and he'd be overwhelmed.

Something had to give. JaKobi needed to break the stalemate before he lost due to inaction. When in doubt, he took a strategy straight from George W. Shock and Awe. This fight needed an offensive explosion to get things moving along. While he didn't have any special bombs like he'd used against the werewolves in Tristholm, he did have a few jars of oil he'd been saving for the right occasion.

JaKobi loved spending time thinking of ways to expand his capabilities without magic. It never hurt to tinker a little, and the last thing he wanted was to become so reliant on his spells he forgot to think outside of the box. Having a non-magical way to spread his fire and make it last longer was something he'd been working on, but it was their fight against the Daughters that gave him his newest idea.

Adding a few jars of accelerant to his inventory felt like a natural evolution of the process. Instead of trying to match Vizerene spell for spell and hoping to get off a lucky hit that would bring her down, JaKobi changed tactics completely.

He used his Flame Shield to block her attacks as he slowly worked his way around the courtyard. Each time he moved to a new location, he tossed one of the jars on the ground behind himself and waited for the contents to spread before moving on. He tried to look desperate the entire time, as though he was running out of strength, and his shield was the only thing keeping him alive.

It took a little running and some acting on his part, but eventually, he circled the entire area and backed out of the fort. He tried to look as weak as possible while backing up, doing his scant best to deflect each of her attacks. It was hard not to laugh when he had her right where he wanted her.

Vizerene smiled. "Is that all you've got?"

JaKobi grinned from ear to ear and launched into the Carlton dance from *The Fresh Prince of Bel-Air* while singing, "You can't start a fire, you can't start a fire without a spark."

Vizerene thought he'd lost his mind as he let the last note trail off until his voice broke. With a flourish, he created a whip of fire in his hand and snapped it forward. As it cracked in the air, the smallest spark flew from the tip and glided down to the ground as gently as a snowflake. His opponent must have noticed the smell for the first time. Her eyes went wide as they followed the little glowing ember's progress.

The ember hit the accelerant with a wet fizzle, and nothing happened.

Vizerene looked up at him, a smile spreading across her lips as her eyes filled with smug satisfaction. "Look who couldn't get it up."

One second the world inside the fort looked as it always had, and the next, flames filled it from end to end. It didn't happen like in the movies where the flames chased around in a circle for dramatic effect. This fort went up like someone had dropped a nuclear bomb in the center.

"Maybe a little less accelerant next time." JaKobi opened his notepad and made a short notation before turning and looking for his camel.

Vizerene screamed once, but it cut off as the flames destroyed her.

The camel was waiting for him right where he left it with a look on its face that said, was all that necessary?

JaKobi sprang into the saddle, and they started the long journey back to the oasis. "Don't worry, friend." He patted one of the camel's humps. "The violence is all done for today."

He leaned back to get into a comfortable position and pulled out the book he'd been reading earlier about arcane spellwork. One thing JaKobi knew for certain was that he didn't mind these long trips. It gave him time to do the research he'd been slacking on. If he could figure out the spell and rub it in the faces of the people at the mage's college, it would make his day.

He truly did love to make things burn, and the shinies that came along with doing so.

He hadn't spent a lot of money since coming into the game, and with the crazy stupid bonus Tim paid him, it was probably time for him to buy Cassie a present. What did a guy buy for a mouthy little tank that he loved? Maybe he'd know it when he saw it.

JaKobi made a few small adjustments to get comfortable before letting out a contented sigh and turning the page of his book. The future would come to him soon enough. There was no reason to hurry.

CHAPTER THIRTY-SIX

"Balls." Cassie snorted under her breath.

She watched JaKobi ride off into the desert on his camel, and all she wanted to do was go with him. The guy couldn't function without her. He needed her, and she loved that about him. What kind of self-respecting mage goes toe-to-toe with an enemy when they could have their girlfriend take the heavy hits for them?

Sure, their relationship turned traditional stereotypes on their heads, but who cared? She certainly didn't, and she would be the one kicking all the ass. Being little and ignored gave her all kinds of reasons to get up in people's faces. Truth be told, part of why she became a tank was that people said she couldn't.

Cassie loved proving people wrong.

If they said it couldn't be done, she'd do it. That was who she was. Sometimes it worked out to her detriment, but she kept pushing. No one liked it when you were all up in their face, about everything, all the time. She was working on that, but meaningful change took time.

At least here she could take out her aggression on the bosses.

People always said it was wrong to express your feelings by

punching people's faces in, but as a tank, she never had to worry about that. Her job was to get in front of the big uglies and hit them as hard as she could repeatedly. Once the bosses were trying to kill her and only her, she knew she was doing her job right. Not a role for the faint of heart, but no one had ever accused her of lacking courage. If anything, she was a little too ballsy.

Now that Cassie found a man who appreciated her finer points everything was fine.

She sat and poured a glass of the honeyed tea. Despite what Tim thought about teas in general, she thought this might be the best drink she'd ever had. There was something about it that was more refreshing than a simple cool beverage. It was as though after drinking the tea, everything felt a little better.

It was like drinking the happy juice from *Big Trouble in Little China*.

Now that she was in the right state of mind it was time to grab a horse and get out of here. The others could ride camels if they wanted, but she wasn't into it. They spit, and the saddles weren't nearly as comfortable as the one on a horse. There was a reason you never saw the fearsome warriors riding into battles on camels.

Because horses were better.

Cassie mounted and gave the horse a long rub on the neck. "Get me where I'm going and back, and I'll make sure you're well taken care of."

The horse turned its head, focused one big eye on Cassie, and nodded once before taking off at a gentle trot.

Damn, she was in for it now. Making a promise to a horse was the same as making one to a kid. They never forget when owed something cool. It could be a candy bar or a new video game, but once promised, you had to deliver. In this case, Cassie would have to track something special down for her buddy. Oats and hay weren't going to cut it for her big guy.

She patted the horse's neck again and pulled out her letter from

Khalid. The envelope opened, revealing a single golden hieroglyph. It was so pretty she couldn't help running her finger across it.

Quest Received: Be Our Champion

Drix is a warrior nomad who earns much of his income from capturing resistance fighters and selling them to Jabari for interrogation. He has a shipment of our men on the way to the palace now. Catch up to the caravan and use Drix's fondness for gambling against him. Challenge him for the slaves and face his champion.

Reward: Ten gold coins

Despite Khalid being a cagey old bastard, she was starting to like the guy. This quest felt hand-tailored for her. All she wanted to do was be a hero, to show people that anything was possible if they put their minds to it. A person could learn to do almost anything if they cared enough to put the time in or wanted to give a big middle finger to the person who told them it wasn't possible.

She wasn't saying everyone was born to be a star, but a good teacher could get a raven to caw in the right keys.

While simply working hard might not make someone a starter, every coach loved someone who put in the daily grind without complaint. Head down, nose to the grindstone, making the most of every single opportunity given. That was the kind of person Cassie wanted to be. So basically, the same thing she was doing now with a little less punching when things went wrong.

Still, what was life without a little punching between friends?

If there was something to be done, she wanted to be doing it. Staying idle wasn't on her radar, not when she could be out living. JaKobi, on the other hand, could plunk his fine ass down anywhere and be as content as a bug in a rug. She wished she had his quiet resolve. They were total opposites, but it worked for them so she didn't fight it.

She watched the horizon for any change, then checked her map and tried to guess how long it would take to get to her destination. The answer was too fucking long. How could she have expected anything else in a land where everything looked the same? It was like being trapped on a raft at sea. Only here the water was the desert, and her horse was the raft.

And her only company.

"Wake me up when we get there." Cassie patted the horse's neck and closed her eyes.

She needed to save her mojo for when she got to their destination. If she took a little nap, it would keep her mind from running a mile a minute as it tended to do. That was why she tried to stay so busy. She couldn't shut the damn thing off unless she was sleeping. At least the problem didn't keep her up at night.

Most nights anyway.

Cassie jolted awake when her horse stopped moving.

"Thanks for the heads up." She gave the horse's neck an affectionate pet. "You keep doing good things, and I'm going to run out of gold keeping your belly full of apples."

The horse nickered in appreciation as Cassie dismounted.

She wondered if Khalid kept spare apples around or if she would have to hunt some down. Did they even have apples in the desert? If they didn't, what did they give their horses for being extra good boys?

A problem for another day.

As her feet hit the ground, Cassie took in her surroundings. There was a small cluster of tents to the right and a single larger tent on the left. Between them stretched a caravan of covered carts, only they were big enough to carry Khalid's men instead of supplies. Seeing the covered carts filled her with more rage than she expected.

Anger was good when you could harness it for the right reasons. The trick for her had always been finding the correct times to apply her rage. Cassie tended to fly off the handle before it was called for. A caravan full of people being sold off to be tortured seemed like the right kind of thing to throw down for.

Who was she trying to kid anyway? She loved a good fight and a fat stack of coins.

Cassie boldly walked into the camp and shouted, "I need to see Drix!"

A large man robed head to toe in luxurious green fabric strolled from the big tent on the left. Two armed guards huddled in the entrance behind him. "I do hope you have something interesting to say. I'd hate to think you came all this way just to die."

Cassie smiled. It was the same one she got on her face when some asshole asked if she needed help reaching the top shelf. "I heard there was a man in the desert with a cargo of resistance fighters and said to myself, that's a man I have to meet."

The guards behind Drix bristled, but he only looked her over with an appraising eye. "From the looks of things, I doubt you can match what Jabari is paying. Stop wasting my time. It's too hot out for such foolish nonsense."

"A wager then?" Cassie grinned.

Drix hesitated for a moment while rubbing his fingers through the stubble on his cheek. "What did you have in mind?"

"I take on your greatest warrior. If I win, I get the resistance fighters." Cassie tried her best to look innocent, but who was she kidding? She was a cocky bitch.

Deep rich laughter bubbled from Drix's lips. "What do I get if I win, your mangled corpse? There isn't a lot of resale value for broken girls. No deal." He turned and headed back into the tent.

Shit!

Cassie was missing her chance. Offering him nothing for winning clearly wasn't the kind of bet he wanted to take on, and a few gold coins wouldn't be nearly enough to cover the cost of the fighters. So she had to make an offer that wasn't enough, but one that would allow him to save face for accepting win or lose. Cassie reached into her inventory and separated a hundred gold coins into a bag, along with a hundred silver to make it seem heavier.

The bag of coins landed at Drix's feet. "Then let's make the wager a little more interesting."

Drix looked at the bag and back at Cassie. "Now I think we have something to discuss." He pointed at the caravan. "If you win, this rabble is all yours. My champion wins, and I keep the coins, and maybe get to sell what's left of you with the rest."

Cassie smiled sweetly. "You've got a deal."

Drix gave her an apologetic smile and bent to pick up the bag of coins. "I'll hold onto these until the decision is made. I'd hate to have you run off and leave me with nothing."

"Running isn't what I do," Cassie replied through gritted teeth. Being accused of cowardice made her bristle. She had to be sure she didn't get sucked into a Marty McFly moment. No insult was worth putting herself at risk, and taking on Drix plus an entire caravan's worth of guards would certainly put her at risk.

Drix clapped once, and men swarmed out of the tents on the right like ants. They moved the caravan out of the tents' protection and formed them into a circle.

The old warrior nodded as they finished setting up the fighting area. "Everyone says they won't run. Not all of them live up to the promise."

Cassie snorted. If the man wanted a little bravado, she could provide some. "Saving the men is merely a bonus for me. The only reason I'm here is that I like taking on the best. I heard you have a worthy challenger."

She pointed at the circled wagons. "Maybe it's time to stop the chatter and start the fighting."

Drix whispered something to one of the guards, who ran off. "I like you. Are you sure you wouldn't rather have a job than be the job?"

"I'm fine with the side I've chosen, but I appreciate the offer." Cassie walked toward the circled carts.

Drix huffed a few times as he ran to catch up. He laid a hand on her arm. "It's just that it would be such a waste to see such a pretty thing destroyed."

"Better back the fuck off before this pretty thing destroys everything you hold dear." Cassie grabbed the staff from her back and glared at the warrior.

All she wanted to do was beat that smug little smile off his face. Was being pretty a crime, or being a woman for that matter? She was going to make this arrogant shit eat his words for underestimating her, and it would be glorious.

Holding up his hands in surrender, Drix motioned for the carts to part and let her in. "Sometimes the voice of reason sounds like madness. Once you enter the ring, there will be no backing out."

Fuck this guy.

Instead of dignifying that with a response, she walked into the open circle as though she owned it. Intimidation didn't work on her. If anything it only served to harden her resolve. Cassie wasn't going to get the opportunity to take it out on Drix, but she was going to break his champion in half.

The ring of carts closed behind her, and Drix climbed on top of the nearest wagon. "Today another has come to challenge me, and in my place fights the one, the only, Fraxus."

Guards climbed on top of the caged wagons all around the circle. All of them chanted the name of their champion repeatedly. Cassie hoped the guy lived up to the hype because if he wasn't amazing, this would be one hell of a letdown.

Wagons at the far side of the circle split apart, and a man walked in holding a sword in each hand. He gave the weapons a few furious swooshes and screamed. The cheers doubled as he lifted his arms and drank in the appreciation of his people. Cassie watched it all with icy detachment. So far she wasn't impressed.

Fraxus moved toward the center of the circle. "Ready to die, little flower?"

"I'm ready to shove your big furry balls so far inside you that singing like a girl would be considered a compliment." Cassie bellowed and charged.

As she ran, she split her staff into two parts to match his twin blades. They crashed together a moment later. Cassie played to her strengths while she waited for Fraxus to make a mistake. His hands were fast, and his footwork was impeccable, but hers was better. She had an answer for each of his attacks. The cocky-ass smile Fraxus wore when entering the circle was quickly fading.

"Turn that frown upside down." Cassie grunted as she pushed him back a few steps and snapped her staff back together.

She launched herself at him without another word, putting every ounce of strength she had into each of her strikes. The single staff moved faster than his two swords as Cassie dodged and weaved around Fraxus' weak counters. She could tell he was getting upset, and upset people made mistakes. Maybe she could push him to further stupidity with the right insult.

"And to think, I was looking forward to this." Cassie dodged a round of attacks and then delivered a hit with her staff to his back.

She put every ounce of cockiness into her smile as she watched his eyes for the next move. "I should have stayed home. Khalid didn't need me to beat the likes of you."

Drix looked worried, but it was the kind of nervous twitching that led to cheating rather than running away. As if on cue, the warrior reached inside his green robes and pulled out a small vial.

He tossed the container to Fraxus. "Don't let me down."

The champion snatched the vial deftly out of the air and drank the contents in one fell swoop. His pants and shirt ripped as his muscles enlarged. Fraxus bellowed as the pain of transformation ripped through him. He stood panting in heavy, ragged breaths. When Fraxus' head snapped up, his eyes had turned solid black and were locked onto Cassie the way hers latched onto a slice of cake after dieting for three months.

Instead of being scared, she was excited. "Now that's more like it."

Fraxus charged across the space between them with his swords raised to come in from different angles of attack. In every fight, there was a moment. An instant where the fighter knew they won or lost based on a single attack. The champion's charge was what Cassie had been waiting for. Despite his bigger size, or maybe because of it, Fraxus was coming at her off balance and out of control.

The hook on her belt was the weapon she needed. Fraxus bore down on her, and Cassie stood stock-still, looking like a deer in the headlights. The idiot was soaking up every second of it. When Fraxus was ten feet away, she rolled forward and to the side as she tossed the hook.

Big ol' Fraxy must have been surprised when he ended up eating a face full of dirt instead of cutting her in half as he planned. But hey, that was the way the asshole crumbled.

Cassie never gave him time to get up.

The back of Fraxus' head made the sound of a coconut being cracked in half with a sledgehammer. His limbs flopped around as his body tried to fight the trauma. She'd never been into seeing anything suffer so she pulled a dagger free and slipped it in between the vertebrae on his neck.

Fraxus' life ended with a single thrust.

Cassie looked up at Drix on top of the cage wagon. "I believe you owe me some gold and the keys."

She could tell he was thinking of ordering his men to attack. The way she beat his champion into the next world so easily gave him pause. Even after Drix cheated it still hadn't been enough for his champion to win. Would his regular men fare any better? The wheels were turning, and she was enjoying watching the man squirm.

Eventually, the idiot would realize he didn't have a choice but to do what she asked of him.

"Fuck you. I name you Scourge of the Desert. If you ever enter my camps again, my men will kill you on sight." Drix tossed the bag of coins she'd put up for collateral at her feet.

After spitting on the ground, Drix reached into his robes and pulled out an iron ring with keys on it. He threw them next to the gold. Turning away from Cassie, he shouted at his men, "Break camp. It's time to go."

The men on top of the wagons all scurried away, and Cassie could hear the sounds of them breaking down tents in great haste. It seemed Drix was a poor loser, that or he might have been scared of what would happen when she opened the wagons and released the prisoners. There was no time like the present to get it done. She had an oasis to return to, and maybe she could sneak in a few more glasses of that honeyed tea before JaKobi made it back.

CHAPTER THIRTY-SEVEN

ShadowLily kind of missed questing alone.

It wasn't that she didn't love her friends. It was more that her style of play was easier to accomplish in solo situations. In the big boss fights, she spent way too much of her time positioning for damage that didn't have the same impact as she did when sneaking up on someone and gutting them from behind. She almost hated to admit it, but she felt a certain thrill right before delivering the perfect execution.

Deadly and methodical, that was how she handled her business.

She planned every single one of her kills down to the moment her daggers went to work. Sure, there were the occasional mishaps, but with enough planning, she avoided most of an assassin's pitfalls. It wasn't her fault most of her stabby brethren were more of the "run in, kill the target, and try to evade capture" types. Those kinds of players had their place, but she liked to think of herself as a well-oiled killing machine.

When she took a contract, she liked to watch her target for as long as possible. It wasn't as if she had the time to scout a sling as she wanted because their adventures kept her pretty busy. Still, showing a little restraint had saved her ass on more than one occasion. There was no reason to be hasty when a few minutes of simple observation would lead to the perfect kill.

Smart assassins don't end up dead.

Sometimes she almost felt more like a thief than a master assassin. Mostly because she spent her time sneaking around in the same way a master burglar would. Only, instead of stealing something at the end of her quests, she plunged her dagger into it. Lock-picking was also something she picked up along the way, although she used the skill to sneak into buildings, not to open chests.

ShadowLily liked to think her perfect kill streak would earn her a little respect in the assassin world, but most of the assassins were self-absorbed loners. It wasn't exactly the kind of profession that lent itself to having close friends in most circumstances. She found a way to make it work.

There was also a chance it wasn't only her friends that set her apart but her code of honor. For her, it mattered who she killed and why. If a job appeared on the board asking for help, she would take it. Evil landlord, strict overseer, rapists, murders, pretty much any job that fell into the protecting the little guy or avenging the wronged, and she was on it. Those jobs didn't normally pay as well, but they left her conscience clean.

A few people tried to take advantage of her generous nature once word got around. Setting up someone innocent for death was the kind of thing that ShadowLily despised. If she found out anyone did that to her, she killed them herself or put out a contract on their head. It didn't matter the price. No one pulled one over on her. Thankfully most of her brethren didn't share her concerns about who they killed, only the sound of coins entering their purse.

Unfortunately, her ambitions had to be put aside for the time being. There would be time for her to right the small wrongs of the world later. Right now they were working on saving a nation.

How cool would that be? Not many people could say they helped do something on such a grand scale. After this, they only had to topple a goddess. No big deal.

At least she'd have Tim by her side. She'd almost written him off when he'd broken out into a song at their graduation, but something told her to give him a chance. What do you know? She'd met the first guy in a long time who wasn't a total piece of shit. ShadowLily didn't know what it was with her fondness for bad boys, but having a good man in her life was a game-changer. Even if he was addicted to coffee.

There were worse things. Her last boyfriend had been addicted to his ego.

Arrogance was such an unbecoming trait. It was okay to recognize the greatness in others, but always talking about being the best was tiresome. A person didn't have to be the best at everything or own the coolest new things to have worth. Some of the best people she knew worked their asses off at jobs that earned them little or no respect but kept food on the table and a roof over their families' heads.

Everyone talked shit about plumbers until a pipe burst in the middle of the night with your family in town for the holidays. Then that plumber was the most respected person in the world. Sometimes saving the world took a big sweaty ass and some low-hanging jeans.

Her ass might not be big or very sweaty, but she liked to think since coming into the game, she'd helped more than a few people solve some unsolvable problems. Maybe instead of an assassin, she could call herself a fixer. Had a nice little ring to it and none of the "I'm always a breath away from killing you" vibe that the word assassin connotated. Although, it might have been a bit disingenuous since she only solved problems one way. By killing them.

ShadowLily jumped into her camel's saddle and pulled out the card Khalid had given her. A quest prompt opened as she stroked her thumb over the golden hieroglyph.

Quest Received: Dancing with Deception

When is an assassin not an assassin? When she's a thief, of course. There is a location I need you to break into and retrieve a bundle of letters from inside a locked chest. A red ribbon will tie the letters together. Normally I'd put your blades to better use, but with Jabari's generals defeated, this is the task that needs doing now.

Not what she'd expected, but the wording was wildly complimentary so she was willing to branch out a bit.

Quest Reward: Ten gold coins

Bonus: Complete the mission without killing anyone and receive an additional five gold coins.

And a challenge.

Khalid might not be the best at sharing secrets, but he was a hell of a quest giver. He left her the ability to kill with one hand while offering her an incentive not to do it with the other. ShadowLily was starting to think this wasn't the kind of man to get on his wrong side. He was playing a long game, thinking seven steps ahead of everyone else.

She guided her camel onto the right course and leaned back in the saddle. After plucking one of her daggers free, she started to sharpen it. The weapons didn't need sharpening, but it made her feel like she was doing something to respect them so they wouldn't let her down in a moment of need. Or in this case, she gave them loving caresses because she wouldn't be using them for a while.

***

This fort looked more like a small town.

"This quest would be so much easier at night," ShadowLily huffed as she watched the guards moving on patrol by the gate.

The only thing she knew for certain at this point was she wouldn't get inside on her camel. A small grove of palm trees outside the fort looked like a tailor-made place for her to leave her horse. She didn't tie it in place in case she died and didn't make it back in time. This was a game, but ShadowLily didn't want the camel starving to death because of her.

"I'll be back." ShadowLily patted her mount and dropped into stealth.

Her skill wasn't strong enough to make her disappear in the bright desert sun, but it did make it harder for people to notice her. Now she needed to wait until a group of people went in or out of the fort so she could slip in among them. Once she was inside, she'd have to follow Khalid's map to the chest.

As if on cue, a large group of people—maybe ten or twelve trailing behind a wagon and two or three in front of it—passed her. ShadowLily doubted this would happen on a loop so she had to go now, or she'd miss her only opportunity until nightfall. Damned if she wasn't tempted to say fuck it and just kill everyone.

She didn't need the extra gold, but Khalid had sucked her in with the challenge.

ShadowLily burst from cover, running in a low crouch. Her stealth ability provided her enough camouflage that unless someone looked directly at her, they wouldn't see anything but a shimmer. The trick wouldn't work on the gate guards since they tended to look at people. It was kind of their job. She needed to find a way to blend in with the crowd behind the wagon or find a way to wedge herself under it.

Getting under the wagon held the most appeal to her, but that would mean weaving through the people walking behind it. From there she'd either have to pray someone didn't see, or they would keep their big fat gobs shut as they went through the gate.

There wasn't much she could do about it now. The group was already closer to the gate than she would have liked. As she ran, ShadowLily noticed that the men and women behind the cart had their feet chained together. None of them appeared to want to do anything except stop walking. It was like watching the walking dead. Most of them didn't even have their eyes open. She moved through their numbers like a gentle breeze and dove under the cart.

There wasn't a lot to hold onto beneath it, but she managed to wedge herself into a small gap. Hopefully, the guards would pass the cart through the gates quickly because she couldn't hold herself in this position forever.

Not yet, anyway.

"We've got a delivery for Kyron." A woman from the front of the caravan called. "New batch of workers for the mine."

If this fort had a mine, it explained why it was so much bigger than the other ones. There was more wealth, then Jabari would need more men to guard it, and ten times as many laborers to see the mine operated at its full potential. Nothing said big extra profits like free labor.

The guards must have motioned for the gates to open because the caravan moved forward again. "He's in a mood today. You better hurry."

The woman laughed. "When isn't he? At least Kyron won't be disappointed with this lot. Sturdy workers, every last one of them." She banged her hand against the cart for emphasis.

The guard watched the progression of the sorry caravan start to move forward. "I doubt that." Some laughter from the other guards. "That kid can't be more than twelve. If he can swing a pickaxe, I'm a captain of the guard."

"We all know after the number ten the next one might as well be fifty. There's work in the kitchens as well," the woman quipped.

Just like that, ShadowLily and the cart were inside the fortress. The large wooden gates closed behind them, sealing her inside the fort with a *crack*. A quick check of Khalid's map and she knew where she needed to go. All she had to do now was figure out the best way to get there. The cart was still going that direction, but she'd be better off approaching on her terms than trying to stay wedged underneath it.

Falling flat on her ass, too tired to stand, let alone use her daggers wasn't an appealing thought. If she were going to die, it'd be fighting not hiding like a coward. Skipping the dying part was probably number one on her to-do list for the day.

ShadowLily waited until there was a gap in the buildings, then rolled out from under the cart into an alley between two structures. She came up next to a low stone wall, slunk over it, and knelt. The three-foot-tall retaining wall gave her a chance to scan the fort ahead. Not a lot to be thankful for stared back at her. This section appeared to be guards for the mines.

Part of her already wished she'd stayed with the cart.

At least the next part of the quest was simple. All she had to do was get from where she was now to her target location. If Shadow-Lily could pull that off without a problem, the rest would fall into place. How hard could it be to sneak in, steal some shit, and get out? Stealing had to take less effort than killing people, right?

This was a great time to test the limits of her skills, and ShadowLily was more than up to the challenge. Ninety percent of staying hidden was planning. It paid to know or be able to guess where and when people would be looking. If she could stay ahead of being full-on spotted, her stealth would do the rest.

Easy-peasy.

ShadowLily jumped the wall, sprinted to the other side of the street, and dove behind some crates. Her heart was thumping now. Getting caught here would most likely result in deadly consequences. Death was the kind of thing that would put a crimp in her plans, so she decided to avoid it at all costs.

No one called out in shock, and her jackhammering heart slowed to dull thudding. Attackers didn't surround the crates she hid behind, and no one was running off to sound the alarm.

"I need to pull it together." Shadow Lily drew a few deep breaths to calm herself, and then she was moving again.

Most of the men must have been busy working their shifts because it was easier to move through the fort than she anticipated. A few times she thought for sure that she'd been busted, but the guards kept moving. She didn't know how spies did this. Sneaking into places you weren't supposed to be was the most stressful thing on the planet.

For the next twenty minutes, she gritted her teeth in suspense every time she heard a noise, but ShadowLily made it to her destination without being seen.

"Would have taken me five minutes to kill them all." ShadowLily stayed low and stuck to the alleys as she scouted her destination.

The outside looked clear enough.

One door led inside the building, and four men guarded it—two on the inside and two on the outside. Going through the door and earning the extra gold wasn't going to be an option, and ShadowLily wasn't quite ready to forgo her bonus. She continued scouting the perimeter, looking for a secondary entrance. Any of the windows would have been perfect, but it looked like they were all closed against the heat of the day.

Maybe there was a balcony?

Circling the property again revealed a small Juliet balcony on the second floor hidden by some superior stonework. The door leading to the balcony was open, and all that was stopping her from getting inside that way was about twelve feet of height and a willingness to go for it.

"I'm no Jackie Chan, but I got this." ShadowLily started to run.

She leapt into the air, kicked off the wall, and flew toward the ledge.

When ShadowLily's fingers closed around the stone, she knew she made it. Now she had to get inside before someone saw her dangling on the side of the building like an idiot. What a mess. It wasn't exactly stealth one-oh-one to be hanging from a balcony in broad daylight. At least an alarm hadn't sounded. If she hurried, ShadowLily might get inside before that happened.

With the strength of a professional rock climber, ShadowLily pulled herself up and inside the building. Not the graceful cat burglar entrance she'd wanted to make, but it wasn't like anyone had caught her yet. Sometimes a good thief needed a little luck. It certainly helped that the guards were looking for wayward miners and not an attack from inside. A person would have to be nuts to break into the fort, then into a building without looking inside first.

Gaston would be so disappointed.

The room was empty, but that was a coincidence. If she wanted to get out of the building unseen and alive, she would have to do a much better job of paying attention to the details. The plus side of being an assassin was that she could normally stab her way out of trouble, which sadly wasn't an option today.

ShadowLily crept forward and stopped by the door. In the comparative darkness of the interior, her stealth was much more effective than it was outside. No sound came from the other side of the door, but that didn't mean much in a world full of magic. If she wanted this to go smoothly, she had to play it safe.

This quest felt a lot like she was playing *Hitman* or *Thief*. In those games, patience was the key. ShadowLily wasn't always the best at waiting around and usually ended up fighting for her life and having to replay the level a few times before getting it right. Today she was going to take a page from Tim's book and take things slow and steady.

The knob turned slowly but was well-oiled and didn't make a sound. As she slipped the door open, one of the hinges squeaked. Her heart rate increased, but no one cried out in alarm as she continued to pull the door open. From her current vantage point, ShadowLily could only see down the hallway in one direction. The only way to check the other side was to open the door further.

No one stood in the hallway, but things couldn't be as easy as climbing onto a balcony and walking out with the letters. The tension of this job was getting to her. Every breath, every noise, felt like it would make the world crash down on her.

The chest was located two doors down on the right.

Once she was in the hallway, there was nothing to hide behind. Not being spotted would take a hundred percent commitment. Any hesitation or indecision could get her caught, and she hadn't suffered through all this bullshit to give up those extra coins now. Slipping one of her throwing knives free, she placed it between her teeth and took another in her right hand.

Khalid said she couldn't kill anyone, not that she couldn't maim or wound them. If there ended up being a room full of armed guards around the chest, then she could stab a few legs and maybe still get out of there without failing. It'd be risky, but she might be able to pull it off.

God, she loved a challenge, even when it pissed her off.

She moved into the hallway and gently pulled the door closed behind her. The first entry on her left was closed, and she cruised right past it. The next one on her right was open, but it sounded like someone was sleeping in there. A glance confirmed only one person inside, and they were in bed. Part of her wanted to close the door to be safe, but any noise wasn't worth the risk.

A crash sounded in the room to her left, and a man swore. It was the kind of noise someone made when they spilled something on themselves and had to clean it up. Her only choices were to move forward before that happened or go back into the room where the man was sleeping and hope she could hunker down until the coast was clear.

She was out of patience. It was time to move.

The door on her left burst open as she reached her destination. She heard a man stumble into the hall behind her while cursing quietly to himself. ShadowLily stepped inside the room and shut the door behind her. She rested her back against the door, closed her eyes, and drew a few deep breaths.

I'm inside.

The man in the hallway wasn't screaming for her head. No one slammed into the door. Next time she did something like this, ShadowLily needed to remember that patience was key, and being safe didn't necessarily mean run as fast as you can. Sometimes it paid to take time and be cautious.

She sighed in relief, tucked the knife in her hand back into the bandolier around her chest, and moved the knife from her mouth to her hand. Then she looked up for the first time since walking into the room and froze in place like a possum caught in the headlights.

A guard stood in front of the chest. He looked at her with the same shocked expression she must have been wearing. The only difference between them was the guard had a glass of wine in his hand, and she had a knife. They both stayed frozen, neither knowing what to do next, then everything turned to shit.

The guard threw his wineglass at her.

It was easy enough to dodge the glass and throw her knife, but the noise from the shattering glass would be loud enough to bring help. Her blade sank into the guard's thigh as he reached for his sword and called for help. It would have been easier to kill him, but the guard limping toward her was using his sword more like a cane than a weapon. The guard stumbled forward, took a wild swing at her, and fell flat on his face with a grunt.

While rushing past the downed man to the chest, ShadowLily realized his attack wasn't as wild as she thought. There was a long gouge in her leather pants, and a small amount of blood leaking through the split in the armor. That had been close, too damn close.

"I fucking love these pants!" It wasn't exactly honorable to kick a man in the face when he couldn't stand, but this one had tried to cut her leg off so ShadowLily gave herself a pass.

His nose made a sickening *crunch* when her foot slammed into it. The snap was also pretty satisfying, kind of like when she snapped one of her late-night KitKats. After the kick to the head, the guard stopped moving. It might have been a little overkill, but a quick check of the guard's pulse confirmed he was still alive.

That was more than she'd be able to say about herself if she didn't hurry.

ShadowLily ran for the chest, flipped open the lid, and snatched the letters. Khalid didn't mention anything about not stealing anything else, so she helped herself to a few of the more interesting items she saw right away and closed the lid. It felt kind of funny that she was risking her life for what looked like old love letters and none of the jewelry or coins.

Fuck it.

She'd never been that good of a thief so she shoved a couple of handfuls into her inventory and closed the chest, the entire time reminding herself it was a game. Once when she was a kid, she stole a candy bar from the store. All she could think about for days was how she'd done something wrong. As soon as she got her allowance, she went to the store and confessed everything. It made her feel better knowing she was honest, and going back wasn't something her dad made her do.

Stealing gold from assholes didn't bother her nearly as much, and if her conscience felt a little too heavy, she could hand over the loot with the letters. ShadowLily was sure the resistance could use all the financial help they could get.

A man burst into the room with a knife in one hand and rubbing sleep from his eyes with the other. It was simple enough to slip inside his guard and deliver an uppercut straight to his chin. The man crumpled like a suit after a sixteen-hour day at the office. ShadowLily took one step to the side and let his unconscious body fall past her into the room, and she was out in the hallway with the two unconscious men behind her.

It sounded like more guards were coming up the stairs to her right so she sprinted toward the room with the balcony. From there, it was simple enough for her to jump out the window and run. Her stealth was on, but it wouldn't be good for much while moving at full speed in the sun. All she could do now was hope that by the time someone did a double-take, she was gone.

Running wasn't her specialty.

ShadowLily was a swimmer, and when it called for it, a wicked good dancer. Dancing wouldn't get her out of trouble here, and she didn't see any water. With her two favorite methods of escape off the table, she did what any busted thief would do. She ran like a life sentence was chasing her.

Vaulting over crates, running through open doors, tip-toeing across roofs, she did it all on the way to the gate and her freedom. This was where things would get tricky. ShadowLily couldn't hobble four armed guards, then get on her horse and ride away. It would be too easy to follow her into the desert, and she risked leading Jabari's men back to the oasis.

"This shit isn't worth five gold coins." Still, ShadowLily knew she wouldn't kill anyone, not when she was this close to getting out.

Maybe it was time to pull a Sparrow.

Jack Sparrow might have been a shitty pirate, but he was good at getting out of trouble. With direct confrontation off the table, she had to find a new way to handle things. Just like when she needed to ditch an overeager guy at the bar, it was time to get creative. It was time to pull a Sparrow.

ShadowLily paused and pulled out one of JaKobi's prototype fire pong balls from her inventory. She had no idea why she kept the damn thing. It was one of the early prototypes, and only JaKobi could touch the damn things without burning himself. It was just the thing she needed now to get out of this mess. The ball appeared in her hand, and she yelped as the flames burned her skin.

Before the burns could get too bad, she tossed the flaming sphere into a pile of crates.

A minute later, a nice little blaze burned not far from the gate. A bell rang somewhere behind her, but with the smoke rising into the air she hoped most of the guards would think it was for the fire and not from her exploits stealing the letters. As the men scrambled to contain the blaze, she slipped through the gate and sprinted toward her horse.

Once ShadowLily was in the saddle and off to rejoin the others, she felt terrific about how things had gone. Hopefully, Tim would be waiting for her at the oasis when she got back and could heal her hand and leg. JaKobi's little death balls might not work as intended, but they did work, and that had to count for something. She wrapped a spare piece of cloth around her hand and directed her horse toward the oasis.

Maybe she wasn't such a bad thief after all.

CHAPTER THIRTY-EIGHT

Lorelei was having a blast.

The desert itself wasn't that great, but Neema was phenomenal. It was as though she finally met someone who got her. There was this thing that happened where they knew what the other one was thinking even if they didn't say the words out loud. She'd never felt like this with anyone else before.

The only thing holding her back was that she knew it wasn't real.

Eventually, she'd have to leave the game and Neema behind.

It was funny what a person could rationalize away when they wanted to. Neema might have only been code, but she was brilliant code that made Lorelei feel wanted. At the end of the day was the woman any less real? She could see, hear, touch, smell, and taste her. If that wasn't real, maybe they were all bits of random code, and God was their developer.

Things might not be that simple, but they could be however she wanted them to be. Inside the game, she was the boss and created her destiny. Right now Neema was part of that, and she loved every minute of it.

"Neema, where are we going?" They'd left so quickly that she hadn't opened her quest card from Khalid.

The Desert Wolf turned in her saddle so she faced the ranger. "Why don't you open your quest and find out?"

She hated playing games. It was like bitch, if you know where we're going, tell me already. Then there was a part of her that knew that wasn't how videogames worked. If she wanted the quest, she had to accept it.

Those were the rules.

Lorelei reached inside her vest and pulled out Khalid's envelope. It took her a moment to pull the card free. Then she downloaded the quest information the way Chuck flashed on the intersect.

Quest Received: It Takes Two to Tango

Hidden treasure doesn't need to be hidden all that well when it has a guardian. Find the tomb of Nemset, and secure The Viridian Shroud. Our people need a symbol to show them they can trust us. The Shroud is a symbol of Eternia we can display for all to see.

Quest Reward: Ten gold coins

Lorelei accepted the quest.

Entering a tomb and killing the guardian to retrieve an ancient piece of treasure sounded like a quest that was right about her speed. The fact that she could hand Neema the shroud and further her goals for the resistance was a bonus. One she hoped the Desert Wolf would pay back with a kiss.

Gold, treasure, girls—just another day at the office.

Things might not have gone her way since she entered the game. Still, a broken heart and a horrible rebound weren't enough to keep her from stepping up to the plate to take another swing. What good was the ability to love if you were too scared to use it?

"Now that you see where we're going, are you excited?" Neema was grinning from ear to ear, thrilled about the possibility of a treasure hunt.

Lorelei jumped from the back of her horse and landed behind Neema, easily swaying with the her new mount's movements. She turned the warrior's head to kiss her. "I'd be more excited if we were back in your tent, but a treasure hunt comes in a close second."

"Good, now get back on your horse and settle in. We have a long ride ahead of us." Neema leaned back and gave her another kiss.

Jumping from Neema's steed back to hers, Lorelei felt herself finally letting go. There was no reason for her to be worried. Things felt so natural right now, as though this was where she was supposed to be. She'd learned a long time ago to trust her instincts about people and places. They weren't always right, but they served her better than she liked to give them credit for.

Her gut told her she could trust Neema with her life. So that's what she did. Lorelei leaned back in her saddle and tried to get comfortable for the journey. If she could fall asleep for a while, it would feel like they got there in an instant.

Treasure hunts were never really her thing.

She did have a little crush on the women who played Lara Croft in the movies. It didn't matter to her if it was Angelina or Vikander. Lorelei thought both of them rocked the outfit with their brand of sexy. Who wouldn't be attracted to a billionaire with a penchant for danger and adventure? It was like Lara was Batman and Indiana Jones rolled into one.

Smart and badass were the new sexy.

She had her version of smart and sexy dismounting right in front of her. They had reached the Tomb of Nemset, and it was time for them to go inside. Lorelei slid from her saddle and pulled her bow free as soon as she hit the ground. She looked over the weapon enjoying the feel of her new toy.

Neema saw Lorelei's selection of weapons and yanked her sword from its sheath. "I'll lead the way."

The Desert Wolf pulled a torch from her inventory and walked into the square archway. Was it odd that the tomb's entrance wasn't sealed? This place was out in the middle of nowhere, but surely someone would have found and looted it by now.

Unless the guardian killed them all.

As the quest said, a tomb didn't need a door when there was a scary-ass monster waiting inside. Neema stepped into the Darkness, and Lorelei followed. The torch gave off a good deal more light than she thought it would, but right now she would have killed for one of JaKobi's little light balls. It was funny how she got so used to her group's perks. Doing things the old-fashioned way felt harder than it should have.

There was plenty to be thankful for. She had a light, and she wasn't as alone as the rest of her guild was right now. Looking on the positive side of things wasn't her specialty, but she was working on it. Why be grumpy all the time? Life had become so much easier to live when she stopped worrying about what other people were doing and focused on what made her happy. Like going on treasure hunts with super sexy girls.

The view from behind Neema was exactly the kind of content she was into.

Lorelei forced her eyes away from Neema to look at their surroundings. It wouldn't do her any good to die because she was too busy checking out Neema's ass. The cavern around them wasn't much larger than the entrance had been. She'd expected the space to open up relatively quickly, but it was as if they were walking down the world's longest hallway.

"Wow." Neema sounded awed as she stopped moving.

Lorelei closed the distance between them and looked over Neema's shoulder. "It's beautiful."

A single ray of sunlight penetrated the cavern from above. The hallway they were in must have sloped down the entire time they were inside. Lorelei was kind of surprised that she couldn't tell as they walked. She usually was more in tune with the environment around her.

The sunlight wasn't strong enough to illuminate the entire space, but it did highlight a stand with The Viridian Shroud draped over it at the far side of the room. "I don't see the champion."

Neema inched forward. "Nor do I. Maybe it died. There can't be a lot of food out here."

"Just idiots looking for treasure." Lorelei's voice dripped with sarcasm.

Pausing again at the entrance, Neema looked back at her. "You know, just once, I'd like to get lucky."

"I can help you with that after we get the shroud." Lorelei winked at her.

It could have been the firelight, but Neema might have also blushed. "Let's see what we've gotten ourselves into first." She handed the torch to Lorelei. "Care to do the honors?"

Lorelei took the torch but was unsure of what to do with it. Neema pointed past her to a sconce on the wall. It didn't take much thought to figure out what to do from there. She walked to the sconce and lit the torch resting inside it on fire.

Flames snapped and crackled as the old dry torch lit. It took a moment for the fire to take hold. Then it burst to life as if waiting for this very moment to shine. One by one, torches lit all around the cavern. The entire space was as well-lit as if they stood outside in the bright desert sun.

Lighting the room didn't accomplish much more than that.

Now it was easier to see the wide-open space between them and the shroud, but nothing else had changed. Sadly there weren't any secret characters revealed on the floor leading the way to the artifact. A champion hadn't yet appeared to challenge them either. Maybe they were going to get lucky.

The door behind them started to rumble closed.

Luck didn't appear to be on the menu tonight, but at least they were being offered a chance to back out if they wanted. The door slid closed at a pace that would allow them to dive back under if they wanted to. Part of her was screaming to roll under it and take Neema back to her tent for a lovemaking session. The look of pure excitement on the Desert Wolf's face made her dismiss that idea out of hand. They came to get the shroud, and that was what they'd do.

The door's rumble stopped, and the floor started to shake. The earth in the middle of the room broke apart as if something large was digging its way out. Whatever was coming for them must have been giant—and pissed off. Lorelei was starting to get a bad feeling. Rocks shifted, and something emerged.

One giant pincer appeared, and another one.

They were in the desert. It sure as fuck wouldn't be a lobster crawling out of the ground. That only left one creature she could think of, and Lorelei wasn't pleased. The full scorpion burst from the cavern floor and shook the dirt off its dark golden carapace. Now that the monster was free, its multitude of eyes searched the room for the cause of the disturbance.

"That's not what I was expecting," Neema breathed out in a low whisper.

Not what she was expecting?

All Lorelei wanted to do was lie in bed all day exploring the wonders of Neema, and now she had to face off with an ancient monster. Why couldn't the tomb's champion be some asshole she could fill with arrows from far away?

Fuck it. She could fill a bug full of arrows as easily as a person.

The first arrow hit the scorpion on the back and skittered off into the cavern. "Maybe not as easy as people." Lorelei looked at the creature, trying to decide how she could make a bigger impact.

Neema didn't seem worried by Lorelei's effectiveness. She ran into the battle with a smile on her face. She bounced her blade off one of the arachnid's armored legs. "Aim for the gaps, as you would with plate mail."

Look for the cracks between the plates. She could do that.

The problem was the plates kept moving, and the opening was there one second and covered the next. It was going to take her a minute to figure out how to fire an arrow that would damage the scorpion. There was a chance she might be better off running in and stabbing the fucker with her new hunting knife. Eight legs and a tail dripping with poison was a lot to worry about, but if she couldn't do damage from a distance, Lorelei would have to get up close and nasty.

The scorpion was fully focused on Neema now. The warrior was holding her own, but for how long? Without help, all it would take is one missed step, and the Desert Wolf would be dead. Not that the warrior noticed. She smiled at death as if this fight was a welcome distraction from all the others.

Two more of Lorelei's arrows bounced harmlessly away, and the ranger started to wish she had a giant fucking hammer. There was no better way to kill a bug than by squashing it into a paste. Since she lacked a dwarven war hammer and the strength to use it, she might as well try to use what was available.

This felt like the time when Tim would come up with some kind of crazy realization that saved all their asses. Lorelei looked at the top of the cavern, expecting to see some rocks she could knock loose with an arrow, but the top of the cave was smooth. Where was that big-brained bastard when she needed him? She had to be missing something. One thought kept running through her mind.

What would Tim do?

Nothing jumped out at her so she decided to take a much less subtle approach. Lorelei put her bow away and grabbed her new knife. She'd been trying to upgrade her skills with small blades, but finding the time to fit it in during boss fights was hard. This felt like the perfect opportunity to get some quality work in.

At least it's not a giant spider.

Was it wrong that spiders felt more creepy when a scorpion was infinitely more deadly? Six armored legs to move on, and that didn't include the two massive pincers. If the pincers weren't enough to convince someone a scorpion was more deadly, all that someone had to do was look at the tail of death and the solid armored carapace. What good were eight legs and a little webbing against all of that might? Yet, she'd rather face two giant scorpions over the one giant spider.

Spiders were the worst.

Neema turned the scorpion to make things easier for Lorelei's approach. The ranger didn't waste the opportunity. Coming in from behind, she rolled underneath the giant bug and waited for an opening. The monster shifted to the right, and she stuck her blade into the gap between plates. Wrenching the knife free, she dove out from underneath the scorpion, sliding across the ground like a baseball player.

The boss did a belly flop that shook the entire cavern.

Dust flew up from the cavern floor as the boss started to climb back to its feet. Realizing that its attacker must have moved away, the scorpion turned and searched the room for her. Lorelei could have sworn she saw eight or ten eyes narrow as the creature locked in on her position. A leg swept Neema to the side as if she were a harmless fly, and the scorpion charged straight for Lorelei.

She used to think of herself as brave.

Facing down two werewolves on her own and escorting a family to the city of Tristholm while being hunted came to mind. The guild faced down bosses that would make the average person shit in their pants, but nothing prepared a girl for having a giant scorpion coming right at her.

And the fucker was *fast*.

Scorpions always looked like slow, lumbering creatures in the movies, but this thing was quick. Lorelei wasn't sure if she could outrun it, and it wasn't like she had a shield to keep her safe.

Dodging around the creature's attacks wasn't that appealing when there wasn't a healer with Cleanse nearby.

So she did what anyone would do. She ran. Not only did she run, but she ran fucking fast, as if her life depended on it.

Road Runner fast.

The one thing the ranger had going for her was that her class had a few viable escape moves. She didn't spend a lot of time running away so the skills weren't as robust as some of her straight offensive powers, but they were useful under the right circumstances.

Lorelei reached into her bag, grabbed a handful of sharpened caltrops, and tossed them behind her. With a thought, she activated the skill Aggressive Evasion, and the caltrops multiplied into the hundreds while spreading out in a fan behind her.

The scorpion slid to a stop, avoiding the metal spikes on the ground, but failed to consider where Neema was. The Desert Wolf let out a fearsome cry as her sword hacked into the scorpion's tail and severed the limb from its body. The guardian whirled around, knocking Neema away.

Lorelei gasped in terror as her lover hit the cavern wall and slid lifelessly to the ground. This couldn't be happening again. Seriously, the game wouldn't be this cruel to her, not when she was so close to having something special.

Never again.

She sprinted toward the scorpion without a thought to her safety and let out a roar that would have made Khalid proud. With her hunting knife in hand, she sprang into the air and landed on the guardian's back. Three bounding steps forward, and the same blade went into one of its massive eyes, turning it into a useless paste.

The screech that filled the room was enough to make her lose concentration for a moment. Lorelei hacked at the boss as she slid toward the ground. On the way down, she managed to sever a leg. She hit the dirt and took a blow to the head as the scorpion danced away from her. Wobbling back and forth as she climbed back to her feet, Lorelei held her blade in front of her and waved it back and forth as if it was Excalibur itself instead of a hunting knife.

Against the guardian, it might as well have been a toothpick.

Her vision started to clear, and Lorelei could see that she was waving her blade at the scorpion's back as it tried to run away. The creature fell to the ground a few steps later and started twitching. The legs curled inward, and the body disappeared in beautiful golden swirls of light, but there wasn't a chest.

It kind of made sense since The Shroud was the reward.

Neema groaned as she pushed herself up. "That hurt more than I thought it would."

Lorelei ran forward and pulled the woman into a hug that probably hurt her more than it had the chance of making her feel better. "Don't ever do that to me again."

"What? Feigning death is my only true survival skill." Neema cracked a weak smile. "Now, let's get what we came for and get the hell out of here."

Together they limped toward the Viridian Shroud and their future.

CHAPTER THIRTY-NINE

Tim's smile made his belly feel warm.

Yes, his smile made him feel that good, or maybe it was the wine? It was tough to tell. They had been at it for hours. He had one eye half-open and was using his left hand to brace himself against the table. If he made this throw, the game was over, and he could finally Cleanse himself and go to sleep.

If he missed, Tim would have to drink the last cup of wine, and there was a chance he'd pass out before getting to Cleanse himself. He hadn't been hungover in so long that he didn't want to start enjoying that feeling again now. All he had to do was find a way to concentrate for a little longer.

Tim deftly held the flaming ball between his thumb and index finger as he tried to aim. The cup was moving back and forth, or maybe that was him. He couldn't figure it out, but it didn't matter. All he had to do was strike when everything lined up. The ball was moving back and forth, and the flames were so pretty.

Concentrate.

Instead of trying to stop the sway, Tim embraced it. He thought of a speech Michael J. Fox gave about his golf game. Addressing reporters on how he could still play golf with Parkinson's disease, he simply said, "I just wait for everything to stop shaking, and I let it rip." It was as good advice for life as anyone was going to give.

Sometimes you've gotta let it rip.

Tim wobbled for a moment, caught his balance, and watched the ball in his right hand move from side to side. He passed his target but was swaying back toward it now. Just before the cup swam back into view, he let the ball fly.

The flaming ball flew through the air and came up woefully short of the cup.

Tim started to curse, but the ball took a crazy hop to the left, hit the rim of the cup on the bounce, and flew straight up in the air. A moment later, the flaming sphere came back down out of the heavens and landed dead center in the middle of JaKobi's last cup of wine with a *hiss*.

Cheering erupted from all around the oasis, and money exchanged hands as JaKobi chugged his final glass of wine.

Always the gracious leader, Tim Cleansed JaKobi before himself.

There was no better feeling than when Cleanse washed the alcohol out of his system in an instant. Well, none better except the fun he had of getting good and drunk in the first place.

Tim moved over to the fire mage and hugged him. "That was a good game. You probably should have won."

Already pouring cups for the next game, JaKobi grinned at him. "Next time, we'll have to play before I'm on a three-win streak. Gets a little hard to aim after twelve glasses of wine."

He almost tried to tell JaKobi he wasn't exactly sober himself when they started, but what was the point? If the fire mage was this good wasted, he'd probably destroy Tim when he was sober. So instead, he tried to enjoy the win while he could. His next one might be a long time coming.

"Just remember, I'm one and oh." Tim grinned, formed his hand into the shape of a zero, and pointed at JaKobi.

Okay, maybe he wasn't as magnanimous as he wanted to be.

ShadowLily appeared a moment later and pressed a glass of honeyed tea into his hand. "Thought you might like a change."

"It's a welcome relief." *And it was.*

Drinking had its moments, but now that Tim was sober again he planned on staying that way until morning. Khalid was going to talk to them about the next part of the plan when they woke up. Phase Three was about to take flight. Tim was pretty sure this was when they were going to take the fight to Jabari himself and maybe push past him to the Pharaoh.

It was about time they got to see what a proper desert city looked like. Until now they'd only seen the outskirts, the dregs of the desert. Tim wanted to know if they had pyramids or tombs. There had to be something more exciting than a handful of forts. The scenery in the desert might not be all that great, but the bosses had been phenomenal.

It could be worse. We could have great scenery and shitty fights.

Tim tried not to let his brain go down the rabbit hole of games he played with amazing potential. There were too many of them to count. Some of them ended up being decent games despite their flaws, while others were flat-out bad. He could almost imagine some asshole sitting at his desk knowing their game was shit and saying to ship it anyway.

Can't recoup losses for investors without units sold.

ShadowLily pressed her shoulder into his. "What do you say we head back to the tent? I never did get that nap."

"I'll be there in a minute." He lifted his glass. "Can I get you a refill?"

She leaned in and kissed him. "I'm fine." Her eyes narrowed. "Don't let JaKobi talk you into another game. I sleep better with you next to me, and if you start playing again, you'll be up for hours."

"I wouldn't." He could see the fire mage waving to him now, but he also knew if she didn't say anything, there was a good chance he would have. So he amended his statement. "I won't."

Tim did his best to ignore JaKobi as he went to fill his glass again. A quick top-off of honeyed tea and he turned to head toward their tent. Before he got there, Tim had one last piece of business he wanted to wrap up before he called it a night. It was officially time to turn in his previous quest.

Quest Complete: Healing The People

You've healed the resistance fighters and cleansed the source of the corruption. Sadly, you've become a victim of your success, and until we liberate Naroosh from Jabari, you'll be pulling double duty as the resistance's primary healer. Welcome to the big leagues.

Reward: Ten gold coins

Was it wrong that his first thought was about how much the healing gig paid? He didn't care, but he knew Khalid was paying the other healers for their work, so it was the first thing he thought of. Tim probably should have been excited about the opportunity to heal extra people. This was the kind of thing he needed to finish upgrading his circlet. If there was anything he loved, it was leveling more than one thing at a time.

Tim gave Cassie a friendly wave and a sly smile at Lorelei as she cozied up to Neema. Things had never been better. They were making new friends, the loot in the desert was phenomenal, and tomorrow they would liberate a city. At least he hoped that was what was on the agenda for the morning. He wanted to crush Jabari and strip as much influence from the Goddess Vitaria as he could. There was a lot of work left to do, but the Blue Dagger Society would be up to the challenge.

The questing would have to wait until tomorrow. Tonight he had a woman to satisfy.

Sometimes life was too good to be true.

<u>List of Tim's Current Stats and Skills</u>

"Tim" level seventeen Battlesworn

Primary Stats

Strength: 13

Endurance: 18

Dexterity: 22

Intelligence: 42

Wisdom: 50

Perception: 6

Vitality: 4

Revitalization: 4

Luck: 7

Notable Gear

Weapons

Simple Dagger of Dexterity, +1 (X2)

Staff of Divine Retribution, +4 Intelligence +5 Wisdom

Orb of Concentration, +4 Wisdom +5 Intelligence

Armor

Tarnished Circlet of Divine Wisdom, +1 Intelligence +3 Wisdom

Wilbur's Fur-lined Shoulder Guards, +1 to Perception Vitality, Revitalization, and Luck

Battlesworn Robes of Justice, +4 Intelligence +6 Wisdom

Jerkin of Unmeasurable Delight, +1 to all base stats

Paul's Gloves of Mending, +4 Wisdom +7 Intelligence

Belt of Wisdom, +2

Hermit's Pants for Special Guests, +2 Endurance +2 Intelligence

Boots of Tranquility, +2 Dexterity +2 Endurance, Increase mana regeneration by 2%

Jewelry and Accessories

Leather Wraps of Divergent Health, 10% chance for single target healing spell to jump targets and heal the secondary recipient for 50% of the value.

Wristband of the Goddess, 10% damage reduction to dark based attacks

Ring of Marginal Transcendence, +2 Wisdom

Necklace of Unshakable Will, +3 Wisdom +1 Intelligence.

Trinket of the Smiling Monkey, +1 to a random stat

Skills

Appeal to the Goddess: Novice rank one

Disturbance: Novice rank two

Infiltrator: Novice rank three

Quick Feet: Novice rank four

Night Vision: Novice: rank six

Snare: Novice rank six

Backstab: Novice rank seven

Throwing Knives: Apprentice rank two

Sneak: Apprentice rank three

Behold My Power: Apprentice rank four

Dodge: Apprentice rank five

Flame Burst: Apprentice rank six

Healing Storm: Apprentice rank seven

Who Needs a Shield: Apprentice rank seven

Small Blades: Apprentice rank seven

Curse of Giving: Journeyman rank one

Weaken Undead: Apprentice rank eight

Cleanse: Journeyman rank one

Divine Light: Journeyman rank one
Healing Orb: Journeyman rank eight

413

Stances
Way of the River: Apprentice rank six
Way of the Boulder: Apprentice rank nine

Buffs
Armor of Eternia: Apprentice rank eight
Attacks of the Faithful: Apprentice rank eight

Open Quests
The Deserts of Naroosh

CHAPTER FORTY

"Bring her to me." The Pharaoh held out his hand.

The virgin had come from his collection. It was a high price to pay to contact the Goddess Vitaria but one he needed to make. The word from Jabari's city of Nar'ha was that the resistance had defeated his strongest warriors and soon his palace would be under attack. The opposition had grown strong and secured outside assistance to aid them in their fight. Maybe if the Goddess was willing to lend them additional aid, they could squash the resistance before it could harm his oldest accomplice and what might be his only friend.

As if his position allowed him such luxuries.

Jabari and the city of Nar'ha were the very foundations of his plans. If Jabari hadn't taken that first step so long ago, none of this would have been possible now. He was the ruler of a kingdom. It was everything he'd ever wanted and then some. Jabari provided the wealth and other than having to sign some bothersome documents now and again, the Pharaoh himself enjoyed the spoils.

There were enough problems for him to deal with inside his walls. All the bloodthirsty bastards he called nobles wanted the top spot, but none of them had the balls to take it from him. Or, more precisely, none of them were strong enough to take on Vitaria's minions to get to him.

Phandar wasn't a fighter. He liked the softer side of life.

He loved gold, drinking, and sex to the point he sold his soul to have it all. Not that he didn't have to bribe, kill, and fuck his way right up to the point when he needed the Goddess' help to further his ambitions. If it took sacrificing a million fucking virgins to make sure he stayed exactly where he was on top of the pile of shit called life, he'd do it with a smile. Whatever the Goddess demanded, he was willing to do.

Phandar bet his soul on her strength, and he needed it now.

The girl tried to pull out of his grasp. "Be still," Phandar hissed.

When she continued to struggle, he slapped her across the face hard enough that her head rocked back. The sacrifice was better received when they were willing, but if they fought it still got the job done. He wanted this one to be perfect though, so if he had to drug the little bitch to make her more compliant, he'd do what he had to.

One of the perks of being Pharaoh was that no one could tell him what to do. He'd sampled mind-altering compounds from across the land and had one for every occasion. What was the point of living if he couldn't have as many delectable options for altering his state of mind on hand as possible? Even if she was stoned to the point of incomprehension as long as she climbed onto the altar herself, it fucking counted in his book.

If you were going to be sacrificed, being stoned was probably a mercy.

After he'd signed his pact with Vitaria, Phandar used drugs to forget. Then he used them because he could, and finally, he was using because he didn't have anything else that he cared about. If the girl thought there was any mercy in him, she'd learn he'd killed it long ago, and now mostly what he felt was hollow.

One thing they never tell you about being the top dog is how badly everyone else wants to take it from you.

Power was a fickle mistress at best, and her jilted husband at its worst. Phandar had grown tired of the game. Holding onto power was a job that kept all his thoughts so occupied that he had no time left to enjoy his success. It was as if his food turned to ash in his mouth, his wine to water. There was no end, only the next task to complete.

He needed a fucking break.

Phandar let out a weary sigh as the girl shied away from him. It was all so tedious. Somewhere deep down, he found a way to replace his anger with a warm smile. "I won't hit you again."

She took his hand, all the time expecting another blow, but knowing she couldn't refuse. If he hadn't done this a hundred times before it would have broken his heart. This was his shame, the price he paid to be the king of nothing. So while he could have hit her until her face was black with bruises and forced her to submit, he hugged the girl to himself as if she were a long-lost friend.

"I am sorry to have lost my temper. Please let me give you something to ease the sting." He said it as though he hadn't hit a hundred such girls, then made them the very same offer.

Sometimes his ability to lie made him sick.

Not that it would stop him from doing it now, or the next time he needed Vitaria's help. He poured two glasses of wine with three pinches of the white flower dust for hers and one for him. The girl wasn't the only one who deserved something to lighten the mood. Phandar looked the girl over again, trying to judge if he'd given her too much. He needed her pliable, not dead.

If she died, he'd have to start the entire tedious process over again.

"Drink this." He handed her the glass and sipped from his to reassure her.

As she drank the liquid, he tipped the bottom of the glass up, making sure she finished every drop. "Enjoy this moment, revel in it, for the next life truly is filled with wonders."

The girl nodded. "My da always told me about the halls of Eternia and how wonderful they were."

"I'm sure they're glorious." Phandar felt the drugs rushing through his system now, and the next lie came out so smoothly he almost believed it himself. "Would you like the chance to see them?"

"Can I? Can I really?" She sounded hopeful.

They always did.

The white flower made it easier to ignore the voice in his head that screamed for him to give it all up. To fill a chest with gold and disappear in the night to build a new life somewhere else. He'd done it before, and it wouldn't be that bad. A simple life without drugs, and death waiting around every corner.

Then he killed that voice.

What had sleeping in the streets ever earned him but scorn? He'd shown those fools. Washed up, a hack, not worth their time. Well, now he told them what fucking time to do things, and they did them or he sent someone to take care of them. If the men themselves were irreplaceable, he sent other men to remind their families how important it was they continued their work.

If the world was a shit heap, it was better to be on top of the pile. He wouldn't go back to slinging it in the muck, and he had to face the truth. A chest full of gold would only last him so long. The more money he had, the faster he spent it. Those whores and drugs wouldn't pay for themselves. Of course, the girl didn't need to know any of this, and the goddess didn't care.

"Take my hand and let me show you the entrance to Eternia's kingdom." Phandar extended his hand to the girl, a fatherly smile plastered on his face.

He hoped the look said he was excited about the wonders they were about to see when he was worried about what might happen next. Not killing the girl, so much as what Vitaria would have to say about Jabari's failures, and his for not handling them sooner.

The girl moved toward the altar, excited about the chance to meet the goddess. If she knew which goddess she was meeting, Phandar doubted she would have felt the same way. He'd worshipped Eternia once, and it mostly felt like he was talking to himself. Vitaria took action, and he was hers whether he liked it or not.

"Let me help you up." The Pharaoh lifted the small girl onto the altar. "All you have to do is close your eyes and think of Eternia with all your thoughts. When you open your eyes again, the goddess will appear before you."

She smiled so warmly that if there were any humanity left in him, he would have sent her straight home to her father. Instead, he smiled as she beamed warmly up at him.

"Meeting the goddess is all I ever wanted." She lay back, looking up at the roof and waiting for Eternia to appear.

"Close your eyes, and trust in me to show you the way." When she closed her eyes, Phandar gently ran his fingers over the lids. "You must not open your eyes for any reason until I give the command. If you open them too early, it will break the enchantment, and Eternia will not appear to us."

"I won't open them, I swear." She was almost crying in her effort to make him happy.

Phandar nodded as she scrunched her eyes shut even tighter. "Then listen to my words, and you will know when the moment is right. I'm counting on you for this. I couldn't do it without you."

Lies were easier to tell when they were rooted in truth.

He reached out and gently crossed the girl's arms over her waist, then started on the other preparations. Candles needed to be lit, and the proper oils and flowers needed to be applied. Each time he lit a candle he said a prayer. Each time he splashed the oil, he called to her.

He begged the goddess to come and provide him guidance on the next steps to take. She would come to help, she always did, but she required a price. He'd gladly pay it to keep himself in power. To seal the connection between Vitaria and himself, he consumed a single sip from a jug of wine containing a splash of Vitaria's blood. Everything was in place and ready to go. All he had to do was follow through.

He was never one to leave a dirty deed undone.

"Are you ready to meet the goddess, child?" A single tear streaked down Phandar's cheek despite his hardened heart.

The girl kept her eyes closed. "Yes." In a much firmer voice, "I am ready."

"Then it is done." Phandar pulled a dagger from inside his robes and lifted it high above his head, where he let the blade linger at its apex.

"Come to me, goddess of the night. Come to me, daughter of none. Come to me, mistress of the eternal. I worship you. My life for you." He brought the dagger down in one fluid motion, slamming it into the girl's heart without an inch of remorse.

His tears were gone now. Showing any weakness to the goddess was a recipe for disaster.

The virgin's eyes snapped open when the blade pierced her heart. A scream of pure agony tore from her lips as she saw the dark Goddess Vitaria rising from the ground in a veil of black mist.

Phandar watched in wonder as the girl's soul rose above her body. She looked at him for a moment, shock and grief etched across her face.

Then Vitaria consumed her. "You called?"

He looked down at his hands still wrapped around the dagger sticking out of the girl's chest, and he slowly unwrapped his fingers. There was always a moment after the sacrifice where he realized what he'd done. He squashed that feeling down where it would never see the light of day and got to the business at hand. "Yes, I have need of you."

"Would it kill you to sacrifice some male virgins in my honor?" Vitaria smiled as she plucked the dagger free. "I'm starting to think you don't understand me at all."

Phandar nodded his head. "Male sacrifices, I can do that."

Maybe killing young men would be easier on his conscience.

"It's certainly a first step in the right direction, don't you think? For our relationship to work, there can't be secrets between us, can there?" Vitaria wrapped an arm around his shoulders and led him toward the throne.

This didn't feel right, but he'd brought the goddess here. Now he had to deal with the ramifications. "Only a fool would lie to you." Phandar was starting to feel like he might have summoned his death right to him.

The goddess gave him a squeeze that almost broke him in half and let him go. "And you're no fool. Is that the gist of it?"

It probably wasn't the time for self-respect, so he tried a different tactic. "No, I'm all kinds of stupid, but the one thing I never take for granted is our relationship."

Vitaria's easy-going smile faded like rain in the desert sun. "You told me Jabari was going to crush the resistance, and now I find myself having to clean up another of your messes." A twinkle appeared in her eye. "Seriously Phandar, what am I going to do with you?"

That bastard Jabari better not have cost him his life or his dick. He was rather fond of both and being Pharaoh wasn't worth a damn without the second. He'd given himself entirely to the goddess already. His pride had been burned away long ago. This was simply about survival now.

Phandar tried to summon the scraps of his courage, but who was he kidding? Vitaria could erase him as quickly as she made him. He tried to hide his emotions and then thought, *fuck, she prob-*

ably feeds off the fear. He might as well use anything he had for an advantage. "I'm sorry for Jabari's failures. All we know is this new band of adventurers isn't from our land and seems to have come from under the mountain."

Of course, he didn't mention the fact she'd promised him the path under the mountain was sealed.

"My sister Eternia again sticks her nose in where it doesn't belong." Black droplets of liquid dripped from Vitaria's shoulders and splashed against the floor, releasing black clouds of steam into the air that were reabsorbed by her dress. "I will deal with Eternia. Your job is to stop these adventurers at any cost."

He dropped to one knee. "Command me, goddess."

Her smile returned with an edge to it. "We will let Jabari fall on his sword. Pull all of your troops back to Naroosh."

Vitaria started to pace back and forth. "With all of our strength consolidated here, the resistance would be foolish to come. If they show their faces, we will crush them."

She stopped pacing, her eyes burning with black fire. "All the while, we will continue to build our strength here. If they don't come to us, we will eventually have to go to them and take back Nar'ha. Eternia can't be allowed to increase her power."

Some of Phandar's trepidation faded as he realized this fight was as important to Vitaria as it was to him. "I trust you have a few surprises in store for them?"

"More than a few, servant." Vitaria stood over him, her shadow growing to fill the room.

Her display left him without the ability even to entertain the possibility of who was in charge, no matter how many times he tried to delude himself otherwise.

The shadows receded, and a cat-like grin spread across her face. "Death is all the resistance will find if they come to Naroosh. My sister's little band of adventurers won't be able to shift the tide in her favor much longer."

Phandar knelt in front of the goddess, making sure to keep his eyes locked on her feet. He wasn't sure what made him do it. It wasn't loyalty, but maybe he suddenly felt a small kinship with Jabari. Shit rolled downhill. Jabari was standing waist-deep in the Pharaoh's shit, and now Phandar was getting a small taste of what it felt like after all these years.

He fucking hated it.

Maybe he owed Jabari more than he thought. "We might yet be able to shift the tide in Jabari's favor. With the help of your special forces, no one would dare attack."

Keeping his head low, Phandar tried one last tack. "He has done much to help us over the years. It would be a shame to abandon such faithfulness now."

Not that he cared two shits for Jabari's well-being. He wanted to get a preview of what would happen to *him* if the Goddess found his efforts lacking in any way. He might very well be looking at his future unfolding before his eyes. It was probably a mistake for him to suggest helping Jabari, but he'd said the words, and it was too late to take them back now.

The goddess moved toward his throne. She sat and tossed her legs over the arm in a display of casualness Phandar hadn't expected. Vitaria had a pouty expression on her face as if she were disappointed but willing to give in to keep the peace. "I suppose we can spare one of my creations, but he will have to do the rest on his own."

If he was judging the moment correctly, and Phandar almost always did, this was a test to see what he would do next. Offer to send one of Vitaria's strongest, and he would appear weak and reliant on others. Send a minion too weak, and everyone would know it was a sacrifice, and he was throwing Jabari and Nar'ha to the wolves of the resistance. Was there one of her minions that somehow fit right in the middle?

Then the idea came to him. He had just the right suggestion. At least he hoped he did. "If the goddess agrees, I think we should send the Juggernaut."

Vitaria gave him an appraising look as if trying to decide if she wanted to indulge her pet Pharaoh. She gave him a curt nod and clapped once, sending a thunderclap rolling out across the throne room. "Done."

With the business of the moment concluded, Vitaria's smile turned seductive. "See if you can round up some promising young men for me to amuse myself. It's been too long since I've felt the pleasures of the flesh. And food. I want to gorge myself."

She paused, licking her lips hungrily. "And drink. I need wine!"

Phandar clapped and was disappointed with the effect after hearing Vitaria do the same thing. Thankfully, the servants hiding in the walls weren't too awed by her to respond to his command. "Wine, food, and men, whatever the Goddess needs, see that it is taken care of."

He turned to Vitaria. "Everything I have is yours, I will seek you out in the morning, or you may call upon me at any time."

Vitaria's eyes moved past him toward the men bearing trays of food and wine. "Don't be early. I plan on indulging myself well into the morning."

Taking a jug from one of the servants, the Pharaoh poured Vitaria a glass of wine. "Serving you is my only desire. I shall take my leave."

He handed her the glass and bowed as he backed out of the room.

Being thrown out of his throne room like a servant so she could indulge herself left a bitter taste in his mouth. He'd let his ambitions override his sense when he'd made a deal with Vitaria. That was the thing no one told you about making a deal with the devil. Sometimes the devil came back. He'd brought this on himself, but it had been one hell of a wild ride so far. Why worry about the ending now?

The scary thing for Phandar was, despite how much he hated

himself now, he'd hated being poor and treated like shit more. Whatever it took not to go back there, he would do it without question. He'd already sold his soul. What else was there to lose?

The throne room doors closed, and Phandar knew that his lovers would see the darker side of his passions tonight.

CHAPTER FORTY-ONE

"What is that sound?" Tim looked around the darkened tent, trying to get his bearings.

ShadowLily got out of bed and lit a candle. "I hear it too."

It was almost silent at first, merely a gentle tapping on the roof of their tent, but then the sound changed. The light tapping became a heavy pounding against the thick canvas, then all sense of individual sounds disappeared completely. For a second he started to panic, then he realized that nothing was coming through the tent. He moved to stand in the open flap next to ShadowLily and looked out into his first monsoon.

It was like standing in a cave behind a waterfall.

The world wasn't normal anymore. It was like someone spilled a glass of water on a painting. Everything was blurry, and the noise washed out any semblance of typical sound. He couldn't make out any individual noises at first, but then he heard the screams. He was about to run into the storm when ShadowLily pulled him back.

"Listen. They're happy." She wore a smile of her own.

Tim stood in the tent flap wondering if he was wasting time, but now he could make out the laughter mixed in with the screams. Rain, even in the oasis, was a celebrated event. It was as if Eternia herself had appeared to smile upon them. Maybe it was a sign of good things to come.

"That storm came just in time. Our meeting with Khalid is in thirty minutes." ShadowLily had the slightly panicked sound of someone late for work.

Tim wasn't worried in the slightest. It was still dark out. There was no way it was almost time for their meeting. He looked at his interface and realized she was right. Why he never simply listened to her was beyond him. "I'll make the coffee while you get ready, then we can switch places."

"As if. I'm ready to go. You on the other hand probably won't make it there in time." She giggled at the wounded expression on his face. "Don't worry. I'll have a few coffee-related excuses ready to save your ass."

That seemed unfair. "Not everyone is a morning person."

"It's ten a.m." ShadowLily had a stern look on her face that was probably a pretty good imitation of Joe's when she tried to wiggle out of something. "Morning ended four hours ago." She shook her finger to emphasize the point.

Tim imagined when your dad ran a breakfast joint, mornings probably started around four. He'd worked on the grounds crew at a local golf course during the summer and experienced something similar. All his friends weren't even off work yet when he was eating dinner and getting ready to call it a night. Now he hated early mornings with a passion no matter what time of the day they occurred.

"Just let me get the coffee finished, and I'll meet you there." He was going to call on a skill he hadn't used in a while, but it felt like something he had to do alone.

ShadowLily was no pushover. She knew he was acting a little weird, but to her credit, she let it go because she knew sometimes people needed a moment to themselves. "I'm going to check on Cassie and JaKobi. Don't be late."

"I'll be right behind you." Tim turned and started making his way to the bathroom.

After ShadowLily left, he took care of the morning business and washed his hands and face before equipping his robe. His first couple of sips of coffee took the edge off nicely, then Tim set the cup aside. There was no way to know if he used this skill whether the goddess would come, but the rain outside almost felt like a hint to pick up the phone.

Tim knelt.

He wasn't sure if the kneeling was mandatory for the spell to work, but it felt right. When one was about to call on the all-powerful, it probably paid to recognize their ability to smite you with a thought. His hands moved through the spell Appeal to the Goddess, and he thought about what he wanted to ask.

"Eternia, I don't know what's coming our way next, but I know we'll need your help. Any advice you can offer would be greatly appreciated." Tim bowed his head and waited.

Beautiful white light filled the space, and the Goddess Eternia stepped out of it. The light formed around her in a dress as she reached down and lifted Tim to his feet. "It is good to see you adventurer, but I have dire news. My sister is already aligning her forces against you, and one of her most fearsome creations is heading to Jabari's palace."

Tim didn't like the sound of that. "What is coming for us?"

"The Juggernaut." Eternia frowned. "The battle against such a creature will not be easy, but it must be dealt with, or the rest of the fight will go poorly for Khalid's people."

Quest Received: Breaking the Juggernaut

The Goddess Vitaria has many vile creations. One of the most monstrous is the unstoppable Juggernaut. The Juggernaut cannot be reasoned with, he cannot be bargained with, he is an immovable force of evil, and he is coming for you. Your job in

the next battle is to stop the Juggernaut before he destroys the resistance.

Quest Reward: Ten gold coins

Tim bowed his head and accepted the quest. "We'll take care of it."

"I never had a doubt." Eternia placed a single finger against Tim's forehead. "Go forth with my blessing, and bring Jabari's grip on his people to an end."

Eternia's dress of light pulled apart, creating a portal. She floated into it, and the light winked out of existence.

The goddess was gone.

"I wonder what level I have to be to learn that?" Tim watched the place where Eternia had been for a moment in absolute wonder.

Being able to portal back to town from anywhere would be super helpful. It would cut their travel time in half. Next time he had a chance to speak with the goddess, he would have to ask her if she'd be willing to share the details of that particular spell with him. If it wasn't something she could divulge herself maybe she could point him in the right direction to figure it out himself.

Better yet, he could put JaKobi on it.

The fire mage loved research, and if he figured out the spell, he could share it with Tim. That was a win-win in his book. He filed the thought away in his never-ending to-do list, powered down another cup of coffee, and ran out into the rain.

It was a comfort to see the fire in Khalid's tent. A few hours ago, Tim would have called it absurd. Why would anyone need one in the desert? All they had to do was step outside, and their skin would instantly be dry. With the monsoon, the temperature had also dropped. Now he was thankful for the fire as it dried the chill from his bones. The older warrior was the only one in the tent so far. Tim had finished his business before ShadowLily could wrangle Cassie and JaKobi out of bed.

No surprise there.

He might as well drop the bad news on Khalid while everyone else was otherwise occupied. The desert warrior might need to change his current plans based on the new information. "Khalid, I have news."

The warrior sat back in his chair as if bracing for a blow. "Tell me."

Tim hoped the news didn't shake the man further. Khalid didn't have too much to worry about since Eternia asked the Blue Dagger Society to handle the problem for him. All he had to do was help them get there and get out of the way. "The Juggernaut is coming."

A low whistle escaped through Khalid's lips as he processed the information. "That changes things." He stood and looked at the map on the wall. "Are you sure?"

"From Eternia's lips to your ears." Tim moved forward so he could see what Khalid was studying. "She also tasked my group with dealing with the new threat."

After tapping the map in a few places, the warrior smiled. "This could work in our favor." Khalid pondered his strategy. "As long as you can handle the task."

He turned away from the map and looked at Tim. "I hope you're up for it."

"We never run away from a challenge." Tim grinned at the warrior. "And we never lose."

"I'm counting on that." Khalid looked at Tim and back to the map. "Jabari isn't going to know what hit him."

The tent flap rustled and the rest of the guild came in along with Neema. The Desert Wolf pointed at the leader of the resistance. "I thought it was too early for our brains to be moving that fast."

ShadowLily laughed as she wrapped her arms around Tim. "You get this one working on a problem, and he never stops. It's like his brain won't turn off until he's figured it out."

Cassie snorted. "Must be a guy thing." She looked at JaKobi.

"Although his focus seems to be limited to things no one else would find interesting, and sex."

"Hey, knowing the airspeed of an unladen swallow is important if you want to vaporize it from the air." JaKobi made a little gun out of his finger and shot a small ball of fire into the air, where it blew up in a shower of tiny sparkles.

Tim made sure nothing was going to catch on fire and grinned back at his buddy. "The real question is, was it an African swallow or a European swallow?"

"Not this again." Cassie groaned.

Suppressing a chuckle, Tim turned his attention back to Khalid. "As always, our better halves have the right of it. Tell us about your plan and what we can do to make it work."

Khalid looked at their group and back at the map. He took a moment to reorient himself after they broke his concentration, then flipped the map over to reveal a second map with a more in-depth look at the city of Nar'ha. "Jabari has enough men to hold the city, but now thanks to our new friends he doesn't have the generals to lead them."

He stabbed a small knife into the largest building on the map. "He will fall back to the palace and make it his last stronghold, but first, he will try to hold us off. Especially if what Tim tells us is true."

"Exactly what did Tim tell you?" ShadowLily shot him a withering glare, clearly not liking being the second person to hear the information.

Before Tim could respond, Neema put her hands on her hips while staring daggers at the map. "That bastard is going to try and use the people as a human shield."

"Yes, once we make it to the city, he's counting on us to be slowed greatly by our inability to attack it directly." Khalid looked at the map and back at the band of adventurers. "The problems for us only seem to be mounting. We can't use the catapults or any of the siege weaponry we secured for the battle without risking harm to the people we've sworn to save.

"If we can break their initial defense, we can bring in the big guns." Khalid looked pained as he said it. "Even then it might do more harm than good."

Tim understood what he meant. What good was freeing the desert people if it destroyed half of the city and the people were all slaughtered? Trying to protect people in a war was a messy business. It was always easier to burn things down than to build them or save them from destruction. They were supposed to be the saviors so they had to hamstring their efforts to save as many people as possible.

"I thought we'd surround the city on these three sides, forcing Jabari back to the Palace." Khalid drew a small half-circle around the city to illustrate his point. "He won't be able to put up a significant defense across that much space."

Tim looked over the map. Coming in from three sides would create a lot of confusion. It would also leave an individual side vulnerable to being completely overrun if Jabari committed all his forces in a single direction. Being so spread out made them vulnerable to a concentrated assault, and it also would expose the palace. Would Jabari risk it, or was protecting himself more important? That was the gamble they faced now. Then there was the surprise Tim dropped on Khalid.

The Juggernaut.

"And that thing we talked about earlier?" Tim looked at the map with a hopeless expression on his face. "Where do you think the Juggernaut will strike first?"

Khalid looked at the map while tapping a thoughtful finger against his chin. "No way to know for certain. Our best bet might be to hold your party in reserve until Jabari commits the Juggernaut to an attack. When Vitaria's monster strikes, it will be your job to stop it."

"Juggernaut?" Cassie sounded disappointed. "Some fucking clown in a shiny hat? That's nothing. Let's go get this guy."

Tim sipped his coffee. "Somehow I don't think we'll be facing that Juggernaut, Cassie, just one of some kind."

JaKobi was grinning like Thomas Edison when that first lightbulb finally lit the night. "We've got our Juggie. Let's see if we can find her a shiny hat."

"Are you saying I'm fat?" Cassie rounded on JaKobi faster than a mongoose on a cobra.

Tim couldn't stop the coffee from spraying out his nose as he laughed. The look of pure horror on JaKobi's face was that priceless. Every man had been there before, said something totally innocent, and been hit with the whammy. He wanted to grab Cassie and shout, yes Juggernaut is fat, but that isn't what he was saying. The stupid bastard was trying to imply she was tough as nails.

Tim did the inventory trick on his robes, but Khalid's rugs weren't so lucky. Maybe there was a way he could bail his buddy out. "So what I heard is their Juggernaut versus our very slim and sexy tank. Is that what you heard, JaKobi?" Hopefully, he'd thrown him a large enough lifeline.

"Exactly what I heard." The fire mage started to inch back.

Khalid looked at their group again, shaking his head as if he couldn't believe they were able to beat the generals. "You'll wait in the back with the rear guard. When the Juggernaut attacks, you'll stop it." He turned to Neema. "Then you'll lead the assault from the other side."

Neema looked worried. "You'll lead the assault from the middle?"

"Someone has to draw their attention. Jabari won't commit the Juggernaut to the battle until he knows I'm there."

Pulling Khalid into a fierce hug, Neema whispered, "Just be careful."

"Always." The desert warrior returned her hug with a fatherly expression on his face.

ShadowLily moved to get a closer look at the map of the city. "Once we've secured the city, what then?"

"Then we move to the palace." Khalid gave Neema one last squeeze and moved to the map. He circled a small area in red chalk. "After the Juggernaut is defeated, meet us here."

Khalid looked at the secondary staging area. "Jabari will have many surprises waiting for us when we assault the palace. Hopefully, I'll be able to give you more intelligence before we head inside and continue the battle."

Tim felt pretty good about their plan so far. Their job was to hang back and take on the big nasty when he showed up. After they kicked the Juggernaut's ass, they would move to the staging area and find out the next steps. It was easy enough to remember and gave a lot of flexibility for when things fell apart. In the end, it wasn't much of a plan, but it was all they needed.

Khalid turned from the map and met the eyes of each member of their party. "I've waited for this moment for so long, to pull our people back into Eternia's light. Now that the final battles are upon us we must wait a little longer. We will leave tonight and attack with the sun."

He reached under his desk and pulled out a small jug of wine. "I will see you this evening. Make the most of the time you have left before the fight for our future. Once the battle starts your options for resting will be limited until its completion." He walked out of the tent with the jug in his hand.

Neema watched him go, but her eyes were full of purpose. It was easy to see the Desert Wolf was concerned for Khalid but knew she had a million things to do before the final fight. Turning to Lorelei, she gave her a quick kiss. "I'll meet you back at the tent in a few hours."

Lorelei pulled her back for a much longer kiss, let her lips linger for a moment, and whispered, "See you then."

Tim tried not to grin. There was something about seeing two hot women kiss that was sexy as hell. Although the more it happened around him, the more the novelty of the situation wore off. Kind of like how he felt watching other straight people kiss. There might as well have been a sign over their heads that read, nothing to see here. As time went on it became a normal occurrence, and he was okay with that.

Addressing the rest of the group as Neema left the tent, Tim couldn't keep the excitement from his voice. "You heard the man. The day is yours to do whatever you want. Tonight we ride. Tomorrow we take back a city and return it to the light."

"I feel like there should have been cheering." ShadowLily giggled. "It was a damn fine speech."

"Guess I need better soldiers." Tim wrapped an arm around his girlfriend and led her from the tent. "But every great leader makes do with what he's given."

"Tell me about it." ShadowLily slapped his ass and took off at a run.

Tim stopped chasing her at the tent flap and turned to look at the others. "Don't be late." Then ran out of the tent and into the rain.

He had a sexy lady to catch.

CHAPTER FORTY-TWO

With the dawn came the call to arms.

Tim had never been part of anything so large in his entire life, and he'd done forty-man raids. The host of warriors assembled dwarfed his largest raid group by a mile although he went through a *Lineage 2* phase and some of those siege battles with multiple guilds on each side were epic. What they needed to do now was evolve their combat, more like a certain canceled science fiction MMO.

Technically, gaming had evolved past the standard MMO years ago, but he was a sucker for the classics. Standing back and watching the mass of armed soldiers moving ahead of him made Tim feel more like he joined the army than was living in a game. The last time he'd been around this many people was back when they were fighting to save Tristholm. There was a certain amount of organized chaos to a force this big.

It was amazing that one man could command all this.

Khalid didn't seem to be having any issues controlling the force as he shouted a never-ending stream of orders at his men. Riders came and left from the command tent almost by the minute. Throughout it all, the warrior had a smile on his face and kept the mood light for the others around him. They were going to lose a lot of men today, but it would be worth it for their people.

The old warrior let everyone he came in contact with know how much they meant to him. This was his life's ambition coming to fruition, and he wouldn't have been able to do it without their help. Although he might die, Khalid didn't look worried. He didn't care about his life as long as they carried the day.

ShadowLily watched the resistance moving to surround the city. "It is something, isn't it?"

"Like ants swarming over a crust of bread." Cassie watched, fascinated.

JaKobi bounced a ball of flames between his hands. "Like people fleeing the stadium after a bad loss."

Everyone looked at the fire mage. "What? I don't just read books and nerd out over magic."

"Whatever you say." Lorelei grinned.

Tim knew what JaKobi meant. He might be a total nerd himself, but he still had other interests outside of gaming. It wasn't as if he was devoid of culture. He enjoyed music and movies as much as the next person. Just not the stuff that won awards. Seeing the films that always won kind of showed him how out of touch Hollywood was with the rest of the world.

Here in *The Etheric Coast,* they didn't have to impress people or win awards. All they had to do right now was deal with the Juggernaut when it showed up. Thankfully they had the skills and the magic that would have made the best of the best back in the real world totally jealous. Sending in the Blue Dagger Society was like dropping a tactical nuke.

They always got the job done.

"I hate all this waiting." Cassie gripped her staff and willed the Juggernaut to make an appearance.

A moment later, Neema pointed at a disturbance along the left side of their battle formation. Something down there was wreaking havoc on their men, and they were falling back.

Tim couldn't make out what was waiting for them through the giant clouds of dust, but he knew it must be the boss. Whatever was attacking the men down there was huge, and it needed to be stopped. This was their time to shine.

If they wanted to take the city they needed to get down there quickly. "Get to the horses!"

He started to run, but their horses were only steps away. The battle was just starting, and he was already so excited he'd forgotten where the horses were. Tim climbed into the saddle and drew a couple of deep breaths to calm himself. He'd never had the chance to be part of a revolution. It was intense.

Viva la revolution!

This was the battle that would determine whether the people of Nar'ha would get to experience freedom. Tim was a big believer that everyone deserved a chance to choose their path in life. Each person should know that they could walk in the sunlight and know that tomorrow, with enough determination and hard work, they could become anything they wanted to be. He was willing to fight and die to give the people of Naroosh the chance to experience the same feeling he woke up with every day.

Tim looked over the battlefield, and a smile spread across his lips. "Let's ride."

They were about to make a difference.

"The goddess' light shines upon you!" Khalid roared as they rode past. "Neema, take your men to the right!"

Tim felt some of the riders following them peel off and head toward the right flank. A small contingent carried on with their group. These men would reinforce the ones lost to the Juggernaut before their arrival. At least that was what he thought would happen. Instead, more and more of the warriors stopped to fill in gaps in the line as they rode. Soon it was only the five of them galloping madly across the open desert toward the boss.

The giant cloud of dust in front of them started to settle, and Tim pulled back on his reins, slowing their racing horses to a slow walk. The Juggernaut looked down at the battlefield with hunger in its eyes. It was as if the destruction of so many lives filled him with happiness, or maybe it was a desire to cause more devastation.

Now that Tim knew what they were facing he kind of liked being in the dark better.

Half of the Juggernaut's head looked like someone had dipped it in molten metal. It was the kind of look that was scary as hell on a person, but when it happened on the head of a minotaur, it was a hundred percent shit-inducing.

He wasn't wearing brown pants, so Tim found a way to control himself.

Seeing the burning red eyes looking out over the battlefield through a mask of steel indifference was terrifying, but what made the creature a Juggernaut? Melting a little metal on a monster didn't make it special. It just gave the fucker a chrome dome. There had to be something that gave the boss that moniker. He couldn't only be a minotaur with a shiny head.

The Juggernaut pulled something from his inventory with a grunt of effort. It looked like a single wheel with grips on the sides. What in the fuck was going on? Vitaria was one crazy bitch if she thought a minotaur on a unicycle would be enough to slow them down.

The Juggernaut gripped the bars on either side of the wheel and let out a war cry that froze everyone in the vicinity in place. Then he lowered his head over the wheel and ran forward, using his head as a battering ram. The wheel crushed anyone unlucky enough to be directly in its path, and the boss' horns did the rest.

Men screamed as they were impaled and tossed aside like bowling pins.

When the devastating attack was over the Juggernaut stopped running, and Tim could see the moisture coming from the boss' nose as he drew deep, bellowing breaths. He reached up, pulled a few bodies free from his horns, and tossed them to the side. A trail of bent and broken bodies lay behind the minotaur, but the monster was already scouting the field for his next target.

The resistance couldn't suffer another blow like that without folding entirely.

"Cassie, you're up." Tim grinned at her while thanking Eternia for the millionth time that it wasn't his job to run headfirst at that thing. "If you see him grab that wheel thing, get the fuck out of the way."

The tank rode past him, taking the lead. "Don't get ground into paste. You always have such helpful advice before the fighting starts."

"I can heal a lot, but don't think for a second that I can blow you back up like Judge Doom in *Roger Rabbit*." Tim decided that wasn't the right tactic and tried to be more encouraging. "Once you're paste," he failed to come up with something clever. "You're paste."

They were close enough now that Cassie leapt off her horse and approached on foot. "Hey, bull for brains, let's fucking tango!"

Tim looked at JaKobi. "Not bad."

"We've been working on it." The fire mage's robes burst into flames, and he ran to catch up with the others.

Tim scanned the field around them while trailing the group as usual, but it didn't seem as if the battle raging around them would be a huge factor. Although the fighting was fierce, there was a very clear perimeter around them now that Cassie had engaged the boss. The game was setting the mood for them, but making sure the fight was fivo-e-mono.

Just the way they liked it.

The Juggernaut put his death wheel away and pulled a much more sinister-looking ax from his inventory. Now he looked like the mythical monster from all the games and shows Tim had ever seen, except much larger. He was pretty sure this massive mad cow fucker could have given Paul Bunyan a run for his money. The boss was easily twenty feet tall and had shoulders as wide as a VW bus.

He'd need them to swing that big-ass ax.

Tim wondered how Cassie felt. Splitter had been one hell of a weapon, but each head of this massive ax could have been one of Dracon's swords. The Juggernaut seemed like an unstoppable force, but there had to be a way for them to win the fight. Cassie slammed into the boss with a shriek, and Tim went to work.

Curse of Giving was what he used to start the fight and quickly followed it with Behold My Power.

There was no reason to be shy.

He sent out a round of Healing Orb as the rest of the DPS got to work. From here on out, his only goal was to make sure Cassie had whatever she needed to survive tangling with the Juggernaut up close. As long as she was at full health and no one else made a major oopsie, he could keep his eyes on the boss and look for any openings or signs that something bad was coming their way.

In every fight, there was usually a trick. So far this battle seemed pretty straightforward. They were due for a more traditional tank and spank kind of encounter, or even a loot pinata. It had been a long time since they'd faced an easy battle, but this probably wouldn't be it. Despite the fact the minotaur was alone, there were hundreds of men and women fighting around them. Almost any scenario was possible.

Cassie had her hands too full dodging the minotaur's hooves and ducking under the ax to make any meaningful contribution to the DPS. Lorelei made some progress with her bow, and JaKobi was doing what he liked doing best, trying to light everything on fire. ShadowLily chose that moment to appear and landed a critical hit from behind that staggered the boss for an instant.

The Juggernaut flashed red.

"Get away!" Tim screamed as he cast Who Needs a Shield on the tank.

ShadowLily didn't hesitate. After their fight in Dr. Zacharias' lair, she wasn't taking any chances. Having your friend fill you with arrows because you were too slow tended to have that kind of effect on someone.

A little extra DPS wasn't worth dying for.

Meanwhile, Cassie was rooted in place. Tim was pretty sure from the look of panic on her face that she wasn't trying to show off. Something was wrong, and he had to figure out what before they lost their tank. His user interface didn't show a debuff on her that he could remove. It didn't show a debuff at all. Was she really stuck there?

What in the fuck was going on?

Now that Tim had no idea what was going on, he got pissed. Now wasn't the time to start playing games or showing off. If Cassie died, they all died. That was it. While he was impressed by the extra damage JaKobi and Lorelei were throwing down right now, risking her life wasn't worth it.

If they died, the Juggernaut would roll through Khalid's army like a wet paper towel.

Cassie must have had some sort of plan, but Tim had no idea what it was. He hit her with a Healing Orb and cast Healing Storm on the entire party to ensure everyone was topped off from the damage Behold My Power was doing.

Thankfully the powerful curse was about to flip from doing damage to dishing it out. Maybe Cassie counted on the boost from his spell to save her ass but that was risky business. Tim had already noticed in multiple fights that the bosses had skills that basically hit pause on all player abilities while they landed a devastating attack. If she was wrong and the boss paused his curse, this fight was over.

All they needed was one more second.

The double-headed ax hit Cassie so hard her feet sank into the ground a solid foot. The tank absorbed the blow, and somehow her staff didn't crack. What did break was her health bar. Getting hit almost made Cassie look like she'd jumped off a tall building and shattered her legs completely.

Sitting at just under thirty percent health, Cassie struggled to move let alone defend herself.

JaKobi was screaming at the top of his lungs, casting spell after spell to distract the Juggernaut. Lorelei followed close to him, filling any gaps in his tanks with arrows, but the minotaur didn't care. He knew that Cassie was injured and wanted to take her out of the fight completely.

Behold My Power hit, and Cassie's health shot over sixty-five percent in a single blast of healing energy. A second later she was at seventy-five percent and back on the move. She had her chain out and launched herself back into the fray before he could top off the rest of her health. She hit the boss hard, keeping the minotaur's attention focused on her as Tim worked on casting another Healing Orb.

The closer she got to full health the better he felt, and it gave him the ability to slip into conservation mode. Once he'd recouped enough of his mana, he could rejoin the fight at full throttle.

"Let's not do that again." Tim ran to get back into position.

Cassie growled as she diverted one of the Juggernaut's attacks. "Have to say he hit a little harder than I expected. Even with popping my cooldowns, it almost wasn't enough."

"New rule," Lorelei shouted as she rotated to stay with the group. "Avoid all the mechanics."

That was a good rule of thumb in every game Tim ever played. It was always better to survive than top the charts, especially early in the game's lifespan. Early on, players couldn't count on superior gear to cover their mistakes, so taking things slow was usually the right course of action. They didn't have the luxury of superior gear, and taking another hit like the last one would be enough to deplete his mana. Then they would be moments away from meeting their caseworkers.

It looked as though Cassie had the boss back under control.

ShadowLily hacked at the Juggernaut with her daggers, only this time from the side instead of directly behind. Maybe she thought her assault from behind triggered the attack mechanic. Tim tucked that thought away for later.

Despite their little hiccup, the fight was going pretty well for them. The boss was at seventy-five percent health and going down at a steady rate. They'd learned what one of the boss' mechanics was and how to survive it. From here it was rinse and repeat until the minotaur threw something new at them.

Cassie kept their group rotating in a small circle.

Tim assumed this was happening naturally since their tank had to dodge attacks instead of standing and eating the damage the way a more traditional tank would. The only person who couldn't attack on the run was JaKobi. The fire mage would run forward to the point where he was just out of the frontal cleave and launch attacks until he was about to run into the rear cleave. Then he sprinted forward again and restarted the routine.

For the first time, it felt as though ShadowLily had a small advantage for DPSing. She was used to moving as she fought, so it was nothing new for her. The others had the luxury of standing back and firing without doing a lot of running in most fights, but not here. All of them were rotating, and it was the assassin's time to shine.

Tim loved watching her reach her deadly dance as she slipped fully into attack mode.

When the Juggernaut's health hit sixty percent, he pulsed red again. Tim looked down and realized there was a circle of red mist at his feet. He couldn't move. Why the fuck couldn't he move? The rational part of his brain fought against the panic. This was nothing. He could handle it with Cleanse so he cast the spell.

Nothing fucking happened.

Tendrils spread out from the boss, each of them leading to one of the trapped players. As the black tendril coming in his direction connected with the red mist around his ankles, Tim started taking small amounts of incremental damage. He sent out a round of Healing Orb to counter the effect and tried casting Cleanse on someone else.

The spell still had no effect.

Maybe this was one of those unbreakable boss mechanics, and yet it felt like there was something they could do. He simply had no clue what it was.

The Juggernaut flashed red again, and it yanked all of them forward. This was getting out of hand. Everyone's health was fine, but they all looked a little worried. If Cleanse wouldn't get them out of this, he only had one option left.

Disturbance.

The boss didn't have any beneficial icons on his status bar. Using his only buff remover now might waste it completely. What if after this attack there was something he needed to remove? Fuck. Why didn't he spend more time working on his new skills? What was he going to do? Should he wait or cast the damn spell now?

The effect yanked Tim forward again, and his health took a hit.

There was probably only one more tug of the spell before all of them would be standing directly in front of the boss. Whatever mechanic the Juggernaut was going to employ would happen then. Tim could waste his time casting something that might not work, or he could get Healing Orb on everyone and hope for the best. He sent out the round of healing and waited to see if he made the right call.

The group jerked forward again, and now they were all just feet away from the Juggernaut. The minotaur laughed at them and blew out the most atrocious smelling fart. It was like something had crawled up in that giant cow ass of his and died. A smile spread on the beast's face as he jumped in the air and landed on his ass with a giant *whomp*.

The move threw all of them to the ground, and the cloud of putrid gas washed over them again.

It was worse than the time Xander ate nothing but ranch-style beans for a week. They hadn't lived in that house for over a year, and he bet the landlord was still airing it out. Tim had always thought of that week of farts as a ten on the stink scale, until today.

At best, Xander was a four.

Tim looked at his feet and realized they were mist-free, and he could move again. "Someone please kill this fucker. If I have to eat another fart, I'm seriously going to lose my shit."

He didn't need to scream. The others had already realized they were free and felt as disgruntled as he did about what happened to them. No one liked being farted on.

Trust me fellas. Girls don't think it's cute.

The Juggernaut still looked dazed and in recovery from his deadly gas attack, but Tim was starting to get worried. Something that smelled that bad couldn't be good for them. He sent out a round of Healing Orb, hoping the minor cleanse attached to the spell would be enough to remove any debuffs they might have suffered from the fart.

The Juggernaut climbed back to his feet, looking rather pleased with himself despite the fact his health had taken a severe beating. The boss was at forty-five percent health now but was also carrying a new buff.

Buff: He Who Dealt It, Made You Smell It

The Juggernaut knows being an immovable powerhouse doesn't apply to his farts. For each person gassed, the Juggernaut receives a five percent reduction in damage taken.

The last half of this fight would take forever if the boss took twenty-five percent less damage the entire time. Tim wasn't going to have the mana to keep them alive long enough to live through repeated rounds of the gas cloud and ax attacks. If they couldn't find a way to speed this up, they were going to get their asses kicked. Maybe this was the right time to cast his buff remover.

Tim cast Disturbance.

One of the five stacks of He Who Dealt it, Made You Smell It disappeared. Not the best news in the world, but a twenty percent reduction in damage was better than twenty-five. As soon as Disturbance was off cooldown, he could cast it again.

Cassie was back on the boss, and their slow rotation continued.

The tiny tank dodged and jumped but was taking a little more damage now. Tim got her back to full health, then the ax bounced off her shoulder plates, and she took a hoof to the gut. Tim kept his heals focused on the tank as they kept the boss' health moving ever so slowly downward.

The boss flashed red again at thirty percent, but before he finished flashing, Cassie and ShadowLily were on the run.

When the Juggernaut's special attack failed to hit anyone, their entire group took a twenty percent blow to their health. Tim was kind of pissed off about it. Now he had to heal the entire party because they correctly avoided the mechanic. The real question for next time was, what was worse, Cassie at thirty percent or all of them at eighty percent health?

Tim knew the answer without having to think about it.

One cast of Healing Storm was enough to get everyone back up to full health, and now they were in the final stretch of the battle. Tim was able to cast Disturbance again, bringing the minotaur's damage reduction down to fifteen percent. The boss didn't look thrilled about the new development, and his eyes flashed briefly red as they locked onto Tim.

The Juggernaut slammed his ax into the ground and pulled his wheel free.

Tim knew that matadors didn't fear the bull because they had a sword and a fancy red cape. Kind of made you wonder if the stories about bulls seeing red came from their times spent being slaughtered in the arena. He was pretty sure if someone stabbed him every time they showed him a swirling red cape, he'd have a pretty fucking adverse reaction to the damn thing as well, whether he could see the color or not.

Tim only hoped to avoid becoming a new color mashed into the sands.

Cassie was taunting the boss, but it wasn't doing anything. This was one of those unavoidable moments. He had to man up, and maybe he could soften the blow a little. He cast Who Needs a Shield on himself and a Healing Orb for good measure. Tim cast Snare as the boss rolled forward, but it had zero effect.

This was going to fucking hurt!

Watching death charging at you wasn't exactly a new experience for him, but now he fully understood what the term Juggernaut meant. Even at full health he probably couldn't survive a direct hit, but he had one spell left in his arsenal for just this occasion. He activated Quick Feet and sprinted to the side.

The Juggernaut's horn clipped him on the hip as he tried to dive clear of the attack.

Tim hit the ground hard and was relieved to see his leg was still attached. He was so focused on healing himself that he didn't see the boss crash into the invisible barrier around their fight and fall stunned. The sound was what made him look up, and from there it was easy enough to piece together what happened.

The boss had no way to block their damage while unconscious and his health fell faster than a wrestler's weight on Ex-Lax.

After climbing back to his feet with a grunt, Tim fired off Divine Light every chance he could. The boss was down to five percent health now and clawing his way back toward the group. The minotaur's burning red eyes inside the metal skull lost their shine, and the Juggernaut fell to the sands defeated.

Cheering erupted from the resistance members watching the battle.

The city was theirs. Now they had to take the palace.

CHAPTER FORTY-THREE

G olden motes rose into the air like rain in reverse.

Tim loved seeing the beautiful golden lights for two reasons. One, it meant that they won the fight. No matter how much he downplayed it, winning was something he loved immensely. He loved it almost as much as he hated losing. There was no rush like that of pulling out a victory from the jaws of defeat. The second reason he loved winning these big fights was the phat gobs of shiny new loot. Every gamer in the world loved the sweet, sweet digital glorification of new gear.

He'd seen players fight over stat increases so small they made Chihuahuas look like Great Danes.

The Etheric Coast solved the problem by creating individual loot pools. Tim was sure they'd see some crafting materials and other things that needed distribution and that they'd drop with frequency at some point. When the materials came, Tim would dump them in the guild bank until someone needed them. There were only five of them, and they all had full access to add and remove items whenever they wanted. He might have to rethink the policy if their numbers ever swelled, but he knew he'd never have to worry about waking up to an empty guild bank with who had access now.

After taking a moment to top off everyone's health, Tim scanned the battlefield. The fighting had resumed around them, but Jabari's men were being pushed back inside the city. Neema's forces overwhelmed the right side of Jabari's army as the warriors fled toward the palace and their last sanctuary.

Khalid rallied the troops in the middle of the battlefield and the day was theirs. Their next stop was the palace, where they would finally get their shot at Jabari. This would end today. Nar'ha would be in safer hands by sundown.

Cassie cleared her throat. "If you've finished staring off in the distance, we can get started." Her hand hovered over the chest.

"Don't wait on me." Tim wasn't shocked that Cassie's hand touched the chest before he finished speaking.

When she turned to look at the group, Cassie was grinning like there was one slice of pizza left and she called dibs. "I won't bore you with the awesome piece of loot I received, but I will guide your eyes to this shiny new pin."

Tim followed Cassie's pointing finger to a tiny pin of the Juggernaut on her leather vest. "It's our very first piece of flair."

"The thing with flair is that you can't ever have enough." JaKobi grinned as he walked toward the chest and laid his hand on it.

The fire mage triumphantly held up his pin as he wrapped an arm around Cassie's shoulders. "Hopefully, we all get one. Plus, I nabbed this wicked cool Ring of Sulfurous Intent. Adds a flat one percent bonus to my base fire damage."

"He gets the best loot because he's always getting hurt." Cassie punched JaKobi lightly in the side. "Just making sure he's ready for his next epic drop."

Tim tossed a Healing Orb at JaKobi and returned his attention to Cassie. "You know, I was the one the Juggernaut almost crushed. Let's not forget how the Daughters double-dipped me. I don't think numbers have anything to do with it. Loot is random."

"There will be no double-dipping while I'm around, mister." ShadowLily punched Tim's shoulder as she strutted past him on her way to the chest.

"Boots of the Silent Mouse. They give a bonus to my stealth and sneak ratings out of combat, and in combat increase my dodge-slash-parry chance by one percent." She equipped the boots. "On top of everything else, they don't look half bad."

Lorelei moved forward as ShadowLily put her new pin in place. "Waistguard of the Raven. Increases my precision and crit chance by one percent."

"Plus, this pin looks legit on my bow." She held out her bow to show everyone.

The little Juggernaut pin was affixed by the arrow rest so it looked like he was throwing the arrows. Tim thought it was pretty cool they could use the pin in a bunch of different ways. He'd been so busy thinking about the battle and what was next he completely missed that ShadowLily had gone before him, and the group was waiting for him to pick up his loot so they could continue.

"That looks awesome." Tim wondered if he could put the little Juggie on his staff with a similar effect.

JaKobi had his pin attached to his big floppy wizard's hat, and Cassie's was still on her chest. ShadowLily's kept disappearing and reappearing in different places as she tried to figure out where it looked best on her gear. Tim was kind of excited to get a fun piece of flair. It was a nice little display that let everyone know they were badass enough to down the Juggernaut.

Not wanting to keep the group waiting any longer he moved forward and placed his hand against the chest.

Item Received: Ring of Luminosity

While this ring won't make you shine as bright as a star, it will enhance your wisdom and intelligence quite nicely. +3 Wisdom, +2 Intelligence, +1 Endurance.

Sometimes an item didn't look like a significant upgrade on the surface. Some of his recent drops had much larger numbers attached to them, but this ring was the perfect upgrade. Tim's new Ring of Luminosity would replace his old ring, which only had a bonus of +2 to Wisdom. Every little stat increase helped, and now he was only one point away from hitting his next stat threshold for endurance.

One nice thing about the gaming in early MMO's was a player didn't have to worry too much about stats while leveling. Any increase was a good increase. Once players made it into the endgame, they had to deal with diminishing returns and balancing flat-out healing or DPS with items that offered special affixes.

For now, keeping their stats moving up was a bonus. If the item had a special power, it was like when the contestant guessed within two hundred and fifty dollars of the showcase on the *Price is Right*. It was a hell of a bonus but totally unexpected. So far the guild had a couple of fantastic items fall into their laps, and having better gear certainly made their progress in the game easier.

"What's the plan now, boss?" JaKobi asked as the sunlight reflected off his Juggernaut pin, drawing everyone's eyes to it.

The only instructions they'd received from Khalid for after the battle was to get to the staging area. Tim knew exactly where to go on the map and headed in that direction. If he could pick up some extra credit on his item quest for healing the wounded on the way, he'd do what he could to help.

After they defeated Jabari, they could bring down the Pharaoh and secure the deserts of Naroosh for the Goddess Eternia.

The city of Nar'ha was beautiful.

It was hard to judge the scope of its size as they ran from the gates toward the center. Tim wouldn't have been surprised to find it was easily the size of Promethia, maybe even larger. The streets around them were empty. The fighting in this part of town seemed to have ended almost as soon as the city fell. Now and then, they passed a courtyard or a wider thoroughfare full of fighters who surrendered and men making sure they didn't pick up arms and rejoin the fight.

It looked like the coin Jabari paid these men only carried their loyalty so far. Most of them weren't willing to die on the losing side for a few extra coppers. Once Jabari's grip on the city and his power waned, most of his mercenaries tossed their weapons aside. Khalid's men worked their way through the ranks of prisoners, sending some home and others back to fight for the right side this time.

None of the destruction Khalid's army did to the outer walls extended into the city. Since almost all of the resistance fighters were from Naroosh itself, they weren't interested in pillaging. It was probably the most peaceful sacking of a city in the history of *The Etheric Coast,* but it wasn't their city yet. The Blue Dagger Society still needed to make it to the command tent, then take the fight inside the palace grounds.

Tim's higher endurance made all the running they were doing now slightly more bearable than it had been before. There was a part of him that knew he'd never enjoy running and that was okay. At least he wasn't lagging as far behind the group as JaKobi was.

The fire mage had faded from a jog to a walk behind Tim about a minute ago and didn't show any interest in picking the pace back up. It was kind of funny to see the three women looking back at the two men and urging them forward.

His ego had taken worse beatings.

Slowing to a walk, Tim waited for JaKobi to catch up. "Is it me, or was this a lot easier when all you had to do was hold down 'W?'"

"Tell me about it." JaKobi's breath came in heaves. "I haven't run this much since high school gym class."

Lorelei ran back to them. "Hurry up, guys. We're almost there."

"Go ahead and find out how Neema is doing." Tim motioned for her to skedaddle. "We'll be there in a few minutes."

Cassie passed the ranger on the way back to the boys. "Don't worry. I'll make sure they don't pass out and die on the way."

"I'll come with you." ShadowLily joined Lorelei. "In case there happens to be trouble."

The ranger gave her a quick nod of acceptance and took off at a run. "Thanks for the company."

The three of them walked the remaining way to their destination. It gave Tim a little time to admire the craftsmanship and color that ran through Nar'ha's byways. Everywhere he looked, the stones on the buildings, even some of the paved streets, were dyed different colors. There was art painted on the walls. Pools of bright blue water flowed through carved channels leading from the river in the distance. The birds and fish were happy calling this city home. If it weren't for the armed soldiers, it would have been beautiful.

Peace would look good on Nar'ha.

When Khalid spoke of a command tent, Tim hadn't expected the very same one from the oasis to be present. It probably shouldn't have shaken him. Tents were made to be moved from one place to another. It was also kind of nice to enter a familiar setting in a very unfamiliar place.

The three of them stepped inside to join the others.

Tim let out a little squawk of surprise when Khalid mashed the three of them into a giant bear hug. The desert warrior released them a moment later and held them at arm's length as he beamed at them. He had a new cut on his leg but otherwise didn't look any worse for wear.

Khalid stepped back to give them some room and motioned for them to join him by his desk. "Your victory against the Juggernaut is what carried the day. I hate to rush you into another fight so soon, but are you ready to hear the next steps of the plan?"

Tim looked around, making sure everyone was ready to go. This was one of those key moments where it paid to check his gear and all his little knick-knacks to make sure he was ready for battle.

He didn't have any health or mana potions to worry about for the time being, and his armor and weapons were fine after a quick cycle through his inventory. He quickly recast his buffs and returned his attention to the warrior.

A Healing Orb took care of Khalid's leg, and a last nod from Cassie confirmed they were all ready to go. "Tell us what's next."

Before Khalid could speak, Lorelei jabbed Neema in the ribs with a finger. "I told you he'd heal his leg."

"I never should have doubted you." Neema grinned in a disarming way. It was a smile that said I was wrong, but I'm so cute you have to forgive me. "How was I supposed to know he was the only healer in the world who works for free?"

Tim coughed. "That's a healer who doesn't charge, sometimes."

"Whatever, we all know you're a big softie." ShadowLily patted him on the back. "That's why we like you."

Khalid flexed the leg. "Good as new. Thank you, my friend."

Moving to the map, Khalid stretched the leg as if he couldn't believe how good it felt. He stopped by the desk and pointed to a spot on the map. "There isn't a lot left to say. Jabari has barricaded himself inside the palace. Either in the throne room or the theater. Most of his guards have abandoned their posts, but his most loyal sycophants will fight to the death to protect him."

It made sense to Tim. The men closest to Jabari would be extremely devout and wouldn't want to see their power and wealth stripped away when the resistance broke their ruler's grip over the city. Those closest to Jabari would fight to the death not to lose everything they had. Tim wasn't sure how the five of them would fare against waves of organized troops.

"Neema and I will neutralize the guards inside the palace with the help of the resistance. Then we'll head to the throne room." Khalid paced back and forth. "I need you to head to the theater."

The desert warrior stopped and spun, locking his eyes onto Tim's with fierce intensity. "I do have to warn you, whichever of us doesn't face Jabari will probably run into his last protector. The Goliath."

Tim smiled as he reached out to grasp Khalid's extended hand. "We have a saying where we come from. The bigger they are, the harder they fall."

"Then today you will truly put that to the test." The old warrior broke their shake. "With the Goliath and Jabari out of the way, Nar'ha will be free, and we can turn our eyes to the capital."

"Just so you know." Neema stared at Khalid with righteous fury. "You aren't killing that bastard without me by your side. After what he did to my family, I deserve the right to put an arrow in him myself."

Khalid pulled her into a hug. "As you say it, so shall it be. We'll fight him together." He released Neema from his grasp and looked at Tim. "Will you help us?"

Quest Received: Take her to the Theater

Have you taken ShadowLily out on a date since you've been in the game? No? Then now is a good time to start. Who doesn't love a night out at the theater when it includes a boss fight or two? Oh, you wanted to know what you have to do to complete this quest. Get to the theater and handle whichever of the bosses waits for you there. Who will be behind curtain number one, Jabari or the Goliath? Either way, you'll need to be ready for one hell of a fight.

Reward: Ten gold coins

Tim hoped everyone's quest text didn't look the same as his. That would be rather awkward. He accepted the quest and tried not to blush.

"When we finish with the theater, we'll look for you in the throne room." Tim shook the warrior's hand one last time.

Khalid was beaming from ear to ear as he clapped Tim on the back. "We've been waiting for this moment for so long. I can hardly believe it is upon us. Fight well." He laughed as he thought about the glorious battle to come and turned to face the Desert Wolf. "Come, Neema. We have work to do."

Neema watched Khalid leave and gave Lorelei a quick kiss. "I'll see you when all this is over."

"No one is looking forward to that more than me." Lorelei watched her go with a hungry expression.

Tim pulled everyone's attention back to the moment. The biggest fight of their lives was coming up, and they had to be locked in. "Everyone buffed up and ready to go?"

"Does Hungry Jack's do a dollar off slices on Monday?" Cassie quipped.

Tim couldn't help but chuckle. "I'm going to take that as a yes."

"Damn straight it's a yes." Cassie looked around the room as though she couldn't wait to get out of there and kick some ass. "Let's go break this big fucker."

JaKobi nudged Tim. "Holding 'W' was nice, but what I really miss is being able to hit one button while I was playing and having my favorite pizza order show up thirty minutes later. Was it dangerous? Yes, but it was also amazing."

ShadowLily looked like she was going to snap. "Don't even get him started on pizza. It's all he talks about. I have Joe working on it. So get your head in the game, or no one is ever going to get pizza again."

"No pizza?" JaKobi cried.

"Ever again?" Tim wailed.

"Men." ShadowLily threw her hands up in disgust. "They're such drama queens."

Cassie pulled her close and pretended to whisper, "I know what you have to do. Make it easier for them to understand."

Holding up a finger as though an idea just came to her, ShadowLily turned and made sure the guys' attention was fixed on her before speaking. "I'll make it simple. You kill boss, get pizza. No boss, no pizza."

JaKobi looked at Tim. "You know what this means, bro?"

"I'm still trying to figure out if I was being insulted, but all I heard was pizza. Then I tuned everything else out." Tim couldn't keep the visions of all that cheesy pepperoni goodness out of his head.

The fire mage jumped up and down. "No man, it means we get to have a pizza party!"

"What are you, five?" Cassie looked exasperated.

ShadowLily put an arm around her shoulders. "You've got it simple. He only has to light stuff on fire. I gotta keep Tim's mind off pizza, or we're all going to die."

"No pizza for losers." Lorelei looked at them. "So get your shit together and let's do this." She took the lead as they walked toward the palace.

Tim watched her go. "Little rough around the edges, but I kind of like her."

"What's not to like?" Lorelei called back with some sass and put a little swagger into her walk.

"That's what I meant to say." Tim looked at the ground. He was hopeless with women, even the ones that liked other women.

Lorelei was right. It was time to stop dicking around. Pizza and beer could come later. Right now, they needed to worry about making it to the theater and taking care of business.

Tim spun his finger in a circle above his head. "Okay, adventurers, let's get to adventuring."

They followed Lorelei's path out of the tent and headed for the palace.

CHAPTER FORTY-FOUR

The palace courtyard was more spectacular than he imagined. The rest of the city had been beautiful, but this was next level. Even with the dead bodies strewn around the grounds and the occasional fountain spraying pinkish water, Tim could see the beauty hidden underneath it all. Manicured gardens, stylishly painted murals, and handcrafted sculptures lined the walkways.

There was so much to see, and they hadn't made it inside yet.

"No wonder Khalid wants back in here." Cassie snorted. "Talk about an upgrade."

JaKobi wiped some blood off a tile to get a better look at the picture underneath. "The oasis is nice and all, but this is like going from a strip mall hotel by the airport to a private resort in Bali."

There wasn't much else to be said so Tim started moving forward again. The place was awesome, but it kind of reminded him of the formal living room at his friend's house. What was the point of an entire damn room if no one ever got to use it? It was like having dedicated dining rooms. It was a large space with a giant table that was probably only used a few times a year. Kinda seemed like a waste to dedicate so much space to something not that functional. In other words, he liked things he could live in.

Having to worry if his shoes scuffed the marble wasn't his type of thing.

Not that Tim couldn't appreciate expensive things when they were around. The amount of work that went into every detail of this place was astounding. What he'd love to do was see some of these people create their art. Even without the ability to watch the artists, being here and living in this moment was a million times better than any museum he'd ever visited. He moved toward a wall and rubbed his fingers against a thick hemp tapestry with an image of Jabari woven into it.

It was like being able to touch history.

Tim turned away from the fabric, looking for something else that was cool, and saw a group of three men charging toward them with their swords drawn.

He turned away from the palace entrance and gently pushed Cassie in front of him. "You're up."

"What are you talking about?" The tank squawked as Tim spun her to face the charging soldiers. "Oh."

Cassie's staff appeared in her hands a moment later as the shock left her face. "Eat a bag of dicks, you Nazi fuckers!"

JaKobi shrugged as Cassie charged at the men who were clearly not actual Nazis. "No one likes Nazis."

"Fuck it. I can get on board with that." Tim smiled as he fired off a burst of Divine Light. "Even saw a movie where someone made Bratzis."

Once someone turned the Führer into little dickish sausage monsters, the world certainly felt like a more hilarious place.

Cassie was in the midst of all three of Jabari's soldiers now and taking a steady amount of damage. He quickly cast Who Needs a Shield and followed it up with a Healing Orb before going back to do more damage himself.

The fun thing about trash packs for him was that he got to play a different style because the healing needs weren't so dire. Tim rapidly cast Curse of Giving on all three men, providing Cassie with a constant stream of heals as she tried to keep their attention.

One of the soldiers turned away from Cassie and sprinted at the ranger. There was nothing any of them could do to stop the attack as the man blurred across the open space. A blink of an eye later, and then he seemed to appear behind Lorelei. The ranger got her bow up in time to ward off the worst of the blow but still took a nasty cut across the arm.

At least it wasn't her head.

Tim hit her with a burst of Healing Orb and blasted the fucker who attacked her with Divine Light. Before he could follow up, the man flashed forward again, this time slashing at ShadowLily's back. Healing her through the damage wouldn't be a problem, but this fight was now pulling on his resources almost as hard as the one with the Juggernaut.

"All DPS on the slippery fucker. The other two can wait," Tim called as the man blurred again, this time coming straight for him.

He activated Quick Feet and dove to the side, avoiding the worst of the sword thrust. Tim cast Snare on the man hoping to trip him up before he could attack again and climbed back to his feet. He healed himself as he waited for the others to kill the man.

Flames washed over Mr. McStabbyPants as JaKobi went to work. It seemed that being quick didn't make the soldier any less combustible. With their one surprise out of the way, the other two soldiers died almost instantly. The fight had been a little more than Tim bargained for. Maybe the game was giving them a subtle hint that shit was about to get real, and the difficulty of the encounters was about to get kicked up a notch.

It had been a while since they faced trash mobs going into a fight. While not having to face them between every encounter was a welcome reprieve, he wasn't surprised the trash mobs had made a reappearance. Normally these fights were pretty simple, but this one had almost rocked their world. He was pretty sure that if they faced the same encounter again, it would go much better for them.

"I thought Khalid would have emptied this place by now." Lorelei looked around, confused.

Tim shrugged. "Guess Jabari had a few more reserves than Khalid planned for. Now that we know they're here, Cassie will take the lead, and the rest of us will follow her."

"I kinda like the sound of that." Cassie turned to address the group. "As your new leader, I'd first like to say thank you for the vote of confidence. I know that our last leader lacked many of the natural qualities normally associated with..."

"Hey," Tim cried. "You run forward and get hit a lot. I'll try and decide if you're worthy of heals based on your performance." He tried to make his statement sound serious, but they all knew he was a softie at heart.

Cassie blew him a giant raspberry and moved forward again.

Trash fights were kind of fun, but in most games, they served two primary purposes. The first was to make the instance take longer. If players went in and only faced three bosses and a mini-boss, they would burn through the content before the developers had a chance to work on something new. When the business model was based on keeping players subscribed to a monthly service, making the content take longer to beat was the key to generating more profits. The second reason was that it gave the developers a chance to give players some coin to balance out what they lost after dying to the bosses and repairing their gear.

So far the inventory trick had worked on everything except Cassie's completely shattered staff. That required a repair shop to fix, but even then it didn't cost a fortune. The trash mobs in *The Etheric Coast* dropped some coins into their inventories, but it was usually only a few coppers or silver. Nothing to write home about. These fights inside the palace were no different.

"Follow me. If one of them starts zipping around, focus on that asshole first." Cassie moved down the corridor with a confident swagger.

The next group of three soldiers charged them instantly, but their group makeup looked different. Tim hadn't been paying too much attention to the first set of fighters they faced, mostly because he was so surprised to see them, and he was trying not to get shivved. One thing he was pretty sure of was none of the guards in the previous group had shields, and all three of these men did.

"Watch for new tricks," Tim called to Cassie as he cast Curse of Giving on all three men.

Never one to mince words when actions would speak louder, their tank charged into the fray. Her bō staff rose and fell as she ducked and dodged around the men. So far Cassie didn't seem to be doing a ton of damage, but the tank certainly had the attention of all three men, and that was all she needed to accomplish for the DPS to go to work.

There wasn't much to be said about Jabari's warriors' battle plan. They each had big-ass shields and decent-sized spears. If the shields were a little larger and didn't have a small spike in the center, they would have looked like the famous ones used by the Spartans. While he loved watching Leonidas kick ass, Tim was less than enthused by the prospect of what would happen next.

The three men moved quickly, surrounding Cassie, and lifted their shields as they ran forward.

"At least we know what the spikes are for." Tim gritted his teeth as he cast Who Needs a Shield and Healing Orb.

Cassie got crunched by the shields, the spikes piercing her from three sides. "You better not call me a fucking kebob!"

ShadowLily appeared a second later and dropped one of the guards from behind. "At least it was the enemies that did it to you."

"Next time if saving your ass requires filling it with arrows, I'll just let you get roasted," Lorelei quipped as she fired at one of the remaining attackers.

Tim didn't mind the witty banter since it kept them calm and focused. ShadowLily would get over being shot a few times by her friend eventually. Right now, they appeared to have the fight well in hand, but they needed to focus and ensure they finished off their attackers before getting too distracted.

Cassie broke free as the guards split apart. One of the men faced the group, and the other hovered over Cassie, keeping her out of the fight.

ShadowLily dodged a spear thrust and rolled backward, coming up next to the ranger. "I'd rather you keep saving me. Just expect me to keep bitching about it if said saving involves arrows sticking out of me." She winked and disappeared.

The guard saw Lorelei as an easy target and ran forward. "Death to the infidels!"

"Shit." The ranger got her bow up and fired a half-assed shot that bounced harmlessly off the guard's shield.

Tim switched his attention from Cassie to the ranger, knowing she'd need heals soon. Her bow was no match for the giant spike on the front of the guard's shield.

ShadowLily reappeared behind the soldier, easily cutting him down before he could reach his target. "These are my kind of fights."

Lorelei smirked as she jumped back a step to avoid the tumbling body. "It isn't very sportsman-like to stab people in the back."

"But it is effective." ShadowLily disappeared again, no doubt running toward the last target.

The last guard fell as a flaming spear pierced through his chest from behind. JaKobi turned, looking extremely satisfied. "That wasn't so bad."

Cassie pushed her entire hand through one of the rips in her tattered leather vest. "Not so bad? Those three spikes fucking hurt, and I'd really like not to have a repeat incident if we can avoid it."

The tank's armor disappeared and reappeared fully repaired a moment later. She looked at Tim. "Do you think we'll see a lot more of these packs?"

"I don't have a clue, but unless the game is trying to make up for lost time, there can't be too many more before we reach the theater."

"Let's keep moving." Lorelei prodded them along.

Tim sagely nodded as if it was his idea. "You know what guys, I think it's time to keep moving."

"Fucker." The ranger tried to hide her smile, but it was impossible with how warmly it glowed.

Tim laughed. "Lorelei is right. Let's keep pushing forward. Cassie, you have the lead."

As the tank started moving again, Tim made sure to follow at a distance while keeping his spiel going. "For the groups with a speedster, attack him first. For the three shields, we'll have to play it by ear and try and take down one of them before they can crush our lovely Miss Cassie."

"In other words, get used to having sharp spikes driven through your body," Cassie grumbled.

"That's why you get the big bucks." Tim laughed to himself.

It wasn't much of a joke, but he felt giddy. Things were going well for them, and while one of their biggest challenges was still on the way, the future felt rife with opportunity. He wanted to get to the theater and find out if they would get a crack at Jabari or be stuck facing down the Goliath. The next group of trash appeared, and his thoughts turned back to the fight at hand, knowing they'd be standing in front of the boss in no time.

CHAPTER FORTY-FIVE

The last pack of trash before the boss went down.

At least he hoped it was the last pack. After his bold statement about how soon they would reach the boss, Tim was shocked at how many groups they'd run into. Five or six pulls between bosses was all fine and dandy, but that was trash pack number thirteen and Cassie wasn't the only one starting to grumble. The only good news was Jabari couldn't have many men left.

Cassie led them around a corner, and Tim let out a huge sigh of relief. A giant set of golden double doors marked the entrance to the theater. As their group approached, both opened as if to invite them inside. From where they stood outside, he could see the massive room beyond.

Looking through the doors, Tim wouldn't have been surprised to find they could have easily fit a football field inside, or at least half of one. It was the biggest theater he'd ever seen, but it wasn't as though they had movies. So if they wanted to reenact large-scale battles, they needed some space. It wasn't what he was expecting, and the area was big enough that anything could be waiting for them inside.

This was going to get interesting.

"Double-check your buffs." Tim knew they should all be good, but checking everything before a battle was a hard habit to break.

ShadowLily popped back into existence. "This has to be the boss. Whatever comes our way, roll with the punches and wait for Tim to make the calls."

"You keep giving instructions like that, and I'm going to be out of a job." Tim didn't mind if she wanted to be in charge.

He was kind of their leader by default. Their group was so competent he didn't have to do much in the way of actual leading. During the fights, he made the calls because he was in the best position to do it. If they ever had to start recruiting, he wouldn't want to be in charge anyway.

"Only a crazy person would want to run a guild." ShadowLily laughed. "I think you can hold onto that responsibility for a while."

Cassie stood in the entrance waiting for the rest of them to stop yapping and catch up. "Stay behind me, and everything will be fine."

"Words to live by." JaKobi gave her a sly grin. "Let's do what the little lady says."

Lorelei moved into position. "You better pucker up before you kiss an ass that hard."

"How I pucker and where is none of your business." JaKobi was grinning from ear to ear at the expression on Lorelei's face as he turned to look at Cassie. "I think it's safe to proceed."

Cassie glanced at Tim. He nodded, and she stepped into the room. The rest of their group quickly followed her inside, and the faint red glow showed that the room had sealed and they wouldn't be able to leave the area unless they died or killed the boss.

Now that they were inside the theater, Tim noticed a series of box seats above and to the left of them and a massive suite looking down at the center of the space. Tim guessed that was the royal box or the VIP section. The upper right-hand side of the room was devoid of any seating options.

As Tim finished looking over the area, the sound of a door opening came from in front of them, and a man appeared in the royal box. He moved down the rows of seats until he stood at the waist-high railing looking down upon them. The sneer on his face was of near-mythical proportions.

This must have been Jabari.

The ruler of Nar'ha wore beautiful blue and white silk cloth from head to toe. His robes were probably worth more than half the damn city. Tim stopped trying to count the jewels that hung from his neck, wrist, and fingers. However, the entire outfit wouldn't have been complete without the crown.

Made of solid white gold and shaped to look like a cobra rising behind Jabari's head, it was one hell of a sight. The amount of craftsmanship that went into making something like that must have been unreal. A man like Jabari didn't deserve something so beautiful, but he didn't only have a crown.

There was a matching scepter.

It must have taken a hundred masters a hundred years to make something so intricate. The scepter itself was made from the same white gold as the crown but was broken up by solid blue lines at matching intervals until they reached a round ball on top. Sitting on top was a spider made of onyx.

It was the only thing Tim would have changed about the ruler's entire look. Why ruin such a badass outfit with spiders? Snakes he could get, maybe even an alligator, but why a freaking spider?

"Camel Spider, maybe," JaKobi whispered just loud enough for Tim to hear as he clearly tried to work out the same problem.

Jabari's thick black goatee bobbed up and down as he spoke. "Khalid's dogs. Why am I not surprised? I'm sorry that he tricked you into an early death. It's what he is known for around here."

His sneer was full of arrogance. "Next time you see the old bastard, ask him how many have died while he sat idly by? Then ask yourself how many lives could have been spared if he had simply walked away."

From the balcony to their left, Khalid roared, "You're the one who kills innocent people. You're the one corrupted by Vitaria's taint."

Tim turned to see the old warrior and Neema making their way down the rows of seats to the railing. The Desert Wolf let an arrow fly, but the arrow simply vanished a foot from Jabari. There was no trail of smoke or ashes. It was simply there one second and gone the next. Tim would've said it was a glitch, but he didn't think such a thing was possible inside *The Etheric Coast*, which meant it was probably a clue.

He was half-tempted to tell Lorelei to try one of her arrows so he could see the effect happen again, but he was afraid it would start the fight prematurely. Part of his brain was still trying to play catch-up because Jabari was above them and it wasn't the Goliath waiting for them in the room.

Jabari's sneer could have curdled milk. "You say those things as if the trail of bodies you leave in your wake is any smaller than mine. The only difference between you and me is that I gave up the pretense of being good while you cling to your morals like a baby with a new toy.

"Such things are beneath men like us." Jabari forced a neutral expression onto his face. "There's still time for you to give up this folly and join me. I can see that it was wrong of me to cast you out all those years ago. Let me welcome you back now with open arms." He held his arms wide as if waiting for an embrace.

Khalid stared across the space with hatred burning in his eyes. "Your father was a man of respect, a man I would have followed until I died. For him, I would have given my life."

The old warrior spat over the edge of the railing. "As for you, Jabari, I wouldn't work for you. I'd rather be dead." Khalid's laughter was full of malice. "Tell me truly. Now that all your ambitions have turned to shit in your mouth, how does it taste?"

"You've been living on the taste of my shit your entire life." Jabari moved toward a seat so he could watch whatever was about to happen next. "I hope you like a show because after my Goliath finishes with them, I'm coming for you."

Neema jumped on the railing overlooking the space between them as if she might be able to leap for it. "Still hiding behind your pets and your threats? The only thing new about you is how little support you have left."

Khalid moved forward, pulled her back, and kept an arm around her. "I've failed the people of this land many times in my life, but I've never abused their trust in me. We will see you humbled today, servant of Vitaria."

Laughter spilled from Jabari's lips, but he had a weaselly, about to flee, look in his eyes. "The Goliath will end your band of adventurers. Then I'll take your precious Khalid from you. Finally, when you have nothing left, I will send you to the pleasure houses to be utterly broken."

Jabari kept his eyes locked on Neema, knowing he could get under her skin much easier than he could Khalid's. He tapped his scepter on the stone railing. "See what your foolishness has wrought?" He pointed down at Tim. "And your trust."

The upper doors snapped shut behind the boxes and sealed. Thick bronze bars slid down from the ceiling, cutting Khalid and Neema off from the rest of the room. There were slots in the bars wide enough they might be able to wriggle through, but Tim expected the metal was sharpened, and they were angled the wrong way to make it easy. The floor shook.

The Goliath was coming.

The doorway below Jabari swung open, and something slowly squeezed into the room. Tim wasn't sure what he saw at first, but then the man made it through the giant door and turned to face them. That's right—the Goliath was so big he had to squish through an opening that the five of them could have walked through side by side at the same time. He made the doors look child-sized instead of made for a group of full-grown adults.

The fucker was massive.

Tim's mouth must have been hanging open because Shadow-Lily tapped the bottom of his chin to make him close it.

He'd expected an epic warrior—a Hercules, a Samson, an Achilles—but what he saw was more like Chris Farley stuffed into armor made for Chris Hemsworth. The Goliath's massive belly hung below his chest piece. Scars lined the fatty surface, so the extra bulk clearly wasn't a recent development. Not what Tim imagined when he'd heard the boss' name, but being fat wouldn't make the Goliath any less deadly.

The Goliath flexed his massive gauntleted hands. Each of those big steel-covered mitts was big enough to pick one of them up and crush them. Or shove them in his mouth for a little snack. *Please don't have him eating us be a thing.* He'd seen that in plenty of games, and getting chomped on wasn't a fun way to die.

Imagine the shirt Barbara would make.

As if to prove a point, the Goliath let out a roar that made his neck wobble from side to side. He could have easily eaten a full-sized person. Hippos did it all the time, and they were about five times smaller than this guy. The boss had grown so large that the helmet sitting atop his head almost looked like a kippah instead of the face-covering plate mail it used to be. However, when Tim looked at the boss' face, all he could see were the teeth.

Big enough to eat you with, my pretty.

It was as though they were facing Gluttony from *Diablo* or Dante's *Inferno* but without all the demon stuff. This boss was big, he was pissed off, and he might be looking for a snack. They had some serious work cut out for them if they wanted to win. The Goliath took one wobbling step forward.

It took everything Tim had not to take a step back.

Khalid looked down on them through the bronze slats as he made the sign of Eternia over his chest. "May her light guide you to victory."

"Kick some ass!" Neema pumped her fist in the air.

Jabari's sneer grew more pronounced as he watched their little display with disdain. The motherfucker's sneer was like the Grinch's heart the way it kept growing. The ruler of Nar'ha barely acknowledged the group as he sipped from a glass of wine and picked over a tray of fruits and cheeses. "They're all yours."

He tapped the railing in front of him again, and the Goliath took another shuffling step toward the group.

"What are we going to do about the egg with legs?" Cassie quipped.

Tim would usually be above fat jokes, having gone through a rather portly phase himself, but in this case, he was willing to let it slide. The Goliath was big enough that a normal-sized human might look like a footlong sub, and there was a time Tim could have eaten three of those bad boys in a single sitting. Tim didn't want to be the next sub sandwich the boss demolished.

He looked too good to be food.

Before the boss got to them, Tim took a final chance to address the group. "Hit him hard, and try to stay away from his mouth."

A string of drool dripped down the Goliath's chin as he drew closer.

"Not going to be a problem." Cassie snorted. "I have a firm no kissing on the first date policy."

JaKobi mouthed at Tim, "Not with me."

Tim didn't have any idea what to say to that so he kept his mind working on the fight in front of them. "Stay sharp, focus on the exposed bits, and try to have some fucking fun." Tim was feeling it now. It was go time.

Cassie let out a war cry and ran forward. "No one takes the last slice of pizza from me."

Tim tried not to laugh as he imagined Cassie always being the smallest person at the dinner table and having to fight off her family so she could have her fair share of the grub. After their talk earlier, pizza was clearly on all of their minds. At least the tank wouldn't have to think about it for long. She'd be too busy dodging and trying to stay alive while he'd be stuck thinking about that ooey-gooey goodness for at least another ten seconds.

The Goliath didn't slow his ponderous steps as Cassie approached. There was a chance he couldn't stop running forward without some help. Getting that much bulk to stop moving all at once would have been damn near impossible. Thankfully, the boss didn't have to worry about slowing on his own. Cassie handled that for him by flying through the air and landing both feet against his chest.

Their tank bounced off what remained of the steel breastplate, flipped in the air, and landed gracefully on her feet. "Try to keep up."

Cassie went to work with her staff, and the rest of the group started their DPS rotations. Tim watched the tank for a moment to make sure she wasn't going to get manhandled straight away, then scanned the battlefield as he cast Curse of Giving. Nothing seemed out of place in the rest of the room so he got to work on his rotation and cast Healing Orb on Cassie.

With his initial burst of healing out of the way, he had to decide if now was the right time to toss out his big damage spell or to wait for a more opportune time. No one but Cassie was taking any damage, so now felt better than later. With a thought, he cast Behold My Power and tossed out a round of Healing Orb to soak up the damage he was causing.

No one batted an eye as his spell crashed into them. The instant the damage was done, his heals took care of it. They were too good of players to let a small thing like a little pain keep them from doing their jobs effectively. From his spot in the back, he could already see several arrows and a few scorch marks lining the boss' massive belly. They weren't doing a ton of damage yet, but they were just getting started.

For the most part, the Goliath seemed to be doing his own thing. He tried to punch Cassie a few times, but when he realized she was too fast, he ignored her. It took everything the tank had to keep the boss focused on her. Jabari watched from above with a disgusted look on his face as if this whole thing was taking entirely too long and was utterly beneath him.

Jabari clapped his hands. "Eat."

Hidden doors opened along the walls and servants ran into the room, tossing whole cooked chickens and hams at Goliath's feet and scurrying away as fast they could. One of the boys wasn't so lucky, and the boss snatched him off his feet with one massive hand. The kid screamed right up until the Goliath crunched into his top half as if it was an apple. He tossed the boy's legs away and picked up some of the other items as he finished his snack.

The boss' health hadn't gone up with his feasting, so that was a plus. Tim had been worried when he saw the food coming out that they'd be starting at square one as soon as he finished the snacks.

What he hadn't expected was the boss to keep eating until he let out a room-shaking fart. A cloud of noxious green gas shot from his ass and hung in the air. What was with these last two bosses? Yes, he knew developers liked to give you mechanics and expand on them but was doing it with farts the right way to go?

"Watch the gas!" Tim called.

The green cloud didn't move, but it did hang in the air. If the gas lingered for the fight's duration, they would have to start moving the boss around the room. Tim got the feeling if the Goliath kept expelling gas in the same place, then the cloud would slowly expand until they ran out of room. If they moved the boss, they could control where he disbursed the clouds, and it might buy them the time they needed to win.

Who would have thought farts would become so fucking important to their survival?

Cassie moved the boss with a not-so-deft touch. Getting the big motherfucker to shuffle was no easy task. She split her staff in two and whaled on the boss with every step she took. The frustration on the Goliath's face slowly grew. It was like watching an old time cartoon where the person drank something hot, and the steam slowly moved up their face until it came out their ears.

Only this cloud of steam came from somewhere else.

Tim was half-tempted to tell JaKobi to try and light the farts on fire the next time one came out, but with their luck, the clouds would all light at once and his little plan would incinerate them all. It wasn't worth the risk of trying for extra damage when the opposite effect might be dying by fart fire.

There was no reason for them to rush. Goliath's health was already down twenty percent, and all of them were at full health. All they had to do was rinse and repeat until the fight was over.

Goliath's health pool must have been massive because Tim hadn't even noticed when Behold My Power took effect. Normally the damage was pretty spectacular, but here it was just a tiny blip. This fight was taking much longer than he planned, but his mana looked good. Nothing too crazy happened yet unless you counted a kid getting eaten like a Tootsie Pop.

ShadowLily must have landed a critical hit because the boss' health jumped down to seventy-five percent in a blink. The Goliath jumped up and down, and the effects shook the entire palace. Dirt drifted down from the ceiling. A little dirt was the least of their worries. With every single jump, their entire group took damage.

Tim shot out a small burst of Healing Storm. "Try to jump right before his feet hit the floor!"

He soaked up the damage from the next jump, waiting to time his next attempt perfectly. Right before the Goliath's feet hit, Tim jumped. The floor was still a little shaky when he landed, but other than almost falling on his ass, he didn't take any damage at all. Then his life turned into a simple routine of jump, land, and hit whoever mistimed their jump with a Healing Orb.

That went on until the Goliath ran out of energy. The boss gave one last mighty leap, but instead of landing on his feet again, he landed on his ass. Everyone in their group missed the jump and all of them were stunned in place. Tim felt their moment of opportunity slipping away and could only hope their punishment for missing the final jump meant they would only get half of the boss' moment of opportunity to do big DPS.

"As soon as the stun wears off give him everything you've got until the bastard gets up again." Tim tried to Cleanse himself to see if it set them free, but it didn't work. He cast Divine Light on the boss, and it also didn't work. For better or worse, they were stuck until the game said otherwise.

Nothing felt worse than when the boss had an unbreakable mechanic that hit everyone. In some games that was it, fight over. *The Etheric Coast* was a little more generous, or maybe they'd gotten lucky, and the Goliath happened to get stunned at the same time as the rest of them. Throwing temper tantrums was never a good way to win a fight. Tim was pretty sure they would live through this stun, but now he wasn't sure if they'd seen the last of the boss' tricks.

Suddenly, the spell ended.

Tim could move again, and he didn't waste a second before he started casting. He quickly reapplied Curse of Giving and sent out a Healing Orb to anyone who needed it. The group's overall health looked good for the moment so he fired off a quick blast of Divine Light before dropping into a wait and see approach.

A group of servants ran into the room with massive poles and a few large barrels. Lining up behind the boss, the men fit the wooden poles over the barrels and used them as fulcrums to help the boss back onto his feet. The Goliath teetered for a moment as if he was unsure his legs were working, then turned to face the group.

Ripping off his metal helmet, the Goliath cried, "I want more." He chucked the helmet up at Jabari's seating area.

"Enough of this!" Jabari roared. "Kill them, and I will place a feast at your feet so great even the gods will be envious."

Spittle flew from Goliath's mouth as his voice quivered with rage. "I'm hungry now."

"Fine, but if you fail me in this you will never eat again." Jabari clapped his hands and the servants bearing food ran into the room again.

Tim caught Lorelei's attention and made a shooting motion with his fingers.

Nodding to confirm she received the message, Lorelei turned and fired in one smooth motion. The arrow flew through the air and vanished a foot away from the boss. He'd been pretty sure that when Jabari was speaking to the Goliath it was some kind of in-game cutscene, but if they missed out on a chance to do damage when they could have, it would have put the outcome of the battle in jeopardy.

They couldn't have that.

Servants ran into the room again, dodging the Goliath's attempts to snatch them up as they threw food at his feet. Once again, one of Jabari's servants was too slow and met the same fate as the first boy. *I mean, why settle for turkeys, chickens, and hams when you could crunch up a perfectly good person?* Tim almost laughed hysterically at the thought.

What were they, ogres?

It was one thing to read about man-eating monsters, but to see someone getting snacked on was something else entirely. Whatever Vitaria had done to make this man into a monster it had clearly changed his appetites for the worst. Tim was pretty sure he hadn't even tried to eat any of the other food this time. Apparently, the top halves of children were enough to satisfy his hunger.

The meal didn't do anything for Goliath's health, but it did start the fart train again.

Cassie was doing her best to move the boss before he exploded with gas, but it wasn't going to happen.

Goliath rumbled with laughter, belched, and farted like he'd spent the last week eating chili four times a day. He turned his massive ass as he expelled the noxious gas, creating a semicircle of hanging fart for them to deal with.

"Just do what you can," Tim called to Cassie as he blasted her with another heal.

The tank gritted her teeth in frustration as she kept slamming her staff into the boss' legs. "Kind of already doing that."

Note to self, don't tell the tank to tank.

Tim looked at the boss' status. He was getting closer to fifty percent health now. Whatever the rest of his group was doing it was working the right way. His mana looked good, and the fight seemed well in hand as long as they kept up the pace.

Was this really going to be so easy? He should have known better than to ask himself that question. Of course, it wasn't. This was the last fight before they took down the big baddie. There was no way they were only going to have to dodge some farts and avoid becoming a snack.

Something else was coming. They had to be ready.

He pulled up the Goliath's stat sheet to take a quick look. The boss wasn't carrying any buffs right now, but he was starting to wonder if there was a window where he might be able to stop the feeding or the farting for an extra moment of opportunity. Whenever a boss was stunned in this game because their group dodged or broke a mechanic, it made the bosses more susceptible to damage for a short time. It didn't happen in every fight, but when they did receive a moment of opportunity they had to make the most of it.

Goliath's health hit fifty percent.

Jabari rose from his seat screaming, "Enough!" He pointed his scepter down at the group and made a sweeping motion.

Tim let out a startled shout as an unseen force picked him up off the floor and flicked him to the side like an ant off a picnic table. That shit fucking hurt, and he didn't think anything they could have done would have stopped the attack as he flew through the room. Of course, Jabari's attack made sure that each of them passed through the fart cloud.

Tim tried to hold his breath, but it was like when his mom cooked chicken on Monday, and he forgot to take out the trash until Thursday night. That stench of rotting chicken bones and bacteria was exactly what Goliath farts tasted like. The fucking smell was so bad by the time they got to the other side of the room, all of them had a debuff, and their health was rapidly plummeting.

It was the perfect time to break out his Cleanse.

He took care of himself first, then Cassie. Cleanse was a good spell to have but it could get pricey with five casts in a row. As soon as the tank wasn't coughing out green mist, she ran back into the battle, and Tim got to work on the others.

His mana pool didn't look so great now. Jabari had nearly wiped all of them out with one simple attack. This fight was winnable, but how would they face off against Jabari in the next one? He'd almost killed all of them, and Tim wasn't sure it had been an attack. If Jabari could repeatedly cast that spell, they'd never get within ten feet of him.

What a fucking day.

On the plus side, the room was now clear of gas. Not that it made up for having to eat a buffet of Goliath farts. Nothing would ever make that right again unless it never happened to him, and everyone else still had to suffer. Then he could sit back and enjoy that fart without a mouthful of stink. Instead, this would become one of those "We never talk about it again" moments that the best of friends often shared when out on adventures together.

Their DPS was rolling now. None of them wanted a repeat of Jabari's attack and the fart-tasting incident. Tim started wondering if they could kill all the servants to stop the Goliath from snatching one of them and releasing more gas, but they didn't come here to slaughter children.

They were here to make sure no one tried to eat them again.

When the Goliath's health hit thirty-five percent, he shimmied and jumped. They'd seen this mechanic before and were ready for it. They still mistimed a jump now and again, but overall the group did much better than the first go-around. All they had to do from here was avoid the stun at the end.

"Get ready for it!" Tim called as he watched the boss bounce.

The Goliath jumped into the air and came down hard on his ass. A little extra gas squirted out at the end. It was almost enough to make Tim laugh, but they had timed their jumps correctly and missed the stun. This was their chance to do as much DPS as possible, and all of them were going all-out.

It didn't look like they were going to be fast enough to end this before Jabari swept them across the room again, so Tim slowed his DPS in the hope he'd have enough mana to heal them through another round of the worst attack possible.

Watching the boss for a buff he could dispel, Tim prayed to avoid their second pass through the land of unimaginable farts.

Jabari stood as the Goliath came out of his stupor. The servants ran out to help him back to his feet, but the boss looked pouty.

"I'm hungry," he roared. "More." He moved his hand to his mouth almost like a baby.

Jabari's eyes almost bugged right out of his head. "There are five meals down there right now. Eat one of them."

Tim realized his mistake at the last second. He was watching Goliath for an interrupt, but he should have been watching Jabari. As the ruler of Nar'ha lifted his scepter, Tim kept his eyes focused on him. He might have missed his chance this time, but next time he'd be ready to stop the attack. While he might not be able to keep them out of the cloud, this time he was going to keep his fucking mouth shut.

No one should be forced to eat someone else's ass cloud.

Tim started casting Cleanse as Jabari's spell dragged them through fart central. The Goliath was back on his feet now, and the servants were dumping as much food for him to eat as quickly as they could. None of them wanted to be the next snack.

So far the boss hadn't been able to snatch one of the boys, but he'd come close a couple of times. His frustration at not being able to grab his favorite meal was starting to make the Goliath upset. When all of the servants made it out of the room alive, he roared in rage.

Cassie ran forward, and the DPS went back to work as soon as she made first contact. The boss's health was at ten percent now. Tim reapplied Curse of Giving and made sure no one was suffering from any lingering effects of the fart debuff. Everything looked under control, right until the boss started shoving the food from the floor into his mouth.

Then the fucker's health started to go up.

"JaKobi, burn the food," Tim screamed, not wanting the boss to gain any extra health.

A look of intense pleasure washed across the fire mage's face as he went to work. "Any day I get to burn is a good day to be alive."

The Goliath screamed as his snacks disappeared. He looked up at Jabari, moving his hand to his mouth again. "I need more."

Jabari grimaced with disgust and waved his scepter again, but none of the servants reappeared. All of the Goliath's food was gone, and none of the servants was willing to become his next snack pack. Being killed for insubordination had to be better than getting eaten alive.

While looking down from his box, Jabari jumped up and down screaming, "Kill them!"

When the Goliath realized no more food was coming, he started to pulse with a red light. A small beam of the same light highlighted the floor, and Tim knew what that meant.

"Keep doing damage, but remember red is dead." Tim had the feeling whatever was coming next would be a one-shot mechanic.

The Goliath ran from one corner of the room to the next with superhuman strength, using the walls like the ropes of a wrestling ring. Stones fell from the ceiling, forcing the team to dodge flying debris as each of his attacks threatened to bring the theater down on top of them. The Goliath charged toward Jabari's royal box with one last scream. Right before the boss reached his destination, his foot caught on something, and he fell forward at full speed sailing headfirst into one of the pillars holding up the seating.

The pillar cracked as the Goliath's skull crashed through the stone, and Jabari's seating area shook.

When the pillar broke, Tim thought for sure they were all fucked, and the entire palace would crash down on them regardless of their victory. Instead, a large section of the roof crashed down, burying the Goliath and cutting off Khalid and Neema from any chance of joining the fight against Jabari.

Their fight with the Goliath was over, but the one with Jabari was about to begin.

CHAPTER FORTY-SIX

Khalid screamed in fury as he beat against the wreckage of the bronze slats trying to find a way through.

"No! Not now. I was so close." The old warrior smashed his sword's pommel into the metal until his arm gave out from exhaustion.

Neema pulled him away from the barrier. "We'll find another way."

"There is no other way!" Khalid cried in frustration, dropping his sword and pulling at the bronze slats with his hands.

The scene playing out above them was hard to watch. Tim tried to imagine how Khalid must have felt at this moment. The warrior had spent most of his life waiting to take revenge on Jabari, and now circumstances had snatched his chance away at the last possible instant. It must have been devastating.

Seeing how strongly Khalid felt, Tim knew they couldn't let him down. Jabari would die here today, but not in the way he'd initially thought. If he had to find a plus about the upcoming fight, he doubted Jabari would fart on them. The Juggernaut and the Goliath had played out that gimmick, and the truth of the matter was the ruler of a city should have a little more class.

"Let's get into formation." Tim moved toward the back of the room.

The rest of the party moved into their usual spots, with Cassie at the tip of the spear. Tim didn't know when the fight would start, but they had to be ready. It looked like Jabari was heading toward the doors at the back of the royal box, but that didn't mean he hadn't signaled for help. After their fight against the Goliath, they knew there were a ton of hidden doors.

Jabari reached out and grabbed the door handle, but he couldn't wrench the door open. He kicked it a few times with no better result, then pulled his scepter free. He waved it at the door, and nothing happened. He cursed in frustration while trying the trick one more time. This time the wooden door disintegrated in a shower of splinters, revealing a slab of stone blocking his exit.

"It's not possible." Jabari reached out and touched the stone.

Neema rattled her bow against the bronze slots to get Jabari's attention. "Not so funny now, is it fucker!"

"Your opinion on the matter is of little importance." Jabari turned away from the blocked passage and slowly made his way back down the aisle toward the railing.

Stepping onto the railing then off it, Jabari fell thirty feet to the floor below. When he landed, the asshole barely even flexed his legs. When he looked at the band of adventurers, his eyes burned with the intensity of a caged rat. "Would you be so kind as to step out of my way?"

"Not going to happen, fucknuts," Cassie growled.

Jabari smoothed out his robes and gently brushed some dust from his shoulder. "It seems when you stop killing people on your own, people forget that you're capable of doing the deed yourself. Maybe it's time for me to give them a proper demonstration."

He moved toward the group and stopped about twenty feet from them. He stood with casual grace, his body not giving away the slightest hint of nervousness. It was too bad Jabari's eyes couldn't do the same.

"I'll give you one last chance to walk away with your lives." Jabari's back was straight as a rod, his chin tilted at just the right angle to say fuck off, and I'm better than you all at the same time.

JaKobi moved to stand next to Cassie. "You heard the lady, spunk bucket. You're not going anywhere."

Tim was getting a rough idea of where all Cassie's improved one-liners were coming from. If the only person she bounced ideas off was JaKobi, she was bound to run into some recycled material at some point. He did give them points for sticking with a theme. Insults seemed to dig a little deeper when they came in bunches.

A look of utter shock replaced Jabari's sneer. Tim got the feeling it had been a long time since someone had said no to him. It was funny how such a simple word held so much power.

The sneer and the attitude of confidence returned as he quickly recomposed himself. "You must take me for some great fool. Many dared to think so. All of them are dead now."

The scepter he held clattered to the floor as Jabari started shaking. His body followed it a moment later as he fell to his knees and hunched over onto his hands. He looked up at them as a scream tore from his lips and he spat a gobbet of blood onto the floor.

Tim watched in growing horror as Jabari convulsed. Two black limbs tore out of his sides, and all he could think about was *The Thing.* At this point, if Kurt Russell walked in with a blowtorch and lit the man on fire, he wouldn't have been surprised, any more so than if those limbs turned into wings.

It turned out they weren't wings, but something much worse.

Hanging in the air supported by his four new limbs Jabari looked down upon them with a hungry expression. His body continued to twitch as another set of legs appeared, and finally the last pair, giving him a total of eight massive legs.

Jabari's eye twitched as if he couldn't control it anymore, but his voice was firm when he spoke. "You could have left, but now you will meet the monster. I do so hope you enjoy it."

Black fog swirled about the man—if Tim could call him a man anymore. He had a decent idea of what was about to happen next, but like when he thought Jabari would sprout wings, he could have easily been wrong. Whatever was going to come out of the fog, it would be big, have eight fucking legs, and a bad attitude.

They had to be ready.

"JaKobi, get back in formation. Cassie, be ready for anything, but especially something with eight fucking legs." Tim hoped it wasn't a scorpion.

Hearing about Lorelei's and Neema's encounter with the Guardian left him a little jealous but also happy he didn't have to fight it. Scorpions were like cockroaches with extra armor and a big pointy stabber. People always said roaches would rule the world after people wiped themselves out, but he always thought it would be the scorpions.

Webbing shot out of the cloud and wrapped around Cassie, pulling her forward. Then there was always the other kind of eight-legged monster. Some might have called them eight-legged freaks. It'd been a while since they'd faced a spider of any kind, but he wouldn't be surprised if this were some kind of new monster with eight legs and webs. Since they'd entered the palace, the only thing Tim was sure of was that he didn't know what to expect next.

Tim tried casting Cleanse on Cassie, but it didn't do anything to the webbing. If he couldn't Cleanse the webbing, there was only one other solution. "DPS the web!"

Flames rippled down its length, and their tank staggered backward as she broke free. "That was fucking gross. Why can't the bosses be people-sized people and not giant spiders?"

"I think what you meant to say was, why do all these bosses shoot things at me with their asses?" ShadowLily tried to hide her grin as she helped Cassie strip away the last of the webbing.

"That was going to be my next point of emphasis. I swear to God if something shits on me in this game, I'm going to break the servers." Cassie whipped some webbing off her bō staff.

The group slipped back into their standard formation as the black fog cleared.

Jabari, ruler of the most beautiful city along the river, had transformed into an abomination. It wasn't as if he turned into one of the famous Driders, half-spider, half-human creatures that were almost like centaurs. He'd turned into an actual spider. There was no humanity left in the monster before them unless you looked at the face.

Tim had never seen a spider with a human face.

Jabari had eight fucking eyes. Two very large, very human-looking ones on each side of the spider's head. Under each of the much-too-human eyes were three very spider-like orbs of blackness swiveling around as they took in the room. His mouth was now a grotesque mashup of lips and pincers, but at least there was some humanity to it. The rest of his body was gone, cast aside like a tarantula's shell, and in its place was a spider so big Tim wished JaKobi could burn the entire theater down to the ground.

Then they could nuke it from orbit.

As far as he knew, spiders weren't supposed to have legs ten feet tall or a body the size of a bus. But what was considered shocking in a world of magic? A few moments ago, the spider had been a normal-sized man. Now it looked like it could eat an entire village.

If these were the perks for working with Vitaria, why would anyone ever do it?

If the best she had to offer was gut-wrenching pain and a transformation into a creature so hideous even its mother would try and eat it, what was the point? Even if the only benefit of working for Eternia were that he would never end up looking like Jabari did now, he'd pick that choice over the other every single time.

Thankfully, besides not requiring him to turn into a spider monster, Eternia had been incredibly generous.

"You should have let me pass." The Jabari monster's pincers twitched, and saliva leaked from his mouth in anticipation of a meal.

Tim looked at Cassie. "He's all yours."

"Such a gentleman." The tank turned and looked at the spider as a tiny bit of poison leaked from his pincers. The droplets hit the floor and sizzled.

Cassie took a moment to look at where the poison hit, then looked into all eight of Jabari's eyes. "And you, I don't know what the fuck you are, but I'd suggest asking for something better next time you barter your soul for a little power."

The spider arched its back and shot another web at Cassie.

JaKobi was on this one the second it slammed into her. It seemed that dodging the webs would be a real problem for them, but as long as they could DPS them down fast enough, they would be able to overcome the obstacle. Still, time spent on the webs would take away from DPS on the boss. It would be better to have a dedicated person on web duty. Their job would be to burst down any webbing that showed up before going back to the boss.

The task would be a mess for ShadowLily. Having her run all over the place was out of the question. Lorelei's arrows weren't nearly as effective as JaKobi's fire. So that put the fire mage on Team Webby until further notice.

Tim cast Curse of Giving and Behold My Power on the boss. "JaKobi, you're on web duty. Everyone else, focus on the boss."

"What looks like a spider but talks like a man?" Lorelei quipped.

There was a riddle he'd never have been able to answer before now.

Cassie was getting up close and personal with Jabari and doing her best to keep his attention by whacking his legs with her staff. She took pretty decent damage whenever one of the legs brushed against her. The damn legs must have barbs or blades because being hairy wouldn't explain the spikes in her health that he saw.

A Healing Orb stopped Cassie's health from dropping, and it slowly started ticking back up. Tim checked his status effects to make sure she wasn't suffering from any kind of debuff. She was clear, so Jabari's basic attacks hit hard. With eight legs to dodge, there wasn't a lot she could do to avoid them all.

ShadowLily entered the fray from behind, landing a critical hit to one of Jabari's back legs. Grinning from ear to ear as she fell into her rotation, the assassin went to work doing what she did best. Any Guildmaster would have appreciated the ruthless dedication she had to pumping out high numbers and surviving fights. Every group needed one of those players to carry the load.

If you had two or three like they did, it made things easier.

Getting two large daggers shoved into his leg from behind must not have been Jabari's kind of thing because he spun while kicking out at ShadowLily. One of his massive feet slammed into her stomach, tossing her aside like a child's favorite toy during a tantrum.

Tim hated seeing her go down.

He checked his interface to see how much time was left before Behold My Power did its thing. Seeing that there was only a second left before it went off, he switched his Way of the Boulder stance from Cassie to ShadowLily, and cast Who Needs a Shield on the tank to give her a defensive boost while he stripped away her other protections.

If he played this right, things would work out perfectly.

ShadowLily shot back to her feet looking like Uma Thurman in *Pulp Fiction*.

There wasn't time for him to think. He had to act. With a thought, Tim flipped his stance back to Cassie and blasted her with a Healing Orb to take care of any extra damage she received while not getting the reduced damage benefit from his stance. The boss's health seemed to be moving downward at a slower pace now.

Turning away from what he was doing, Tim scanned the battlefield looking for a reason. It didn't take him long to find the culprit. JaKobi was stuck in a web, and all of them were so wrapped up in their things that none of them had noticed. They couldn't afford to fall behind on them or they would be in real trouble. Despite the slowed DPS, if enough of them got webbed, they wouldn't be able to recover, and they would die.

Tim *really* didn't want to get eaten by a spider.

"Get JaKobi out of that thing!" Tim shouted at Lorelei as he cast a bolt of Divine Light at the webbing to help speed up the process.

Lorelei stopped DPSing the boss and went to work trying to free JaKobi right away. Tim trusted that the ranger had things under control and turned back to see who else needed help only to find Cassie also encased in webbing. ShadowLily had the boss on her and was kiting him to avoid a quick death. She wasn't in any position to help break Cassie free as the boss was right on her ass.

Tim switched his stance again, hoping it would be enough to keep the assassin alive until they freed their tank.

"JaKobi, get Cassie free the second you're out of that shit." Tim turned away and fired a Healing Orb at ShadowLily and reapplied Curse of Giving.

"Yurumph, goit, bothe." JaKobi spat, reached up and pulled some webbing off his lips, and started spitting like he had hair caught in his mouth.

JaKobi clapped once, sending a flaming Phoenix straight at his girlfriend. The flames engulfed the webbing and vanished in an instant. "That's what I'm talking about." He pumped his fist once and sent his next spell at the boss.

Cassie ran back to the fight with her staff above her head. Tim didn't envy Jabari. She was pissed off, and he was going to feel it.

Tim splashed ShadowLily with another heal and flipped his stance back to the tank for what he hoped was the final time.

Cassie had Jabari focused on her now, and all of them were free to do their jobs again. It wasn't easy for him to admit how close a call that had been. If they had noticed JaKobi in the webbing any later, they all would have been dead.

Their reward for surviving was they were now twenty-five percent done with the fight.

Jabari was pushing them now. His attacks came faster than before, and the damage was pretty constant. It was all Tim could do to keep everyone afloat. Contributing any DPS right now was an experiment in wishful thinking.

There was no way to know if the whole fight would be like this or not. The group was taking a lot of damage, but none of them had a debuff. Getting webbed did a small amount of incremental damage until the webbing was removed but didn't seem to have any lingering effects. Something else was draining them, but he didn't know what. At this rate, he would be out of mana before they reached fifty percent. Something had to give.

What was he missing?

Tim looked around the room, but nothing had changed since the Goliath died. There wasn't a super-secret button he could hit to give them a momentary reprieve from the battle to recharge. What they needed was a break in the action and what he was getting was more heals going out than he'd ever cast before.

Everything turned into a blur.

When Jabari's health hit fifty percent, a blast of webbing shot out and engulfed their entire party. His spider form teetered around the theater for a moment and fell onto its back. The legs curled up in the way dead insects tended to do, and the body melted in on itself. A puddle of goo spread out as the spider continued to melt, but rising from its center was a man.

Jabari rose back to his feet like a Terminator sent back through time. Dark visceral fluid that stank worse than one of the Goliath's farts covered him from head to toe. Looking at their party with hatred burning in his eyes, Jabari snapped his fingers, and the servants came running.

The men and women cleaned and dressed him. One of them found his scepter on the floor and returned it to him. When it became clear that their master was satisfied, the servants streamed from the room as quickly as they'd come. Now Khalid's nemesis stood before them again as if he hadn't turned into a spider so big Tim would have gladly left the continent to avoid even seeing it.

The man looked slightly haggard as he plucked an errant thread from his robes and tossed it aside. The webbing surrounding them started to deteriorate, letting Tim know the fight was about to resume.

He didn't know if he needed to thank Eternia or if they had pushed the phase change soon enough, but the break was just the thing he needed to recharge his dwindling mana supply. Now they had new problems to deal with. With a spider, they knew what to expect. With the man, they had no idea what was coming.

Except that Jabari's scepter could be deadly.

"Watch for magical attacks," Tim shouted to Cassie.

The tank grunted as she broke out of the last of her webbing and started running. "Spider-man, spider-man, goes splat in the way only a spider can." Her staff whistled down at Jabari's head.

It stopped an inch away.

Magic was in the air, or more to the point, Jabari had some kind of magical shield that prevented Cassie from making contact with him. That put their tank on defense. All she could do was dodge and poke at him to keep him interested. Flames washed over the shield and arrows bounced harmlessly away.

How did you beat something you couldn't hit?

Tim's mind was racing. Normally he would have applied some out-of-the-box thinking to the situation, like having JaKobi heat the area around Jabari and make it so hot he had to break his shield. If the solution was that simple, anyone could think of it, but why was he bashing his head against the wall when he could call on his lifeline? No one knew Jabari better than Khalid and the Desert Wolf.

"Khalid, we need some help down here," Tim called up to the section where the old warrior and Neema were trapped.

Khalid's face appeared in a gap as he watched the fight. "Hold on!"

"Easy for you to say." Cassie was hit by an invisible force and thrown to the floor.

Tim was on healing duty so he missed the first part of what came next as he brought Cassie up to full health. While he hadn't seen what happened, he heard Khalid shout a warning. Then he picked up something flying through the air right at Jabari's head.

"Now!" Khalid roared.

Neema stepped to the slats, aiming an arrow through a small gap. All Tim could do was watch as it sailed across the open space. Somehow she hit the bag right as it crossed above Jabari's head.

He crouched, expecting an explosion.

Instead of a blast, the arrow simply pierced the bag and continued on its way. Light golden dust filled the air and slowly trickled down to Jabari. He looked up and tried to get out of its path, but Cassie and ShadowLily kept him corralled. They hammered at his shield with brutal efficiency, forcing him to stay where he was and let the sparkling dust land on him.

Whatever Khalid had thrown at them stuck to the surface of Jabari's shield. It looked as though the shielding covered his entire body but only a few inches away. Cracks were forming in the surface of his shield now, and the top started to melt away. It was weird to watch something invisible melting even when bright golden dust outlined it.

Jabari screamed in rage as his shield finally broke apart. He waved his scepter in a vicious arc, sending them all flying into the opposite side of the room just like when they had fought the Goliath.

"Not fair, asshole," Cassie growled, ready to charge back into the fight.

She was clearly ready to kill this asshole before he could turn back into a spider. It wouldn't have surprised Tim in the slightest if she was pissed about being forced to take damage while not getting to deal any. Sure, her role wasn't to do a ton of damage, but hitting things was an oddly satisfying way to work out some stress.

Jabari might have been a shitty ruler, but he was even worse at reading the situation. No one wanted to deal with Cassie when she was mad.

Nobody.

Waves of electrical energy rolled across the floor in front of them. The boss was at the other side of the room and to get there, they would have to navigate the pattern without getting hit. Tim loved movement-based combat. It wasn't all that hard to stand in one place and blast off spells, but it was hard to be moving, jumping, dodging while doing the same thing. A little challenge never hurt anyone.

Unless they died.

The best part about this situation was that they would probably get to deal extra damage for a short duration once they made it to the boss. They couldn't waste a moment of opportunity like that. He was tired of dealing with Jabari. He just wanted the fucker to be dead already.

The downside to a fight like this was that traditionally any missteps on their run toward Jabari meant instant death. Tim couldn't think about that now. He needed to figure out the pattern so they could get across the room. He formulated a plan and hoped he was right.

"Everyone follow me." Tim looked back to make sure everyone was huddling behind him, then sprang into action.

The key to these puzzles was to find the right bit of movement and go with it. He ran into the room, almost looking as if he were trying to kill himself by immediately running into the bar of crackling blue energy. Tim wasn't trying to off himself. He simply knew that for them to make it across, he would have to play it a little fast and loose. Otherwise, there wouldn't be enough time for the others to follow him.

Pushing forward, they crossed the room, never stopping. They came close to getting fried a couple of times as Tim waited for the right moment to run, but soon enough they were standing in front of the boss as he struggled to maintain the spell.

Jabari's hands shook, and he dropped them as he fell to his knees in exhaustion. His breaths came in ragged gasps as he tried to regain his energy. "It isn't possible."

"Guess the impossible is possible!" Cassie roared as she charged forward.

Tim cast Curse of Giving and Divine Light before stepping back to assess the situation. None of them were too banged up, but they'd taken a few scrapes from being dragged across the room and slammed into place. A single blast of Healing Storm fixed most of their pressing issues.

Jabari was getting hammered now.

The boss had started this phase of the fight at fifty percent health and was dipping below thirty percent now. Tim made sure everyone's health was topped off and cast Behold My Power.

At twenty-five percent health Jabari waved his scepter again and swept the group across the room. Now the boss' outline pulsed with a slightly red glow. It was enough to let them know if they didn't defeat him after this trip across the room, things were going to get real interesting. Like, splat, you're dead interesting. The last thing they needed was for Jabari to turn into some kind of crazed spider they couldn't defeat or had to fight while waves of blue death balls covered the room.

This time, not only did the pattern on the floor change when Jabari cast his spell, there was an additional wave of fire added to the mix. Now they had to watch their feet and periodically duck or jump to make sure they didn't get roasted by the fire. It was the same thing as last time, only on steroids.

Time to level up.

Tim watched the pattern for a few moments and motioned for the group to get ready. "Follow me like last time, only this time I'll be making calls to jump or duck as we go. No matter what the call is, we always have to keep moving, or the floor will get us."

The rest of them didn't look so sure about the situation, but he was feeling the flow. Tim was the human *Frogger*, the master of intricate patterns. He drew a few deep breaths and prepared himself. "When we get across, hit him with everything you've got. We need to end this now."

ShadowLily winked. "You get us across, and we'll do our part. We've got this."

"Just make sure I don't get fried. My hair doesn't look good with static." Lorelei looked like she was locked and loaded.

"Feuer frei!" JaKobi cried with enthusiasm.

Cassie laughed. "Whatever he said."

It was hard not to feel the love as Tim looked over the group. Not one of them had questioned his ability to get them through the danger safely. All of them were lined up and willing to bet their lives on him. That was the kind of friendship money couldn't buy.

"Let's fucking do this." Tim held up a fist and dropped it as he started moving.

They were cruising along nicely when he saw the first wave of red coming in low. "Jump!" They ran for a few more steps. "Duck."

That's how it went as they crossed the room. He had to send out waves of Healing Storm a few times, but for the most part, it went better than he expected. These were the kind of sequences in fights that simply got easier the more times a player did them. He wondered why more games didn't have training rooms for boss mechanics. It would certainly cut down on the frustration for players learning new fights.

The last beam of fire was different than the others. It was coming right for them, but where the others had been high or low, this one was coming at them right at waist height. Tim was somewhere between jumping and ducking when he finally tried to throw his body over the top. He hadn't made a call, but everyone but JaKobi was doing fine.

JaKobi didn't take nearly as much damage as Tim thought he would, maybe because of his affinity to flames. Still, they couldn't afford to have him out of the fight for more than a second so Tim started healing the fire mage as his top priority. By the time JaKobi cast his next spell he was almost back to one hundred percent health.

Jabari fell to his knees. The magic he'd used to flood the room had exhausted him. Behold My Power hit him damn near instantly, taking five percent of his health in one big chunk. Then the real DPS kicked in. All of them poured everything they had into it. Tim's mana was flatlining, but even when he only had enough left to cast Flame Burst repeatedly, he did it without hesitation.

Nar'ha's ruler staggered to his feet and waved his scepter one last time, sending them across the room. Tim didn't know what happened. The boss' health stopped dropping at one percent. Jabari didn't have full control of his regalia though so its magic flailed around the room, threatening to bring more of the roof down on them. Jabari stopped the spell, but not before it had ripped away some of the bars blocking Khalid and Neema from joining the fight.

The desert warrior stepped through the breach with his sword raised high above his head. "Today, you pay for your crimes against the people of Nar'ha."

Jabari held up his hands, pleading for his life, but the blade was already falling. An explosion of beautiful gold and platinum motes burst into the heavens as Jabari's head caved in from the blow. The beautiful lights swirled through the air, then winked out of existence as if they'd never been there at all.

In place of Jabari's corpse was the most ornate chest Tim had ever laid eyes on.

Today was a good fucking day.

CHAPTER FORTY-SEVEN

Vitaria's anger was palpable, and it was making Phandar uncomfortable.

Everyone thought being Pharaoh was great, but there was always someone more powerful. He'd given himself wholly to the Goddess Vitaria, and now he saw that decision come full circle. His usefulness to her was ending. There was still a chance he could save himself, but he was no longer sure he'd get out of this alive.

Now he had to break the news.

As Phandar knelt in front of the goddess, she spoke. "The Juggernaut has been defeated, and we have one less guardian to secure your empire. Do you see now why I said to let that fool Jabari die alone? The man was worthless."

He'd always thought of Jabari as a close confidant, a man that could be trusted when called upon. None of them had foreseen this band of adventurers coming from another land, backed by the power of their goddess.

"It was wrong of me to question you. It will never happen again." Phandar lowered his head in submission.

If she was going to relegate him to the position of a servant, then he'd be the best damn servant he could be, right until he found a way to get rid of her. For now, it wasn't his job to ask questions. He'd done that, and it almost cost him his life. All he had to do now was wait until the resistance quieted down, and she went home with a smile on her face.

"It was wrong of you to doubt." Vitaria lounged on his throne. "Now that you have seen the errors of your ways, I like that you are quick to amend them."

Phandar looked up and met her eyes. It was a bold choice, but they knew each other well enough that deceits between them never lasted long. He needed to show he was willing to serve but also had the backbone to lead. "Your command is my greatest desire."

"Then sit and do nothing." Her smile looked more like she was mocking him than about to tell him some good news. "I have taken control of the army and have them arranged around the city. Only a fool would attack us here."

She sipped her wine and ate a bite of cheese. "So all I ask you to do is nothing."

The Pharaoh thought about what she was asking for a moment. Vitaria was right to make the resistance come to them. Khalid's army of farmers was better trained than he thought, but his army was bigger and full of Vitaria's minions.

With the goddess' monstrosities aligned outside the gates, Khalid would have to be a madman to come here. In this case, necessity would drive the desert warrior into action. For Khalid to succeed, he had to conquer Naroosh. For Phandar to win, all he had to do was stay put. Maybe there was a way out of this for him yet.

If he could do what Vitaria asked everything would be fine. All Phandar needed to keep going was a little glimmer of hope at the end of the tunnel. He didn't want to die and would do just about anything to prove it.

"I will build our strength here, and when our numbers are large enough, we will take back Nar'ha and complete control of this land." Vitaria stood from the throne and made her way down to a table laden with fresh fruits and cured meats. "Until then, we sit, we wait, we grow stronger."

She turned to look at the Pharaoh while eating a grape. "You have what I requested?"

Her abrupt change of subject caught him off-guard, but for the goddess, their conversation on the matters of war was over. "I would not have dreamed of returning without it."

Phandar rose from where he had been kneeling by the throne and moved to stand next to Vitaria. He reached inside his robes, handed her a sealed package, and took a respectful step back.

He had no idea what was inside the package. If there was one thing he knew for certain, it was that poking his nose into Vitaria's affairs was a sure-fire way to end up dead. All Phandar knew was that whatever was inside was worth more to her than the hundreds of lives that were lost collecting it.

It was kind of sad that this was what he'd been reduced to after his climb to the top. The goddess merely had to clap her hands, and he was like a dog willing to do anything to make her happy. He wasn't the ruler of a nation anymore. Phandar was only a first-class ass-licker. It was starting to grate on him, but unless someone could kill the goddess, there wasn't much he could do about it.

At least for the moment, his continued survival meant keeping his ego in check. Phandar had never excelled in that department. It was how he ended up in this situation in the first place. So for now, he would sit and fetch her things when she asked like a good dog. When she finally left, he would find a way to end her.

And they said enemies couldn't be friends.

Vitaria took the package from him, and it vanished in an instant. "That will be all." She walked back to the throne, dismissing him as if he were worthless.

It was a mistake to dismiss him so callously.

Being embarrassed inside his palace was an insult Phandar

couldn't live with. How could he command the respect of his men if they all saw him as weak? As a leader himself, he understood exactly what she was doing. Vitaria had set a boundary between them, reminding him that he was only there because she wished it to be so.

"On your way out send in Ruban and George." She thought about it for a moment. "And that girl with the brown hair and chocolate eyes."

Phandar bowed low. Now wasn't the right time to do anything but serve. He kept his head down as he backed toward the door. "It will be as you command."

But maybe not for as long as you think.

He left the room shouting commands. It felt good to have some semblance of control, even if it was a lie. Fuck, he needed a drink. Maybe that was how he would spend the rest of this war—drunk on wine or high on that stuff they peddled in the back alleys. Surely his contributions from here on out wouldn't make much of a difference.

"Wine!" He strode to his new quarters to wait for his next summons.

CHAPTER FORTY-EIGHT

Brilliant white light flooded the theater.

Tim took a step back and covered his eyes, but even peeking through his fingers, it would have been hard for him to miss what was happening. The damage to the palace was repairing itself. He could hear the people outside screaming in joy as the entire city transformed before their eyes.

Eternia had come to Nar'ha and reclaimed the city from the darkness.

While he couldn't see outside yet, he'd experienced these types of changes in other games. The city of Nar'ha would now be a place of light. Eternia would protect the men and women, or at the very least, Khalid would find good people to protect the citizens. Gods were too busy to be everywhere at once. That was why they gave people the tools to protect themselves.

The theater they stood in was now fully restored. Paintings on the walls had changed from scenes of warring armies to farmers in the fields. The room itself felt more inviting somehow. Maybe it was a trick of the light, but Tim didn't think so. The theater felt the way it did because Eternia had claimed Nar'ha for herself.

Even Cassie stopped her mad dash toward the chest to watch the last of the transformation. Now that it was over, she looked at the chest. "We should probably get this out of the way before Eternia shows up."

"Do you really think she'll come?" Neema sounded worried.

"I don't think she did all of this not to make an appearance." Cassie laid her hand on the chest, then broke out in a happy dance so epic it would have made Spice Adams jealous. "Leather Cuirass of the Bold. Basically certifies that I'm a badass."

"You know how we do it!" JaKobi strutted up to the chest.

Lorelei laughed. "Stick with the bookworm thing. It works better for you."

"I am kind of good at being me." The fire mage placed his hand on the chest. "Staff of the Burning Phoenix."

JaKobi broke out in a weird little shuffle that might have been considered a dance if the person in question was blind, with a bad sense of timing.

"I take it back. You can say whatever you want. Just don't do that again unless you include me." Lorelei was grinning ear from ear as she tried to repeat his moves.

ShadowLily broke tradition and went to the chest next. "I don't know. The dance is kinda starting to grow on me. Maybe it's one of those things where it looks better if more people do it."

The assassin reached out and touched the chest. "This must be the best loot we've ever gotten from a single chest." She spun some new daggers around. "Daggers of Silent Night."

Tim grinned. "Creepy and cool, I like it."

He never really minded going last when it came to loot so he motioned for the ranger to go next. "It's all you."

"Don't mind if I do." Lorelei stopped dancing and walked to the chest to claim her share of the loot.

The ranger took a shocked step back, looked at the chest, and back at the group with a bewildered expression on her face. "I got two things. Gloves of the Falcon, and Boots of the River."

"That's fucking awesome." Tim was happy for her.

One thing he was learning to do more often was celebrate others' success with them. It didn't matter if they climbed a small hill or an entire mountain. When one of his friends did something or won something, he wanted to cheer them on.

Did a small part of him also hope for double loot? Of course, it did.

Now that it was his turn to touch the chest, Tim didn't know what to expect. There could be one great item in there for him, or a couple of good ones. This game never stopped surprising them. It felt like something new was happening all the time. If it wasn't loot, it was the fights. If it wasn't the fights, it was the location. It made it easy to want to keep moving forward when every day presented new and unique opportunities.

Item Received: Belt of Divine Inspiration

Sometimes working hard isn't enough. A person also needs the right idea to sink their teeth into. This belt will help you do that.

Wisdom +4, Intelligence +2, Endurance +1

Tim was excited to see that endurance was dropping on some of his gear and not so excited about only getting a belt. He'd been so busy going over the stats he also missed the fact he received a second item. He'd been joking with himself about getting two pieces to drop, and now it happened.

Item received: Wristband of the Faithful

Eternia has watched you fight for her cause time and time again. This wristband is not only a symbol of your devotion to her but of hers to you. Welcome to the big leagues, warrior of light.

+1 Endurance

Special Ability: Recharge

Once every ten minutes, the wristband can double a player's mana regeneration for ten seconds.

That was pretty sweet.

There were a couple of times where his mana was almost gone recently, and the ability to pick up a little extra during a boss fight would be a huge bonus. It was a damn good item, and with it, his endurance also went over the first threshold of twenty. He was finally there. No one needed to mention what his strength looked like compared to his other stats. Lifting heavy things was never going to be his strong suit while inside *The Etheric Coast*.

That's why he kept the women around.

Tim equipped his new items and would check out his stats a little later. He knew after their recent battles he'd have a few skills to go over as well, and that was always something that took a little time to do right.

The chest in front of him disappeared, and Tim turned to face Khalid. "So what now?"

"Now we get to sleep in a palace." JaKobi started doing his little dance again. "Don't hate the moves."

Neema came over to stand by him and joined his dance. "I like the way he moves."

"You've got to be kidding me." Lorelei laughed.

JaKobi was grinning like a fool. "Come on, do it with us. It'll change your life."

They were saved from hearing her response as the room filled with light again. Eternia made her presence known by floating down from the royal seating area above them. She descended as slowly as a feather, her feet stopping inches from the floor. Now that the goddess was on their level she looked over their party, her eyes settling on Khalid.

"You have won a great battle here, but there is still work left to do. Even now my sister Vitaria gathers her forces in hopes of defending Naroosh." Eternia frowned, and the room seemed to dim.

Khalid fell to his knees. "Goddess, we don't have the men to take Naroosh by force. I don't know what else I can do."

Eternia reached out and laid a calming hand on the back of Khalid's bowed head, then gently lifted the warrior back to his feet. "You've done enough. No one in this land has done more for the light than you have. There have been many horrible sacrifices, but in the end, I hope you found the future in something new." She let her eyes linger on Neema for a moment before returning them to the warrior.

Khalid stood and moved to the Desert Wolf, pulling her into a fierce hug. All of them could feel the fatherly love he had for her. "We're a different kind of family, but family all the same."

"Damn right we are." Neema blushed. "Sorry."

Eternia smiled down at them. "A little swearing never hurt anyone, and after such a monumental victory, one should be allowed a few liberties. This is a fucking theater after all." The goddess winked. "I have much to discuss with this band of adventurers. Then we'll celebrate your victory together."

She turned to Khalid and gave him a warm smile. "See to your men and share with them the news of our victory. Tell them the goddess of light stands beside them."

"It will be done." Khalid looked ready to spring into action. "If you wanted to say something as well, I'm sure the resistance would appreciate it. This victory and all that comes after it is because of your guidance."

Eternia gave them that all-knowing smile and a tiny bow. "The people of Nar'ha watched me descend from the heavens and rebuild their city from the ground up. For now, that will have to be enough to satisfy their curiosity." She motioned for him to go. "I will find you later tonight. There is something I've meant to give you, and now seems like the appropriate time."

"Neema, with me," Khalid ordered and walked toward the door.

The Desert Wolf pulled the goddess into a quick hug and stepped back, looking almost shocked at herself for being so bold. "Thank you for looking out for us."

A tear dropped from Eternia's eye. "It has been my pleasure to watch you grow into the woman you have become, Neema. I do hope you will join us at the party. There is also something I have been saving for you."

"Wouldn't miss it for the world." Neema turned away from the goddess and went to Lorelei. "We'll talk soon." She kissed her and left the room in a hurry to catch up with Khalid.

Tim felt pretty good about how things went, but he wondered what the next step would be. Khalid told the goddess they didn't have enough soldiers to take the fight to Naroosh, and they couldn't camp out here and wait for the Pharaoh to decide to come and kill them all.

They needed to end this fight sooner rather than later.

"Brave adventurers, you have done much for the people of this land, but I must call on you to do more." Eternia looked over their group with an appraising eye.

Another quest from the Goddess was what they needed. Saving the city was awesome, but Tim had started to crave the experience boost that came from turning in quests more than he cared about loot. Once he reached level twenty, there was the chance to change his class again, and he wanted to see what other options being a Battlesworn had to offer.

Without hesitation, Tim dropped to a knee and lowered his head. "We are yours to command."

He might have been laying it on a bit thick, but when dealing with a goddess, it was probably better not to take chances.

"There is a secret way into the Pharaoh's palace, but the challenges waiting within will be numerous and daunting. Are you willing to risk your lives to save the people of Naroosh from the same fate suffered by those in Nar'ha?"

Quest Received: The Tomb of Nemset

You must enter the pyramid of Nemset and find the key to unlocking the secret entrance to the palace. Many dangers

await you inside, and the journey will not be easy. Once you make it to the palace, use the portal stone I've given you to open the way for Khalid's army of resistance fighters.

Reward: The Goddess Eternia will let you select an item from her hoard.

Her plan made sense to Tim. Why fight an army when you could sneak right past them? This upcoming battle felt like it was an all-or-nothing thing. It wouldn't do them any good to fight their way to the Pharaoh and not be able to finish him. Having an army behind them swayed the odds significantly in their favor.

Plus, the goddess said something that had his mind buzzing with excitement. Pyramid. That was what he'd been waiting for since they came to the desert. He'd been so jealous that Lorelei got to go to an actual tomb. Now they got to go to one together, in a real pyramid.

Tim accepted the quest, but one thing was bugging him. "If the Pharaoh has an army guarding the city, how will we get to the pyramid?"

"I'll take you there myself." Eternia looked over their group. "We'll leave in the morning. Tonight we celebrate, and tomorrow you help save the world."

"No pressure." JaKobi mimicked knocking back a drink.

Cassie looked ready for a real drink. That fake nonsense wasn't going to cut it for her. "Partying is what I do best."

"She's not lying." Tim couldn't stop his smile from spreading. "Imagine how good we'd be if Cassie cared as much about tanking as she did about drinking."

The tank rounded on Tim. "I'd beat your ass if the goddess weren't standing right behind me."

With a mischievous look in her eyes, Eternia's smile slowly spread across her face, and she winked at Cassie. "Don't stop yourself from following your heart on my account."

Oh shit.

Tim ran for the door. "See you at the party." Then he activated Quick Feet and hightailed it out of there.

Some things were worth dying for, but snarky comments weren't one of them. It wasn't the most graceful exit he'd made in front of the goddess, but when an angry lady with a big stick was chasing him, it was better to just get the fuck out of Dodge.

CHAPTER FORTY-NINE

Before the party, he really wanted a bath.

It was funny. After all his bitching about needing a shower, the bath was becoming Tim's happy place. After spending an entire day getting his ass kicked and getting pulled through clouds of stinky gas, he wanted a bath. The warm water took a lot of the sting out of his sore muscles, and there was no better place in the world to go over his stats and skills.

As long as he didn't fall asleep.

Skill Increased: Appeal to the Goddess

Rank: Novice level three

Whenever this spell is off cooldown, you should consider using it. Not everyone is fortunate to have a direct lifeline to the goddess. Use it or lose it, bub.

Tim hoped he couldn't lose skills by not using them, but it would make a certain kind of sense. While a person might always be able to do something, to do it at a very high level took a daily commitment. Contacting the goddess more often wouldn't make him commit that often. He'd have to reach out to her once a week.

Skill Increased: Infiltrator

Rank: Novice level four

You're kind of good at sneaking into places and doing dastardly deeds. Are you sure you picked the right class? Maybe it's time to get a little more stabby-stabby and a little less with the splashing people with water act.

Snort.

Tim looked around, hoping ShadowLily wasn't nearby. That snort sounded suspiciously like a fart, and despite what some of his best friends thought, most women weren't interested in getting romantic right after someone ripped a big one. After the day they had, if she heard him rip one now, the fartfender might not get any for a while.

While the thought of switching to something with a little more damage was sometimes appealing, as much as he liked stabbing things, Tim liked healing more. There was something about keeping people alive that called to him. Maybe it only made him feel important, but Tim kind of liked the added pressure that came with playing a healing class. Unless he fucked up and his chat turned into a tirade of healing hate.

Skill Increased: Quick Feet

Rank: Novice level five

Running from Cassie probably shouldn't earn you an increase, but you were running, and she was probably going to hit you really hard.

Tim rubbed his shoulder.

Although he'd healed himself and the giant bruise was gone, he could still feel it. Cassie didn't pull any punches when she was pissed, but she also didn't break his arm, so there was something to be thankful for. JaKobi didn't know how good he had it with those gentle jabs to the ribs.

To be fair, she apologized for about ten minutes straight after she'd smacked him a good one, which wasn't really necessary. It was all in good fun, and he deserved it. What he was pissed about was the game didn't recognize any of the other times he used Quick Feet, only the most embarrassing one.

Skill Increased: Disturbance

Rank: Novice level six

Removing buffs and interrupting actions. You're doing it all with this spell. While not every fight will allow you to use Disturbance, when you do get the chance you better use it, or it's going to hurt, real bad.

Tim didn't like the sound of that, but he'd experienced how much missing the opportunity to use this spell hurt when they faced the Two Daughters. He would have to make sure always to watch the boss for effects he could stop. Hopefully, one of the others had the same kind of spell because he spent most of his time watching them for status effects and a lot less time worrying about what the boss was doing.

Skill Increased: Backstab

Rank: Novice level one

Sure, you're a healer, but let's face it. You enjoy delivering some justice, and if you can do it from behind, you like it even better. You've reached the Apprentice ranks and picked up an additional five percent chance to critical attack when striking from behind. Keep sneaking up on people and killing them to level this skill.

It was true. After an initial reluctance to hurt other humans, he'd become quite adept at stabbing people. Tim could do it from the front or behind, but the game was right. He preferred to do it when they couldn't fight back. Sleeping, mid-coitus, taking a dump, all great places to stab someone without them being able to see it coming.

Tim didn't get the chance to pull out his daggers and DPS very often, so when he did, he appreciated it. It was as though Khalid had known what he needed at that very moment in time. He didn't see an update for his throwing knives, but he knew that he'd made some progress to the next level there as well.

Apparently, he needed to throw his knives at more people.

Skill Increased: Snare

Rank: Novice level one

People wanna go, go, go, and you want them to stop in their tracks. Now that you're in the Apprentice ranks, that's more likely to happen. Any time someone is going somewhere you don't want them to be, use this spell to slow their roll.

P.S. It works great for babysitting.

Tim didn't know if everyone did a stint as a babysitter as a teen, but he'd spent his fair share of time trying to wrangle kids to bed for ridiculously small amounts of money. Also for free when it was his siblings. It was funny how that worked. The ones he got paid to take care of listened to him, and the two brats he didn't get paid to watch tried to make his life a living hell.

They'd probably knocked a good ten years off his life via stress, but he still loved them.

Skill Increased: Sneak

Rank: Novice level five

Some people like to get freaky. You like to get sneaky. Sneaking from room to room and slaughtering your enemies is a time-honored tradition for assassins, not so much for healers. Although you did pick a class that does damage as well as heal-ing, so maybe being sneaky is right up your alley.

That wasn't exactly nice.

Tim was sneaky because he didn't have the strength to be anything else. Walking up to people and bashing them head-on took a certain amount of fortitude he didn't have. His options were to blast them from afar or get sneaky with it. If there was a real threat from someone with big muscles, he had to call on one of the ladies to deal with it. Sure, it was a little humbling to have your girlfriend winning fights for you, but if he'd learned anything, it was never to let his pride get in the way of results.

So when Tim wanted to win solo, he did sneaky things.

Skill Increased: Dodge

Rank: Novice level seven

You have a certain flair for not getting hit. Yes, sometimes you get scared and get klutzy running away, but the amount of minimal to small damage you seem to miss per encounter is rather staggering. Just keep being you and this skill will level on its own.

In other words, keep screwing up and trying to get out of it by running. Putting his life on the line to level a skill seemed a bit reckless. He'd rather skip out on the dodging and running for his life parts and get to the loot, but there was a reason they made you fight the bosses.

It was fun as fuck.

Getting loot for doing absolutely nothing was a way to lure suckers into a game that wasn't good enough to stand on its own. *The Etheric Coast* didn't have that problem. This game was awesome, and every day was like a new adventure.

Skill Increased: Flame Burst

Rank: Novice level seven

Burning down the house is a catchphrase, but you should always be looking to burn as many things as possible if you want to level this skill. Let's be honest. It's come in pretty handy for you, so you should probably show it a little more love.

The system understood how to reach him.

A little poking, a gentle push in the right direction, and he was more than willing to listen. Only an idiot would ignore what the game was telling him to do. If the system wanted him to burn stuff, then he'd do it all day. So far, all the skill messages he received served to keep him on track for what he needed to accomplish. It would be as easy for him to toss out a Flame Burst now and again instead of Divine Light.

The savings in mana alone would make using Flame Burst more often worth it.

Skill Increased: Small Blades

Rank: Novice level eight

So you have a thing for knives, huh? There are worse things you could spend your time doing than slicing and dicing your enemies, but now you won't have to. Using blades shorter than eighteen inches in length will increase your base damage and critical hit chance.

There was a certain sense of satisfaction to clipping someone from behind, but he was much more comfortable casting from a distance while others soaked up the damage. Fighting was all well and good when they couldn't see it coming. Getting stabbed, beaten, and kicked—that shit was for suckers.

Skill Increased: Behold My Power

Rank: Novice level eight

This spell goes boom-boom-boom. Actually, there's only one boom, but it's rather spectacular. The reduced cooldown has helped you use this spell more often and with great results. Keep using Behold My Power to crush your enemies, and you'll get stronger. In strength there is power, and you will show them who wields it.

That was a little dark.

It sounded like he would be the next Sauron or something, but that would never be the case. The only reason he would have gone to the dark side is if those damn Jedi wouldn't get off his back about the love thing. It was never wrong to seek balance in the Force. Wait, all he had to do here was keep working with the goddess of light, and he was bound to come out on the right side of things.

Vitaria could promise him the moon, but Tim knew it was all bullshit. This was where he was meant to be, and he was damn sure that he was fighting on the right side of things.

Skill Increased: Healing Storm

Rank: Novice level nine

Healing rain falls from the heavens and makes you look like a badass. Large groups of people with injuries aren't a problem

anymore. You've used this spell to help not only your group but others in need, and that's been noticed. Reach the Journeyman ranks for new and exciting bonuses.

Any time one of his healing skills received an upgrade it was a good day. If all his other skills suddenly stopped being useful, but he could still heal his ass off, Tim would find a way to make it work. Healing Storm in particular was invaluable, especially if he was going to keep receiving items where he had to heal a certain amount of people to block further attributes.

Being able to heal multiple people at once was more useful than he'd initially planned, even if it cost more mana.

Skill Increased: Who Needs a Shield

Rank: Novice level nine

This is one of those spells that not only benefits the target but everyone in your group. It's probably something every healer wishes they had in their hip pocket, but not all of them do. Reach the Journeyman ranks to unlock new benefits.

This was probably his most useful spell when it came to mitigating damage. The only thing that even came close was the target of his stance. The nice thing about both the spell and the stance was he could cast them on the same target or different targets at will. Anytime someone would eat a lot of damage, he could lessen the load quite a bit by using one or the other.

At the end of the day, Who Needs a Shield saved him from having to heal damage that could have been easily prevented in the first place.

Skill Increased: Cleanse

Rank: Journeyman level two

Is there anything more important in a fight than immediately removing negative status effects from your party? Probably not, at least if you want to live. This spell does wonders for you now. Imagine what it will be like when you become a master.

Cleanse was pretty standard in every healer's toolkit like

an interrupt should be for a DPS. He used it whenever he thought it was appropriate, but like every healer, he was guilty of tunnel vision at times. Nothing caused him to pay attention to what was going on like seeing someone he was supposed to be keeping alive's health plummet like a barrel over Niagara Falls.

Then Tim called on his favorite little spell, and all was right in the world.

Skill Increased: Divine Light

Rank: Journeyman level two

Just like stabbing things with your knives, you really like blasting things until they die. Once you admit that you enjoy hurting the enemy, things will go much easier for you. Seriously, what kind of healer picks a class where they hurt things to heal them? It's kind of sadistic.

Tim didn't think it was sadistic.

Using his curses on the enemy was good common sense. While he'd never be able to put out as much pure healing as someone who was a more traditional-styled healer, his damage helped take the pressure off his DPS and end fights sooner.

He was such a good guy that it felt kind of fun to be a little naughty.

Plus, sitting in the back and never doing anything but healing was kind of boring. It was nice to know he brought a little utility to the fights. If they needed more DPS, he could manage it. If they needed more healing, he could swing it. He'd always be a better healer than a DPS, but their group had a leg up on any group with a more traditional healer.

At least he liked to think so.

Skill Increased: Curse of Giving

Rank: Journeyman level two

Taking what you want and inflicting pain is all part of your average day now. Some people might even call what you do a form of necromancy, taking the life of one thing and giving it

to another. I'm not saying that's what you are, but others might not take too kindly to your spells.

You've been using this skill exactly how it should be used, and if you continue to do so it will continue leveling as quickly as it is now. Cast this curse on as many people as possible and take their precious life for yours.

I guess they call it a curse for a reason.

Tim didn't care what someone wanted to label his skills. Labels didn't define him. Outside of Healing Orb, Curse of Giving was his most effective skill, and in a battle with multiple enemies the sheer healing power it provided was monumental. This was his go-to, his old faithful of the curse department. He knew a time was coming soon where he might get more curses, and he was looking forward to it, but for now, he'd use this one every chance he got.

Skill Increased: Healing Orb

Rank: Journeyman level nine

You've almost reached the master ranks with one of the very first spells you were given when entering the game. That's a pretty impressive accomplishment and a milestone that you shouldn't ignore. Keep using this spell to keep people alive, and you'll be a master in no time.

A master, imagine that. Tim didn't know if he'd be the first person in the game with a master-ranked skill, but whether he was the first one or the millionth, no one would be able to take it away from him. He was on the verge of crossing a threshold, and the next step after master was grandmaster. He'd get there eventually, but for now, he needed to focus more on their next quest.

Leveling up his skill would happen naturally as long as he kept playing the game.

Stances

Skill Increased: Way of the River

Rank: Novice level seven

This is the skill you use when healing multiple people quickly is paramount to your survival. Not every situation calls

for this stance, but when it does, make sure you take full advantage of the moment.

The only bad thing about Way of the River was that it didn't provide any additional protection for the tank. If it could keep Cassie safe and provide extra healing for the others, he'd use it all the time, but that wasn't how the spell worked.

Tim thought he did a pretty good job with Way of the River, but he would have to keep his eyes open for additional opportunities to master the spell.

Skill Increased: Way of the Boulder

Rank: Journeyman level one

Getting hit by things sucks, even when you're a rock. That's why your stance's target now also benefits from a five percent increase in their dodge rating, plus the previously listed benefit of damage reduction.

This stance already gave a flat-out ten percent reduction in damage. Add in another five percent dodge chance, and it would help him do a little more damage during their fights. That or the amount of damage their group would take in fights was about to spike again.

Way of the Boulder should at least give him a little flexibility so Tim wouldn't be stuck at the back of the fights the entire time while struggling to keep people alive. He wanted to bring more to the battle than reduced damage and rock-solid heals.

Buffs

Skill Increased: Armor of Eternia

Rank: Journeyman level one

Eternia is pleased with your progress to the Journeyman ranks. As your adventure continues, the goddess understands that the way you protect yourself and your allies must adapt to the circumstances. At the Journeyman rank, this buff no longer provides a five percent reduction in dark magic but a flat one percent reduction in all damage received. Before, this spell also provided a five percent chance to avoid succumbing to weak-

ness. A five percent chance to resist any status effect replaces it, and if the effect isn't resisted, then its duration will decrease by five percent.

Holy shit!

None of his other skills had ever changed so dramatically when they updated to a new rank. Not only was this a big update but a significant one. His Armor of Eternia spell had been incredible in certain situations but wasn't effective in all their fights.

Now it would be.

Eternia must be pleased with their progress if she was willing to help him out in such a big way. He hoped some of the others also received cool improvements to their skills as they hit new skill ranks. They were moving out of the little leagues and into the big leagues.

More danger, bigger rewards. This was going to be awesome.

Skill Increased: Attacks of the Faithful

Rank: Journeyman level one

The Goddess Eternia's understanding of your needs continues to evolve as you do. As an adventurer, even a healer must realize there's a time when they can no longer simply play defense. Having the right buff for the right job is key in any situation, and this one is no different. Now, instead of converting a percentage of your base damage into holy damage, you and your party will receive a one percent increase in all damage done.

Again, this spell was a huge upgrade over the older version. Getting buffs to only one type of damage was pretty lame unless the enemies you were facing also had a weakness to that particular affinity. Flat-out damage increase was incredible, and Tim was pretty sure his group would love it. If their buffs also received increases like this, they might be able to cruise through the next set of fights without too many problems.

That didn't sound right.

It was far more likely the game was setting them up to scrape by their next set of encounters. No one liked being handed victories or getting completely obliterated time after time. Tim swore that wasn't going to happen. They were going to rock this next adventure like Prince did *1999*.

Their adventure to the Pyramid of Nemset would be Tim's little *Tomb Raider* moment. He didn't have cute little shorts or Alicia Vikander's rockin' bod, but he did love Lara's swag. If he were honest, he'd pick to be Lara Croft over Indiana any day of the week.

It was like being Indiana Jones with James Bond gadgets.

System Message: You have gained a level

How had he missed this notification? Getting his skills increased was nice, especially with the changes to his buffs, but a level increase was fucking awesome. Two more levels and he'd get to take on his next class change. He really wanted to find out what options he would have available for that and what parts of his new class would be different than they were right now.

Since it looked like Tim would start getting Endurance on his gear along with increased Intelligence and Wisdom, he decided to put the point into strength. When he got his strength to twenty, he'd give up on boosting his secondary stats and dump everything into Wisdom like a good boy. It felt like in this game, hitting the first threshold was an important milestone. He didn't want to walk around for his entire life thinking his staff weighed two hundred pounds when it probably weighed closer to twenty.

With his strength up to fourteen, Tim lifted his arm above the water and flexed.

"Impressive," ShadowLily commented as she walked past the tub to get something from the counter.

Tim lowered his arm in shock. He didn't realize she was in the room. "Can you tell the difference?"

"Not really." She giggled at the crestfallen look on his face. "But you looked cute doing it so I had to say something."

He climbed out of the bath and dried off. "I wonder if hitting twenty will be noticeable."

"I'm kind of surprised you aren't dumping everything into Wisdom." ShadowLily leaned against the vanity as they spoke.

Tim was kind of surprised too. Normally he was a min-max kind of guy, but in *The Etheric Coast* where everything was so real, it felt like having a decent baseline was a good way to start his adventuring life. Then he would follow his usual affinity for dumping everything into his primary stat and reap the rewards. If nothing else, he was all about playing the long game. There was no time for now. He was always looking toward the future.

"It'll happen soon enough." Tim equipped his clothes.

ShadowLily moved toward the door while motioning him to follow. "Come on. Everyone is waiting for us."

"Hey, I'm not late this time." Tim checked the in-game clock and hurried to catch up. "Is everyone already there?"

She laughed. "It's not that you took longer than usual or that you're late. It's just that no one else was willing to risk cutting it close when we're going to meet the goddess."

Tim knew that being late to a meeting with Eternia would be incredibly embarrassing. It would be like showing up to work late. The bossman never cared why, only that someone was late and they had to cover the missing person's work until they showed up. Except in this case, the boss was a goddess and disappointing her wasn't like being a few minutes late for a minimum wage job.

He needed her support to accomplish what he wanted to in this game. Having her on their side was doing wonders for the guild's progress, and there was no reason to put their relationship in jeopardy because he wasn't on time. Although it looked like they would be early, Tim picked up the pace.

His dad always told him that if you cared about something, being on time was as good as being late. It was time to put his father's lessons into practice.

"Let's hurry." Tim started to jog.

CHAPTER FIFTY

The morning after a party used to suck.

Now that he didn't have to suffer the effects of the previous night's debauchery, the morning after didn't have to be that bad. With the floor not spinning and his head not throbbing as he prayed to throw up, Tim was able to notice more of the little things. Like Khalid's giant new sword and Neema's quiver of magical arrows. The goddess hadn't been lying when she said they would receive amazing gifts.

Light flooded the theater, and the Goddess Eternia descended from the heavens.

Tim always felt kind of awkward in these situations. He was a Christian by definition, meaning he went to church on the big two. Whatever time service was for Christmas and Easter, his family was there. The rest of the year, not so much. So it wasn't that he felt blasphemous or anything. He knew the difference between an in-game deity and God. He just never knew if he should bow or kneel.

It was like meeting royalty, only on a grander scale.

One thing Tim did know for certain was that standing there

with his mouth hanging open wasn't a proper sign of respect, so he dropped to a knee and lowered his head. Kneeling on one knee and bowing his head was the kind of thing a knight would do in an Arthurian tale, and it felt right. He was a warrior of light, after all.

He didn't bother to see if the others in his group followed suit, but Khalid remained standing.

When he could see Eternia's feet hovering above the ground, Tim stood and met her gaze. "Goddess."

Eternia flashed him a beautiful smile and addressed the group. "Today I ask you to put your faith in me, and together we will finally bring peace to the desert."

When no one interrupted her, the Goddess continued, "Khalid, I need you to muster all your forces. The task I have set before you is to march to Naroosh. This band of warriors needs to be large and bold. I want trumpets sounding their coming from the moment they leave these walls."

"That's suicide. Phandar's army will slaughter us all." Neema's mouth twisted in fury.

Khalid reached out and placed a calming hand on her arm. "The Goddess knows our limitations."

"And I would not send you to die." Eternia's light dimmed a little, making her appear almost human. "Massing your resistance fighters will be for show, to keep my sister's gaze pointed in this direction. All Vitaria understands is power and strength so she'll think we will do the same."

Eternia turned away from Khalid and her eyes locked directly onto Tim's. "The rest of it will be up to the Blue Dagger Society. The five of you will have to make it through the Tomb of Nemset and into the palace before Khalid's forces draw close."

She pointed at Khalid. "When I say I want your army moving slowly, I mean broken wagon wheels, long stops for water, camping early. The two-day journey should take five. If at any point my adventurers fail, I want you to turn around and return to safety."

"Your commands from my lips." Khalid bowed to the goddess. "As much as I would like to stay, there is much for me to prepare."

Eternia crossed the space between them and gave the warrior a single kiss on the forehead. "There will be time for us to speak after this is over. I owe you much, servant of the light, and if your wish is within my power to grant, then it will be done."

Her gaze turned to Neema. "I will do the same for you. Without your efforts to secure the oasis, where we are standing now wouldn't be possible."

Neema looked like she was about to cry but held the tears back. She nudged Khalid gently. "Let's go rally the resistance together one last time."

"So we will." Khalid wrapped an arm around Neema's shoulders and gave her a quick hug before returning his attention to the goddess. "I will see this through to the end if necessary."

"Let us hope it never comes to that." Eternia laid her blessing upon both of them, and the warriors left together.

Tim was putting the pieces together.

Khalid's army was a distraction. It would be their job to work their way through the tomb and breach the palace's inner defenses. From there, they could use the item Eternia provided them to create a gate for Khalid's men to enter, completely bypassing the army waiting outside the walls of Naroosh. It was a damn fine plan, and it all hinged on their success.

No one said saving the world would be easy, only that there would be a cheerleader.

There was only one question left for Tim to ask. "When do we leave?"

Eternia moved her finger, creating a portal out of thin air. "I'm ready when you are."

Cassie shouldered her way to the front of the group. "Just in case there are any surprises." She jumped into the portal and disappeared.

"Tell her not to run off looking for trouble," Tim called to JaKobi as he went through the opening.

Lorelei stepped up next. "Don't worry. I'll keep an eye on them."

Tim sighed in relief. It was nice to have one adult in the bunch. Granted, if someone else was in charge of running their little band, he'd probably be twice as bad as the rest of them. It was a good thing that responsibility looked good on him. Most of the time, he'd rather be off looking at every cool thing and pushing buttons or pulling levers he had no business touching.

The last time he'd stopped to look at a tapestry, it almost cost him his head.

"Don't take too long." ShadowLily kissed him and disappeared.

Tim knew this probably wasn't the right time to ask, but he figured if he didn't do it now, he might not get the chance again. "Goddess, is there any chance you can teach me how to do that?"

Eternia laughed, but it wasn't a mean one. It was the kind a mother has when her child asks if one day they can grow wings and fly. "Maybe one day, brave adventurer, but for now you must be content hitching a ride."

Tim wasn't even disappointed.

What he heard when Eternia said "one day" was there was a serious chance he could learn how to create a portal. Hope springs eternal and all that nonsense, but he would cling to this hope like it was the edge of a cliff, and the only thing waiting at the bottom was the sound of him going *splat*.

"See you on the other side." Tim stepped into the portal, felt his gut twist, then he stood on the steps of Nemset's tomb.

He was standing at the base of a pyramid. This was so fucking cool.

Cassie was in the lead, and everyone had taken their regular positions behind her. So far there wasn't a threat in front of them, so Tim felt pretty good about turning and looking the other way. He could just make out the bulk of Vitaria's forces aligned outside the city of Naroosh in the distance. From here the soldiers looked like ants, but he could also make out large-scale siege weapons dotted across the landscape. Not to mention more boss-sized monsters than they could possibly take on.

He wouldn't want to face that army with a hundred adventurers by his side.

Eternia appeared before them. "I cannot stay long, or my sister will detect me."

They moved toward the pyramid's entrance, where the goddess cast a spell and the doorway opened. "You must first make your way to Nemset's resting place. Find the key, and use it to escape to the palace."

She motioned for them to move inside. Tim could see the strain on her features as she held the door open for them.

"Once you beat the final guardian and enter the palace, use my token. Khalid and the resistance will be only steps away."

As soon as their entire party stood inside the doorway, Eternia disappeared, and the door started to close. This was their last chance to back out of the instance. If they wanted to go or needed extra supplies, this was it. Tim looked at their expectant faces and wanted to pull them into a giant hug. Of course, they were ready to go.

He shouldn't have been surprised.

"Let's do this." Tim grinned at Cassie, motioning for her to lead the way. "Keep your eyes open for trash packs. Let's follow the stairs up. If I know anything about ancient leadership, it's that shit rolls downhill so the treasure will be at the top."

Cassie tapped her staff on the ground. "As if it will be that easy. Bastard's probably twenty feet tall and shoots those bugs from *The Mummy* out his ass."

Tim laughed so hard he started to cry. The last thing he ever wanted to do was be in another fight where anything came out of anyone's ass.

"We all know that no one likes beetles in their ass." JaKobi wiped a tear from his eye.

Tim's laughter hadn't subsided much since they started talking. "I know the last couple of bosses had some gastric issues, but I'm pretty sure the Goliath was the last we'll see of that nonsense."

He looked over his group seeing a few unbelieving faces. "If the next boss shoots beetles from its ass, I'll give you each ten gold and a hearty apology for my ignorance."

"I've never prayed so hard for a fart in my entire life." Lorelei cracked a smile.

Cassie spat on the ground. "Speak for yourself. You're not the one who has to stand in the cloud. One of you guys farts, I might start having PTSD."

"All right then, people, tighten up those assholes. We can't have an incident." Tim scrunched his buns together really tight.

The effect was lost on the others because of his robe.

"Fuck off." There was a little *toot* sound and Cassie spun to glare at JaKobi. "That better not have been what I think it was."

Tim started moving into the corridor. "Maybe we should get going just in case."

He didn't have to ask twice.

Cassie took the lead, and the group fanned out behind her. Tim looked at JaKobi and mouthed, "You're playing with fire."

"That's what I do." The fire mage had a reckless grin on his face.

He ignored the man for now. If he wanted Cassie to beat him up later, that was his business. Tim focused on what was in front of them. He expected if they were going to see trash mobs, it would happen sometime soon.

The entrance to the Tomb of Nemset wasn't all that spectacular. It was merely a square room with a flat floor. None of the walls had been decorated. If any thief broke into this place, they would have thought it was empty. The only feature the room had was two stairways. One led up, and the other led down.

Neither looked very appealing. Claustrophobic was the word

that came to him. Tim was a big fan of horror movies, and in more than a few of them, people got trapped underground and attacked by monsters. He would always say that won't ever happen to me. I'm not stupid enough to do something so asinine, and yet here he was walking single file up a flight of stairs thousands of years old and hoping for the best.

At least there was magic in this world, so the ruins were probably a little more secure than they would have been back in the real one. Tim was starting to think there would only be a cave-in if they triggered some kind of trap. Wait...didn't the ancient Egyptians line their tombs with traps to keep people from stealing, or was that only something he'd seen in a movie?

"Keep your eyes open for anything that looks funny," Tim called to Cassie. It was vague, but he had no idea what to tell her to look for.

"Explain funny?" Cassie shouted back. Having a conversation with three people between them wasn't ideal.

"Traps." Tim had no idea what one would even look like.

If this passage were much smaller, he wouldn't be able to stand normally. All it would take to wipe them out was anything coming down at them from above. There was nowhere for them to run, or duck, or hide. With JaKobi and Tim at the rear, anyone up front was totally screwed.

Cassie sighed. "Next time you think there might be traps, we should probably have ShadowLily or Lorelei lead the way."

"I'll grab you if I see anything." ShadowLily tapped Cassie on the shoulder to get her moving again.

The rest of their trip up the stairs went without a hitch. Tim felt as if a weight had lifted from his shoulders as they stepped into a small antechamber. They were still underground. Well, technically they weren't underground, but there was enough stone sitting on top of them they might as well be. Something about not being so confined in the tunnel and having a little breathing room made him feel normal again.

Hopefully, they were done with small spaces for the foreseeable future.

The door into the next room was already open, and Cassie stood on the threshold peering inside. JaKobi sent a ball of flames past her and into a large urn in the center of the wide-open space. Flames raced out across the floor in the four cardinal directions, and a series of smaller urns lining the walls lit up, covering the area in warm orange light.

This was the kind of room Tim imagined when they talked about treasure. Large statues lined the chamber. They looked as if someone had carved them from the solid stone to make it look as though the people were holding up the roof. Miniature versions of the same servants were scattered through the room. Some of them were bronze, and others were even more precious metals.

Vases lined the tables, and incredible pictographs covered the walls. It would have taken an army of archaeologists a hundred years to decipher and catalog it all. And yet, it didn't feel like a treasure of wealth. This room felt more like these items and pictures were meant to tell a story. Most likely the one of Nemset's life. There was probably something they could learn in this room that would help them in the next fight, but he had no idea what to look for, and the room was huge.

For now, it was probably better if they moved on.

"Hands off the loot." Tim looked at all the things he'd love to see in their rooms back at the inn. "If you want something, mark the location, and grab it on the way out."

ShadowLily nodded. "This time, I'm with the paranoid one. Taking things that don't belong to you never works out well in the movies."

They moved through the room, heading slightly upwards as they did. It was hard not to marvel at all the cool artistry, but they were here to do a job. When they reached the opposite side, there was a staircase wide enough for all five of them to ascend simultaneously.

Tim sighed in relief. When they hadn't run into any trash mobs, his imagination started to get the best of him. Part of him was still waiting for every statue in the room to come to life and try and murder them. Instead, they made it to the exit without an incident.

Together they moved up the stairs but in their normal battle formation. Tim didn't know what would come next, so he was happy everyone was staying disciplined. It wouldn't be long now before they were in their next battle. He could feel it like the hairs standing up on the back of his neck.

The room at the top of the stairs was open to them. There wasn't a door, and there didn't need to be. The only thing in the room was a giant sarcophagus. It was so large it would have taken an army to lift it, and even then, it wouldn't fit down the stairs.

They'd run into something like this once before, but tombs buried in the mountains weren't nearly as cool as the ones from ancient Egypt. They needed to get in there and find a way to trigger the fight.

One night off, and he was itching to kill some shit.

As soon as Tim's heels crossed the barrier to Nemset's burial chamber, there was a low rumbling sound. Pillars of stone rose from the floor, trapping them inside the room. At first, he wondered if it was a boobytrap, but then he realized they were being locked inside for their next encounter.

"Get ready, Cassie. I have a feeling this will be a wild one."

CHAPTER FIFTY-ONE

Tim was expecting the sarcophagus to open.

It didn't take much imagination to see the lid slide back just enough for a mummified hand to reach out and push it the rest of the way open. He watched the center of the room waiting, almost willing it to happen, but it didn't. The room was silent except for the sound of their breathing.

This place was a tomb in every sense of the word.

Since nothing was happening, Tim looked around for a clue. Maybe there was something they had to do to start the fight. Statues of Anubis lined both sides of the tomb. Only, these were different from any of the ones he'd seen back in the real world. These versions had two sets of arms, one sculpted to look as though they were holding up the roof and the other holding a shield and a sword.

He wasn't much of a scholar when it came to decoding messages, but these certainly looked like protectors of some sort. They were holding up the weight of the world and yet ready to attack to protect their master. If you got rid of the creepy "inside an ancient tomb waiting for a boss fight" vibe, the place was kind of beautiful.

There wasn't much to look at other than the statues, and the air vents cut into the upper walls. At the far end of the room was a smaller staircase leading to what must be the treasure room.

"Every time I say this it ends up badly, but maybe nothing is going to happen." JaKobi walked toward the treasure room.

Cassie smacked the fire mage on the back of the head. "He knows it ends badly, but he still has to say it anyway."

"Typical." Lorelei snorted. "But to tell the truth, I'm with him. I want something to happen."

Tim looked around the empty tomb, kind of feeling the same way. This place was beautiful, and he was enjoying poking around, but that wasn't what they came here for. Khalid and his men were marching to Naroosh as a diversion for them to get inside this tomb. Now that they were inside, they needed to make it past the bosses and get to the palace. Otherwise, Khalid's distraction would turn into a rout.

He didn't want to be responsible for the death of the resistance.

"Normally I'd never go for this, but let's head to the treasure room." Tim walked toward the smaller staircase at the rear of the room. "What's the worst that could happen?"

Cassie froze in place. "Did I hear that right? What's the worst that could happen?" She pointed at JaKobi. "And right after this guy just said, 'I know it ends badly.' What are you trying to do to us?"

"Maybe he's turning over a new leaf," ShadowLily replied casually. "A less scared and timid leaf."

Tim paused. "Prudence isn't scared, and I've never been very timid."

"He's got big balls." JaKobi grinned as he made cups out of his hands and moved them up and down between his legs as he walked.

"For fuck's sake, this is worse than that Grail stuff." Lorelei sounded exasperated. "Someone please step into the treasure room so I don't have to listen to a song about balls."

Tim snickered. "It's not about balls. It's about big fucking balls."

"If it's Christmas time, they might even be Schweddy Balls." JaKobi was really busting her balls now.

They could all see Lorelei smiling although she pretended to be angry. "Then I vote, Cassie goes first."

"I'm on team slow and prudent, this time." Cassie hadn't moved an inch since she froze to chastise them for being impatient.

"Not!" She sprinted toward the treasure room.

Black mist cut off the stairway as Cassie neared. She ran into it at full steam, and it sent her flying back into the tomb. Tim tossed a Healing Orb at her and turned to see what was in store for them. A giant four-armed Anubis was climbing the large staircase leading to the entrance.

Tim knew it wasn't the Egyptian god, but the figure looked so much like him it was the easiest way for his mind to process what he was seeing. The four arms were throwing him off, or maybe it was the two swords and two shields. With a sword and a shield on each side, the boss could block and attack multiple fronts simultaneously.

This was going to be one hell of a fight.

"I am the guardian of Nemset and will not tolerate thievery." The stones moved from the floor and ceiling to seal off the stairwell behind the guardian as he entered the tomb.

Tim was still trying to piece together what they were in store for so he tried to buy them some time. "Would you believe we were taking in the sights and got lost?"

"The only thing you will see here is your death." The guardian's smile revealed rows of sharpened canine teeth. "It has been so long since I've enjoyed fresh meat."

Tim looked at Cassie. "Guess that was a no-ereno on the sightseeing. Looks like you're up."

"It's about damn time. Let's see if dog breath likes getting hit with sticks." Turning to face the guardian, Cassie shouted, "Hey, Cujo, I'm going to put you down." She sprinted forward with her bō staff lifted high above her head.

While it wasn't the line of the century, it had one up on fuck-nuts. Tim let a little laugh escape from his lips. Now that the fight was starting, he felt the weight of expectations falling away. It was so much easier to focus on the moment than it was to worry about every little thing and what could go wrong. He spent a lot of time making mountains out of molehills when he should have been looking on the bright side of things.

The loot side of things.

He didn't wait to see how the fight was going to start. The guardian had shields and swords so it seemed pretty self-explanatory. Cassie and ShadowLily should be the only ones at risk for any kind of damage early on. It was the perfect time to start the fight with Behold My Power. He'd never cast the spell to start a battle before. He always started with a heal. Still, there was a first time for everything.

With the big hitter out of the way, Tim cast Curse of Giving to get the healing ball rolling.

Before taking a second to look over the room again, Tim hit Cassie with a Healing Orb. He wanted to make sure whatever initial damage she took was swallowed up pretty quickly. The last thing he wanted was for her to take a critical hit from the boss, followed by one from his spell. The feedback from his curse sucked, but the damage was so spectacular he was willing to live with it.

Cassie and the boss were going toe to toe. Her bō staff was giving her the reach she needed to bat aside the boss' main attacks easily. This was the one time her being so small was a huge advantage. The boss was wider than normal because of the extra arms, and Cassie was so small he could only attack or block her with one set of arms at a time. You could tell the guardian was frustrated, and he hadn't met ShadowLily yet.

Watching the fight from the back of the group was kind of like watching a movie. As Cassie dodged and attacked, he could almost tell what would happen next. She was a little slow coming up out of her roll to the side. The guardian used his shield like a ram and knocked the tank off balance and right toward his other sword.

ShadowLily made her appearance, and it was super-clutch like so many times in the past. Her daggers knocked a killing blow off track, and while Cassie had been stabbed in the arm, she certainly wasn't dead.

Behold My Power hit and restored Cassie to full health in a blink. The guardian looked surprised when her staff smacked him in the back of the head. If nothing else, he probably thought his blow would have kept her out of the fight longer than an instant.

Maybe he'd underestimated the threat this boss posed. The guardian was already dealing them pretty substantial damage, and they hadn't made it to a phase change yet.

Tim had no idea what to expect when the boss hit his first threshold. The only thing he knew was that it wouldn't be farts, and he was pretty sure the whirlwind attacks were going out of style. Whatever happened next should be new and interesting.

Lorelei was all business during this fight. Her bow *thrummed* constantly. The boss' shields blocked half of her arrows, but for every one he blocked, one of them also got through. Not to mention the distraction from all those arrows caused additional attacks from ShadowLily and JaKobi to land as well.

Despite his initial fears, they were making fantastic progress on the boss. They had dropped the guardian's health by twenty-five percent already, and it didn't look like their pace would slow anytime soon. Whatever they were doing right now was working perfectly and clearly had the Guardian off his game.

They only needed to keep it going for as long as they could.

The guardian hit seventy percent health, then sixty. Tim's opinion of the encounter was rapidly flipping from one extreme to the other. He was starting to get worried that this fight was too easy. Maybe Eternia dropped them off at the wrong tomb, or this was the beginner's version of the fight. Something didn't feel right, and those tiny inklings went from running to the bathroom right into a total shitstorm in the blink of an eye.

"Watch for something to happen at fifty percent," Tim called as he sent out a burst of Healing Storm to make sure everyone was topped off.

At fifty percent health, the guardian slammed his shields together sending a shockwave through the room. He tossed the shields aside and pulled a pair of matching scepters from his belt. "For thieves, you put up a valiant fight, but your time amongst the living has come to an end."

"Just once, it'd be kinda nice if the boss was like, 'Hey, you know what? This isn't working out so well for me. Here's some treasure, now get the fuck out and don't come back.'" Tim hated being called a thief the way Marty McFly hated being called chicken, so he took things a little personal now.

Cassie snorted. "Seriously. My favorite part is when they blow up in pretty golden lights. I'd kill him a few times just to watch him explode." She turned her attention back to the boss. "Less talking. More dying."

The guardian of Nemset smiled his wolflike grin while lifting the scepters. Clouds of dark energy formed across the roof of the tomb and flecks of dark energy dropped out of them like the dying leaves of the Ellcrys slowly falling to the ground.

It wasn't hard to fathom that getting hit by one of the floating leaves of energy would be a bad thing. Now they would have to move the boss through the room with care or risk taking additional damage. This almost felt like one of those fights that would turn into a healing check.

Cassie was back on the boss now, but all Tim could do was keep watching the leaves of energy as they slowly fell to the floor. One of the dark energy drops touched the stone, and it created a pillar of dark energy between the ceiling and the floor.

Oh shit, this isn't good.

"Shoot the energy leaves." Tim sent a blast of Divine Light, eliminating one of the guardian's magical leaves before it could touch the floor.

The leaves of darkness fell all around the room, and whenever their group wasn't fast enough to destroy them before they landed, they created a pillar. It didn't take a genius to figure out that running into the columns would be bad. Tim hadn't noticed the hazard for what it was quick enough, and now pillars filled the room, waiting to zap them.

Once they eliminated the last of the dark energy drops, the columns started moving around the room. As far as Tim could tell there was no pattern to the madness of it. If the pillars hit each other, they changed directions. The same thing happened when they hit a player, except his team also took a considerable amount of damage.

It was like playing bumper cars of death.

His entire life now consisted of running and healing. Quick Feet saved his ass once, but then all he could do was cast Who Needs a Shield and pray for the best. The guardian was at twenty-five percent health now, but he was lifting the scepters again. They weren't going to live through this if they didn't do something now.

"Any cooldowns, any special skills, anything you've been holding in reserve. Now is the time to drop it." Tim kept the heals going out. "Ignore everything but the boss. If we don't kill him now, we won't survive the next Pillar Phase anyway."

The guardian's diminished health seemed to be slowing him a little, but the magic flowing into his spell hadn't slowed at all. The leaves fell faster now, almost like snowflakes in a storm. They wouldn't have long until pillars of dark energy filled the entire room. When that happened, they were dead.

Tim made sure everyone's health was topped off and cast Divine Light like it was going out of style. The boss's health was plummeting now. Twenty seconds later, he was at five percent.

The first of the new pillars snapped to life, then a second and a third. They were happening all over the place. They hadn't stopped a single bit of the dark energy flakes from landing, and they were paying for it. Maybe he'd picked a shit strategy, and they were all going to die.

Three percent.

Two-thirds of the room was full of bouncing pillars of darkness. All of them were getting hit and ricocheted in every direction, and there was nothing they could do about it. Tim stopped trying to DPS. His extra one percent wasn't going to matter if they were all too dead to talk about how little DPS he did during fights compared to the big three.

He cast Healing Storm and channeled all his mana into it.

Two percent.

"Holy fuck, why does that last percent take so long?" Tim had a pillar pressed against him now, and there wasn't anywhere else for it to go so it was starting to crush him against another of the dark energy beams. The constant pain in his arm made it hard to concentrate, but he refused to drop the spell.

Everyone was hurting now, and he was pretty sure Lorelei's vest was on fire. The guardian was flailing around as he died, but it sure didn't feel like it was happening fast enough for all of them to come out of this alive. With one final wail of disbelief, the guardian disappeared, and the pillars of darkness winked out of existence with him.

Tim fell to his knees. The skin on the right side of his body was a shriveled mess. Some of the others were doing even worse, but they were still alive, if barely. They might have looked like the walking dead, but they were still alive.

Now that the fight was over his mana flooded back into his system.

Tim wanted to fall over and pass out, but that wasn't going to work for any of them. He lifted his ruined arm into the sky and cast Healing Storm again. The fat drops of liquid fell onto them, and he could feel his skin knitting back together. The burned skin sloughed off like a cicada shell, and his arm looked fresh and new.

Magic was so fucking awesome.

The rest of the group was standing now, looking around the room almost in a daze.

"That wasn't very fun." Cassie had taken the most damage, but she looked better thanks to the continued healing.

Tim gave her a quick hug, hoping it would shake off any bad mojo she felt. "You know what is fun?" He pointed toward the treasure room. "Loot. Let's go check it out."

"I feel like this is exactly how the last fight started, and I'd really like never to do that fight again." Cassie walked toward the stairs. The fear of death would never be strong enough to keep her away from the prospect of collecting new shinies.

Getting burned alive was in Tim's top three worst ways to die, so having the pillar crushing him and burning him at the same time wasn't exactly the best experience. When they got through all of this, he'd have to sit back and analyze the fight to find out what they could have done better. Then he could apply it to the next battle, or this one if the instance repeated at a higher level.

He was a big fan of when developers brought low-level dungeons or even bosses back at endgame.

When Cassie breached the stairs to the treasure room, nothing happened. It looked like they were in the clear.

CHAPTER FIFTY-TWO

There was nothing better than getting to the loot after a close fight.

Although in this case, Tim wasn't expecting much. Normally when they got a big quest where the quest-giver was willing to part with something from their hoard, the bosses they fought didn't drop much. It could have been a figment of his imagination, but when Eternia dangled the carrot, they usually had to work for it.

Cassie led the way up the stairs and into the treasure room.

Piles of gold and jewels littered the floor and the walls. They were stacked waist-high in some places. Tim reached out, trying to touch one of the pieces, and found he couldn't pick it up. It was as if his fingers hit an invisible shield.

Cassie was trying the same thing in front of him. "Maybe it's only for looks."

It would make sense if the treasure in here was only for looks. Regularly giving the players this kind of money would devalue gold until it was worthless. Tim did spot a single chest in front of them. It was about an eighth of the size they usually saw after battles so he wasn't expecting much. If anything, Tim was starting to think their quest item would be in there and not a lot else. After their last fight, he was okay with that. All he wanted to do now was get what they needed and move on to the next boss.

Facing off against Egypt's denizens was about as crazy as he thought it would be. It felt like it had been a long time since he had to run, dodge, and jump like that during a fight. And of course, there was a certain mysticism about the place, especially if whoever came through here next loved reading *Wilbur Smith* as he did. It was so cool when the developers mixed fantasy and reality. It hit harder.

Tim didn't know about the others, but his magical defenses were pretty bad. He assumed that was probably pretty standard across the board except for Cassie. All their recent fights included magical attacks of some kind, something new for them to deal with. Hopefully, some of their new gear would come with resistance. They were going to need something amazing, especially if the fights only got harder from here.

Cassie reached the small chest, and she looked back at Tim for approval before laying her hand on it. She was probably checking to see if it was a trap, and he hadn't considered that before saying yes.

Her hand came down on the chest before he could shout a warning.

Cassie turned with a small square cube in her hand. "Five freaking gold and this hunk of junk." She tossed the cube to Tim. "Eternia better have some fancy shit waiting for us, or I'm going to be pissed."

"I'm guessing it will be the best gear we've seen to date." Tim started looking at the cube. "This is what we came up here for. So, mission accomplished."

The tank turned and headed back in the other direction. "It's not what I came up here for. I wanted something shiny."

"She gets cranky without her loot." JaKobi rested his hand on the chest. "I'll see if I can cheer her up. Maybe we can talk more about pizza. That seems to calm her down." He ran to catch up with Cassie.

"That's probably not a..." ShadowLily's sentence trailed off as JaKobi sprinted away. She shook her head as she looked at Tim. "Have an extra heal ready for him when we catch up to them." She laid her hand on the chest, then followed the others out.

Lorelei walked up to the chest with a smile on her face. "Five gold is five gold, am I right?"

She was totally right.

"Any loot is good loot." He'd played a few games where loot only came at the very end of every long encounter, and it just didn't feel right. He didn't mind getting some of these epic quests done for amazing rewards, but he also liked the instant gratification that came from looting the boss.

Having a little extra coin never hurt anyone. Tim would always rather have the money and not need it than need the money and not have it. They all had bills to pay. Rent on their rooms, or taxes if they owned property as he did.

One thing he didn't know about making a lot of money before now was how much it cost to start and maintain so many businesses. In many ways, he still didn't feel the full brunt of the workload. Mr. Applebottom handled almost all of that for him. All Tim had to do was supply the startup money and get out of the way.

When he thought about it for more than a second, that poor guy probably deserved a raise. Tim looked over his bank account and sent a message to Mr. Applebottom to take whatever he was making and double it for now, with the understanding that if rents dried up or something went haywire, he might have to lower it again in the future.

The way Mr. Applebottom ran things, Tim was pretty sure he'd be doubling his salary again before ever having to consider making a reduction.

Tim laid his hand on the chest and collected the five gold

before checking his inventory to make sure he hadn't missed anything. There was nothing new in there except the cube Cassie had given him so he pulled it free to examine it on the way out of the room.

A dusty old bronze cube wasn't much to look at initially, but after putting it in his inventory and pulling it out the cube was clean, and Tim could make out more of the details. On each side was an intricate design of Earth, Air, Water, and Fire. On the cube's top was a small raised bevel that looked like it could be inserted into something, and on the bottom there was only a small circle.

The circle reminded him of a certain box *Pinhead* liked to send out into the world.

He shuddered thinking about how badly some of those movies scared him as a child, but he had more realistic problems to deal with than the Cenobites. With the key in hand, they had everything they needed to reverse course and head back down to the pyramid's lower levels.

Traditionally, there were three things at the bottom of a pyramid. An emergency escape hatch, servants to serve the entombed in the next life, and often a wife or priestess so they could enjoy immortality with the pharaoh.

Imagine watching as Anubis weighed your heart.

Tim shuddered at the very thought. Not because he was worried about the outcome but because of what the scales meant. It'd be like watching someone flip a coin to decide if they were going to kill you. On one side a heart and on the other a feather, it might as well have been heads or tails.

The others were waiting for him so he slipped the cube back into his inventory and hurried to catch up. He didn't want to get left behind in a place like this. It was creepy enough, but probably not as bad as a mausoleum because of the sheer size. In a mausoleum, the bodies were typically packed in pretty close together. He'd always imagined them all coming to life and chasing him.

No big surprise that when Tim was left alone, his imagination tended to run away with itself.

Cassie was waiting for him in the tomb's center, and everyone else was milling around the stairs on the far side of the room. "What do you think we'll find down there?"

"Honestly, I have no idea." Tim shook his head as they walked. "I thought we'd be facing off against Nemset in here, and not only his guardian. From here on out, anything is in play."

Cassie pulled her bō staff free. "Do you think that cube will open the passage?"

"Eternia hasn't let us down yet. It will get us there." Tim didn't know why he trusted the goddess so much. He simply knew that it felt right to put his faith in her.

Back in the real world, it depended on the time and place as to which gods or God you worshipped. The one thing all religions seemed to have in common was that if you followed another one, you needed to be converted. Merely hearing the word converted made him think of the *Chronicles of Riddick*.

There will be no conversions here.

Tim looked over at Cassie, grinning from ear to ear. "Finding out what's next is kind of like playing the lottery. You can't win if you don't play."

"Then let's stop dicking around." Cassie picked up the pace.

It turned out none of them were too keen on trying to snatch any of the items on the way back down through the gallery. Tim hoped maybe he could buy something similar to them from the vendors in either Nar'ha or Naroosh when this was over. Part of him still thought the grand gallery's items were a trap, mostly because they could touch them, unlike the mountains of coins in Nemset's treasure room.

Maybe when they finished, Tim could lead Khalid here. There was no doubt in his mind the warrior would use the gold to help rebuild the kingdoms of Naroosh. Maintaining two cities and the needs of their people had to cost a fortune. His parents had enough problems feeding three kids.

They finished traversing the grand gallery and back down the single file stairs of death into the tomb's entrance. From here they needed to descend another single file staircase before finding out what was waiting for them below. Tim gritted his teeth, hating every second of being in the confined space. All he wanted to do was get to the boss. Dying in combat would be a million times better than getting crushed to death in a collapsing passage.

Cassie must have felt the same way because she was going down the stairs two or three at a time. ShadowLily was right behind her looking for traps, but at the rate of speed they were going, he doubted either of them would be able to stop in time if they saw something.

Either luck was on their side, or any traps inside had been disabled by other adventurers' deaths long ago. Their group poured out of the stairwell flushed with excitement and from the exertion.

All of them were breathing hard, but JaKobi sounded like a fish on land.

"Next time, slower would be better." The fire mage tossed himself on the floor, gasping for breath.

Cassie looked at Tim. "Don't even say it."

"If you'd been wrong, I wouldn't have to say it. We'd all be dead." Tim winked at her. "I didn't want to be in that stairwell any longer than you did."

"Seriously, cavers are the craziest people in the world." Lorelei looked around the room and defended her position. "What?

Imagine someone climbing into dangerous underground places for fun. Might as well write the obituary before you go."

Tim got where she was coming from. He didn't have the kind of courage it took to do something crazy like that back in the real world. That was why he did it here. It was also kind of cool to think they were exploring something no one else had seen before. Other than the people in the pyramid right now, it was possible no one had entered the place since Nemset was mummified.

"I wouldn't last a second." ShadowLily gave a nervous laugh. "If I was caving or scuba diving and my light went out, I'd freak. Panic would kill me before anything else."

JaKobi laughed. It was a good, hearty sound that brought them all out of their grumbling. "Come on, guys. We're in a fucking pyramid, and if we die here we can come back to life. Why don't you try living a little?"

"So the scared rabbit passes the master." Tim bowed his head. "You're right. This place has been awesome, minus the stairs."

JaKobi was feeling it now. "Magic elevators. Has to be a market for it."

"You're just the guy to make them." Tim knew what the fire mage was doing, but it worked anyway.

Just like that, any funk Tim had been feeling since coming into the pyramid was gone, and he was ready to roll. It was amazing what a good friend could do for a person. Sometimes all it took was a laugh to readjust someone's perspective. If he wanted to be honest with himself, this place was pretty badass. He hoped that when they found the secret passage, it was bigger than the stairs and not the tight little tube the android crawled through in *Aliens*.

A noise sounded from in front of them and they all spun from where they'd been looking and zeroed in on it. It almost sounded like a cane or a staff tapping against the tiled floor and the scuffle of feet. Something was out there in the darkness, but Tim couldn't make it out. They needed more light.

"JaKobi." Tim didn't have to finish his sentence before the fire mage had orbs of light flying through the air.

The room in front of them was smaller than the one above. Where that tomb had been the size of a football field this one was maybe half of that. The sculptures down on this level were as intricate as the ones above. The only difference Tim could tell in the amount of loot piled up was the quality and quantity. The tomb resting in the center of the space was also much smaller. Where Nemset's final resting place looked more like a boss' size, this one looked like it was for an average-sized person.

Tim's eyes moved over the tomb to the man beyond. He was older and bent over a scepter like it was a cane. He shuffled from one spot to another always looking up at the wall and muttering, "They stole it from me, and I want it back."

What they stole and what he wanted back Tim had no idea. It was always a bad idea to disturb a ghost, but he had a feeling there was no way around it. "Excuse me, good sir, is there something we can help you with?"

There was no reason not to be polite.

He found it was always better to make things sound like a question. The last thing he wanted was to rile up this spirit if they didn't have to.

The old man turned, and when he saw the adventurers, his eyes went wide. He stopped using the scepter as a cane and waved it in the air. His body solidified as it grew in size. Gone was the weak old man they'd seen before them and in his place was a nine-foot-tall man glowing with the radiance of youth.

Nemset himself glared down at them. "Return what you have stolen, thief, and I will send you to the afterlife quickly."

This wasn't going how Tim planned at all, and why was everyone calling him a thief?

Was looting really thieving?

It wasn't like they were breaking down the windows of Target and running out with free clothes. When they killed a boss, they earned the treasure at the end. In his mind, whatever they scrounged up was bought and paid for by their victory. Saying that to Nemset wasn't going to get them anywhere.

Tim thought it wouldn't hurt to see if they could get around this situation without a fight. Sometimes in RPGs with the right dialogue options, a player could skip something that others wouldn't be able to. "Maybe if you told me what you were looking for we could help you find it?"

Cassie elbowed him. "What are you doing?"

"Hoping there's an easy way around," Tim whispered back, eyes locked on Nemset.

The ancient Pharaoh glowered at them. "And yet you have the key to my salvation in your hands." He pointed at Tim. "Give me the key, and I will let you scurry away like rats."

Wow, the boss could tell he had the key on him? It must have been an extremely powerful magical item. So much for being tricky. Instead of coming here, killing some bosses, and summoning Khalid's army, their fate might simply be decided by what he chose to do with the key.

"What happens if I give it to you?" Tim looked up at Nemset.

It was highly possible he was wasting time with his questions for absolutely no reason. Even if Nemset had a sob story or a legitimate grievance and said their paths aligned. How could he trust him? If he handed Nemset the key, he could disappear, leaving them here to die.

It was too big a risk.

"If?" The ancient Pharaoh chewed on the word as if it had an unpleasant taste. "What I do with my property is no concern of yours, thief." Nemset extended his hand. "Give me the key."

"Listen here, Nemmy. We killed the guardian. The key is ours. If you want it back, you're going to have to take it." Apparently, Cassie had finished talking.

Nemset lifted his scepter into the air, the polished head of

Anubis shining in the light. "If you are begging for death, you've come to the right place."

"I've begged for a lot of things, but death isn't one of them." Cassie turned and looked at Tim, waiting for the go-ahead.

They didn't have a plan for this fight so he motioned for her to get to it. "Do your best." He had no idea what to expect. Now that these bosses were using magical skills, nearly anything was possible.

Magical energy shot from the tip of Nemset's regalia and branched out across the room. Beams of electrical energy shot between the open mouths of the statues lining the walls. There were about ten statues on each side with an open space between each pair of figures of nearly identical size. It looked like right now all of the beams were active, then would shut off for a few moments and reactivate.

It was a simple pattern to master. The real problem was the boss didn't have to worry about getting cooked and they did. The arrangement also didn't have to stay the same. If this was going to be a fight based on movement, anything was in play. After almost getting crushed by the mechanics in the last one, they had to be ready to battle on the move. Constantly moving during a fight also tended to have a negative effect on the DPS numbers, but they were all skilled enough to handle the challenge. The stairway behind them was sealed off.

Their only way through was forward.

Nemset waited for them at the end of the room with a haughty expression on his face. "You wished for death. It stands before you."

"This is some bullshit," Cassie grumbled. "I clearly stated that I *did not* wish for death."

Tim pulled the tank close. "Make sure you don't take a hit from one of those beams. I hope there will be a signal or something if the pattern changes, but be ready for anything."

"Hit the boss, try not to get incinerated, all pretty standard stuff for an average Monday at the office." Cassie was grinning now.

She did love a good fight.

Tim looked at the others. "Is it Monday?"

"Our leader doesn't even know what day it is. Guys, I think we're in trouble." JaKobi slapped Tim on the back.

It was amazing how the days blended when you didn't have to be somewhere at a certain time everyday. He was living a task-oriented lifestyle. Days were merely numbers on the calendar as they tried to save the world. Jack Bauer didn't know what day it was. That motherfucker was living life one hour at a time.

"Go hit the boss and stop giving me lip." Tim smacked JaKobi on the ass. "Get in there, tiger."

Cassie led the way.

They made it past the first beam and stopped in the gap. Then went past the next and stayed in the gap. Were they going to do this all the way down the room? It was taking forever, and he was already bored.

"Go for two next time," Tim shouted as the beams stopped.

They all ran forward, making it past two beams with time to spare. They took a second to catch their breath and did it again. The third time they made the run, Nemset moved. It seemed that even the bosses in this game ran short on patience.

The ancient Pharaoh moved through the beams of electrical energy as if they didn't exist. It must have been nice for him not to worry about such trivial details as not being electrocuted.

One of the perks of being the boss, I guess.

Cassie ran forward a square and picked up the boss, giving them some separation. It was a good tactic. The two ranged DPS and himself weren't taking any damage. He cast Curse of Giving and Behold My Power. The initial burst of the fight always seemed like the best place to drop his heavy hitter. It didn't activate until well after Cassie had control of the boss' aggro table, and normally the first ten percent of fights were relatively easy healing-wise.

The real fun came when the mechanics started, and Tim highly doubted a few beams of light were all Nemset had in store for them.

Tim sent out a splash of Healing Storm and cast a quick Healing Orb on Cassie. She was taking pretty steady damage, nothing too crazy yet, but that would change at some point or if the boss landed a critical hit. The nice thing about having an avoidance tank was that they shrugged off a lot of the damage. The only time it was a big deal was if she took a critical hit.

While a regular tank might absorb a couple of big blows, Tim had to be Johnny on the spot if Cassie got sucker-punched.

He liked the tradeoff.

A little lighter healing load for most of the fight let him contribute in other ways besides healing. Bringing a little utility to the battle was the spice of life for him. A splash of DPS, a hint of interrupts, and a powerhouse of healing, all wrapped up in one super handsome package.

Behold My Power went off, freeing up more of his resources.

Whatever they were doing to Nemset was working. The boss was almost down to seventy-five percent health, and the fight had barely started. The one thing Tim liked about these fights was the bosses with magical abilities tended to take more damage. The developers were kind of like the ancient gods in that regard. They like to give with one hand and take with the other. While the boss' health went down faster, his attacks also hit harder.

When Nemset hit seventy-five percent health, the mechanics swept them back to the starting area. The pattern of the beams stayed the same but now the sections without them had something on the floor. He didn't want to call it lava because that was a kid's game, but you wouldn't see him testing his luck with the molten liquid.

For now, the coals seemed to follow the same pattern as the lights. The only difference being, as the beams ended, the coals came to life. Tim watched for a few more moments and realized that the rays didn't have a tell, but the lava did. The floor would glow softly, and when the beams turned off, it burned bright orange for a moment before returning to the regular flooring.

The new development would make things tricky because now they would be continually flirting with danger. Get out of the beams too late—zappo. Leave too early—burn-o-rama. Both situations were lose-lose. They had to find a way to live in between the two spots. It didn't mean they had to stay together, but if they did, there was less of a chance that they missed moving to the safe zone in time.

Sometimes all it took to get someone's ass moving was seeing someone else running for cover.

"Cassie, can you kite the boss back and forth?" Tim looked at his tank, trusting her to have a solution even if she couldn't do what he asked.

"He's been moving pretty easy. I can do it." She was grinning like this was the most exciting thing she'd ever done.

They were ready to go. "Everyone stay on Cassie's ass like it's your dream home and you want to live there forever."

"Hear that, babe? Your ass is my dream home," JaKobi blurted, then slapped a hand over his mouth.

Maybe Tim could save him by shouting instructions. "Let's go, Cassie. We all move as one."

Cassie sprang into action, and the rest of them followed in a tight knot behind her. They made it past two sections of beams and stopped to wait. The floor under their feet started glowing brighter. Heat cracked through the stone, then the rays turned off, and they were moving again. Sadly, they could only move one square forward at a time because either the beams or the lava was cutting them off at any given moment.

Nemset didn't give them a break this time. He made them cross the entire space before joining the fight. Now the real work began. They needed to keep moving the entire time. When the floor turned to lava, they had to move and dodge back as quickly or risk getting melted by the beams.

Tim didn't have time to think of anything but the fight. His entire mindset focused on where his feet were and his teammates' health bars. He knew JaKobi took a hit mostly because he heard it. Stopping to make sure would only slow him so he sent a Healing Orb at him and looked at his status to confirm the spell hit.

They were all taking pretty steady damage now, so Tim switched from Way of the Boulder into his Way of the River stance.

Cassie would take more damage now that she'd lost a big chunk of her protection, but it was easier to give her a few extra heals than it was to top everyone off continually. The fight was going well, and by that, he meant no one had died from sheer stupidity, and the boss' health was going down rather quickly.

Nemset hit fifty percent health and swept them back to the beginning of the zone.

The beams of energy and the lava on the floor stayed the same. When one was active, the other was off. Nemset himself had an aura around him now that sent off blasts of air in seemingly random directions. Cassie not only had to move the boss back and forth but dodge gusts of wind that could push her into the active danger zones.

The boss took a step to the side. The indicator under him changed directions, and the blast of air went off in the opposite direction than the time before.

So this fight wasn't only going to be tricky for the tank. It would be for all of them. The DPS would have to rotate to avoid the blasts of air. One wrong move and whoever got hit would have a really bad day, like, the opening credits to *Terminator Two* bad.

"The time has come for you to meet the goddess. May Vitaria take pity on your souls." Nemset beckoned them forward.

Cassie led the charge again.

So far they had this part down. It was tricky with the two

different traps going across the room, but it hadn't stopped them yet. The little gusts of air coming off the boss were new, but Tim was pretty sure they could handle it.

Nemset and Cassie clashed together scepter on staff. Tim wasn't watching the fight anymore. He simply picked up hints and traces of the battle as he stared at the little blue arrow under Nemset's feet. There had to be a way to figure out which direction it would turn next without endlessly watching.

Tim cast Curse of Giving to ensure it was still active and went back to figuring out where the next gust of wind would go off. Right now the arrow pointed away from all of them but was rotating to where Cassie stood.

"Watch for the air," Tim called.

He almost called it a fart, but the Pharaoh wasn't farting. It was more like he was summoning small gusts of wind and throwing them at them.

The arrow turned toward Cassie, and she rotated the boss. As the boss turned, the indicator under his feet stayed pointed in a fixed direction. She dodged to the side as the attack went off and moved into the spot where the air attack occurred. Tim's extensive staring told him two things: the next blast would miss them but the one after was coming for all of them, and the second was if they couldn't DPS the boss down fast enough all four of them would have to do some fancy footwork to get out of trouble.

A quick burst of Healing Storm ensured everyone's health was topped off as the blue arrow shifted toward the group. Tim went left, JaKobi and Lorelei went right, and ShadowLily joined Cassie in front of the boss. Then they all flipped back into their previous positions.

All of them took a little damage from the beams, but it wasn't anything Tim couldn't take care of with a round of Healing Orb.

After three more rounds of fancy footwork and dancing around, Nemset's health hit twenty-five percent. The boss swept them to the side of the room and bent over panting. Channeling that much mana must have been exhausting, not to mention the ass-beating he was taking. The smugness Nemset had exuded since they first encountered him was gone.

Tim felt as though the ancient Pharaoh was slipping into survival mode now and would break out every trick he had at his disposal.

The pattern from the beams changed.

Now five of them went off at once, then the next five. The lava on the floor did the same thing. Wherever lava was active, the beams weren't, and vice-versa. It was a cool effect visually, but it made the fight a little simpler because they would always have a safe spot to stand. The arrow under the boss moved faster now, forcing them into quicker rotations.

They could handle all of that.

The new additions were the problem. Now they also had to play the high-low game Jabari had thrown at them. Beams, lava, gusts of air, and now columns of magic energy. This wasn't a fight so much as a battle of wits and movement. The good thing was all of it was manageable. The bad thing was one mistake, and it could turn into a tidal wave of errors really quick.

They needed to kill the boss before that happened.

Nemset had a faint purple glow around him, letting them all know that during this phase he was taking extra damage.

"Just keep your wits about you, and we got this." Tim made sure their health was full and got ready to run.

Cassie led the charge into the room, and he was so close to her that he felt like a creeper at the bar. When she jumped, he jumped. When she ducked, he ducked. Tim wondered if this was what the others felt like during their fight with Jabari. The only difference being no one was shouting instructions. All of them were so focused on what they were doing that it was dead silent.

It was almost like someone turned up the noise-canceling headphones to Cone of Silence levels.

His feet were a blur.

Up down, circle to avoid the wind, up, down, jump to avoid the lava. Heal until his arms hurt and repeat. Nothing would break his focus. This was one of those times the house could have been burning down, and he was too locked in to notice.

All that mattered was winning.

Lorelei mistimed a jump and got blasted into the lava. Shadow-Lily had her out in an instant, but then they were busy dodging a beam now instead of DPSing. They were alive though, and that was all that mattered. If they could keep up this deadly dance a little longer, they would make it through this just fine.

Tim channeled Healing Storm as he continued to move. He wanted to know if everyone was okay, but he couldn't look at his interface. All he could focus on was keeping his feet moving, running and jumping, ducking and dodging.

He sprang into the air, and the lava under him disappeared before he crashed into it. Tim hit the floor with a *thud*, knocking all the air out of his lungs. He rolled over while groaning and was in time to see the last of the golden motes swirling their way into the heavens. He sighed in relief.

The fight was over.

CHAPTER FIFTY-THREE

After this fight, there wasn't a chest.

Those were the breaks sometimes, but delayed gratification could be the best kind as long as the prize at the end of the tunnel was worth it. With Eternia, the payout was always worth it. The goddess hadn't let him down one time since he entered the game. Some might even say she'd gone above and beyond to help them out. Eternia saved Cassie's life, gave him the buffs he used in every fight, and set him on the path to helping the High Priest.

From there, the rest was kind of history.

Tim was trying to cheer himself up and it wasn't because he needed loot right away. The last fight had been draining, physically and mentally. Having to move and execute spells while keeping track of where the boss was letting off a separate attack while dodging beams and lava was nuts. These bosses with magical abilities were always something else. Sometimes a guy wanted a tank and spank or a loot pinata.

Something so simple wasn't in the cards for them right now.

Everyone still looked a little shell-shocked from the fight, so he sent out a round of Healing Orb. Their health was full, but everyone needed a little something to lift morale. The last battle had been a doozy, but that was what they signed up for. They were the ones out leading the curve. No one was figuring these fights out for them. Sometimes that hurt a little but being one of the first, if not the first to do something came with a sense of accomplishment.

Plus they still had a key and a secret door to unlock.

Tim pulled the key from his inventory and walked toward the wall at the back of the room. "JaKobi, can you get some light over here?"

"Sure thing, boss." A small light flew from the fire mage's hand and illuminated the area.

Tim held up the key so everyone could see it. "Look for something that has these symbols on it."

JaKobi held up his hand. "Do you want me to tell you where, or do you want to look for a little longer?"

"I'm all for skipping ahead." ShadowLily casually flipped a dagger in her left hand. "This place kinda gives me the creeps, and I can't wait to see what Eternia has in her little goody bag."

Lorelei motioned for JaKobi to get on with it. "You know me. I hate wasting time and love kissing ladies."

"Don't we all." Tim winked at the ranger and turned to face his buddy while holding out the key. "Care to do the honors?"

JaKobi held out his hands in protest. "No way, dude. I've seen too many movies where the guy gets his hand cut off, or crushed, or trapped when using something like that."

"You know I can heal you through it, right?" Tim waved the key at him, but JaKobi wouldn't take it.

The fire mage's impassioned speech seemed to have worked on the others as well because none of them wanted any part of the key.

Tim knew the only way this would get done was if he did it himself. "Fine, I've got this. Point me in the right direction, Broham."

"It's over there." JaKobi pointed to a spot on the wall.

When he reached the location JaKobi singled out, Tim looked around for a moment, then found a small recess where he could slide in the upraised portion of the key. He lined up the hole and the key and shoved it in. The key only went in a little bit. Then it stopped.

"It won't go in." Tim tried pushing harder.

Cassie snickered. "That's what she said."

Oh my God, JaKobi was turning her into one of them. Soon she'd be asking about elevenses.

"But seriously, do you need some help?" the tank finished.

They pushed on the key together, but it wouldn't go in.

Finally, he got an idea. Tim ran his finger over the circle on the back as they did in the *Hellraiser* movies. The designs on the cube's sides folded down and were a perfect match to the recessed engraving on the wall.

The key still wouldn't fit in the fucking hole.

"Just fit." He slammed his open palm against the flat side of the cube, and his world exploded in pain.

A small blade stuck out of the cube's back and had impaled his hand. Blood spattered on the floor as the key fit snugly into place. A door didn't open. The wall didn't slide away to reveal a hidden passage. The only thing that had changed was now the key's back had a pointed blade sticking through his hand.

It fucking hurt.

"You're not going to like this, but you have to turn the key to the left." JaKobi grimaced at the thought of it.

Tim rotated his hand to the left. "I blame George Lucas for this."

"We all used to. Then we saw how bad it could be without him." JaKobi was willing to say anything to help him through the pain.

His hand hurt but bitching about it wouldn't open the passage any faster. Blood leaked from Tim's hand as he kept applying pressure to the cube. If he had to turn the key much farther, he would need someone to lift him because human arms didn't bend the way the game wanted his to go.

Click.

"Did you guys hear that?" Tim stopped turning his hand.

There was a series of sharp *cracks*, and the entire wall shook.

Tim pulled his hand from the key and quickly healed himself. Now he knew what every guy who ever had a knife slammed through his hand in a movie felt like. It certainly wasn't the greatest, but at least with magic, there would never be any lasting damage.

The key fell out of the lock and closed back into an innocent-looking cube. Tim quickly picked it up and stuffed it in his inventory. He didn't know if they would need it again, but there was always the chance.

"If we have to do that again, I'm calling not it." Tim hoped his face had the appropriate amount of *don't push me right now* written all over it.

JaKobi punched his shoulder. "You can't call *not it* in advance."

"I think we can let it slide this time." ShadowLily pointed at the stairs leading down. "What do you say we go and find out what's down there?"

Lorelei moved to the entrance. "When she's got a good idea, she's got a good idea."

"Whatever the fuck that means." Cassie shook her head. "Still, let's get her back to Neema before we all have to suffer the wrath of the Desert Wolf."

Tim gave Cassie the go-ahead. "Let's do it."

The secret passage was about what Tim expected.

It was dark and dusty and utterly devoid of anything interesting. Walking down the corridor almost felt as if he was in the loading screen again, except that the walls were very real and much closer to him than he would have liked. At least the passage wasn't forcing them to walk in single file. The three women walked side by side in front of them with room to spare, and the ceiling was a respectable ten feet off the ground.

Knowing how far the palace was from where they started, Tim imagined different things the ancient desert people could have used it for in all kinds of different scenarios. Sure, his mind started down a dark path, but it ended up with this being the kind of tube a space fighter shot from in a science fiction movie. He pictured bright lights streaming by as his fighter picked up speed. Then he was out in the void.

Tim's imagination had a way of running away with him sometimes. When everyone else got bored sitting in total silence, he spent the time making up stories in his head, working out problems from games he was playing, and living out a plethora of fantasies. He was a pilot, a cop, owned a dispensary, fought for Mars in the rebellion, was James Fucking Bond, and that was a typical morning.

Walking for hours in the tunnel provided him with a wealth of entertainment, but even Tim had limits for how long he could walk in a straight line without anything happening. Even his pants that encouraged him to have conversations with himself had run out of ideas to talk about. Shit was getting real.

At least it felt like they were walking upward now. For a while, Tim thought Eternia tricked them into entering the Underworld to fight her sister.

Of course, the Goddess would never do such a thing, but his mind played out every conceivable outcome whether he wanted it to or not. An overactive imagination had its drawbacks sometimes, but it came in handy when it counted.

At least he liked to think so.

Cassie turned her head to look at them. "I think I see stairs."

"I can confirm the presence of stairs," Lorelei added as she pulled her bow free from her back.

Tim felt his spirits rise instantly. This was their moment. One last boss and Khalid's army would storm the palace. Eternia would bitch-slap her sister back to the Underworld, and they would have saved the day. *Cheerleader not included.* He didn't know if it was the fighting, the partying after, or the fact they were making progress that got his blood pumping, but he was ready to sprint up those stairs and take on the boss this instant.

Then he saw how many stairs there were.

Stairs were almost as bad as running, worse if there were a shit ton of them like right now. Stairs were the things that got his calf muscles burning. At least he had better endurance now, and his strength was working its way up from abysmal. JaKobi would be the one who suffered the most, but he had an idea that would help with that.

"Hey Cassie, do you think you could carry JaKobi up the stairs for us?" Tim couldn't keep the twinkle out of his eyes.

The fire mage placed a hand to his forehead and pretended to swoon. "I don't know what I'll do about all these stairs. Save me, save me."

Tim had been expecting JaKobi to get mad, maybe psych him up a little for the long climb, but instead, he loved it as Cassie scooped him up in her arms as if he was a baby instead of a full-grown man and started running up the steps.

ShadowLily saw Tim looking at her. "Not a fucking chance."

"That's cold." He started walking up the stairs.

Lorelei laughed. "Cold will be when we make it to the top and see you're not there. Then I send Cassie down to drag you to the top by your feet."

"Remind me not to get on her bad side," Tim quipped to Shad-owLily as he picked up the pace.

Lorelei made a sound like a cracking whip. "It's all about finding the right ways to motivate people."

"I could stand to be a little less motivated." Tim kept pushing himself up the stairs.

It felt like it took them days to reach the top, but if he was honest with himself, it was probably only an hour. An hour of climbing a steep-ass set of stairs had left them all feeling a little pissy.

This boss wouldn't know what hit him.

He felt the others casting their buffs and reapplied his as he walked toward the wall. "JaKobi, find Waldo for me."

The fire mage moved up to the wall and cast a few additional lights. He clearly wasn't seeing what he wanted so he moved away from the wall blocking their way and searched the sides and floor.

About ten yards back from the end of the passage, JaKobi stopped and waved Tim over. "This is it."

"Are you sure?" Tim slid the key into the lock, and the sides folded down as before. All he had to do was hit the switch.

The pain wasn't any better the second time around as the spike pierced his hand, but he felt like one hell of a team player for taking the hit and not asking anyone else to do it for him. He tried to turn the key to the left, but it wouldn't budge. The abrupt stop shot pain up his arm and down his opposite leg.

"To the right this time," JaKobi added helpfully from behind.

Tim turned the key to the right. Eventually, it clicked in place, and the blade retracted. Now that he was free from the cube, a quick heal fixed his hand. He couldn't help but wonder who devised this system as he bent to pick up the key. Even if a person found it, there was no guarantee they would ever make it this far. He knew that he wouldn't have without his friends' help.

The doorway rumbled open, and they looked out into an empty coliseum. At least that was what he was calling it although he'd never seen one carved out of solid stone. Instead of the open air, there was a cavern roof. It was unpainted, and he could clearly see the sandstone's deep golden hue against the onyx columns leading to the sandy floor.

In all honesty, it could have just been an arena, but it reminded him of the kind or place the Romans watched the gladiators or where the Greeks held the Olympics. It even kind of looked like Soldier Field in Chicago. The only thing missing was the boss.

"Cassie, this is your show. Remember everything we've seen so far." Tim probably didn't need to remind her. They all knew the developers liked to build on previous mechanics to deal a wicked knockout punch with the final boss.

This fight was going to be hectic enough without him trying to control everything. Whatever was coming next, they would have to go with the flow. Tim bent over, stretching out his legs. If he'd learned anything from the previous fights, it was that he was going to be doing a lot of running and couldn't risk cramping up.

"All right guys, follow me." Cassie made her way into the arena.

The tank froze in place as a breeze moved through the chamber. The light breeze turned into a gale-force wind, pushing them back to the far end of the room. All of the sand covering the floor was pushed aside, then simply disappeared from the chamber, leaving a stone floor in its place.

Tim noticed that the floor wasn't solid. Instead, it was sectioned into little six-by-six squares across the coliseum. Looking back on their previous fights, he knew it would come into play, but not exactly how. No statues lined the walls, but the columns could come into play, or the boss could have some kind of other magic at its disposal.

Speaking of the boss, where in the hell was it?

Cassie moved to the edge of the first square and tapped her toe on it. When flames didn't burst up and engulf her, she moved to the next.

Maybe his paranoia was getting to them, but if this was a boss fight, whatever the squares on the ground did wouldn't start happening until they were in combat. "I think we can risk it."

Cassie stopped checking each square and walked forward at a normal pace. "If we end up sitting in the lobby to meet our caseworkers, I'm going to give you a big fat I told you so."

"You might be waiting for a while because if you get incinerated, I'm going to stop moving forward." Tim couldn't keep from giggling.

"What a dick." Lorelei gave Tim a playful punch to the shoulder. "Of course he should run headfirst into the fire after you."

ShadowLily laughed. "Maybe after me, but after Cassie, I'd give him a pass."

"I'd run into the fire for you, baby." JaKobi looked dead serious.

Cassie started moving again. "At least I know one of you cares enough to follow me into the afterlife."

"My guy has cookies." JaKobi winked. "So it's no great hardship."

Cassie sighed. "Even my boyfriend would only die for me because of the cookies."

Hey, everyone loved cookies.

They were spared from further debate as the doors at the far end of the room opened. Beyond the doorway, Tim saw a rising staircase. That was where they needed to be. At the top of those stairs, they could open Eternia's portal. All that stood between them and victory was whatever was coming down the stairs to greet them.

He started having *Chamber of Secrets* flashbacks when he saw a snake's body, but this wasn't a basilisk. What was slithering into view must have been the king of nagas or the great serpent of the underworld. The snake-like body had to be at least twenty feet long and strong as hell to support the massive human-like torso above it.

This creature was more like the naga Tim had grown up looking at pictures of and slaughtering in games. Instead of a human torso plunked on a snake's body, it felt more like this monster was born this way. His face was more serpent than man, although you couldn't quite call it reptilian. The arms were human enough, minus the razor-sharp spurs jutting from the naga's elbows.

Tim looked at the boss with no weapons in hand and back at the floor full of squares and knew this would be one hell of a fight.

"The Tomb of Nemset is to remain closed." Apep's name flashed briefly across their interfaces as the boss slithered down the final stairs. "Any who dare open the way must be punished."

Cassie put a hand on her hip. "You know, if this was Friday night, and you were a little more human, we might have something to talk about."

"She does like getting punished." JaKobi was grinning as if reliving a fond memory.

Tim smacked his palm against his forehead. He didn't need to know these things, and neither did the boss. "Any chance I can hand the key over, and you'll let us go?"

Hissing laughter filled the coliseum. "The die has been cast mortal. Prepare to live with the outcome."

The doorway leading from the arena filled with dark mist, cutting off any chance they had of trying to run around the boss. Behind them didn't look any better. All they could do was run down a shit ton of stairs right back into the bajillion-mile passage, into a pyramid they couldn't leave. There was nothing for them to lose. It was time to rumble.

"Get it on like *Donkey Kong*," Tim whispered to himself as he gave Cassie the green light.

Cassie walked forward again. "Listen here, Apep. I've had my fill of snakes, farts, and death for today. I'm going to fucking kick your ass, so I can chill and knock back a few cold ones."

"Amen to that." JaKobi's robes burst into flames.

Tim was starting to see why they were perfect for each other. While the two of them got places in different ways, they ended up at the same destination. What more could you ask for from a significant other?

Cassie started jogging. "So if you're going to bring it, then BRING IT!"

Apep didn't need a further invitation. The boss waved his hand in the air and cast a spell.

Tim noticed a section of blocks to their right receive a faint red outline around them, and a few seconds later they burst into flame. "Watch the floor. Red is dead."

Cassie sprinted at full speed, then leapt into the air after pulling the chain from around her belt and tossing the hook at the boss. When the weapon landed, she pulled the chain taut and flew directly at Apep with both feet out. It was like watching a wrestling move executed by Bruce Lee. This shit was epic.

The only person in the room not thrilled by her attack was Apep.

Now that she'd thoroughly engaged the boss, Tim cast Curse of Giving and Behold My Power. He followed that up with a round of Healing Orb and started to run as the tile under his feet changed colors. Tim didn't care where he went next as long as it wasn't in Cassie's way and the floor wasn't red. Ideally, the three ranged players should stay together, but the shapes' randomness wouldn't always allow that to happen so he simply moved and hoped they'd regroup soon enough.

ShadowLily was on the boss now, and she immediately started taking periodic damage. She didn't have a debuff on her, so he didn't waste time with Cleanse. Instead, he sent a Healing Orb in her direction and looked at the boss to see if it had any buffs. Aura of Reflection. The tooltip only said it returned a portion of the damage received back on the dealer if they were within five yards. There was also a little red line around the icon. Tim guessed this meant his Disturbance spell couldn't remove it.

Had he always been able to see this information on the boss? It felt like a new development that would make it easier for them to figure things out in the future. It wasn't the time to think about it, but he loved it when games received good quality of life features in updates and not only things for the cash shop.

He'd spend time digging into the menus later. For now, he had to worry about keeping ShadowLily alive. Curse of Giving and the reduced damage Cassie put out compared to ShadowLily meant his curse was keeping the tank topped off just fine, giving him the ability to be a little more flexible with his healing.

"ShadowLily, if you get low on health get away from the boss." Tim sent out another round of Healing Orb and waited for Behold My Power to take effect.

A lot was already going on in this fight, but not so much that he was surprised by how far along they'd come. Apep was down nearly twenty-five percent of his health, and he felt as though they were barely scratching the surface.

Apep hit seventy-five percent health and screamed, "Enough!"

All of them were swept to the back of the room, and the light slowly faded from the coliseum. Tim looked over at JaKobi. "Lights."

"You got it, boss." The fire mage began to cast.

The room kept getting darker. "JaKobi?" Tim looked at his friend.

JaKobi cast again and again but nothing was happening. "The spell is working, it's just whatever this is," he waved his hands at the darkness in front of them. "Is eating them up."

Apep's laughter filled the chamber. "My mistress Vitaria welcomes you to the darkness."

A beacon of light formed in the middle of the room as Eternia clawed her way up through the stones. "To me, adventurers. Stay inside the light."

She didn't need to tell them twice. The five of them ran for the goddess and the protection of her light. The entire time they were in the dark, all of them took periodic damage. Tim was working on bringing them all back up to full health when Eternia started moving.

"My sister fights against me. I cannot remain here for long." Eternia's voice wavered.

Apep reached into the light, his skin sizzling from the contact.

He grabbed Cassie and tossed her out into the darkness before any of them could do anything to stop him.

Tim started healing her, then got an idea. "Use your hook." He felt something tighten around his waist then pull him to the floor as the tank used him as an anchor.

Cassie landed next to him a moment later and held out her hand to help him up. "Quick thinking."

Before Tim could respond, the light around them faded. "I must leave you for now." Eternia disappeared.

The darkness closed in quickly, and Tim cast Healing Storm. As the first drops of healing rain landed on them, the light started to return to the room. Apep looked around, startled by the turn of events. Apparently, not many people brought a goddess with them to beat the darkness phase of the fight.

The fight continued just like their first go-around.

Cassie had the boss, and the rest of them were dealing damage. Now and again, random segments of the floor burst into flames. Things went on like this until the boss lost another five percent, and things changed.

Apep smiled as a red circle appeared under JaKobi's feet.

"Why is it always me?" The fire mage started running, but the red circle followed him from square to square.

Eventually, the red circle dropped from his feet and moved to outline the square he was standing on. He jumped into a clear space, and the red square fell away into nothingness. "Holy shit."

Tim looked at the gaping hole in the floor, and his mind processed what was going on. More holes, fewer places for them to avoid the fire, and if they fucked up which squares disappeared, no places to stand. JaKobi's was out in the middle of the room. From here on out, they would have to do better.

"Anyone but the tank gets targeted, they need to make it to the outer edge, or we'll run out of places to stand." Tim looked down in the hole and whistled. "We don't want that."

This phase turned into a battle of wills. They kept hitting the boss, and he made parts of the floor disappear. Other than Cassie almost getting flash-fried once, they were handling the new development pretty well.

When Apep hit fifty percent, the lights went out again. None of them needed to be told what to do. When Eternia appeared they all ran for her, and Tim healed them as they went. He didn't know if the floor was solid during this phase, but there was no way to see where the missing tiles were so they had to hope for the best.

The boss reached into the circle and Lorelei squawked as he threw her into the darkness. The ranger rematerialized next to them a moment later. "I have a handy get out of Dodge quick spell."

Tim reminded himself if he got tossed out into the darkness that he needed to use Quick Feet.

Eternia's light faded, and Tim cast Healing Storm to keep them alive through the transition.

Apep reappeared looking extremely pissed off. Clearly, no one he'd ever faced had made it this far. His breath was coming in heaves as he glared at them. "Do you have no honor? This is your chance to die with dignity, to spend eternity with the Goddess Vitaria as your master. Why do you resist?"

Tim glanced at JaKobi and gave him the big balls dance from *Major League*. This was where he should drop the perfect one-liner. It might have been childish, but it would be fun.

"Deez nuts!" JaKobi howled with laughter.

The flat-out disrespect was palpable.

Their entire group broke into laughter and Apep glared at them, his eyes burning red.

"You dare to mock me?" Apep raised his arms and cast another spell.

Bars of blue electrical energy ran from one side of the room to the other. Each of the horizontal lines differed in height. As with their earlier fights, they would have to duck or jump depending on the circumstances.

This was getting outrageous.

The floor was fire if it was even there at all. Now they would also have to jump up and down. Might as well ask them to sing a show tune while they were doing it. Tim was starting to understand why the naga's health was so low. If players had to keep this up the length of a normal fight, they would have lost their minds.

It was like taking down Avatus for the first time in *Wildstar.* Tim still wasn't sure what happened during that fight. Run, jump, dodge heal, holy fuck we're all going to die had pretty much been the gist of it.

Right now he was pretty sure they would make it out of this in one piece as long as they kept their wits about them. The one thing they couldn't afford to do was panic. One chunk of the floor missing in the wrong place and a shit roll of the fire floor, and they were toast. So while it was going to be chaotic, they had to take things slow.

"Cassie, you've got this. Everyone else prioritizes staying alive over DPS." Tim ran with the group as Cassie moved.

Run, jump, duck, dodge to a square that wasn't red. Rinse and repeat. Keep Curse of Giving on the boss the entire time, and heal anyone who needed it. Part of him wanted to flip to his Way of the River stance, but he didn't want to chance Cassie not having the extra protection when she needed it.

Shit!

There was a circle under his feet. When did that happen? Tim activated Quick Feet, turned, and sprinted away from the group, aiming for the edge of the room. When his feet stopped flashing red, he ran back to the group while casting heals. Hearing the floor drop out of existence behind him was one of the scariest noises he'd ever heard. Thankfully, he avoided the drop and could slide back into his normal rhythm of jumping and ducking.

Apep hit twenty-five percent health and instead of sweeping them away as usual, bursts of dark energy shot from his body. The little floating spheres came out in a pattern with small gaps in between. Now they were being challenged vertically and horizontally, all while moving to avoid the flames.

People's feet weren't turning red anymore so they were avoiding that issue altogether. Behold My Power wasn't off cooldown yet, so Tim cast Divine Light and a few Flame Bursts, but mostly he was holding back his mana for the final push.

At ten percent health, the room grew darker, and they were all taking periodic damage again. The squares on the floor stopped shooting random gouts of fire into the air, but now they were disappearing one at a time. They'd reached the critical point of the fight.

The Burn Phase.

"Give him everything you've got!" Tim cast Who Needs a Shield to help with the damage and made sure Curse of Giving was active before he flipped the switch on his Wristband of the Faithful, doubling his mana regeneration for the next ten seconds. With his mana regeneration in overdrive, Tim started casting Healing Storm.

His mana plummeted like a rock, but it let the DPS focus on what they needed to do. JaKobi wasn't even trying to dodge anymore as he cast spell after spell. Lorelei's arrows never stopped coming, and ShadowLily's daggers were dedicated to destruction.

Apep didn't stand a chance.

The darkness cleared from the room and Apep exploded in a fireworks display of golden motes. The wispy golden lights swirled up into the heavens, and the fight was over.

CHAPTER FIFTY-FOUR

"That was intense." Tim climbed to his feet and started healing the leftover damage.

The others were slowly standing. There wasn't a single one of them that wasn't burned, battered, or busted up in some way. Right at the end, Tim was pretty sure they were all toast.

Another couple of seconds and they would have been.

"Five fucking gold." Cassie turned and glared daggers at Tim. "All I'm saying is Eternia better come up big time, or I'm going to be so pissed."

Lorelei pulled her into a hug. "No one ever said making the big time would be easy."

"Do you really think we're big-time?" JaKobi asked with a wistful tone.

ShadowLily grinned. "The biggest."

"I kind of like the sound of that." JaKobi walked toward the stairs.

Tim leaned over and whispered to ShadowLily, "What exactly are we going to be the biggest at?"

"I don't know. He sounded so excited about it that I wanted to keep it going." ShadowLily straightened her back and twisted her head and neck until something *clicked*. "Let's go."

They walked to catch up with the others. "Eternia didn't say anything about meeting additional resistance during this part of the plan, but keep your eyes open in case."

Cassie gave him a quick nod, and the set of her shoulders changed as she continued up the stairs. "Better be worth it," she grumbled.

JaKobi flashed Tim a quick thumbs up. "Remember babe, we've got pizza coming."

"I want all the pizza in the world. Big-ass slices falling from the heavens like one of Waterboy's spells." Cassie kept her pace consistent as she continued climbing.

ShadowLily nudged her grumpy companion with her shoulder. "Just give him some time. Joe will figure it out. He always does."

"All I want is some pizza, a beer, maybe a little sex, and a nice long nap. Is that too much to ask for?" Cassie hung her head.

"Fuck no!" Tim shouted. "That's exactly what I want."

That broke the tension they'd all been harboring from the fight. It was amazing what good friends could do for one another when they stuck together. They had one part left to accomplish, and they would be able to rest.

They reached the top of the stairs and Cassie poked her head out of the little alcove, then waved them forward. As soon as Tim knew they were inside the actual palace, he pulled the stone from his inventory and looked at it. Maybe instead of asking Eternia if he could make portals, he should have asked her how to activate the damn thing.

Tim set the stone gently on the floor in the center of the hallway. He backed away, then called on the only thing he could think of. He used his lifeline to the goddess.

The words to Appeal to Goddess tumbled from his tongue, and a moment later she was there.

"You have done well, warrior of the light, all of Naroosh thanks you." Eternia reached down and touched the stone.

A moment later the hallway was filled from end to end with a portal. The resistance fighters streamed through the opening and right into the heart of Phandar's palace. The ground shook with their presence.

Neema and Khalid emerged at the end of the trail of warriors.

Khalid stopped and extended his hand to Tim. "Thank you for this, my friend. If you ever need anything and it's in my power to give, it's yours." He looked over the rest of their group. "That goes for all of you."

Neema kissed Lorelei. "I'll see you after the battle, yes?"

"Yes," Lorelei responded with a throaty growl and dove in for another kiss.

Khalid was grinning, but his eyes had a serious set to them. "Neema, it's time to go. Goddess, I will see you up there." He turned to follow the resistance fighters.

"Wait." Eternia reached out and grabbed the warrior by the shoulder. "All of you take hold of me quickly."

Tim knew when to ask questions and when not to.

This was one of the times not to. He ran forward and grabbed Eternia's arm, and saw JaKobi and Cassie touch her feet. Then they were all too close together for him to see much of anything at all. Brilliant white light erupted around them, and Tim buried his head against the goddess, trying to keep it out.

There was a screaming sound, and everything went black.

What in the fuck?

Tim reached down and touched comfortable bedding. Shadow-Lily wasn't around so it must have been late. He was having the worst dream. They went on this really long quest and right before they were about to hit the big payday everything went fuzzy. Had it all been a dream or... He jumped out of bed and equipped his robes.

Right there, right where it was supposed to be, was his little Juggernaut piece of flair.

So it was real, but how did he get here?

There was only one way to find out. Tim got up and headed down the stairs into the inn. It was crazy to think how far they went, and he was right back where he started at the Blue Dagger Inn with Ernie behind the counter, Gaston drinking beers in the middle of the day, and Liz running around trying to keep everyone else happy.

ShadowLily ran to him. "Thank Eternia. You're awake."

"Yeah, but I'm a little fuzzy on the details." Tim made his way to a chair and smiled as Liz brought him a steaming hot cup of coffee.

The brew was just the way he liked it, dark and full of flavor. A good cup of coffee went a long way to ease his mind. Right now Tim's mind was spinning, and focusing on the liquid goodness coursing down his throat was helping him find his calm center.

It felt good to sit although he'd just gotten out of bed. Why was he even in bed? They were about to storm the palace. Then everything went fuzzy. Tim sipped from his mug and looked up at the woman of his dreams. "What happened, and where is everyone else?"

ShadowLily still watched him as though she expected him to keel over. "Everyone is fine. Cassie is with JaKobi. Lorelei, Neema, and Khalid are fetching us food from Joe's. Hopefully, we'll find out more when they get back."

"Did we finish the quest?" Tim laughed at the thought of adding one more completed quest to the pile he already needed to turn in.

What he really wanted was a little downtime to get everything squared away so he could focus on what was coming next.

The assassin grinned at him. "When have things ever been that simple on a major questline?"

Never.

Tim nodded as he thought about what she was saying. Vitaria had done something, and Eternia saved them. At the moment, those two facts were all he could be certain of. Only one person could fill in the details, and she wasn't here right now. It wasn't like goddesses hung out in inns like the rest of them.

Another sip or two of coffee, and Tim felt his muscles start to relax. Everyone was fine. They merely needed to come up with a new plan of attack. He let his eyes wander around the room as he tried to wrap his head around being back home. Then he noticed Eternia sitting in a big cushy chair by the fire.

What in the fuck?

Eternia's sapphire eyes looked dim as her gaze locked onto him. "The quest to save this world from my sister is not yet complete, adventurer. Can I count on you to see it through to the end?"

Tim put his cup of coffee aside and dropped to one knee. "The Blue Dagger Society is yours to command."

List of Tim's Current Stats and Skills

"Tim" level eighteen Battlesworn
    Primary Stats
    Strength: 14
    Endurance: 21
    Dexterity: 22
    Intelligence: 46
    Wisdom: 53
    Perception: 6
    Vitality: 4
    Revitalization: 4
    Luck: 7

· · ·

Notable Gear

Weapons

Simple Dagger of Dexterity, +1 (X2)

Staff of Divine Retribution, +4 Intelligence +5 Wisdom

Orb of Concentration, +4 Wisdom +5 Intelligence

Armor

Tarnished Circlet of Divine Wisdom, +1 Intelligence +3 Wisdom

Wilbur's Fur-lined Shoulder Guards, +1 to Perception Vitality, Revitalization, and Luck

Battlesworn Robes of Justice, +4 Intelligence +6 Wisdom

Jerkin of Unmeasurable Delight, +1 to all base stats

Paul's Gloves of Mending, +4 Wisdom +7 Intelligence

Belt of Divine Inspiration, +4 Wisdom +2 Intelligence +1 Endurance

Hermit's Pants for Special Guests, +2 Endurance +2 Intelligence

Boots of Tranquility, +2 Dexterity +2 Endurance, Increase mana regeneration by 2%

Jewelry and Accessories

Leather Wraps of Divergent Health, 10% chance for single target healing spell to jump targets and heal the secondary recipient for 50% of the value.

Wristband of the Faithful, +1 Endurance, ten seconds of double mana regeneration

Ring of Luminosity, +3 Wisdom, +2 Intelligence, +1 Endurance

Necklace of Unshakable Will, +3 Wisdom +1 Intelligence.

Trinket of the Smiling Monkey, +1 to random stat

. . .

Skills

    Appeal to the Goddess: Novice rank three

    Infiltrator: Novice rank four

    Quick Feet: Novice rank five

    Disturbance: Novice rank six

    Night Vision: Novice: rank six

    Backstab: Apprentice rank one

    Snare: Apprentice rank one

    Throwing Knives: Apprentice rank two

    Sneak: Apprentice rank five

    Dodge: Apprentice rank seven

    Flame Burst: Apprentice rank seven

    Behold My Power: Apprentice rank eight

    Small Blades: Apprentice rank eight

    Weaken Undead: Apprentice rank eight

    Healing Storm: Apprentice rank nine

    Who Needs a Shield: Apprentice rank nine

    Cleanse: Journeyman rank two

    Curse of Giving: Journeyman rank two

    Divine Light: Journeyman rank two

    Healing Orb: Journeyman rank nine

Stances

    Way of the River: Apprentice rank seven

    Way of the Boulder: Journeyman rank one

Buffs

    Armor of Eternia: Journeyman rank one

    Attacks of the Faithful: Journeyman rank one

. . .

Open Quests
    The Deserts of Naroosh
    Breaking the Juggernaut
    Take Her to the Theater
    Tomb of Nemset

Before I start with any actual notes, I wanted to give a special mention to my beta team. They always tell me when I'm getting off track, and I really appreciate their notes and feedback. I can't say enough nice things about my editor Lynne. Let's just say when she gets my books she has her work cut out for her and always does a fantastic job. Of course, none of these books would exist if Michael didn't take a chance on a new face. I'm always going to be grateful for the opportunity to work with such a great company like LMBPN.

A few other noteworthy mentions.

Without my wife Becky, I'd be completely lost. She does so much work around the house, has a demanding full-time job, and takes care of me in so many ways I couldn't even list them all. She's the reason things get done around our house. :-) Plus, she takes care of our four fur babies Blizz, Jackson Bower Bates, Cisco Ramon, and Lucyfur.

I'd also like to give a special shout-out to Mathew from Grow Sciences here in Phoenix. I got to meet him at a little event, and he's the real deal. You're not going to meet another guy in his industry who cares as much about their customers, and their experience as Mathew does. Grow Sciences is always checking the pulse of the community, and striving to be the best. When a great product is backed by amazing people, it's a match made in heaven.

So much changed while I was writing this book. I found myself struggling early on but just found a way to keep grinding and refining the story until I was pleased with it. Of course, COVID happened, and it certainly changed our lives. There were moments of hope watching people sing to each other from their balconies and moments of despair like when we saw Keyontae Johnson collapse on the court. My hope for all of you is that you and your family and friends are safe and healthy.

2020 was a weird year for me personally. I turned forty, normally that would be a milestone, but this year it just kinda felt like a blip. The writing community lost a dear friend in author T.S. Paul. Scott really helped me out early on in my writing career, just by talking to me and keeping me motivated to keep going.

Scott and I met about six years ago, probably a week after Michael did his big throwdown on Kboards which might as well have been the big bang as far as the publishing industry was concerned. We wrote together, we laughed, we did all the things friends do. I won't ever forget the time we had dinner at Hofbrauhaus in Vegas. Singing, laughing, there might have been a little dancing, and I still have these two giant ass beer mugs I've never used.

Scott was a big hunk of love, and he will be missed. If you haven't checked out his Federal Witch Series you're seriously missing out on an amazing story.

Let's get on to the fun stuff.

Despite the fact that whenever you run into someone now you have a moment from Gladiator. "Still alive, Quintas?" things will get better. 2021 will be the year we get on top of the virus and show it who's boss. When I think of 2021 and what the future holds, what I feel is hopeful. If 2021 is the springboard, then 2022 is when we will really take flight.

For the next couple months, I'll be locked in the writer cave working on book four. I'm enjoying where the story is going so far, and am even more interested to see how the book ends as the plot points come together. Tim has become a personal buddy of mine. I sit down to play a little Valhalla or Cyberpunk and think what would Tim and the crew do in this situation, how would they handle it.

Normally, I just channel my inner Cassie, scream a one-liner at the TV, and charge into the fight without a care in the world.

That's how we roll!

~Bradford

First, thank you for reading both this story, and here to the back in the Author's Notes as well!

Scream our inner Cassie… I like that.

I, also have a bad habit of stifling my inner expression that I'm too embarrassed to let out. Well, except on the page of course.

I can't pinpoint a time in my life where I felt that embarrassment was a feeling that was so abhorrent, I shrank from doing things that might bring about even a small chance of creating that feeling in myself. Why try when I can do it naturally all the damn time?

I walk across a perfectly flat floor.

I trip myself.

A particularly awkward comment to a girl in my teenage years.

Open the mouth and let it fly.

If I had the ability to turn on my inner Cassie, I'd try it within boundaries because I'm built that way. However, for those of you who leave your inner Cassie turned 'on' all of the time?

I salute you.

Cooking / Baking in 2021.

This is going to be a short mention. I'll tell the whole story in another set of author notes but here is the punchline.

When grabbing flour out of the pantry to help with purchased refrigerated pizza dough, realize that both flour and white powdered sugar look similar. If you are not paying attention, you might grab the wrong container (especially if your wife has put them both into clear containers with no labels.)

The main problem is white powdered sugar will make the dough taste a bit sweeter.

It's not a good thing.

I hope all of you have a fantastic 2021, and I'll work on letting my inner Cassie out!

Ad Aeternitatem,

Michael Anderle

The Marchenko Incident

Smuggler for Hire

Origin Ice

The Fairy of Salem

Witching Hour

The Wild Hunt

Standalone Titles

Crimson Stars

BOOKS BY MICHAEL ANDERLE

Sign up for the LMBPN email list to be notified of new releases and
special deals!

https://lmbpn.com/email/

For a complete list of books by Michael Anderle, please visit:

www.lmbpn.com/ma-books/

CONNECT WITH THE AUTHORS

Connect with Bradford Bates

Facebook:
https://www.facebook.com/bradfordbatesauthor/

Twitter:
https://twitter.com/Freetheblizz

Website:
http://www.bradfordbates.com/

Connect with Michael Anderle

Website: http://lmbpn.com

Email List: http://lmbpn.com/email/

Social Media:

https://www.facebook.com/LMBPNPublishing

https://twitter.com/MichaelAnderle

https://www.instagram.com/lmbpn_publishing/

https://www.bookbub.com/authors/michael-anderle

ABOUT BRADFORD BATES

Bradford Bates is a full-time author, husband to an incredible wife, and father to four furry rescue dogs. He lives in sunny Phoenix, Arizona, trying to not melt in the oppressive heat of the summer. When he isn't busy writing the next book, you can find him playing video games and watching scary movies.